To Jim Van
Enjoy

CARETAKER'S
SONG

K. J. OLSON

PublishAmerica
Baltimore

Softcover 9781462694488
PUBLISHED BY PUBLISHAMERICA, LLLP
www.publishamerica.com
Baltimore

Printed in the United States of America

Also by K. J. Olson

Fire Song
Kailie's Song
The Path Between

To Kay Marie

And in loving memory of my parents

Acknowledgments

Books take precious time to write. Though I thank him with each book, words, my stock in trade, cannot fully express the gratitude I feel for the time and space, for the love, the encouragement to continue my writing, and for the unending support given to me by my husband. Frank, may you always walk with dragons.

Scott, Christian, Gabrielle, and John, thank you for the love and encouragement you all give me. *Caretaker's Song* is another part of the story of your dragons. I hope you enjoy it.

Janet, I promised you a dragon and here she is. She is as beautiful as her namesake.

All my family and my friends who have taken an interest in my writing, thank you for your continued support.

Author's Note

I found that a story is never quite complete, even though I thought I had ended it. I felt with the completion and publication of *Kailie's Song*, the first book in this series, that I was done with the characters and story line I had created. Not so. There was more to the story and *Fire Song* followed. Now the story was complete. Well, not quite. There was still more to tell; the dragons still sang to me; there were new characters waiting to be born, perhaps even another dragon or two.

So, here is *Caretaker's Song,* the final part of the story I began several years ago.

Or maybe not.

KAENOLIR

Sinnich Isle

Lorn Isle

Strait of Tears

Cliffs of Sorrows

Dark Land

Thanion Woods

Shiptown

Landsend

Gathorn Isle

The Diarmids

Ferry Landing

Milton Hills

Skara River

3 Rivers

High Ghilana Plain

Guardians' Fort

Wall of Rhade

Campeonn Marsh

River Gate

Fort Gate

Riversend

North Fork

Skara River

South Fork

Horn of Valor

Kalora Bay

Lake Country

Fairtown

Lowlands

Hranor Hills

Round Stones

Stonetown

Trayonian Sea

Balagorn Sea

Fjords

chapter one

TIME

A gale blew in during the night, waking Kailie Fairchild from her dreams. A bucket she had left near the back door went clattering noisily away, carried into the thrashing grasses of the dune behind the small stone cottage that had been her home for decades. Fitful lightning and rumbling thunder announced the storm. With a sigh she pushed back the coverlet and rose to light a candle, knowing there would be little sleep for the rest of this night. Howling wind accompanied the crash and roar of the sea while rain mixed with ice pellets pounded the little cottage. Kailie paused for a moment to murmur a prayer for those unfortunate sailors caught out in the violent storm.

With movements slow and somewhat unsteady she pulled on woolen slippers before drawing on the heavy robe left at the end of the bed. She picked up the candle from her bedside table and with careful steps left the room and moved down the short hallway that led to the main room of the cottage. A few coals still glimmered in the hearth, and a fire, she decided, would chase away the gloom of the storm. At her approach a great gray wolf of Faerie, silver now with age, lifted his head. With a soft murmur of greeting, she placed the candle on the table beside her chair. With practiced movements of a task repeated throughout her long life, she added kindling to the coals, and when the sticks caught fire, she added a log and then another. With the fire crackling brightly, she swung the water pot over the flames to heat. Yes, a cup of tea would warm her on this stormy night.

Kailie sat before the leaping flames and sipped the hot sweetened tea she had prepared. The wolf stood, shook himself, and came to lie beside Kailie's chair. Torar had guided her out of the Dlarmid Mountains of Kaenolir, down a sheer cliff and over raging seas to help free her father, imprisoned by the Darkling Prince in the fiery depths of Mt. Sinnarock. He had come to help her when Kaenolir needed the power of her Song not long ago as pirates attacked River's End. When she returned to her cottage after helping Timis and Kaenolir fight the evil that Aldward Finton had created, Torar had awaited her. He remained by her side, ever a faithful companion.

She reached down to knead her fingers through the thick fur of his neck, his presence a comfort to her.

"Old friend," she whispered to him.

Warm and content with the wolf beside her, she would think now about the dreams that came more often of late. They did not disturb her sleep. No, she welcomed these dreams. For in her dreams, her beloved Alexander walked with her, laughed with her, spoke with her.

And loved her once more.

"Come, sweet Kailie. Walk with me."

She smiled as she remembered all the times they had walked together on the Wall of Rhade or along the banks of the Skara River, most often just as the sun was setting, when his work as Captain of the Highland Guardians of Kaenolir could be set aside for a time.

Her tea grew cold as her memories gathered around her. She set the cup aside, then leaned her head against the back of the chair. Her eyes fluttered shut and she slept. Torar sighed, laid his head on his paws and stared into the shifting flames. Soon he slept as well.

"Come, Kailie, it's time. Come, love." Alexander held out his hand to her; in her dream she took it and laughed when he kissed each finger.

"Kailie Fairchild, come."

Another voice.

She knew this one well, too, but the figure who spoke remained in the shadows.

"Talanor?" she murmured. "Is that you? Alexander? Alexander."

The dream figures dimmed, then slipped away. She awakened to hear, not the voices of her dreams, but the keening of wind and the chattering of sleet against the windows. Torar raised his head and whined softly. The fire had gone out leaving the room cold again. Weak, watery sunlight slanted for a moment across the floor. A new day dawned; there was much that needed doing.

The storm did not abate until the next day. In its wake it left the shore of Kalora Bay littered with logs, branches of storm-ravaged trees, mats of sea grass and kelp, carcasses of fish and crab. Gulls whirled and floated on the lessening winds; crows picked at dead creatures caught in the storm's detritus. A small fir tree lolled in the waves near the shore, its roots tangling with whatever floated by. The next tide would pull it out to sea. The carcass of a large sea lion, slashed and rotting, lay at water's edge just down from the tree. A flipper pulled into the air by passing scavengers, gull and crow, gave testimony to its death. It, too, would be gone on the next tide, returning from whence it had come, providing food to others in the cycle of life that was the sea.

Kailie walked along the hard-scoured sand, her cloak billowing in the wind. She stopped from time to time to examine what the storm had washed ashore. Torar moved ahead of her, sniffing the scattered debris, turning back frequently to make sure that Kailie still followed.

She walked with a cane; though it hurt her pride to admit it, she could not have walked here without its aid. Life was slipping away, she knew, but the life of a Golden One, all in all, had been good. It had given her a powerful Song of magic to save her father and her people; it had given her the love of a good man; it had given her children; it had given her so many grandchildren she could neither name them all nor count them. It had given her good friends and solitude when she wanted it. Then with a grin, she remembered that life had given her the ride of a lifetime on a golden dragon. Her grin turned to laughter and its merry sound floated away on the wind.

Clouds scudded across the sky as she walked in sunlight and shadow until she grew tired. A convenient log offered her a place to rest for a bit before returning to the cottage. She watched the gulls, drifting on the wind, and listened to their shrill squawks. A strand of hair, freed by the wind from its long braid, brushed against her cheek, and she absently tucked it behind her ear. Torar came trotting back to her from his excursions and settled down in the sand beside her to wait. Both wolf and woman looked out to sea, watching the endless ebb and flow, thrust and pull of restless waves. The wind shifted; the air grew chill as the sun slipped lower in the sky. With a tired sigh Kailie rose to make her way back to the cottage. Torar stood and shook sand from his thick fur.

"Torar, we used to walk for miles along the bay. Now we tire before we've gone but a short distance."

The wolf glanced up at her and gave her a knowing grin.

"We are young no longer, my lady."

"Ah, yes. We've had long lives, my friend. But I think mine shall soon be over."

Kailie stopped and Torar turned to face her.

"The Golden Ones are needed."

"Oh, Torar, I'm old and tired. I want to be with Alexander."

"And you shall be. There are other Golden Ones, lady."

"Yes", she murmured. "So there are. Do they know what paths their lives will take, I wonder."

"Not yet, but soon."

The wolf walked on but when she did not follow, he turned back. He nudged her hand with his nose. *"Come. You are tired and cold. But not as old as some."* His wolfish grin made her smile.

"Yes," she murmured. "Time to go." She brushed the errant strand of silver/white hair from her cheek again, and then with her hand on the back of the great wolf, the two of them made their way slowly across the sand.

Wind moaned about the eaves of the cottage as Kailie prepared for bed.

"So tired," she thought as she slipped into bed and pulled the coverlet about her shoulders. She had spent the hours of the afternoon and late into the night writing several letters. With the letters written and sealed, she left them on the table beneath the window where they would be easily found. Books, many of them ancient and dusty, were stacked near the letters. They were books from Talanor Rowan's library, books that held many secrets. She had placed a second stack of her own books next to Talanor's. Another shorter stack sat next to them, three thick leather-bound journals chronicling her long golden life.

In the distance, a night hawk cried as it hunted. Waves slapped against the shore in their endless rhythm and for a moment, time stood still. Kailie sighed as she let sleep come. On the drift of dream Alexander walked toward her, his arms outstretched, laughing with joy. Her laughter twined with his as she ran to meet him.

"Alexander, I've waited so long."

"But no longer, love. Come."

There were others with him, others who smiled and held out their hands to her: her father Alexander Goldenhorn, her mother Katrine Seton. Talanor Rowan, the mage of Kaenolir, stood beside her father, leaning on his staff, and beckoned to her; her daughters were there with Alexander; Highland Guardians who had served with Alexander on the Wall of Rhade, friends all, waited for her.

So many, oh so many.

There, near her father, stood the Golden King, his crown sparkling in the light. He smiled and came to stand beside Talanor. Arm in arm with the King was Rhianna Lanee, the Singer who had taught the Golden Ones their magical Songs.

"We have waited for you, Kailie Fairchild," Rhianna said. *"Come."*

"Yes," Kailie whispered.

With a sigh she joined them.

Torar rose from his place by the hearth. He whined softly, then lifted his head in a long, mournful cry. He padded to the front door and when it opened, he walked out into the night. The sky shimmered with shifting, weaving streams of green, there turquoise, here purple. The air danced and sang with the winds of the gods. Torar lifted his head once more to howl a long wavering ululation of sorrow and farewell. With a last look toward the stone cottage, he trotted away.

chapter two

A ship lay at anchor off Lorn Isle, rocking in gentle swells. Hot breezes stirred the flag of Timis flapping it lazily against the tall mast. Three men had come ashore at dawn, bearing petitions for Camron Thorpe from the people of Timis.

"We need you, Camron. Timis needs you," the spokesman Adam Carland had said. His face was lined with worry; the cares of his people sat heavily on his shoulders. "Before he died, Tiernan Irworth urged us to bring you home, to be chieftain in his place. He named you as his choice in his will, and the people of Timis claim you as chieftain to lead them." He took a scroll bound in black velvet ribbon along with a thick sheaf of papers from the pouch he carried and placed them on the table. "These are for you. From Tiernan."

Camron stood staring out the window of the sitting room of the cottage he and Kitra Fairchild had built on Lorn Isle more than twenty-five years ago. In the valley fruit trees heavy with peaches, plums, apples, and pears slumbered in the heat of summer. Grape vines brought from Timis and Kaenolir climbed the low hills to the west, burgeoning with the wines of winter. A vegetable garden spread its bounty just beyond the flowers that bloomed in a riot of color. He lifted his hand to wipe tears from his cheeks.

"When did he die?" he asked hoarsely.

"Three weeks ago tomorrow," Adam replied. "I wanted to send word to you when he grew so ill, but he would not hear of it. 'Let him be for now,' he said. 'The time will come soon enough when Timis needs him again.'"

Camron turned to face the men, his eyes red and filled with tears. "I would have come if I had known," he murmured as he picked up the scroll. "He was always so strong." He slowly untied the black ribbon and unrolled the heavy parchment. He glanced to the bottom at Tiernan's distinctive scrawl. The words blurred and he turned away again. Kitra came to stand beside him and slipped her arm beneath his. She laid her head on his trembling shoulder, and together they grieved for Tiernan Irworth.

At last Camron blinked away his tears and unrolled the scroll. With words nearly as old as the history of Timis, Tiernan passed the torch of chieftaincy to Camron Thorpe, the man of his choice, as was a chieftain's right.

Kitra looked up at him with a sad smile before stepping back. "You must go," she said softly.

"Yes," he whispered. "I must. It is not my first choice." He rolled the scroll and tied it again with the velvet ribbon. "I would gladly live out my days with you here on Lorn." He shook his head. "Somehow I knew that was not to be my destiny." He reached out to touch Kitra's cheek before turning to the Timisians. "It will be a few days before I can return to Timis with you," he said. "There are things I must do here first to help my family."

Adam nodded. "Of course. Take however much time you need, but I urge you not to take too long. We are to wait for you. When you are ready, signal the ship and I'll send a skiff for you." He stepped away to join the other messengers, but he stopped at the door, then turned back to Camron and Kitra. "These are bad times for Timis," he said softly. "You will find reports in the packet about the latest difficulties we face. I thought once Finton was dead and gone and the dragons had rid us of his spawn, we would live in peace and prosperity for the rest of time. It seems that is not to be the way of it. If we don't find a way to solve our problems, there will be more bloodshed, Camron, perhaps even all-out war with the Arlanders. Come quickly." He nodded and walked out the door.

It was nearly midnight, but Kitra and Camron lingered before the empty fireplace discussing their plans for Camron's leaving. Camron sat with his forearms resting on his thighs, rolling an empty wine goblet between his hands. The door and windows stood open to the cool breezes from the murmuring sea; candles guttered on the mantel casting shadows on the wall. Somewhere close by an owl called softly to be answered by another, farther away. Kitra sighed and rubbed her arms as if she were cold.

"We have only to send word to Rayce and KaynaRee in Shiptown, and they will come to help me with the harvest. I know Rayce will want to see to the wine- making once the grapes are harvested. He may even decide to stay through the winter. If he stays, Ree may well stay here with him. I know that both of them enjoy time with my mother in Shiptown, among people. Even so, they will be eager to return home." She stared out into the night for a moment. "As you and I both know, Lorn is beautiful in its solitude, but lonely in its isolation" she said softly.

Rayce Thorpe and KaynaRee Fairchild had been born on Lorn Isle. Kitra and Camron had settled here after helping Timis and Kaenolir destroy the dark forces of Aldward Finton. Rayce, tall, broad shouldered with dark hair and dark eyes like his father, was the older of the children by two years. He'd be twenty-three on his next birthday and had grown restless during the last year. KaynaRee favored the Fairchild women, tall and graceful with long blond hair. Both children had grown up steeped in the lore and history of the Golden

Ones of Kaenolir. They traced their ancestry to the kingdom of Faerie; magic flowed in their blood. The Caretakers of Timis were part of their heritage as well. The fire beasts of legend were very real to them, for they had heard the stories of So'Kol, of Ke'Shan and Ga'Vrill and Jho'Son from the time they were babes.

Camron sighed and sat up and put aside his goblet. "They may well wish to stay on here, and I think we should urge them to do so, if that's what they want. I hope you will be able to join me in Camlanrein before winter sets in. If not then, surely by spring. But, let's just see what the children want to do. You might also consider sending word to Landsend to ask some of your people to come help you."

"Yes, there are friends who would be glad to come, I'm sure. I can offer to share the harvest in exchange for their help. Rayce and Ree like visiting the mainland, but they are always ready to come home when the time comes. But, I know, too, that if we are not here, Lorn will not be the same for them."

They sat in silence for a time, listening to the night. The tide was turning and the sound of the sea grew gradually from murmur to roar. Nighthawks cried as they hunted and the owls continued to call to each other, though the calls were fainter now, farther away. When one of the candles sputtered and went out in a sudden gust of wind, Kitra rose to close the door and windows. She picked up a shawl she had discarded earlier and placed it around her shoulders before returning to her chair.

"What do the reports Adam brought tell you about what's happening in Timis? Is the situation in Kaenolir mentioned?"

Camron got up from his chair to retrieve the sheaf of papers he'd left lying on the table. He gathered them up and returned to sit beside Kitra.

"We destroyed the evil Aldward Finton created, but in the years since we rode our dragons to aid Timis and Kaenolir, another evil has come to fill the void created by the death of Finton and his minions. You and Kailie subdued the evil that festered on Sinnich. The Warrior Song you sing each morning has kept it dormant, but how long will it continue to lie silent? Evil takes many forms, and it seems it has taken hatred and envy for its mask this time."

For a moment, Camron paged through the report, thinking back over the history of Timis. "Arlanders have been jealous of what the people of our two countries possess, seemingly for as long as time has been recorded in our history books.

"Villages and homesteads were deserted when their owners sought safety elsewhere during Finton's rampage. Arlanders decided that the situation here in Timis was to their advantage, saw their chance and moved in to claim by right of possession what Timisians, and some Kaenolirians, had left behind. Over the years there have been fights aplenty when the rightful owners tried to reclaim their property. Bad feelings continue to fester and grow as more Arlanders come to Timis and to Kaenolir. Many people have been placed in dire straits with no real place to call home. When some Timisians fled to Kaenolir for safe havens, they believed it would be temporary; they'd come back to pick up the pieces of their lives and go on as they always had. It didn't work out that way for many; the Arlanders were already there, and they were not about to leave.

"Our people want what belonged to them, what they and their families built over the generations, but the Arlanders refuse to budge. And, the reports say, more Arlanders are moving into eastern Timis with each passing month. Arland has long been a poor country and its people are becoming more and more desperate. They see Timis as a land of plenty, a land of promise, there for the taking; our people just want their homes, their land back. It is unfortunate that no solution has been found after all these years.

"Some enterprising Arlanders, led by a man named Kelan Dellay, took over the gold mine, according to the report. There's something unsettling about this Dellay, Adam said. How did he phrase it? Something dark and devious about the man, something secretive and sly. He has steadily organized the Arlanders into cohesive groups and seems to be adept at getting people to do what he wants.

"But back to the mine, the Arlanders control the mine, although production has fallen off to near nothing. Still, they refuse to allow Timis to reclaim the mine, which means the wealth the gold brought to our country is a thing of the past, and Timisians are angry about the theft. There have been occasional skirmishes at the mine, but no organized assault to take it back. My people are more concerned with their immediate needs, like food and shelter.

"Then there are the Warders, or what's left of them, to worry about. Finton's Warders, you will remember, were Timisian by birth, and a small group remains banded together. According to Adam, they live secretive lives in a compound in a valley of the Dalrudds, not all that far from where Finton built his castle. They stay to themselves, and we can only assume they live much as Finton prescribed. However, we don't know much about them, for anyone caught trying to go into their valley is run off. There have even been a few reports of men gone missing who were supposedly headed for the valley. How much truth there is to that, I don't know. It could just be a rumor, a way to keep people away. But what are they doing there? No one knows."

Kitra sighed deeply and ran a hand over her forehead. "We have been out of touch, Camron, here on our island. I did not realize so many were cast adrift when the battles we fought were at last over. Perhaps I haven't wanted to know." Kitra pulled her shawl more closely about her shoulders and crossed her arms. "It has been, what, five, six years since we visited Camlanrein? We should not have been so wrapped up in our own little world. Maybe we could have helped in some way. "

Camron shook his head and set the reports aside. "We thought we'd done our part in destroying Finton and the Pales and making a life here with our children."

"Talanor Rowan said once that when good, or what people believe is good, triumphs over evil, evil simply finds another way. Finton is gone but he left behind seeds of hatred, greed and envy."

"And those seeds have sprouted and are growing and spreading unrest and dissention." Camron sighed.

Kitra rubbed her eyes wearily. "Why can't we find peace?" she murmured. "Why can't we be at peace?"

"I don't know the answer to that either. Perhaps man has always had the need for violence. We know from our own histories that we pushed out earlier inhabitants in both Timis and Kaenolir. However, there have always been those who tried to act as go-betweens, men and women who tried to find a peace where all involved could be satisfied."

"And that's what you will have to be, a go-between among all the factions in Timis?"

"Yes, it seems so," Camron said softly. "War must be prevented, for surely that is where we are headed if we cannot find a solution to this dilemma of have and have-nots. War must be viewed as the last resort; it is never an answer." He shifted in his chair and rose. "Come," he said and held out his hand to Kitra. "It is very late and we've much to do tomorrow."

Kitra took his hand and stood. "You did not mention what is happening in Kaenolir, Camron."

"The Arlanders are moving into Kaenolir, too, Kitra. Not as many as in Timis, but they are coming. There are more to oppose them in Kaenolir; the Highland Guardians are better trained to handle the Arlanders. Still, the situation grows more heated as time passes." He snuffed out all but one of the candles, and carrying it he led the way through the kitchen and down the hallway to their bedroom.

In the muted light just before dawn, Kitra was awakened by the long mournful cry of a wolf. Again and again the cry echoed.

"Samar?" Kitra whispered and pushed her covers aside. She moved quietly from the bed, but Camron, too, had been awakened by Samar's howling.

"What is it, Kitra?" he asked.

"I don't know, but Samar doesn't howl like that. Oh." She doubled over, her arms wrapped tightly around her waist. "Oh, Camron, oh. No," she wailed.

Camron rose hastily and came to her side. "What is it, Kitra? What's wrong?"

Kitra straightened and reached out for Camron. He took her in his arms and held her tightly.

"It's Kailie," she sobbed. "She's gone, Camron. She's gone."

"I'm sorry, Kitra, so sorry," he said softly.

She pushed away and Camron released her.

"I must go up to the pinnacle to sing the Warrior Song. For Kailie."

"All right, love. I'll come with you."

By the time Kitra and Camron reached the top of the eagles' pinnacle, the sky had begun to brighten. Samar still cried, but for a moment Kitra thought she heard an answering cry. She called to him. He howled one more time before coming to stand beside her. She reached to pull him close, then knelt and buried her face in his thick ruff. Her tears wet his fur.

"Lady."

It was not Samar's voice which spoke in her mind, but another, one she had heard but once—on the day she had climbed the pinnacle and sung the Warrior Song for the first time. Kitra lifted her head, then stood. She wiped the tears from her cheeks with her fingers, and turned to find a great silver/white wolf standing near Camron.

"Torar?"

"Yes, lady. "

"She's gone then. Kailie Fairchild is dead." Her tears came again with her words, but she did not wipe these away.

"She has joined her loved ones. She would not want you to be sad for her passing, lady. It was time."

"Her Song. I must sing for her this morning. Her Warrior Song, one last time, here on the pinnacle."

"Yes. For Kailie Fairchild.

With a great wolf of Faerie on either side of her and Camron standing beside Samar, Kitra Fairchild lifted her face to the sunrise and sang the first notes of the Warrior Song. The Song began softly, Kitra's voice choked with tears of sorrow, but as the sun pushed above the horizon and bathed first the sea and then the pinnacle in golden light, the Song filled the air with its magic and power. She sang a farewell to Kailie Fairchild. She sang the Song again, this time for Andrew Goldenhorn who slept in the burial mound behind her; she sang for Rhianna Lanee who had taught the Singers their magic Songs; she sang for all the Golden Ones who had walked the land of Kaenolir.

And then she sang the Song one more time. This time she sang for herself and her dragons, for Ke'Shan and Ga'Vrill and Jho'Son; and when she did, Camron added his voice to hers to sing his Caretaker's Song for So'Kol. The last notes vibrated on the sunlight, and for a moment, for just one magical moment, Kitra heard an answering echo. She covered her mouth with her hand and sobbed.

"Goodbye," she whispered at last.

chapter three

KaynaRee Fairchild sighed in her sleep. Music, just on the edge of her consciousness, played softly, calling to her, as it called to her both waking and sleeping. She moved restlessly beneath the coverlet, too warm for comfort. When the music came again, stronger this time but tinged with deep, mournful sorrow, KaynaRee came fully awake. She pushed the covers aside and rose, listening to the music.

"Warrior Song," she whispered as she recognized the music she had heard every morning of her life growing up on Lorn Isle. Her mother's Song. Kailie Fairchild's Song. Andrew Goldenhorn's Song.

And she knew why the Song had come to her.

The Song drifted away into silence with the rising of the sun. She brushed away her tears and pulled a robe on over her sleeping gown as she left the bedroom. Both her brother, Rayce Thorpe, and her grandmother, Mary Fairchild, stood at the window, watching the dawn. Rayce turned to her as she came to stand beside him and put his arm around her shoulder.

"It's Kailie," she whispered. "She's gone, isn't she? Did you hear the Warrior Song, too?" she asked.

Rayce nodded. "Mother was singing. Then I heard father sing the Caretaker's Song."

Mary sighed. "I thought for a moment I heard another voice, too, as the Song ended."

The three stood at the window with sunlight streaming over them, coloring the air around them with gold.

"We planned to leave tomorrow to visit her," Rayce said quietly and hugged KaynaRee against his side.

"The last time I saw her I thought she looked tired, and she moved so much more slowly. I asked her to stay with me here in Shiptown for a while, but she would not hear of leaving Kalora Bay. I said I could stay with her there on Kalora, but she said she needed to be alone, alone with her memories." She sighed again and smiled at her two grandchildren. KaynaRee was the beautiful younger image of her mother, Kitra Fairchild; and Rayce had the rangy good looks of his father, Camron Thorpe. Within both of them flowed the magic of the Golden Ones and the knowledge of the Caretakers.

A blessing, Mary thought, but a burden as well. Deep in her heart, she feared what lay ahead for them, just as she had feared for their mother. She sighed and turned from the window.

"Rayce, if you'll light the kitchen fire, I'll prepare some breakfast. Come give me a hand, Ree."

During a hurried meal Rayce and KaynaRee decided they would leave for Kalora Bay as soon as they could be ready. Mary packed provisions for them while Ree went to the Guardians' garrison to ask Sergeant Sean McAllam to send a courier to Loren Lamond, Captain of the Highland Guardians, informing him of Kailie Fairchild's passing. She also asked that a message be sent to Kitra and Camron on Lorn, telling them she and Rayce were going to Kalora Bay. Rayce left to finish readying his boat, *Dragon Keeper*.

By midday a steady wind and a strong current carried Rayce's sleek sloop south along the Trayonian coast, well on the way to Kalora Bay. If wind and sea continued in their favor, the sailors should not be far from the terminus of the Wall of Rhade by nightfall.

Rayce and KaynaRee, born and raised on Lorn Isle, had sailed the waters around their island home almost as soon as they could walk. They knew the Trayonian and Balagorn Seas as others might know the mountains and highlands of Kaenolir. With knowledge of currents, wind, and shoreline, with a fearlessness born of their heritage, they continued to sail long after the sun had set.

Rayce manned the tiller while KaynaRee slept for a time, but when he grew sleepy, he woke her.

"Ree," he called. "Your turn. I can't stay awake."

With a sigh and a grunt, she pushed her blankets aside and, yawning and stretching, she came to stand beside Rayce. "Where are we?" she asked, her voice husky with sleep.

"We passed the end of the Wall about an hour ago."

"How's the wind?"

"Still steady out of the north, northwest. Moon won't set for another couple of hours, but we can use the Hermit's stars to steer by if need be."

"We shouldn't be too far from the little cove where we anchored last year when Mother came with us to visit Kailie. If I spot it, let's drop anchor there. That way we can both get some sleep."

"Sounds good. Wake me if you need me." With a jaw-cracking yawn he handed over the tiller, took the blankets KaynaRee had dropped, wrapped himself in them, and lay down to sleep. The rocking of the boat lulled him to sleep almost as soon as he settled.

Luffing of the mainsail as the sloop changed course awakened him a short time later. "Did you find the cove?"

For an answer he heard KaynaRee drop the anchor, felt the boat swing about to ride the gentle waves in the cove.

"Good," Rayce muttered and was immediately asleep again. He didn't hear Ree's quiet footsteps as she passed him on her way to the galley to find more blankets.

"Hey," Rayce muttered and sat up as Ree pulled his blankets off.

"Here." She pushed a biscuit sweetened with jam under his nose, then sat down beside him to enjoy her own. She set a bottle of apple cider between them, and they ate and drank in silence just as the sky began to lighten above the rim of dark cliffs that surrounded the cove on three sides.

"What do you think we'll find when we get to Kailie's cottage, Rayce?"

Rayce leaned closer to hear her softly asked question. He shook his head, took the last bite of biscuit and washed it down with a swallow of cider. "I don't know. She knew we were coming, so maybe she is waiting for us." He thought for a moment before going on. "The Goldenhorn is buried on the eagles' pinnacle. Kailie told me he chose not to follow his fellow Warrior Singers to the kingdom of Faerie. He loved Kailie's mother too much to leave her behind, so he stayed on Lorn with her. He buried her on the eagles' pinnacle. When Goldenhorn died, Kailie and Talanor buried him beside her. Perhaps Kailie wished to be buried there as well."

"Or, perhaps Kailie chose to sleep beside her Alexander. He's been gone for a very long time, Mother said. Maybe we'll find something that will tell us if that is her wish." She brushed the crumbs from her fingers. "But then, we may find nothing all."

Rayce stood up, picked up his blankets and began to fold them.

Ree took them from him. "Let me do that while you get us ready to sail."

Dragon Keeper rode the heavy surf around the Horn of Kalora with Rayce at the tiller. Moonlight glimmered off the curling tips of the restless waves as the sloop slipped around the Horn into the calm waters of the bay. Rayce guided the boat toward the dock that jutted out from the northeastern shore of the sheltered inlet near Kailie's cottage.

"Okay. Now," he called to Ree where she waited at the mast to drop the sail and tie it down.

The boat bumped lightly against the weathered planks and Ree jumped out to catch the line Rayce threw to her. She quickly pulled the line tight around a wooden cleat set in one of the pilings of the old dock before straightening to gaze at Kailie's *Highland Guardian* on the opposite side, bobbing in the slight swell.

"Rayce, what should we do?" she asked quietly. "It will soon be dawn. Should we wait for daylight before going up there?" She pointed toward the darker shadow of the cottage set amidst the rustling grasses of the dune.

She heard Rayce sigh. "I'd rather wait, but I think we should go now."

"Thought that's what you'd say. We'll need a light."

Rayce stepped into the galley to retrieve a lantern. When he had it lit, he handed it up to Ree before joining her on the dock. Ree worried her bottom lip with her teeth as she looked at him.

"It will be all right, Ree," he smiled at her. "Kailie is waiting for us."

"I know. I just don't want her to be gone," she whispered.

Rayce reached out to take his sister's hand and together they walked to the end of the dock. As they stepped down onto packed sand, a white shape, huge and silvered in the dim light, came down the path to meet them.

"Torar," Ree whispered and let go of Rayce's hand to reach out to the great wolf. The wolf whined softly as Ree touched him. She couldn't stop her tears, but when Torar whined again and licked her cheek, she smiled.

"Take us to Kailie, Torar," Rayce said and the wolf turned to lead them up the path.

The cottage door stood open allowing a shaft of moonlight to soften the shadows that filled the cottage. Torar lifted his head and his lament carried out across the dune. As he reached out to comfort the wolf, Rayce felt a touch, just for a moment and was comforted in turn.

"Kailie?" he whispered. He set the lantern on the table and turned to his sister. With the great wolf standing between them, they began to sing. Softly, almost gently, though it was not a Song to be sung gently, the words of the Warrior Song surrounded them, a Song they knew but had never sung.

They had heard their mother sing the Song, had even asked Kailie to sing it for them; but she had smiled and said no. It should only be sung when it is needed, and she had not needed her Song since she had sung it with their mother. She had gladly obliged them when they asked her for the story of the dragons, the glorious fire beasts that had come when Timis and Kaenolir had such great need of them, though they knew the story by heart. She had laughed when she told them of the exhilaration she had felt as she flew the golden Ga'Vrill.

"You are a Caretaker, Rayce, and mayhap one day you will need to find the fire beasts again. And, KaynaRee, you may need to learn to sing a different Warrior Song, not like mine,

or even your mother's. One day," she had said and shook her head. *"But I pray not."*

Would those words take on more meaning 'one day', Rayce had wondered then.

The Song ended as quietly as it had begun. The three figures stood for a time until the wolf whined and then padded silently back into the night. There was no need for them to look for Kailie Fairchild in the cottage; she was not here.

"Rayce, if you light a fire, I'll prepare a pot of tea. We should eat something, too."

Rayce stood in silent homage for a few more minutes before moving to the hearth. He soon had a fire burning, the flames adding light and warmth to the small sitting room. Too restless to sit, he moved from hearth to chair, to the front door and finally to the table under the window. There he found the books and letters Kailie had left.

"Ree, come take a look. There are letters for us." He thumbed through them and handed Ree her letter as she came to stand beside him. She offered him a mug of sweetened tea, and he took it from her but set it on the table, untouched. "Here's one for our parents, one for Grandmother Mary, and one for Captain Lamond."

"Oh," she said softly. Ree set her mug beside Rayce's. She took the letter he handed her and turned away to take the chair near the fireplace while Rayce sat down at the table. With trembling fingers she broke the wax seal.

My dear KaynaRee, she read. *Do you know that your name came from the Singer who taught the Golden Ones how to sing their Songs? Her name was Rhianna Lanee and she was very beautiful, as you are beautiful. She lived in the Singers' Hall on the Horn of Kalora. You know the story. I doubt there is much left of the Hall after all this time, but you must try to find it one day. You will know when that day comes, for, dear heart, you are truly a Golden One, although you may not realize that yet. I had hoped to take you to the Horn, but that is not to be. It is left to someone else to teach you your Song. Your Song is found in the Quair, just as my Last Song was there, and your mother's Fire Song. My mother's heart near broke when Talanor Rowan came to take me to the Horn when it was time for me to learn my Song. Your mother's heart will ache, too, for you, dear Ree.*

Take my <u>Highland Guardian</u> as your own and sail safely, Ree. My journals, too, are for you. In their pages you may find answers to your questions. I cannot tell you more than this because I do not know what lies ahead for you. I pray the Ancient Ones will guide you and show you the path you must take. I know only that Timis and Kaenolir will have need of the Golden Ones. I would have it otherwise, for you, Ree, and for Rayce and for your parents.

Do not be sad that I am gone. Three lifetimes I have lived, but now my time is done and I am ready to join my Alexander. I want you to know that you have blessed these end of days for me.

Be strong, my KaynaRee, with the strength and power of a Golden One, the knowledge of a Caretaker.

Kailie Fairchild

KaynaRee wiped away tears as she finished reading, and then she smiled, but it was a sad smile. A log shifted sending sparks up the chimney and she rose to get more wood for the fire. She stood for a time, staring into the flames, thinking about the letter she had just read.

"What had Kailie meant by 'your Song'? Why did she feel I should find the Singers' Hall on the Horn? What is there for me to find?"

She felt a draft and turned to see Rayce standing in the open doorway, looking out toward the sea. Wisps of mist shifted and eddied over the dunes. The waters of the bay hissed and sighed. Somewhere close by, the piercing cry of a sea eagle announced the dawn.

"Rayce," she called softly. He turned and smiled at her.

"Let's walk," he murmured. Together they left the cottage, following the path through the dunes to the water.

"Did you read your letter?" she asked as the mists swirled around them.

"Yes. She asked us to deliver her other letters and to see to the cottage. There are books for me. Some are hers, but I think many of them belonged to Talanor Rowan. I wonder," he said almost to himself, "what will I discover in the books?" They walked a bit farther in silence. "There are books for you, too, Ree, her journals."

"She knew, didn't she, knew that she was going to leave us. She gave you the books because you are the studious one, always asking questions. You asked her once if she would come with you to Cathorn. Remember? Why do you want to go there?"

Rayce merely sighed without answering Ree's question.

"Kailie said I should go to the Horn, to look for the Singers' Hall. She said someone would teach me my Song, though she didn't say, or know, who that 'someone' might be." She shook her head. "A Song, do you suppose, like hers, like Mother's?"

"I don't know, Ree. Kailie said I would walk with dragons." He laughed. "Me? Walk with dragons?"

"Does that mean, do you think, that dragons will be needed? Like they were when Mother and Father needed to find their dragons? Why will dragons be needed? Oh, Rayce, there are so many questions. I hope you will find some answers in Talanor Rowan's books. Perhaps in Kailie's journals, I'll find some answers."

They walked until the sun had risen high enough to burn off the fog and mists before turning back. A sad task and a long, hard day lay before them. For the moment, they put their questions aside and turned to what they needed to do before leaving Kalora Bay.

They packed what they wished to take from Kailie's cottage in the *Dragon Keeper* and the *Highland Guardian.* Rayce shuttered the windows, repairing one shutter with the hammer and nails he found in a basket in the kitchen. He stacked the wood pile that had begun to tumble near the back door, but brought in a large basket of logs to set near the hearth. After seeing to repairs in the cottage, he checked over the *Highland Guardian.*

Ree emptied cupboards of the food that remained and the clothes she found in a chest in Kailie's bedroom. She folded the bedding and put it in the bottom drawer of the chest she'd emptied of clothing. The few pieces of furniture would remain. Looking about the small cottage, it appeared they had done all they could do.

"I've fashioned a lock for the door, though if someone wants to get in, it won't take much to break down the door. It's old and weathered," Rayce said as he pulled the door shut and locked it.

"Thanks, Rayce, for checking the *Highland Guardian* for me."

"For as old as it is, it's in good shape. The sail is fairly new and the ropes were replaced recently, too." He smiled sadly as he thought about the story Kailie had told them of sailing the *Highland Guardian* over the bar into the harbor at Riversend with their mother and grandmother Mary Hamilton in Kitra's boat the *Wanderer*. "She wanted you to have it, so she made sure it's seaworthy."

They walked a short distance down the path to the dock, but they stopped as one to look back at the cottage that had sheltered Kailie Fairchild for so many years. Already the dunes seemed to be encroaching on the small space. For a fleeting moment, Ree thought she saw Torar slip through the tall grass, but she could not be sure.

"What will become of Torar?" she asked.

Rayce shook his head. "I imagine he will join Kailie wherever she is."

It was appropriate, Rayce was later to think, that the sun broke through the clouds just then and bathed the stone cottage in a golden light. When the light faded, they turned and continued to the dock. Behind them, Torar watched them go.

Two days later Rayce and KaynaRee sailed into Shiptown harbor. Clouds were beginning to build in the west, and the sun set in a fiery portent of a coming storm. After securing their boats and packing up several bags of items they didn't want to leave behind, they walked together along the bustling wharf.

"I never asked you what you plan to do with the letter Kailie wrote to Captain Lamond." Ree stopped to rearrange the bags she carried.

"I'll take it to the Guardian garrison and ask Sean McAllam to send it in the courier bag to the Fort."

Ree nodded. "After we visit with Grandmother Mary, I think we should go home for a while, don't you?"

"Yes. Not long now until harvest, so our help will be needed."

"After that, then what? Will you stay on Lorn?"

"I don't know, Ree. I'll probably see to the grape harvest and get the wine in the aging barrels, but beyond that, I can't tell you. Something. . ." He shook his head. "Something seems to be urging me in a different direction."

"What do you mean?"

Rayce laughed. "If I knew, I'd know what I was going to do."

They walked on, dodging loaded carts and fishermen getting ready to head out.

"Kailie said. . ." he paused again. "Kailie said I need to translate Father's book."

"But she didn't tell you why you need to translate it, or how, other than Talanor's books might help?"

"That's about it, yes."

Ree blew out a breath and stepped around a woman hawking fresh oysters. "Okay. After you translate it, then what will you do with it?"

"Look out," Rayce suddenly grabbed her arm and pulled her out of the way of four young toughs coming toward them, laughing and talking loudly. They whistled and made rude remarks to Ree as they stumbled by.

"Arlanders," Rayce said in disgust and hustled Ree away from the carousing four-some. Catcalls followed them.

"Never used to see Arlanders in Shiptown," Ree said. "Those four were already drunk, and it's early yet."

Shouts and obscenities came from the open doors of a tavern as they passed by.

"Sean and his Guardians will have their hands full tonight," Ree said.

Finally they threaded their way from the dock area and trudged up the street which would take them eventually to their grandmother's house.

"I'd like to leave this letter off before we go on, Ree, but I'd rather you didn't walk home alone. Come with me."

Ree sighed. She was tired, weary and sore, but she nodded and followed Rayce when he turned down the street that led to the Guardians' garrison.

"I never used to need an escort through town," she groused.

"Times have changed since we were kids running free here."

"I know, and I don't like the changes. If you listen to what people are saying, the changes can be laid firmly on the Arlanders. It seems there are lots of incidents between 'Towners and the Arlanders with more and more Arlanders coming every week."

"Not a good situation. People here won't hire them, and landlords won't rent homes to them, even if the Arlanders do have money, which most don't. There will be trouble, already is trouble, but it's just going to escalate."

They passed through the garrison gate and crossed the narrow yard before mounting the steps to the main building. Inside they found Sergeant McAllam giving the night patrols their orders. When he had finished his instructions and sent the Guardians on their way, he turned to Rayce and Ree.

"Welcome back," he smiled first at Ree, then nodded to Rayce. "Lady Fairchild is gone, then?" he asked.

"Yes," Ree murmured. "We'll tell you all about it later, but now Rayce has a letter for Captain Lamond."

Rayce set one of his packs on the floor and bent to retrieve the letter. "Will you send this to the Captain with your next courier, Sean? It's from Kailie."

"Of course. And I have letters for you. They just came in today's courier bag from Landsend. I was going to take them up to your grandmother later. Wait here, I'll get them for you." He stepped into his office and returned shortly with the letters.

"Thanks. Perhaps we'll see you tomorrow." Rayce took the letters and hoisted his bags. Ree gave Sean a tired smile and murmured good night.

At the door, Rayce paused and turned to Sean. "You may have a rough night. We encountered several drunks on the dock and the taverns are already doing a brisk business."

Sean sighed. "Most nights are rough," he muttered. He watched Rayce and KaynaRee leave the compound before turning away to deal with the paperwork on his desk.

The night sky had grown dark with just a few stars peeping through the scudding clouds. The wind shifted to blow stronger and colder from the west, pushing more clouds from over the sea toward the land.

Ree shrugged. "Storm coming in tonight. Good thing we made it home ahead of it. Who are the letters from?"

"There's a letter from Father," Rayce said. "It's addressed to both of us, and another from Mother to Grandmother Mary."

"Hm," Ree murmured. "Wonder why father would write to us?"

"We'll soon find out. There's grandmother's house."

The three of them, Rayce, Ree and Mary Fairchild, sat with cups of tea before a fire burning low in the hearth. Rain battered against the windows as the storm blew in. The travelers had eaten and read the letter from their father, but before finding their beds the three of them shared the contents of their letters from Kitra and Camron with each other.

"Your father has had great responsibility placed on his shoulders. According to your father and from what I've heard, Timis is a country in conflict. The situation between Arlanders and Timisians may well come to war. If anyone can find a solution, Camron Thorpe can; Tiernan Irworth chose well."

"I'm not surprised Father was chosen to be the Timisian chieftain; although, I wish the business with the Arlanders was not so explosive."

"Kaenolir may be drawn into a confrontation with Arland, too," Rayce said as he set aside his cup.

"I know," Mary sighed. She placed the letter from her daughter and Kailie's farewell to her on the small table beside her chair. "I see more Arlanders every time I venture out to market. I don't go down to the docks for seafood anymore, at least not alone. I've lived in Shiptown a long time, but I never worried about being safe before. I do now," she said. "Well, there are always problems in life that cannot be solved with simple solutions. We'll just have to work at finding ways we can all live together." She rose from her chair. "You are both very tired, I know. Tomorrow will be a busy day for you. Time for bed." She picked up the lamp she'd lit earlier. "Rayce, would you see to banking the fire and be sure the door is locked before you go to bed?"

Rayce nodded. "Of course. Sleep well, Grandmother. Good night, Ree."

Ree gave Rayce a tired smile before following her grandmother down the hall to the two bedrooms at the back of the house. Rayce saw to the fire, checked the door and then headed for his sleeping pallet in the alcove off the kitchen where he slept when both he and Ree stayed with Mary. He set the candle he'd lit on the kitchen table and retrieved his letter from Kailie from the pack beside his bed. Though exhaustion nagged at him, Rayce pulled up a chair and read Kailie's letter to him again.

Rayce, Caretaker, it began. *The books are for you. Most come from Talanor Rowan's library, a few are mine. I selected these special titles knowing you would find them interesting and enlightening. Helpful, too, I hope. I should have taken you to Cathorn Isle one day, but I waited too long. However, you must go. And you must go soon. What you find there will answer questions you would have asked Talanor were he still with us, questions you would have asked me. You will have many questions, I think, once you begin reading*

You are a Caretaker, like your father before you, and his father, and his, back to the time of the fire beasts, the dragons you always ask me about. You see, Rayce, you know more about the dragons than I do because they are part of your heritage, part of your blood, your bones. Your father has a book written by the last Caretaker to walk the land of Timis, the last Caretaker to walk with dragons until your father did. And it will be up to you, I believe, to walk with them once more. For what purpose I do not know.

So, take your father's book and discover its message. I believe the help you need to translate and interpret what is written there will be found in Talanor's books, in the library at Camlanrein, and perhaps in mine. When you have the words, you will know what it is you need to do, you and KaynaRee. Yes, Ree is part of the answer.

I must go, dear Rayce. Alexander is calling me.

May the spirits of the Caretakers and the Golden Ones keep you strong, and may the Ancient Ones watch over you.

Kailie Fairchild

Rayce folded the letter and for a moment tapped it against his knee, his brow furrowed in thought, his broad shoulders slumped in weariness.

"Kailie called me Caretaker. Caretaker of the fire beasts," he thought.

He had so many questions, so much he wanted to know. But for now, he would rest. He scrubbed his face with his hands and rose to go to bed. As he shed his clothes, he heard the wind whistling about the house and the steady pounding of rain. He lay down, covered himself with the quilt, yawned and closed his eyes.

"I'll think about all of this tomorrow," he murmured and turned his face to the wall.

Caretaker.

A whisper on the edge of his mind, just before sleep took him.

Caretaker.

chapter four

He was tall, gaunt and slightly stooped. A jagged scar ran from his temple through the empty socket of his right eye down his cheek to his jaw. It was a scar made by fire and though he was still a young man when the fire beast's flames touched him, he felt the pain and heat still. Black hair heavily streaked with gray hung below his shoulders. He wore a long robe of dark wool belted with a chain of slim gold links, to mark a position of distinction among his fellows. In his left hand he carried a staff of oak hardened in fire, but in a fire of his own making. The staff was the only aid he allowed himself, for another scar hidden by his robe ran from chest to knee and throbbed and burned with the fire of the dragon.

Gadred Aember limped along the shore of the Balagorn Channel, searching as he had these past years for remnants of Dunadd, the black granite castle Aldward Finton, his master, had built, a castle Aember remembered well, a castle and all its riches and magic reduced to ashes by dragon fire. Whenever he thought of it, he cursed those who had caused its destruction and ultimately Finton's death.

A great stone circle erected by ancient worshippers and infused with powers dark and sinister had stood on the harsh shore below the castle. Finton had called upon those powers and made them his own and made his followers strong. Fire beasts destroyed the stones as well. But there must still be fragments buried beneath the sand, and those fragments would yet hold power. He was sure of it. Memory of castle and stones reached out to him in dreams and in waking, and at times he felt Finton touching him, whispering to him of power and the gold Finton had lost.

"Once," he thought, "we walked with power and magic. If we could but find the source of Finton's power, we would walk so again. We shall walk that way again," he swore. "We shall."

There was power here, and it would be his if he could but find it. His master would want him to have it.

There had been a book, the Storin, filled with secrets of darkness. The book had shown Finton the way to bring Pales from the Abyss, savage and terrifying creatures able to kill and destroy. Did dragon fire destroy the book as it had the stones? Aember remembered the book placed on the center slab of the circle. If he closed his eyes, he could hear Finton reading from the book in a language only Finton knew, could see white flames surrounding Finton. And in the midst of those flames the Pales wrapped Finton in their horrible embrace.

Aember shuddered at the thought of the Pales. They had frightened him, but the Pales had not harmed the Warders. The Warders were protected by Finton's power, by his magic.

High Suzerain, the Warders had called Aldward Finton, high lord, and they became his soldiers, followed him into battle and followed him into death. Dragon fire had killed most of the army of Arlanders and Warders that Finton had gathered, and in the end, Finton and all his Pales died in dragon flames.

"All for naught," he thought angrily. Hate welled up in him and he jabbed his staff angrily into the sand. He shook his fist in the air and cursed, cursed the beasts and their music, cursed those who had ridden them.

It had been the fire beasts, the dragons, he realized suddenly that had been more powerful than even the creatures from the Abyss, more powerful than Aldward Finton.

As he remembered how the fire beasts had destroyed pirate ships whose captains Finton had lured to his cause with gold, how the beasts had destroyed Pales and men alike, how the songs of the dragons and their riders had surrounded them and beat them into submission, his thoughts took a different bent.

"If I could find the lair of the fire beasts, if I could make them mine, mine to command, what then . . ."

The day grew hot and Aember paused to wipe the sweat from his brow. He had been searching since dawn. Shore birds swooped and swirled before him to settle once more in their search for insects and other tiny creatures. As he rested, the wind shifted direction and stilled. "There will be a storm tonight," he thought.

He stood for several minutes, gazing out to sea.

"Lord Finton, show me where the magic lies," he whispered, but there was no one to hear his entreaty, only the wind as it came now from the north, ruffling the waters of the Balagorn Channel as it went. "Lord Finton," he murmured again, but this time with the name came images that filled him with hatred, so intense he could barely breathe. "We had so much—great power, great wealth, a leader we bowed willingly to. And they destroyed it all, the Timisians, the dragons." He ground his teeth together, his breath coming harshly, almost in gasps. "We shall have it back; I swear." He lifted his fist and shook it toward the sky.

Finally, he began to walk again, retracing his steps of the morning. Tired and hungry, still feeling the rage he had felt the day he watched Dunadd and all that Finton had built destroyed by fire and sword, he made his way along the beach and then began to climb the path that led into the Dalrudd Mountains. It was here that he and the few followers of Finton's Way lived in lonely isolation. Where once the Warders had numbered more than a thousand and roamed throughout Timis and into Kaenolir with impunity, now there were but fifty and most of them growing old. They did not call themselves Warders, except among themselves, for that title brought unwanted attention. The people of Timis in particular had no tolerance for the message Finton had brought first with words and then with the power of the sword and the darkness of the Abyss. Thus, after the Warders who survived the flames of the dragons and the swords of the Timisian shed their black robes, most left the path of the Way and the life it had dictated. Some returned to their families, those whose families would have them. Others wandered aimlessly eking out a bare existence, scorned and hated. Still others died unnamed, unwanted and often unburied.

But fifty had banded together under Gadred Aember's leadership, finding they could not nor did they want to live in any other manner than what the Way had prescribed. They built a long low hall of stone and thatch in a deep valley hidden in the mountains above the Channel, not far from where the black castle had once ruled. Here they managed to subsist on the bounty of the sea, vegetables grown in terraced gardens, fruit from an apple orchard, a small plot of grain. Fresh water came from a well dug laboriously by hand and fed by mountain snows and scant summer rains. Bread was baked in an oven they had constructed from mud bricks and stone. They did not venture beyond their valley except to make the trek down to the sea. If intruders dared to come too close, they were run off, or, upon occasion, even killed and buried hastily beneath a cover of rocks and earth. The Fifty, after all, had all been soldiers in Finton's army of Warders, and the ways of a soldier were second nature. Timisians soon learned to give the valley of the Fifty a wide berth.

"My lord," a voice called.

Aember stopped and leaning tiredly on his staff shielded his eyes from the sun and waited for the comrade who had watched for his return to join him.

"Did you find anything?" Younger than Aember by several years, Conn Regan had joined the Warders soon after his thirteenth birthday, a man in the eyes of his family. But the decision to walk in Finton's Way had ostracized him from his relatives and many of his friends. He did not know if his parents and brothers still lived on their farm in the High Champaign, nor did he care. In truth, he rarely thought of them.

"No, Conn, I did not," he muttered darkly.

Regan fell in step beside Aember and offered his arm. The older man sighed as he took it, irritated that he needed the physical support, and the two continued to climb the steep, narrow path that wound into the mountains. When they reached the top, they stopped to rest for a moment before starting the descent into the valley. They watched smoke curl lazily from the center chimney of their communal dwelling and knew that the evening meal was being prepared.

"I'll come with you tomorrow, m'lord, if you will allow me to."

Aember nodded his head. "All right. To search for clams for soup, if nothing else," he said bitterly.

The younger man nodded. "Tomorrow then," he said.

While Aember and the rest of the Fifty slept that night, a storm blew through the Balagorn Channel, its fury unfelt for a time in the hidden valley. The narrow channel funneled the wind and water and whipped the waves into towering peaks that smashed their way through the restraining walls of sand

and mountain. A slab of stone gave way to the relentless pressure it had endured for eons and crashed into the sea, leaving a gaping scar. Surging water scoured the channel walls and in its wake, not far from where the stone circle had stood, it left a piece of gleaming metal melded with a streak of black granite. Sand sifted over the piece until the next wave retreated, leaving a portion exposed.

Spears of lightning were followed by claps of thunder that rolled on and on. Wind whistled and keened a strange and mournful cry as the storm beat its way south. In the mountains above the hollow left by the destruction of Dunadd the wind began to howl like a thing long restrained set suddenly free.

Gadred Aember.

In his bed, Gadred Aember awakened with a start. He had been dreaming and in his dreams he stood in the center of a stone circle; dragons flew above him and then began to settle slowly to the ground around him. With a wild cry they bowed their heads in homage to him. They were glorious, all the colors of the sea and the earth, and the music of their songs filled the air.

And in his dream they were his to command. His.

Aember smiled and rose. As the leader of the Fifty he enjoyed a small room at the end of the hall while the members of the brotherhood slept in a large dormitory-style room. He lit the candle set near at hand on his bedside table and pulled on his robe. Leaving his staff behind but taking the candle, he left his chamber and moved silently past his sleeping comrades.

With the dream still vivid in his mind he settled in front of the low-burning fire in the central room where the Fifty gathered to eat their meals and to rest after their assigned tasks. He searched for elements of power in what he believed to be the areas where Dunadd and the stone circle had stood, but perhaps he had it wrong. Perhaps he should have been searching for knowledge of the fire beasts.

Why had they come to Timis? Had they been called? With magic? The music he had heard that fateful day—sung by the dragons? Or their riders? Or both?

And then he remembered—the Golden Ones of Kaenolir. Their Songs were magical, powerful. He had heard Finton curse them when he left his ravaged army of Arlanders, left his faithful Warders to their fate, and whirled away. Where had he gone? Some said to the Wall of Rhade in Kaenolir, and there the dragons and their riders had destroyed the last remnant of the unearthly Pales. Some believed Finton had not died with the Pales but that he had escaped to Dunadd. If that were true, then Finton died as his castle burned around him. Or had he? Did he yet exist, waiting for Gadred Aember to find him and gather his Warders together once more?

There were names, if he could but remember, names of the Golden Ones and a name just on the edge of his memory, a name of a Timisian who had spied on Finton and the Warders. What was it? Ah, yes. Thorpe, Camron Thorpe. What had he heard him called? Caretaker, that was it—caretaker of the fire beasts. Thorpe and Aldward Finton had once roamed the countryside together when they were young men, but they had parted ways when Finton took up the Way and began gathering followers loyal to him. Where was Thorpe? Where were the Golden Ones? He would check tomorrow with the Fifty; someone might remember more about those last chaotic days as their Way crumbled around them. And surely some would know the histories of Kaenolir and Timis.

Dragon fire, dragon song. Golden Ones, magical songs.

Gadred. Gadred Aember.

Wind whistled under the eaves and rattled the windows; rain began to pound the slate roof. The storm had found its way through the mountains into the valley. Aember rose stiffly from his chair. He had sat for a long time, remembering, and the fire had burned down to embers, leaving him chilled. He rubbed the ache in his thigh and cursed his weakness. He must rest now for with the dawn he would begin to search in a new direction; he would search for the fire beasts. If he found the fire beasts, he might well find his beloved master.

"My lord, the brothers are waiting for you."

Conn Regan had come at dawn, as he did each morning he was here in the compound, to help Aember decide what tasks were to be accomplished this day and who of the men were best suited to complete the tasks. Aember had asked Regan to have everyone remain at the table after breaking their fast.

"Thank you, Conn. Would you have tea and some bread at my place? That's all I require this morning."

Regan bowed his head in acknowledgement and left Aember's chamber.

Aember gathered the few papers he'd managed to keep over the years, but they offered little information except for a note that spoke to the close relationship between the chieftain of Timis, Tiernan Irworth, and Camron Thorpe. He could find no mention of the Golden Ones of Kaenolir. Perhaps some of his fellows would recall more than he could remember. He gave a wry smile, for he had not been the best of students. However, he thought, he had been a faithful follower of Finton's Way.

Aember took his chair at the head of the long plank table. A steaming cup of tea and a plate of warm brown bread waited for him, and he ate and drank while the low murmur of conversation flowed around him. When he finished his repast, he raised his hand and the men gave him their immediate attention.

"I want all of you to think back to the days when you were young." This comment brought a few smiles. "To a time when you still lived among your family and friends." The smiles faded. "I want you to remember when we were soldiers in our Lord Finton's great army of Warders. And I want you to remember the fateful day when life changed for us and all was lost." Aember sighed and rubbed his throbbing thigh. "Some of our memories are hard and I know you have put them away, out of your minds, but I want you to remember everything from our years as Warders and from your lives before becoming followers of the Way.

"Conn, please take notes on what we discuss today, if you will. I want a record we can refer to." Regan left the table to retrieve pen, ink and parchment from the cupboards at the back of the room. When he returned to his place, Aember began again.

"Now, tell me what you know or may have heard about the Golden Ones of Kaenolir and about Camron Thorpe."

The Fifty spent the morning dredging up old memories, and for many, old wounds. Conn Regan took copious, meticulous notes and after the evening meal, Aember excused himself to his chamber to go over them in careful detail.

He had names now to go with half-remembered memories: Kitra Fairchild of the Golden Ones; Camron Thorpe, Caretaker of the fire beasts of Timis; tales of the Wall of Rhade and Kailie Fairchild, of Andrew Goldenhorn and the Warrior Singers of Lorn Isle, of Mt. Sinnarock; of Alpean, an ancient Kaenolirian king, and his brother Maelorn the Darkling Prince. And a name that Aember had heard as a boy, Talanor Rowan, was repeated in several of the stories.

Some of the Fifty had taken part in capturing Banning Village and taking the Cragon gold mine. All had been part of Aldward Finton's army, and the march out of the mountains through Cragon Pass was still clear in their minds. Disparaging remarks were made about the Arlander thugs Finton had lured with the promise of gold, how the Arlanders had not adhered to the battle plan but plunged ahead to pillage what they had all thought would be a defenseless Ross Harbor.

A picture of the Golden Ones became clearer to him, and he was pleased that two of the Fifty had roots in Kaenolir and knew the story of the Golden Ones and the connection between the Singers and the mage, Talanor Rowan. Several men had known Camron Thorpe and Tiernan Irworth.

But there had been questions, too, questions and anger and disagreement. "The fools," he thought.

"Why, Gadred, do you want to know all of this? What purpose will it serve? We have put our old lives behind us and we are content here in our valley. Why stir up these old memories, make us think of what we once were, what we had?" asked Jaston Sonne.

"Gadred, you have been searching the sands and the rocks for years. For what? Do you think you will find Lord Finton in grains of sand?" Desmond Orly asked heatedly. "Many of us are growing old. We are safe here. Leave us be!"

"What we once were we could be again!" Aember shouted. "You were soldiers; we were an army! People did as we commanded them! The gold of Timis was ours!"

"The gold of Timis was Finton's," a quiet voice of calm came from the other end of the table. Morten Cassel, oldest of the Fifty, his white hair and beard shining in the sunlight that slanted through the narrow windows, turned to look at Aember. "Have you forgotten that point, Gadred? Finton took the gold for himself. He raised an army. To get what *he* wanted. He used Pales to kill and frighten because *he* wanted to be a *king*."

"No," Aember shook his head angrily.

"Yes, Gadred. Your hatred has twisted your reasoning. What Finton did, he did for himself, not for us."

"We would have shared in all he gained," Aember cried.

"Where did we store the gold, Gadred? Why did we kill our own people? Answer those questions, for all of us to hear."

Aember rose shakily to his feet and shook his fist at the old man. "Dunadd was the safest place to store the gold, to keep it from the Arlanders." His voice shook.

"Ah," Cassel murmured. "Or was it to keep it from us? He used magic to seal the door to the room where he had us take the gold bars. I was there when he uttered the words. We guarded Dunadd's gates, its walls. How would the Arlanders have entered the castle? How would they have broken the magic seal to steal the gold? Think, Gadred, think. You are remembering a Finton who did not exist!"

A few of the older Warders raised their voices in agreement with Cassel, but others shouted them down.

Aember pounded his fist on the table until the shouting lessened and his voice could be heard above the argument.

"Are you content, then, to die here in this valley, hidden away, afraid you will be found? When there were those who dared to find us, what did we do? We ran them off; we've even killed a few. Why? Why should we be so afraid to be found?"

He pounded his fist again and again on the table. "We are Warders," he shouted. "That should mean something to you!"

"It means, Gadred, that if we dare to venture from our valley wearing our black robes, we will be killed. You know how many of us escaped when Dunadd fell? Look around you, Gadred—fifty of us escaped. Fifty! What can fifty do?" Cassel asked.

Before Aember could respond, Cassel rose from his chair and with great dignity, left the hall followed by six others who agreed with him.

"Bah," Aember waved at the retreating backs in disgust. "Go then, be gone." He slumped dejectedly in his chair. After a moment, he looked around the table at the remaining Warders. "You have your tasks for the rest of the day," he said wearily in dismissal. The men rose and began to take their leave. "Conn, I would like you to stay for a moment." When the last man exited the hall, he turned to Regan. "I have a proposal to make to you. Come with me, to the beach, where we'll not be disturbed."

The younger man nodded and rose to follow Aember, whose limp was very pronounced from sitting so long.

"May I get your walking staff for you?" Regan asked and at Aember's nod, hurried away to fetch it.

The two men walked slowly along the Balagorn shore, the midday sun warm on their shoulders. High above them eagles rode the currents of air, and hundreds of tiny shore birds scurried ahead of them until they took wing together, a silver shifting mass, whirling away above the sand. They soon came upon the massive slab shed by the mountain during last night's storm. It lay in jumbled pieces, and at high tide a huge boulder slivered from the slab would block the narrow beach.

"We may have to forge a new path down to the sand," Regan said.

"Hm, yes, I think so. It's as if the mountain sliced off a piece of itself." Aember walked slowly and carefully among the scattered stones, leaning heavily on his staff.

"Would you like to rest, m'lord?"

"No, let's go a little farther. Give me your arm, Conn. That would help. Yes, thank you," he murmured as he took the younger man's arm. Something called to him and he pressed on. The stones that littered the beach gradually became smaller and fewer in number as the two men trudged on.

"We are nearly to the place where the stone circle once stood, where Lord Finton called the Pales. Do you remember?"

"I became a Warder shortly thereafter. So, no, I was not privileged to see the master call the Pales."

"So much power," Aember said. "All gone now."

"But perhaps, one day," Regan said softly, "there will be power here again. With the Warders."

"Yes. With us." He smiled. "I'm glad you think so, too." They walked a bit farther. "Cassel is wrong," he muttered.

The sun glinted off something just there in the sand, sending an almost searing beam of light into their eyes.

"Conn, what is that?" Aember felt the blood suddenly pound through his body. "Go, quickly, see what the sun has found."

Regan slipped his arm free and hurried to the spot where they had seen the bright burst of light. He knelt on one knee and brushed away the concealing sand.

"What did you find, Conn?" Aember asked breathlessly and he struggled to hurry.

"My lord, look," his voice shook. "It looks like a clump of gold. With a black streak through it. See?"

Aember stood beside the kneeling man, out of breath and shaking with excitement. "Yes," he whispered. "At last, at last I have found what I have been seeking."

Regan reached down to pick up the treasure, but Aember stopped him. Aember dropped his staff and with a concerted effort knelt in the sand. He picked up the clump of gold, about the size of a small, clenched fist, from its nest hidden in the sand. Though small the nugget was heavy, very heavy. Aember turned the piece over, examining it carefully. The gold, he saw, encapsulated the black section that appeared to be granite.

"Yes, yes. Gold, dragon gold, and black granite from the Stones. Yes," he laughed. "So close, so close. I've searched for so long and it's been so close all this time." He clutched the nugget in both hands, pressing it against his chest and as he did so he felt the full impact of the power he held. A piercing, fiery pain shot through his body from the top of his head to the soles of his feet. He screamed in agony and fell to the sand, babbling and frothing at the mouth. His eyes slid back in his head and he laid still, the nugget still clutched tightly against his chest.

"My lord Aember," Regan cried and reached out to catch the man as he fell. "My lord," he cried again and knelt beside Aember's prostrate form. He tried to pry the nugget from Aember's hands but could not pull his fingers away.

The day grew hot but Aember did not stir. Regan dribbled water from the small water flask he carried onto Aember's face and tried to get him to drink. He feared for his master's life, and if he didn't come back to himself soon, Regan decided he must pull him up farther onto the beach and into the shade of the large boulders that littered the sand at the base of the cliffs that rose here above the Balagorn Channel. The death-like grip Aember had on the nugget did not loosen, and after a short time, Regan slipped his hands under Aember's shoulders and began to pull him into a more protected spot.

The older man was heavy and Regan had to pause several times to catch his breath, but at last he reached a cooler shaded area among the rocks. He straightened Aember's limbs and once again tried to remove the nugget from clenched fingers. He could see that the skin of Aember's fingers and palms was fiery red.

"This thing has burned him," he whispered, and thinking to cool the wounded areas poured a little water onto them. But he jerked back in surprise when the water sizzled and sputtered when it touched the clump of gold.

"My lord," he whispered, "what have we found?" He dropped down in the sand beside Aember. Again he tried to get the unconscious man to drink but could not.

The afternoon wore on; the tide turned and the surf drew closer and closer until Regan was forced to pull Aember even further into the rocks. Even so, the tide would soon be running full, and he knew they could not escape the sea. Still, he would not desert the master.

As it grew dark, Regan dozed in exhaustion, but he jerked awake at the sound of his name.

"Conn." Just a whisper. "Do you have any water?"

"My lord? Have you come back to me? Yes, yes, let me get my water flask." He lifted Aember's head and carefully gave him a drink. "Just a little now. Sip it." He set the water aside and lifted Aember to a sitting position. "We must move farther up, m'lord. The tide is coming in. Can you help me get you on your feet?"

Regan pulled Aember's arm across his shoulder and with a grunt hoisted him to his feet.

"Where is my staff, Conn? I could help you more if I had my staff."

"I'm sorry, my lord, I left it on the beach when I brought you up here among the rocks. You needed to be in the shade or you would have died."

"Never mind," Aember murmured. "I can get another."

With Regan bearing almost all of Aember's weight, they pulled themselves upward until they were beyond the reach of the sea. Breathing deeply, Regan slid Aember down and slumped on the sand beside him. The waves hissed and splashed against the boulders below them, and darkness enveloped them. They rested for several minutes, before Regan broke the silence.

"Your hands, m'lord, that thing we found burned your hands. What is it, that lump of gold?"

Slowly Aember opened his fingers enough to peer at what he held. Even in the darkness it glinted, as if from an inner light. "This is what I've searched for since we came to the valley." His claw-like fingers closed again around his treasure. "This is a piece of Finton's power, of dark power, Conn. It is a piece of dragon power as well, and with this we will be powerful again. We will find the way with this treasure." His voice grew stronger. "The black portion of the nugget is the granite of the Stones of Destiny; the gold is the gold of our treasure. Both have been forged and melded in dragon fire. Dragon fire, Conn, so powerful it destroyed even what the Darkness created." He smiled and in the eerie light streaming through his fingers, the smile was grotesque. "With this we shall find the lair of the dragons and make them our own." He laughed and the sound floated on the air above them. "Come, Conn," he said as he rose, unaided. "We have what we need to walk the Way of the Warders. Now, this is what I want you to do."

Aember talked through the night and with the dawn, the two went their separate ways, Aember back to the valley and Conn Regan into the mountains toward Cragon Pass.

Night winds whistled down the valley, sighing through trees and sending leaves swirling into corners and skittering across the courtyard of the Warder's compound. One by one the men found their beds and lulled by the sounds of the night all soon slept, all but Gadred Aember. He did not sleep nor had he slept since finding his treasure, the dragon token as he's come to think of it. He felt no need for rest. As the compound settled into darkness and sleep, Aember paced the confines of his chamber, fingering the piece of gold and granite, caressing it, and passing it from hand to hand. A single candle flickered on his bedside table casting his shadow in giant relief on the walls as he paced.

He was not the same Gadred Aember who had walked the beach and found a treasure, a treasure he believed would restore the Warders to power. The initial burns to his hands when he had first clutched the treasure had all but disappeared, and his skin was smooth and supple, the way it had been when he was young. Although still somewhat thin he was no longer stooped. His shoulders appeared broad and muscled beneath the fabric of his robe, his back straight, his carriage upright. He walked with but a slight limp, his thighs and lower legs once more strong and flexible, allowing him to move with the grace of youth. Although the dragon fire scar still throbbed, he no longer paid it much attention. The scar across his face did not cause him the anguish it once had. His voice, pitched deeper and more melodious, seemed to soothe and cast a spell upon his listeners. Dark, piercing eyes probed deep, found secrets. His lips curved with sinister pleasure.

No, he was not the same Gadred Aember.

However, since finding his treasure, he had been very careful to appear as he had been for the past twenty-five or more years, gaunt and stooped and weakened. No one must see him as he was here in his chamber until he was ready, until the power he craved was firmly in his hands.

He stopped his pacing to stare out into the night, still stroking the gold and granite token with his long, tapered fingers. A smile lifted the corners of his mouth as a plan began to take shape in his mind. He was nearly ready, ready to take his place alongside Aldward Finton as a power to be reckoned with here in Timis. Gadred Aember would take what should belong to the Warders, to him. As the dragons had taken Timis from them, now with the power and fire of the dragons in his hands he, Gadred Aember, would take Timis.

And the dragons would bow in obeisance before him.

He laughed softly. From an inner pocket of his robe he withdrew a silken pouch and placed the nugget in it. With a long golden cord, he fashioned a necklace, threaded it through the top of the pouch and tied it securely around his neck, then slipped it beneath his robe. The pouch with its contents lay pulsing lightly against his chest. He was nearly ready. Tonight would begin the journey to claim Timis. The first step would be to eliminate the Warder who stood in his way. Tonight Morten Cassel would pay the price of dissent.

With silent steps he left his chamber and made his way down the hall to the chamber where the Warders slept. Snores and sighs greeted him as he stepped into the long narrow dormitory. He stood absolutely still for several minutes making sure that no one felt his presence. Carefully, he slipped to the end of the chamber where he found the Warder who had become his nemesis sleeping soundly in the narrow bed.

"You are a fool, Gadred Aember, a fool to believe the Warders can once again be a force to reckon with. We are but fifty aging men. You cannot think to lead us back to greatness. You do not have the dark power that Finton possessed, nor do you know how to foster it." Cassel's words angered Aember anew.

"It is you, Morten Cassel, you are the fool! The power is within my grasp; I carry it with me! I will find the dragons and they will bring Timis to its knees before us!"

Cassel had risen from his chair at the end of the table and with a look of disgust tinged with something akin to pity he turned to leave the communal room where all the Warders had gathered at Aember's request.

"Morten, please stay," the voice of Desmond Orly called, his tone pleading and conciliatory. "Gadred," he soothed, "we all have different memories of our past lives. Surely we can find common ground after all these years."

Cassel had waved a hand in angry dismissal to both Aember and Orly and left the room. He had not missed an opportunity since then to sway how the Fifty viewed Aember's assertions that the Warders could once more become powerful and bring their will to bear on Timis.

But tonight would end Cassel's intransigence. After tonight, he thought, there will be only forty-nine.

Aember stood beside Cassel's bed for a long time, making sure no one was aware of him. Finally he slipped the pouch from around his neck and removed the golden nugget. With a quick movement he bent to press the gold against Cassel's forehead. Cassel gasped and tried to turn his head, but then with a deep sigh he stilled. He breathed in deeply, then slowly let it out and breathed no more. Aember slipped the nugget back into its protective pouch and like a wraith, a mere shadow, he turned and hurried from the chamber. Midway down the row of sleeping men a man sighed in his sleep and turned over as the shadow passed by.

It was Desmond Orly who brought the news to the Warders gathered in the morning to break their fast that sometime during the night Morten Cassel had died quietly in his sleep. After delivering his message he slumped in his chair and buried his face in his hands. He sat thus for some time amidst the cries of disbelief and sorrow that greeted his message, and when he lifted his head he saw Aember watching him. Orly read satisfaction in the set of Aember's mouth, a decidedly dark look in his eyes. Some thought niggled at Orly, something about last night. There had been something, hardly more than a shadow, that had momentarily disturbed his sleep, but with the grief at Cassel's death crowding his mind he could not remember what it was. With a shudder, he rose from his chair and without a backward glance left the room. He felt Aember's eyes boring into his back as he walked away.

With leaded steps he moved to the bedside of his friend. He stood silently with bowed head; tears ran down his cheeks and he wiped them with the back of his hand. "Oh, Morten," he whispered. "What's to become of us? Yours was the voice of reason and calm. Without you, I don't know what will become of us?"

"Desmond?"

Jaston Sonne stood with two others beside Orly, their faces lined with sorrow. "We've come to help you prepare his body."

"Jaston, what will we do without him?" Orly shook his head and wiped more tears away.

Sonne sighed deeply and shook his head. "Come, we've work to do. Let's be about it," he said after a moment.

Orly nodded and stepped away to retrieve a basin, water and cloths while Sonne and the others went to gather a clean robe and blankets in which to shroud their brother Warder's body for burial. As the four men worked silently and respectfully to remove Cassel's sleeping garment and wash his body, Orly noticed a small red mark on Cassel's forehead. Although Cassel's body was cool to the touch, the red mark was warm as Orly ran his fingertips over it. "What is this?" he murmured.

Sonne shook his head. "I have no idea. Perhaps he bumped his head somehow." He continued to wash the old man's limbs with studied care.

"Hm," Orly replied. "Odd."

The four men completed their preparations and Sonne and the others left, leaving Orly to keep vigil until a wooden box in which to lay the body had been built, the grave site selected, and the digging completed. Morten Cassel was the first of their brothers to be buried here, and the men wanted a special location in which to bury one of their own.

The day wore on and others drifted in and out joining Orly in paying silent respect to Cassel. At last, Orly was left alone once more and the afternoon waned and dusk darkened the chamber. With heavy heart, Orly lit the bedside candle and as he did so, his shadow flared for a moment on the wall above the silent figure on the bed.

And he remembered what it was that had disturbed his sleep the night before. A shadow, a man's shadow, near Cassel's bed, turning away and hastening from the dormitory. Just a shadow, and yet, and yet. . .

Morten Cassel was alive yesterday, arguing vehemently with Gadred Aember as he often had. The two had nearly come to blows. And this morning Morten was dead. Orly shook his head in denial at the path his thoughts were taking. Surely Gadred would not have . . .

Fear shivered down his spine and with haste born of that fear he turned away. His bed and the small chest that held his few possessions sat near the back door. He ran to the chest, pulled out trousers, tunic and cloak and began to change his clothes. His fingers fumbled as he fastened the trousers and slipped the long-sleeved tunic over his head. The few things he would take with him—a sheathed knife, a few coins, a pair of warm stockings, a pair of gloves—he thrust into a leather bag. He stuffed the black robe he'd worn to mark him as a Warder under his pillow. Voices interrupted his packing and he grabbed the bag and his cloak and fled, away from the voices, and out the back door that led into the garden. Without stopping he ran through the garden and toward the large storage shed just at the end of the neat rows. There, in its shadow, he paused to look back at the hall where more lights shone now from the windows of the dormitory. He stood in the dark for several minutes, making sure no one followed him. When he deemed it safe to move again, he slipped from shadow to shadow until he stood within the shelter of the small apple orchard. The apples were not quite ripe but he gathered several and added them to his bag. He didn't know when he would find food. He mentally cursed himself for not having taken a water flask in his haste, but it was too late to go back for food or water now. He paused when he reached the last of the trees and listened intently. He thought he heard someone call out his name, but he might have been mistaken.

The night and the silence, except for the occasion chirp of a night bird, deepened around him. Taking a deep breath, he left the shelter of the trees, and moving within the protection offered by the darkness and shadows of rocks and brush, he headed for the hills that crowded the base of the mountains.

The Dalrudd Mountains ringed the valley, and these mountains had kept the small group of Warders safe from the outside world for many years. He prayed they would hide him now when he ventured into them, hide him as they had hidden him and his brothers in the valley, hide him from the man he was sure had somehow killed Morten Cassel.

Desmond Orly had often agreed with Morten Cassel in how the Warders should continue to live. That had meant he often disagreed with Gadred Aember, not as forcefully perhaps as Morten had, but still he had often spoken up to ask questions that angered Gadred. If Morten no longer stood in Gadred's way, if Gadred had in fact eliminated a pesky thorn in his side, was Desmond Orly also a thorn to be removed? He dare not stay to find out. Not if he wanted to live.

Something about Gadred Aember had changed. When he thought no one was looking, he straightened to his full height and walked without a limp. He seemed physically stronger and more assertive. His contention that the Warders would once more have the power, in fact now possessed that power, to take Timis back had become a constant argument during these past weeks. Morten had contended they should stay as they were, safe from the outside world within their valley, while Aember spoke of nothing but the power the Warders had wielded under Aldward Finton. Conn Regan, who often soothed Aember's outbursts, had left the compound weeks ago, and without his steadying influence, Aember's anger against those who opposed him grew. His hatred of the Timisians seemed to shape all his reason, all his beliefs; hatred fed his envy and when the two combined, Gadred Aember became someone who would have his way at all costs. The Warders, except for Morten, Orly, and sometimes one or two others, were drawn in by Aember's desire for power and made it their own. They began to speak openly of the day when they were no longer prisoners of the valley, when the black robes of the Warders were once more feared.

He climbed on, often stumbling in the dark with only dim starlight and a cloud-shrouded moon to light his way. A misstep sent him tumbling down a sharp incline to lie battered and bruised with the breath knocked out of him. When he was able to breathe again he pushed himself to a sitting position. He pressed his back against a large boulder and leaned his head back against the cool stone. The clouds freed the moon and its scant light filtered down to where he rested. Somewhere in the night a creature screamed as its life ended. He glanced up and saw a white owl silhouetted against the night sky as it lifted away on silent wings, a small animal dangling from a claw. When his breathing leveled, he struggled to his feet and moved on. He must keep moving.

When dawn came, he was high above Cragon Pass and by midday he approached the pass with caution. It would be best, he decided, to wait for darkness before descending into the pass. He had encountered no one in his headlong rush to leave the valley, but there could well be others using the pass, both Timisians and Arlanders, and he did not wish to be seen by anyone. Where he would go once he left the pass behind, he had no idea. He'd thought only to escape the valley and certain death, to escape Aember. Perhaps he had overreacted. Perhaps there had been no one in the dormitory but the sleeping Warders. But, then, what was the shadow he'd seen? And he was certain now he had seen something. And that strange red mark on Morten's forehead? What was that? He had not imagined the look in Aember's eyes when he'd stared at Orly, nor the pleasure Orly sensed the other man felt at the news of Cassel's death. It had not been news to Aember, he was certain of it. No, Aember knew Morten Cassel had died in the night.

"I don't know how he died," Orly thought, "but Aember does."

The sun stood high above him when he found a narrow opening between two sections of rock wall and slid into its cool depths. With a sigh he eased himself down to rest against the rough stone. He'd found water in an icy stream and had drunk his fill, but that had been hours ago and he was both thirsty and hungry. In his rush to leave the hall, there had been no time to gather food or water. He would have to find both soon, the apples he'd picked on his way through the orchard were long gone. For now he must rest; he had a long way to go. Wind whistled through the small cave-like opening where Orly rested. It swirled around him and dried the sweat on his heated body. He drew the cloak about his shoulders, glad for its protection, and with a sigh, he slept.

While Gadred Aember set in motion his plans to consolidate the Warders' allegiance to him, Conn Regan spent the time searching the Dalrudd Mountains. He found hidden canyons, climbed high peaks, spent days in dank caves, hiked through the forests on the lower levels of the Dalrudds. He came to respect the power of avalanches, sudden summer thunderstorms, the ferocity of winter blizzards, the ways of rivers and waterfalls. He found the dens of bears and great mountain cats; followed the paths of deer and mountain goats; discovered the nesting sites of eagles and hawks, the dens of foxes and wolves. With his knowledge came a preference for the high places. In the mountains the air was clean and cool, the water pure, the light of moon and stars brilliant. Here he seldom encountered another human being, but when he did he would pause for a while and perhaps share a campfire. In doing so he added more knowledge about the mountains and what could be found here. He also learned of conditions in the rest of Timis and sought more information about the Arlanders and their incursion into both Timis and Kaenolir.

And all the while he searched as Gadred Aember had commanded him to do.

He catalogued everything he came to know. He drew careful and detailed maps and kept meticulous notes of all he learned. The information was important to implement the plans Gadred Aember had begun to make. The knowledge of the mountains Conn Regan brought back to the valley of the Fifty was a part of those plans.

With the coming of spring, he came down out of the Dalrudds, tired and thin. He had been gone nearly six months, but the valley seemed to have changed little. However, the Aember who welcomed him and ushered him into his chamber was not the same Aember who had sent him on his mission. This Aember stood tall and robust.

"Conn, I'm eager to hear what you found in the mountains. Here, sit, sit by the fire." He poured a goblet of wine and handed it to Regan. "You have done well, Conn," placing a hand on the young man's shoulder. "I've not had time to go through your notes or study your maps, but I know they will be invaluable to us." He took the chair next to Regan, poured a goblet of wine for himself and set it on the table between the chairs. He steepled his fingers against his chin and waited for the younger man to begin.

Regan drank deeply, set the goblet aside, and leaned forward in his chair to rest his arms on his thighs.

"It is as you thought, m'lord. There are many caves, some little more than crevasses. But there is an unusual one midway through Malhain Pass, east of where the avalanche occurred all those years ago. It is somehow different from the others I explored—I can't tell you why I felt that way. Just a feeling. When I entered it, something didn't want me there." He shook his head. "There was a presence there, a power, something ancient."

"Did you explore the cave in its entirety?"

"No, m'lord. The opening that led farther into the cave was too narrow. Part of the wall had collapsed. I didn't stay long because I could hear rumbling from deep within the mountain. I feared I would be caught in a slide with no way out."

"Hm, interesting." Aember sat back in his chair, staring for a moment at the fire. "Other caves of interest?"

Regan sighed. "The mountains are riddled with caves. I could not possibly search them all, but I marked as many as I found on the maps."

"Good, good. Did you encounter anyone in the mountains?"

"Only hunters, in the lower foothills." He stretched his legs out toward the heat. "They were always willing to share a campfire and talk." Regan smiled. "Things are not going well for the Timisians."

"Tell me, all that you heard, all that you saw."

Hours later Aember finally sent the exhausted man to his bed and sat contemplating the fire. Morten Cassel was no longer a force to rival him and Desmond Orly, who so often challenged him with his infernal questions, had disappeared from the valley. Conn Regan had returned with what Aember felt certain was a possible dragon lair. What Conn had learned about the Arlanders steadily moving into Timis and causing great unrest could work to Aember's advantage. Perhaps the Arlanders could become a force that the Warders could use to bring Timis to heel. He couldn't promise them the gold that Finton had used to lure them, but he would find an ally among them to bring the Arlanders around to Aember's way of thinking. What was the name Conn Regan had mentioned? An Arlander who seemed to be organizing some of the immigrants into a more cohesive group? Dellay, yes, Dellay.

The fire slowly burned to coals before Aember, too, finally took his rest. There was much to do and once Regan had rested, Aember planned to send him into the cities and villages of western Timis. He was ready to dispatch a half dozen trusted Warders to spy out the High Champaign and the coast of the Balagorn Channel. He'd send others to Ross Harbor and Timthurlen to organize and direct Arlanders in ways to cause mayhem in the two cities. By the time spring came again to Timis, he would be ready.

chapter five

Rayce secured the last shutter on the Lorn Isle cottage. As he worked he thought about the years he had spent here. He and KaynaRee had been free to roam the island, often with Samar leading the way. Brother and sister had come to know every part of their home, had come to appreciate its beauty and tranquility as it changed with the seasons, had come to know the stories of those who were buried here: Andrew Goldenhorn and Katrine Seton, his ancestors; Alpean, ancient king of Kaenolir; the stories he and Ree had asked for over and over, stories about the Golden Ones, about the Warrior Singers; stories in which Kailie Fairchild and Talanor Rowan played such an important part; the stories of Kitra Fairchild and Camron Thorpe and their quest for dragons to save Kaenolir and Timis. The history of Kaenolir was imbedded in Lorn, and he was part of that history.

He had grown to manhood on this island, in this cottage, and now he was preparing to leave it behind. Would he return here one day? He did not know. The Caretaker blood that coursed through his body was urging him elsewhere. His dreams were becoming more vivid, more insistent with each passing night. Dragons slipped in and out of his conscious thoughts, their Songs becoming more and more compelling as the days and nights of fall and winter turned into spring and the waning days of summer.

With the shutters all in place and *Dragon Keeper* packed with his belongings, he walked through the shadowed cottage once more. For the last time? He stopped before the hearth, rested his hand on the mantel and stared into the darkened fireplace empty now of the ashes of his last fire. KaynaRee had gone on ahead to Shiptown. After visiting with her grandmother she planned to go to the Horn of Kalora, though she had shared that information only with Rayce. She'd send a letter to her parents upon reaching Shiptown, knowing they would understand her need to find the Singers' Hall, especially her mother.

Rayce's destination was Cathorn Isle

With a sigh he turned away, walked through the front door and latched it firmly in place. There was no key for this door; his parents had never felt the need to lock it even when they were gone for a time visiting family and friends on the mainland.

A breeze, fragrant with the heat of late summer, fluttered the leaves of the trees that surrounded the cottage on three sides. Four eagles soared overhead and he paused to watch them. He and Ree had climbed to the top of the Eagles' Pinnacle just yesterday to say goodbye to the nesting pair and their latest offspring. Life would go on here on Lorn as it had for ages, but life here would be without Golden Ones. Rayce smiled sadly and continued down the path to the dock.

He did not look back.

"So," Rayce said. He and KaynaRee sat together in chairs their Grandmother Mary put beneath her apple tree in the backyard each year when the weather warmed. "You are set to leave for the Horn then."

Ree lifted her face to feel the warm wind blowing in from the sea. "I know Mother and Father will be disappointed when I don't come to Camlanrein first." She paused to look at Rayce. "But I must go to the Horn, Rayce. I must."

Rayce reached over to squeeze Ree's hand. "I know, Ree. I understand. We are being pulled in different directions, you and I." He freed her hand and rose to stand. "Our parents understand; you know they do."

"They are afraid for us, too, Rayce."

"I know that. I'm afraid, Ree, for you, for me, for what awaits us." He looked down on her. "But I want to know as well what it is that is calling to me. I hear the dragons," he whispered. "I hear them. Day and night they call." He rubbed his forehead and closed his eyes. "But there is something more, something I cannot see." He shook his head in frustration.

"Rayce?" She rose to take his arm.

"They're in danger, Ree. The dragons are in danger. They call for their Caretaker. And I don't know how to take care of them, what they need me to do."

"When you translate father's book, Rayce, just as Kailie told you, then you will know what to do."

Rayce nodded. "I know that. I do know that." He rolled his shoulders to ease the tension there. "I said I was afraid, Ree. Mostly I'm afraid for the dragons. Something powerful. . ." He paused. "Something threatens them." He looked at Ree and she saw the anguish in his eyes. "In the threat to them lies a threat to Kaenolir and to Timis. Something evil is coming, Ree. I feel it. May the gods help me, I feel it in my bones," he whispered.

"Yes," she whispered in response. "It is time for you to go to Cathorn. Just as it is time for me to go to the Horn, time to find the Singers' Hall." She gave Rayce a sad little smile and reached up to touch his cheek. "We'll leave tomorrow," she said softly. "Come, we must tell Grandmother Mary."

"You are truly a Golden One," Kailie Fairchild had written in her letter. KaynaRee had read the letter so many times she knew it by heart.

"Your Song is found in the Quair."

Before her mother left Lorn to join her father in Timis, Kitra Fairchild had taken her daughter aside.

"I have something for you," she had said. "It's time I passed it on to you, just as Kailie passed it to me." Kitra opened an intricately carved chest and lifted out a gilt-bound book. She lifted the cover and slowly turned the fragile parchment pages. "This is the Quair, KaynaRee. " She looked into her daughter's sky-blue eyes, so like her own, and smiled. "You know its story," she said softly.

"Yes, I know the story, your story and Kailie Fairchild's story."

Kitra closed the book and handed it to her daughter. "From one Golden One to another," she whispered.

KaynaRee took the Quair and carefully turned the pages of the ancient book. One after the other, all the Songs of all the Golden Ones lay before her eyes. She came to the Last Song and lifted her head to look at her mother. "Kailie's Song?" she asked.

"Yes," Kitra nodded.

Ree turned the page.

"Fire Song, your Song," Ree said.

"Yes."

When she turned the next page, she found it sealed. She looked at her mother. "And this Song?" Her voice trembled as she asked the question.

"It is your Song, love. I do not know what it will be or who will teach it to you. You must do as Kailie told you to do in her letter: take the Quair to the Singers' Hall. There you will learn your Song."

Ree's fingers trembled as she closed the Quair.

"Yes," she whispered. She told her mother then of her dreams, dreams filled with music, music that wrapped her in its power, pulled her in and would not let her go. In those dreams something else called to her, too, something that was only just there, a shape in the mist of sleep. It called, not to a Golden One but to a Caretaker.

"Oh, Ree," her mother had cried softly. "Oh, my Ree."

And as Kailie had written that her mother's heart near broke when Talanor Rowan came for her, so, too, Kitra's heart near broke, knowing the anguish, the sorrow, the pain that lay before KaynaRee. She had folded her daughter in her arms then and willed away her own fear. She had stepped back at last, her tears resolutely blinked away to smile at Ree. "Go, then, love. Find your Song."

Once again the music surrounded her as she slept. In her dream the great doors to the Singers' Hall stood open while music poured out like a great stream, rolling and surging, to carry her ever onward. Music beat against her, lifted her, touched her as no music ever had. Its harmonies played over and over in her mind, willing her to listen, to hear, to understand.

Come to me, Golden One. Hurry, hurry. Come soon.

Again the shape rose out of the mist of her dream, but it was no shape she knew.

Come to me. Come to me.

"I'm coming," KaynaRee murmured in her sleep. In Kalora Bay the tide churned into the narrow inlet between the Horn and the coast of Kaenolir. Wind whipped the dune grasses in a frenzy of motion. Above the fury of sea and wind the lonely cry of a wolf echoed again and again.

"Torar, I'm coming," KaynaRee answered. "I'm coming."

In the alcove off the kitchen Rayce pushed the coverlet back and rose from his bed, too agitated to sleep. He pulled on trousers and shirt and stuffed his feet into soft boots before making his way from the alcove where he slept. He walked through the quiet of his grandmother's house out into the backyard to the chairs where he and Ree had sat in the afternoon. A sliver of moon moved across the face of the sky, marking its path through a heaven of stars. Though the house sat well away from Shiptown's harbor, night breezes carried occasional sounds of ships and sea. Rayce slumped in a chair, leaned his head back and stared up into the branches of the old tree. He closed his eyes and willed himself to calm. He sat thus for some time and perhaps had even dozed off when a wolf's mournful lament slipped unbidden into his mind.

"Jagar," he muttered. "I'm coming."

chapter six

Dragon Keeper swung around as Rayce shifted the sail to catch the wind. The distance from the Shiptown harbor to Cathorn Isle was only a few miles, but the current running between the island and the mainland was swift and rough. With the late autumn sun warming his shoulders, the wind brisk and steady from the north/northwest, he looked forward to reaching Talanor's island. What he would find there he did not know. More books, he hoped, more books that would point him in the direction he needed to go to translate the Caretaker's Book.

He'd spent the winter and spring and the early days of summer in the solitude of Lorn with the books of Talanor Rowan and Kailie Fairchild. The books were slow to release their secrets, and after his searching and studying he had been able to translate only a few disjointed words and phrases of the Caretaker's Song.

Rheena Aleen. . .Caretaker. . .fire beasts. . .Portal

The word "Song" and "Caretaker" appeared frequently. When he deciphered the phrase *cursed with hiding in memory* he knew he had opened the door to the meaning of the Caretaker's book, but he was unable to translate more. That was when he knew he must go to Cathorn Isle, as Kailie had urged him to do in her letter.

Most of the last days on Lorn had been spent completing the harvest, helping his family's Landsend friends pick the grapes, loading the largesse into the *Dragon Keeper* and the friends' boats, and taking all to Landsend. He'd had little time to search any further for a pathway that would lead to understanding the ancient language.

The dragons called, their cries filling nearly every waking minute. His nights echoed with dreams of them, calling, calling for him to help them, to save them. Frustrated because he couldn't find the answers without knowing what was in the Caretaker's Book, he said his goodbyes to his sister and grandmother and sailed for Cathorn. Somehow he knew he would find some answers there.

He thought of his father and mother as the wind carried him west. The cries his father had heard from the fire beasts had taken him into the mountains of Timis; the call of the dragons had taken his mother to the wild eastern shore of Kaenolir. What would he find on Cathorn? Deep in his heart, he knew that Cathorn was not the end of a journey for him, but a beginning.

And KaynaRee? The dragons called her, too. A Song in the Quair, a Song for a Golden One, waited for her in the ancient Singers' Hall on the Horn of Kalora. There she would begin her journey.

Caretaker.

"I'm coming. I'm coming."

A hazy smudge on the horizon marked Talanor's island, and Rayce steered for it. Another hour brought him around the island to the western entrance of a shaded cove. Somehow he knew it was there, and he slid between the tall stone walls that protected this secret place. He dropped the sail and let the current carry him to the dock still anchored securely to Talanor's Cathorn Isle. *Dragon Keeper* bumped against the old wood and Rayce steadied the boat and snugged it securely against a piling. There on the other side of the dock was a sleek white sloop, looking for all the world as if Talanor had just come back from a sail, tied up, and stepped ashore. Rayce smiled at the thought.

"I hope you don't mind my being here, Talanor Rowan," he whispered. He stepped into the galley to retrieve his pack and the bag of books he'd brought with him. He placed the two bags on the dock and boosted himself up onto the dock. He swung the pack onto his back and lifted the heavier bag and took a few steps before coming to a halt. There at the end of the dock, sitting on his haunches, his steady gaze watching Rayce, was a huge gray wolf.

"Jagar?" Rayce smiled as the wolf rose to come toward him. "I wondered if you would still be here. You've been alone a long time." Rayce held out a hand and the wolf sniffed it; then, as if satisfied, he turned and walked to the end of the dock. He looked back to make sure that Rayce followed before stepping on to the hard-packed sand.

"Lead the way, Jagar."

The trail led up into a forest of fir and cedar and eventually along a meandering stream whose waters sparkled in the sunshine. Birds flitted and fluttered in the low-growing bushes that grew along the banks of the stream. The air felt soft and was almost sweet smelling. Eventually the trail came to an end at a low wall. Jagar passed through a gate and Rayce followed him up a carefully laid path of washed gravel to the large front door of Talanor's cottage.

Rayce stopped to set the bag of books beside the door. Was it locked? Was there a key if so? Rayce laid his hand on the latch and the door opened without a sound. He turned to pick up the bag and motioned Jagar to enter before him. The wolf padded into the room and immediately lay down on a rug near the fireplace. He looked at Rayce as he entered and, satisfied that all was well, laid his head on his paws and closed his eyes.

With hesitant steps, feeling a trespasser here, Rayce stepped through the doorway and surveyed the large room. Sunlight slanted across the floor from the window above the long planked table set against the wall. Two sturdy wooden chairs flanked the table. Comfortable chairs were placed on either side of the fireplace, with small tables close at hand beside them; a basket of wood stood near the hearth ready for the next fire. A sink with a bucket and dipper on a narrow counter and a tall cupboard comprised the rest of the accoutrements of the room. A doorway led into what Rayce assumed would be a bedroom. He would not trespass there just yet. He set the heavy bag of books and his pack on the table and stretched to ease his tired back and shoulders. The large basket of food his grandmother had packed would need to be carried up from the boat and the food stored in the cupboard. With a sigh he turned to retrace his steps.

"Be right back, Jagar," he murmured as he left. The wolf cocked one ear and opened an eye to acknowledge Rayce.

Sunset colored the sky as Rayce finished storing his foodstuffs in the cupboard. A fresh bucket of water had been carried in from the spring behind the cottage; a fire crackled merrily in the hearth. Jagar rose, stretched lazily, then headed outside. Rayce found a pot and filled it with water, set it to heat on the iron hook above the fire. He found a teapot, shook in some tea leaves, and with a tired sigh, sat down in one of the chairs near the fireplace to wait for the water to boil. He stretched out his long legs and took in his surroundings.

The wall opposite the table was filled floor to ceiling with shelves full of books. Here and there among the books were colorful shells, bits of driftwood that had appealed to the old mage, candles in heavy holders. The books drew him from his chair and he read their titles in the flickering firelight. When it drew too dark to read the spines, he lit the candles and placed them in several spots around the room. He forgot about the tea he had steeped and pulled a book down to read.

A History of the Land of Timis the title read. Returning to his chair, he set the thick tome on his lap and opened the cover. The heavy parchment crackled as he turned the pages filled with an almost delicate handwriting. He began to read the rather archaic words set down as a record of a time far in the past.

Jagar slipped back into the room and took his place by the fireplace once more. He watched Rayce for a time before rising to come to stand before the engrossed reader.

"Rayce Thorpe."

Rayce nearly jumped out of his skin and fumbled the book, catching it just before it fell to the floor.

"Baskers. . ." he swore with chagrin. "Jagar?"

The wolf gave him a wolfish grin and sat on his haunches. Rayce set the book on the table by his chair. "Samar speaks, I know, to my mother and Torar spoke to Kailie. I could not hear them, but I can hear you."

"Yes."

"I'm glad you're here, Jagar. Will you stay?"

"Yes."

Rayce nodded his head and took comfort in the wolf's presence. "Good," he said simply and rose to find something to eat.

Feeling less the trespasser and more a welcome guest, he ate his meal of bread and cheese, dried strips of meat and an apple. He sat back to enjoy a fresh cup of hot tea and watched the flickering flames die down. Too tired to do more reading, he finished his tea and rinsed his supper dishes before banking the fire. He extinguished all the candles save one which he left burning on the mantel while he shook out his bedroll and placed it on a pallet he'd found in a chest by the door. The floor and pallet would serve as his bed for now. Perhaps later he would make use of Talanor's bed. Before settling down to sleep, he stepped outside to take in the night sky. A slim crescent moon did little to dispel the darkness. Rayce sighed as he walked down the path for a ways. Starlight cast its faint glow toward a distant earth and he glanced up in time to follow a star as it streaked across the heavens. He wondered, not for the first time, if the brief stream of light signaled the death of the star, or was it simply moving from one spot in the heavens to another. He smiled at the thought that perhaps the gods were moving it to a more propitious place in the sky. Maybe he would find an answer in one of Talanor's many books.

He heard a soft footfall behind him and stopped when Jagar joined him. The wolf pressed against his hip and Rayce kneaded his fingers through the thick fur on Jagar's neck.

"So much I do not know, Jagar," he whispered. "So much. Will I ever find the answers to all my questions?"

"You will find a way, Rayce Thorpe."

Man and wolf stood for a long time, contemplating the night, listening to the soft murmur of the wind and the shush of the sea, the call of a night hawk. Underneath those sounds was a constant refrain admonishing Rayce to hurry, to come, hurry.

At last, Rayce sighed and turned back to the cottage.

Tomorrow, tomorrow, he pledged, he would find more answers.

Caretaker. Hurry.

One day became two, then four. Three weeks passed with Rayce finding little help in Talanor's library. Frustrated, weary of dusty books and illegible writing, Rayce pushed back from the table with an oath and stood, rolling his head and shoulders to relieve some of the tiredness he felt. Jagar, from his usual spot by the fireplace, watched as Rayce paced the length of the room, turned and walked out the door. He followed the path away from the cottage, climbing gradually into the hills behind Talanor's orchard. He stopped to pick a golden colored apple, rubbed it on his shirt, and took a bite. The trail grew steeper and Rayce felt the pull in his legs. "Been sitting too much," he muttered and breathed in deeply. He finished his apple and threw the core toward a chittering squirrel. When Rayce moved on, the squirrel jumped down to claim the sweet feast.

The trail meandered through tall fir trees where the wind soughed and sighed in their many branches. Rayce noticed huckleberry bushes with clusters of small blue fruit hanging thick and ripe. He stopped to pick some and decided to come back tomorrow with a basket so he could pick more than a handful. Enjoying the pleasure of the sweet tang on his tongue, Rayce walked until he had cleared his mind of the jumble that seemed to have accumulated as he searched through Talanor's books.

"Perhaps I'm going about this in the wrong way," he mused. "I've been looking for several books, thinking I'd find a way to translate the words from many sources." He came to a stop. "Maybe," he said aloud, "maybe there is just one source. Maybe I need to find just one book." He turned to look back down the trail and stood, chewing on the inside of his bottom lip. "Huh. Just one book. What would it be? A history most likely. Or stories? A saga?" He ran his left forefinger along his bottom lip. "Yes, a saga, a story of a people." Huckleberries forgotten he hurriedly retraced his steps.

It was nearly two sleepless weeks later when Rayce found his source. True to his assumption, it was a saga, *The Seanan of Reamonnland,* at least that's what he made the title out to be. The book was about the same size as the Caretaker's Book but much thicker. Brittle yellow parchment sometimes crumbled as he turned the pages. The once black ink the author had used was now gray and disappeared altogether in spots. So weary he could barely sit upright, his eyes red from hours of pouring through the book, the words often blurred as he tried to read them.

Slowly, painstakingly, at last the words came. He forgot to eat; he rarely slept but for a few minutes at a time; he grew thin from lack of food and exhaustion. The winds of late autumn cooled Cathorn Isle and whistled about the cottage, but he took little note of the changing season.

Caretaker. Come.

The words echoed and reechoed in his mind as the days passed.

With the Caretaker's Book close at hand, the saga opened the Portal and the words of his father's book took shape and sense before his eyes:

I, Rheena Aleen, am the last Caretaker of the fire beasts, and soon I will pass through the Portal. I ask the Ancient Ones to send another to take my place, and it is for that special one I write these words. To you who read my words, guard well the secrets they reveal.

'Twas the Ancient Ones who from stardust scattered across the heavens in a dazzling stream shaped mighty beasts and gave them fire, gave them Songs infused with magic and power borrowed from music of the spheres. But it is I who keeps alive their memory by writing these words, just as it was I who made of these fire beasts naught but memory.

No more will their Songs be heard. No more will they take flight over snow and ice and mountaintops, over sea and wave and storm.

They wait. They wait for a Caretaker who will remember, wait for a time when their Songs might once more fill the skies with music.

Will they wait in vain? I fear they will.

Read my words, Caretaker, and know.

The Seanan, as my people name themselves, called this island home since the dawning of time. Our tadc, our poets, tell us in story and song that the Ancient Ones carried us across the seas in boats as fleet as those creatures who swam beside us and guided us through sun and storm. Why we felt compelled to journey from a land we must once have deemed our homeland, the sagas do not say, and the tadc have long forgot.

Fire beasts greeted us, so the stories tell, when first we stepped upon these shores and named this land our own. Reamonnland, we called it, land that protects us. Fire beasts flew above us, calling and singing, welcoming us. Their brilliant scales gleamed and shimmered in the fierce light of the sun. So many colors, blue and green, gold and deepest red, purple, shimmering white and silver, blackest black. There were colors of the sea from those beasts which gloried in the water; there was the white of snow and silver of ice from those beasts we learned preferred the aeries and caves of the mountains; there was black from beasts who loved the night's skies.

And, oh, their wondrous Songs, each beast with a Song all its own, unique, unlike any other. Yet when they sang together, as they oft times did, their music was a harmonious blend of magic, of power. Of life. They shared the island with us and there were those of us who learned their language and Songs. We became Caretakers, gifted with keeping the legend of the fire beasts to pass on to those who came after us, tasked with the responsibility of preserving the knowledge we came to possess. And we learned to fly with them, privileged to ride the currents of air high above the earth on the backs of fire beasts.

Oh, the joy of it, to fly and sing with the fire beasts!

So it was for eons of time.

Our homeland was blessed with warm summers and mild winters. Rains brought the fertile land to life after winter's chill and crops grew lush. Grains from vast fields beyond the mountains, fruit from orchards and vineyards filled our larders. Herds of sheep and goats, cattle and horses grew fat on pastures of tall, thick grasses. Our sagas do not say how we came to have the seeds and seedlings to plant, the animals we herded. Perhaps the Ancient Ones provided that which they saw we needed. It is a secret I am not privileged to know.

But I do know the secrets of the fire beasts, the dragons of Reamonnland, for I am a Caretaker and Singer of Songs. The Ancient Ones blessed me with the secrets of the fire beasts, the dragons of Reamonnland; they blessed me with a voice to sing their Songs. But they cursed me as well

The near-idyllic time of my people came at last to an end. Others came from across the sea to our shores. They saw the richness of our lives and desired what we possessed. They saw our homes, our fields, our herds and set out to take them. They hated us, for what we had, for who we were. Why? We were not like them; thus they killed us. No one was safe, neither young nor old.

They ravaged the land, emptied storage barns, burned homes and fields, vineyards and orchards, carried away animals. They took all they could carry back across the sea, leaving death and destruction in their wake.

Why, we asked, did the Ancient Ones turn deaf ears to our pleas, our cries to save us from the marauders? I do not know. I only know the people who escaped fled to the mountains, to caves and hidden valleys, wherever they might find safety.

But the fire beasts had no place to hide. The marauders saw the power and magic the dragons embodied, and they wanted those powers and that magic for their own. They killed all the fire beasts they encountered, drank their blood and bathed in it, cut out still beating hearts and ate them. The magic then, they believed, became the essence of the men who killed the beast. Murderous fools! My heart cries out when I write of the pleasure those men took in shooting the fire beasts from the skies with poisoned arrows, in slaying them with swords and spears in the caves where they sought shelter. They were so beautiful, such magnificent creatures. How could men slay them? I could not understand such a soul that took delight in killing. Perhaps those men, in the end, had no souls.

The time came when I was left alone in a desolate homeland, the last Caretaker, charged with saving the fire beasts that still lived. The Ancient Ones took heed of my entreaties and showed me the way. It was left to me to hide the fire beasts, to still their Songs. It fills me with sorrow as I write these words, as I remember why it is I came to use my magic to bury their magic, to save their secrets but allow only memory to live. It was I who was led to the Portal and shown the way that fire beasts, whose long, long lives were nearly over, would gather with their fellows to sing one last Song together, how they would fly high into the heavens on a mighty crescendo of music, and how they would be lifted by the shimmering winds of the gods through the Portal to return to the stardust that formed them.

The Ancient Ones gave me the Caretaker's Song and when I sang it, its words powerful and savage, the fire beasts came to me. They came from caves high above the sea where the marauders could not reach; others came from hidden places on mountain peaks where men could not climb.

With the remaining fire beasts gathered around me—so few, so few—the Ancient Ones allowed me one last blessing, one last promise, one last curse: As I sang, my music opened the Portal to memory. Memory of their power, their magic; memory of their strength and beauty; of their joy in living; memory of their Songs. My soul touched theirs and they slipped through the Portal to be remembered in story and Song, to be cherished for what they had been.

They were no more.

I was cursed with hiding them in memory.

However, the Ancient Ones were not done with me. I was given two tasks: to save those of my people who were left and to set in words what I had done to save them and the fire beasts. In the words are the promises that my people will live separate and inviolate in a kingdom known as Faerie. They will be given the gifts of magic and Song, and to a select few who come after us the memory of Faerie will come alive and they will remember and know.

The fire beasts, the Ancient Ones promised, the fire beasts will live in memory, and when all else fails, they will take shape once more and come to the aid of those touched by the Faerie, those who hear the Songs of dragons in dreams and waking, to those who cry out against an evil that threatens to engulf them. With their fire, the fire beasts will destroy the evil which man cannot.

I opened the Portal for my people and for my fire beasts. Memory now, only memory. I am left alone in sorrow so deep and abiding I can scarce stand. There is no music, only the cry of the wind mingling with the crash of the sea. Soon I will be but memory. The Portal begins to open before me.

The sun burns hot; my eyes fill with tears; my heart cries out for all that was. I curse the gods then, but there is one more task set before me.

Here are the words of memory, the words of the Caretaker, given to one who comes after. When you read these words you will hear the music of the Caretaker's Song. It is your Song. Listen and learn. In these words lie the power and the magic of the fire beasts.

You will know. You will know.

Rayce was shaking and sobbing as he wrote. Here were the words of the last Caretaker, words meant for the Caretaker who could read them.

"Read these words and know."

Now he knew.

He read the last of Rheena Aleen's words and as he wrote them down, the music, the wondrous, glorious music filled his heart and mind and he did know. He sang, then, his Song.

Wake, you are needed.
Evil walks.
Good lies weak and hopeless,
Hear its petitions.
Come
Slip through the Door opened to your being.
Come
For you are needed.

Come from sea. Come from ice. Come from blackest night.
Dreams give rise and fire beasts sing.
Faerie hear and touch with magic those who listen
And know.
Hear the Songs of fire beast and Faerie.
Come.

When all else fails, memory serves.
The portal opens.
Come.
You are needed.
When all else fails.
When all else fails.

Caretaker.

His Song lifted him and seemed to carry him from his world of being to another, otherworldly place of music and power, magic and fire. His dragon waited for him there, shrouded in the mists of time, beyond the portal.

Caretaker.

The portal opened and the fire beast stepped through it. Huge, gleaming silver, his black-tipped wings folded back along his rippling sides, he sang his Song in harmony with the Caretaker's Song, music wild and powerful, magical and fierce. When the Songs ended, the dragon lowered his head and gently enveloped Rayce in his fire.

Caretaker. I have waited for you. You have come at last.

"Yes," Rayce whispered. "I have come. Tell me what I must do."

Evil comes yet again. There is one who possesses a token forged by the fire beasts own fire. It is a token of gold bound up with a black stone of darkness. With it, power will be given to bring us to him. Find the token. Take it to the sacred circle the Caretakers made.

"Who has the token?"

He is like those we once destroyed with fire. Another Caretaker then. And a Golden One.

"My father," Rayce whispered. "Camron Thorpe and my mother, Kitra Fairchild. They heard the fire beasts who called them." After a moment, he said, "Their fire beasts destroyed Aldward Finton and his Warders with fire. When all else failed."

Yes. Golden One and Caretaker. There is another. A fire beast calls to her.

"KaynaRee," Rayce said quietly.

Soon she will learn her Song. Her fire beast will hear her Song and come to her.

Mists began to gather around Caretaker and fire beast.

You must go now, Caretaker. Fire beasts will come. When all else fails.

The mists deepened and darkened, leaving Rayce to stare unseeing into the shifting darkness.

"Tell me," he called to his dragon, though he could no longer see him. "Tell me your name."

Once, long ago Caretakers called me Far'Lin.

The mists disappeared and Rayce found himself once more in the familiar surroundings of Talanor's cottage. Jagar came to stand beside him. "I've found the way, Jagar. Now I know what I must do."

The wolf leaned against him and Rayce took comfort in the touch. After a few minutes Jagar whined softly then moved away. Rayce watched the wolf cross the room and walk out the door. He turned back once and Rayce raised his hand.

"Will I see him again?" he wondered. With a sigh he rose, stiff and so weary he could barely stand.

Rest now, Caretaker.

He knew the voice in his mind was the voice of a dragon.

His dragon.

chapter seven

With a brilliant sun dazzling her eyes, a racing current, and stiff winds, KaynaRee guided the *Highland Guardian* along the Trayonian coast toward the terminus of the Wall of Rhade. She would tie up at the dock there for the night and continue on to the Horn of Kalora at first light. It had taken her longer to take her leave of her grandmother Mary Fairchild than she had anticipated. Mary worried that she might not see her grandchildren again for a long time, fretted over the unknown into which both sailed and did not want to let them go.

Caretaker and Golden One heritages combined to make a powerful force that neither Rayce nor Ree could ignore. The dragons called them; the music of the Golden Ones sang in their hearts urging them to follow the dictates of ancient powers set in motion once again by an evil that must be found and destroyed. Mary understood all that, but still her heart ached and she feared for her grandchildren as she had feared for their mother.

"Grandmother, I must go. You know I must," KaynaRee whispered as her grandmother held her tight in one last goodbye.

"Yes, I know," Mary said as she released Ree and stepped back. She wiped her cheeks with her fingers and tried to smile. "Go, then, my sweet Ree. May the Ancient Ones and the Golden Ones watch over you. And over Rayce."

KaynaRee stepped onto her boat as her grandmother freed the line and threw it to her. Ree shoved off and lifted the sail, maneuvering among the many craft coming and going in the harbor. She lifted her arm in one more farewell and her grandmother answered with a wave. "Be safe," Mary whispered. "Please, keep them safe for me." When she could no longer make out the small white sloop as it sped toward the horizon, Mary wiped her cheeks once more and turned away.

Ree reached the terminus well after the sun had set and was greeted by the Guardian on night duty as she docked. After helping her secure her boat, checking on her destination (Fairtown, to visit relatives, she fibbed), and how long she planned to tie up here, he saluted her and told her to rest well. After a quick meal from the hamper her grandmother had packed for her, she eased down onto the deck with a cup of cider and listened to the night around her. She sighed in harmony with the breeze that ruffled the water against the *Guardian*. Voices and occasional laughter drifted down to her from the small detachment of Highland Guardians stationed here. Someone called a "good night" and soon the voices ceased.

Rayce would be at Cathorn Isle by now. She wondered what he had found. Talanor had been gone a long time and while the island had been warded during his lifetime, she wondered if the magic binding it was still in place. And the great gray wolf that had been his companion, Jagar, would he have greeted Rayce? She sighed and finished her cider, rose to replace the cup and find her bedroll. She stretched out on the galley bench, which was just wide enough to accommodate her slender form, and settled down to sleep. Tomorrow she would reach the Horn. What would she find there? Someone to teach the Song that was sealed in the Quair? The music that was always on the edge of her mind played softly and a counterpoint echoed. *Come, come. We need you.*

She turned her head to the side and closed her eyes. Tears, unbidden, slipped down her cheeks. "I'm coming," she murmured. Then, "Please, show me what I must do."

The only reply was the wind, whistling softly as it gently rocked the white sloop.

The sky was gray with the threat of rain as she sailed into Kalora Bay. It had been a rough day on the water and Ree was exhausted. The current carried her into the mouth of the bay and beyond the land curved like an animal's horn. She continued toward the northeastern end of the bay where she would anchor. The sail luffed as she turned into the current and she soon came in sight of the dock. She dropped the sail and hastened to maneuver the *Highland Guardian* into position, bumped against the solid piling and reached out to snug the boat against the dock.

"You're home, *Guardian*," she murmured as she tied up to a cleat fastened to the planking. She turned to look toward the old cottage in the dunes where Kailie Fairchild has spent the last decades of her life, but the dune grasses had grown so tall she caught only an occasional glimpse of the cottage as the wind lifted and bent the stalks as it passed through.

Raindrops came with a gentle splash and then as the storm entered the bay, the splash became a deluge and Ree quickly sought the protection of the galley. She had thought to spend the night in the cottage, but with the storm she settled down to a cold supper and early bed. For a time she listened to rain beating a rapid tattoo on the galley roof. Finally, lulled by the *Guardian's* movement, she slept to dream of music and flashes of color that seemed to brush against her.

Come to us, lady. We wait for you.

"I'm coming," she answered. "At last, I'm coming."

Though the storm had blown itself out during the night, dark clouds still sailed before a stiff wind when Ree pushed back her blanket and rose in the early hour just before dawn. A long hike back down the bay to the horn lay before her and she wanted to get an early start. After her morning ablutions and a hasty breakfast, she pushed open the galley door and stepped out. She swung a pack up onto the dock and hoisted herself out of the boat. As she stooped to pick up her pack, she saw him at the end of the dock. As she straightened, he came slowly toward her.

"Torar?" she called softly. "Oh, Torar, you are still here."

He stopped as she dropped her pack and held out her arms to him. She took his snow-white head in her hands and dropped her forehead to his. He whined softly and licked her cheek. She laughed as she stepped back, wiping her cheeks with the back of her hand.

"I have been waiting for you, KaynaRee Fairchild. I will take you to the Singers' Hall."

Ree's eyes opened wide in amazement and then she laughed with delight. He spoke to her just as she knew he has spoken to Kailie, as Samar spoke to her mother. As the watery sun rose above the bay, she lifted her pack and swung it to her back. "Lead the way, Torar, I'll follow you."

The two companions stopped once on their way to the tip of the Horn so Ree could eat and rest. For much of the way they were able to hike along the hard-packed sand beside the bay's western shore, but there were places where rocky cliffs and thundering surf blocked the way. Then they were forced to make their way over treacherous rocks wet with spray. The day wore on and as the sun sank toward the sea, Torar came to a halt.

"I can take you no farther. You must go the rest of the way alone. When it is time, I will come for you."

"But where do I go, Torar?" Ree looked around her in confusion. To her left lay the waters of the bay, to her right an impenetrable forest of fir, cedar, and hemlock.

"Just there, there where the trees are not so thick. There is a path. Follow it."

Ree looked where Torar had indicated and with a nod, shifted her pack to a more comfortable position and set off toward the trees. As she left the sand and moved into the trees, she turned to watch Torar as he trotted back the way they had come.

Wind sifted through the branches of the myriad trees that grew tall and dark around her. The leaves of the bushes and trees of the understudy rustled in a passing breeze. There was a path, just as Torar said, and she followed it for what seemed hours. Night sounds now surrounded her: soft music from wind in the trees, muted rhythms of the waves somewhere beyond her, here and there gentle undertones of murmuring birds and scurrying forest creatures. She felt immersed in music, music that led her ever onward to its source.

A shaft of bright moonlight slanted through the trees and marked the path she was to take, a path that led her ever deeper into the forest until she came to the ruins of a once great hall. A wide door stood open and she knew she must step through it.

Empty frames of tall windows graced two walls that stood roofless, open to a star-filled sky. As she looked around her, she could see flecks of color here and there beneath the windows from the shattered stained glass panels that had filled the openings, flecks of paint from murals that had decorated the ruined walls. Evidence of the mosaic tile that had covered the floor could be seen through the leaves and debris that obscured the scenes nearly worn away by time and the elements.

It must have been a magnificent hall, she mused, taking in everything around her. An intricately carved stand, untouched, it seemed, by the ruin that surrounded it, stood in the center of the great room. Ree walked carefully through the wreckage until she could see the complex detail of the lectern. It was then, as she stood there with moonlight all around her, that she heard the music.

She slipped the pack from her shoulder and with a feeling of awe tempered with fear she removed the Quair and with trembling hands placed it on the stand. She had come, she knew, to learn her Song. Notes of haunting beauty and magical power swirled around her like mist as her hands lingered on the Quair.

Her Song and only she would sing it.

Open the Quair, KaynaRee Fairchild, a melodious voice whispered beside her.

The Golden One stood shrouded in a soft transparent mist that hid her features and form, but the voice, oh the voice, was so familiar.

"Kailie? Mother?" Ree whispered.

No, dear child. I am Rhianna Lanee. 'Twas I who taught Kailie Fairchild her Warrior's Song as I had taught her father before her.

"I've heard mother sing the Warrior Song, but there is another Song that is hers alone."

Fire Song. A Song like no other. The fire beasts taught her their Song for the Warrior Song was already part of her being. Your Song, child, will be a blending of Caretaker and Golden One, just as you are a blend of your parents.

"Caretaker and Golden One," Ree whispered.

Yes. Fire beast and Warrior. Like your father. Like your mother.

The figure stepped forward and took the Quair from the stand.

Take the Quair, KaynaRee, and open it to your Song.

Fear made her tremble, a fear of what she would become when she opened the book, fear of the unknown, and fear of the power the Song would give her.

"I cannot," she murmured and stepped back.

You must, another voice whispered. *You are needed. Evil comes.*

Take the book. Find your Song, the Golden One commanded.

Time stood still for KaynaRee. She had been born for this moment, had been moving steadily toward a task ordained for her by the Ancient Ones, a task to help defeat the evil that had taken yet another form, another course, in this time.

Come, KaynaRee Fairchild, come. The voice from her dreams.

With a heartrending sob she accepted the Quair from the Singer's hand. She replaced it on the carved lectern and opened the cover. One by one she touched the pages of the Songs of the Golden Ones until she came to the Warrior Song. Softly she began to sing, not with the power of Andrew Goldenhorn or Kailie Fairchild, not with the potent force of her mother, but with a power unique to her. The Song vibrated on the air around her and ended with a crashing crescendo. Before the last notes had died away, she turned the page to the Fire Song, her mother's Song. She sang it, too, though she would never sing it again, for it was not hers to sing but this one time.

As she sang a form came forward out of the mists that filled the hall.

Shimmering red with touches of gold around its eyes and great head, along its long back and serpentine tail, on the edges of its folded wings, a huge fire beast breathed softly and fire flickered around KaynaRee, bathing her in the power of the dragon.

The Fire Song ended and Ree stood trembling before the great fire beast. The brilliant deep red of its scales illuminated the mists with a glow that was at once fire and light.

KaynaRee Fairchild, break the seal and learn your Song, your Caretaker's Song, your Warrior Song. Golden One, Caretaker.

Ree did not know if the voice that urged her on was that of dragon or Golden One, nor was it important. She only knew that this dragon for this moment in time was her dragon, as So'Kol was her father's. As the fire beasts of the sea—Ke'Shan, Ga'Vrill, and Jho'Son—had been her mother's.

She took the seal in her fingers and twisted it to unlock her Song.

Chords of infinite beauty like things alive slipped in and out of the mists surrounding the two of them. The music formed a bond with KaynaRee that was at once the strength and savage power of the dragon and the ancient power of the Faerie, unique and like no other, created for KaynaRee Fairchild and the red dragon by the Ancient Ones.

When the Song ended, Ree reached up to touch the magnificent red head and whispered, "I would know your name, beautiful one."

For you alone, I am Ja'Anee. Come, KaynaRee Fairchild. We must learn to fly together.

The fire beast lowered herself and canted a front knee for Ree to climb aboard.

Later, KaynaRee would not remember clambering up onto Ja'Anee's back, would not remember settling between the huge wings and grasping the slender horns at the base of the dragon's neck, would not remember how long they flew. No, all she would remember was the intensity of the emotions that swept through her, emotions she would experience again, but only when she flew into the heavens on the back of a fire beast. Joy coupled with fear, excitement laced with sorrow, pride that magic and power carried her to this place in this time, sadness for what lay ahead.

The red dragon circled and slowly came to rest at the edge of the forest that hid the Singers' Hall. KaynaRee slid down to the ground and leaned against Ja'Anee's side. She could feel the beating of the mighty heart and the beating of her own heart. Ja'Anee swung her neck down and around, sheltering her Caretaker.

You must go now. When you sing your Song I will come to you.

"But how will I know when to sing?"

When all else fails.

Ree awakened to find Torar beside her. He nuzzled the hand that lay across her stomach and she smiled at him. Dizzy and disoriented, she sat up and looked around her. Keen, sharp disappointment brought tears to her eyes. The Singers' Hall was nowhere to be seen; her dragon was no longer beside her.

She was back on the beach with the sun shining brightly overhead.

"Come, lady. We must go." The wolf butted his head gently against her shoulder.

Ree got stiffly to her feet and reached to pick up her pack, no longer heavy with the Quair. She took a deep breath and let it out slowly. "I wonder," she murmured, "if the Quair still rests on its stand in the Singers' Hall. Will there be others one day to break the seal on their Songs?" She shook her head and sighed again, then followed Torar as he led the way along the shore of Kalora Bay.

Caretaker, the breeze whispered. *Golden One.*

chapter eight

A small boat plowed its way through the Balagorn Channel. These waters were difficult to navigate in the best of weather and conditions, and today the narrow waterway churned with swells that threatened to swamp the old fishing boat filled with men, women and children, far too many for the boat to accommodate.

The passengers on this boat were not there to fish. No, they were seeking a new life, an easier life than the one they had left behind in Arland. They were going to find land and homes for the taking in the once proud, once rich country of Timis. Others had gone before them and had found homes and farms abandoned by people seeking safety from war and made them their own. When the Timisians returned, they were the ones turned forcefully away. Much as the Arlanders had done for generations in their poverty-stricken homeland, it was the Timisians who now must lead a hand-to-mouth existence.

Finton's War, as people referred to that terrible time when Aldward Finton, his Warders, and his Pales had nearly taken Timis, had been over for more than twenty-five years, but for many the effects of that war would never be over. Finton had lured Arland's leaders and many hundreds of its men and boys with the promise of gold. The greed of Cedric Raemon had squandered the limited resources of Arland on ships and armaments for Finton.

And nothing had been gained.

There was no gold. Cedric Raemon was dead. Several hundred men who had fought under Finton's banner died in Timis.

The gods of old no longer heard the pleas of Arlanders; rain did not fall on the parched earth; the sun beat relentlessly down day after day on withered crops, on the few scrawny animals that managed to survive, on the starving people who cried out for mercy. What else was there to do but die or flee their ravaged land.

The grizzled captain of the fishing boat swore in frustration as the wind tossed the boat about like so much flotsam and clung to the tiller with all his strength. People screamed as the boat lurched from side to side as it plowed through the rolling seas. Somehow the old tub managed to stay afloat and staggered onward. Pulling the tiller hard right, the boat swung around Lognan Point and into choppy waters of the narrow inlet.

"Drop the sail! Let the current take 'er!" the captain shouted. Letting the current carry it toward the shore, the craft angled for the pier at Blairtown. As the boat drew alongside, one of the crewmen jumped to the dock and turned to catch the line tossed to him. With the boat tethered against the old dock, people began to gather their meager belongings; and handing children up to waiting hands, they straggled off the vessel, grateful to have solid ground once more beneath their feet.

As the last Arlander made his way off the dock and into Blairtown, a scraggly bearded crewman joined the captain at the rail.

"What do you think will become of 'em, Cap'n?"

Caleb Jessrick shrugged and spat in the water. "Who knows? They think they're going to find a better life here, but I doubt it. There isn't enough here to go 'round. Timisians have about had their fill of Arlanders. They're not wanted in Kaenolir either." He spat again before turning to take an accounting of how his boat had fared in the crossing. "Who knows?" he asked again as he walked away. "Get ready to get us underway."

"Poor sods," the crewman muttered as he turned to follow Jessrick. "Most likely they'll find nothing better than what they left behind."

From the bluffs above the dilapidated buildings that housed the cold furnaces that had forged the gold of Timis, a man, Hunter he was called, watched the Arlanders come ashore. He counted the number of men and older boys.

"Uh," he grunted. "Scrawny old men and kids." He stepped back from his viewpoint, picked up his pack and extracted a paper and stub of chalk that he used to mark down the numbers of Arlanders landing at Blairtown. So far this fortnight, there had been sixty-five, but most of them were elderly, the rest women with children. Some of them would find their way to family and friends already living in the High Champaign. Others would find shelter and sustenance where they could. The villages of Stonetown, Waytown, and Malhain had been taken over by Arlanders many years earlier. A few Timisians subsisted in out-of-the-way places among the foothills of the Dalrudd Mountains, but eastern Timis was, for all purposes, an Arland colony, a colony on the edge of starvation and desperation. The rich herds of cattle, sheep and goats, left behind by the Timisians in their flight to save themselves, had once been the staple of the High Champaign. Under the inexperienced husbandry of the squatters, the herds had dwindled to nearly nothing over the years. Too many of the animals were slaughtered for food and hides, leaving too few to reproduce in the numbers needed to sustain the population.

Acres of rich grassland were plowed under and planted in grains, but the land was meant for grass. The Dalrudd Mountains blocked the moisture-laden clouds and little rain fell on the Champaign in the summer, too little to grow grain. Timis had seemed a land of promise offering food and shelter to the people of Arland who had little of either, but in a few short years the promises had withered and died. They didn't know how to live in drought-stricken Arland, and they didn't know how to live on the land in Timis.

Still, they continued to cross the Balagorn Channel. The man who counted their numbers shook his head. They left nothing, had nothing, would find nothing here.

Unless they crossed the mountains into the vast richness of western Timis, or moved northward into Kaenolir.

And that, he thought, was exactly what Kelan Dellay planned to do.

He put the paper and chalk back in his pack, picked up his bedroll and food packet and left the bluff. If the weather held for a day or two, he'd be able to reach Malhain Village where Dellay had established himself as a leader of the dispossessed Arlanders. Himself one of the dispossessed, Dellay was relentless in organizing those Arlanders willing to fight for land, possessions, and a new way of life. He began by encouraging a few men and older boys to join him in learning how to use swords and spears when they could get them, axes, even shovels and staffs when they couldn't. Slowly, over the years, the numbers of men who were willing to take what they wanted, especially here in eastern Timis but eventually in western Timis as well, grew into an army of sorts awaiting Dellay's call to arms.

Hunter crossed the River Roon, hardly more than a summer trickle. The air was hot and still, and Hunter took off his hat to wipe sweat from his brow. He took a swig from his water flask, rinsed his mouth and spit out the tepid water. Settling his pack more comfortably on his shoulder he pushed on until the sun slipped behind the Dalrudd peaks and it began to grow dark. He decided to find a place to camp among the scrub trees and the rocks that littered the ground at the base of the mountains. He'd get an early start in the morning.

By the light of his small campfire, he looked over the numbers he had scratched on a scrap of paper. Of the recent Arlanders coming through Blairtown, only a few might be interested in what Dellay had in mind to do. However, over the last five years, there were many men who were willing to follow Dellay's lead. Hunter was certain that the number was sufficient to lead the push into western Timis, perhaps even to move north into Kaenolir. He stuffed the paper back into his pack, added another stick to the fire and settled comfortably against a large rock. One of the first items on Dellay's agenda was to get the Cragon Mine operating again. Hunter didn't know how Dellay had done it, but he'd found an old miner who had worked in Cragon and was willing, for a price of course, to teach Arlanders how to bring the gold out. The old fellow thought he could figure out how to get the smelting furnaces up and running, too. For a price of course.

The fire crackled and sparked and Hunter's eyes grew heavy. Somewhere in the crags above him a wolf howled and was answered by another and then another. Hunter shivered and added more fuel to the fire.

"Wolves," he muttered and shivered again. He pulled a short sword from his pack and laid it across his lap. After a time, he no longer heard the wolves. His head dropped forward, his chin resting on his chest, and he slept.

Kelan Dellay sat at a rough plank table, a large mug of ale at his elbow. Like many Arlanders, he was of medium stature but with heavy shoulders and chest, a short neck and broad face with a thick head of sandy colored hair, a belly that sagged over his belt. There was nothing about him that distinguished him physically, but there was something, something about him that marked him as a man other men would make way for when encountering him on the same road or path. His deep voice and loud laugh commanded attention and when he spoke others listened. He could quickly take the measure of a man or woman, and when he gave an order, that order was carried out or there would be an unpleasant consequence. He was mean and often cruel. Something sinister lurked in his eyes, something dark and unappealing, not a man to trifle with or take lightly.

A tall, heavy-set woman, shoulders slumped in weariness, trudged back and forth from fireplace to table, bringing platters of venison and roasted vegetables for the six men seated at the table with Kelan. The cottage where she toiled for Dellay had once been her family's home. When she, her husband and two sons, returned from safety in Kaenolir after Finton's war, they found Malhain Village in the possession of Arlanders. Her husband and sons had been killed as they tried to evict the squatters from their cottage. She buried her family and several friends in the burial grounds on a windswept hill beyond the village, and with no other recourse, she had stayed and become the thrall of Kelan Dellay, cooking, washing, scrubbing, fetching, and sometimes sharing his bed—whatever he demanded of her. She had come to loathe him, and prayed each day that she would find a way to make him pay for what he had done to her, to her family, and to the Timisians who once had lived at the foot of the Dalrudd Mountains.

"More ale," Dellay grunted in her direction. "The pitcher's near empty."

The woman picked up the pitcher, slanted a look of disgust toward Dellay and stepped away to do as she was bid. With her mouth tight in anger, she thumped the filled pitcher down on the table at Dellay's elbow, spilling some in the process. He swore and swiped an open hand at her. For all her size, she stepped quickly beyond his reach and left the men to their food and drink.

"Damn sow," Dellay muttered.

"Good cook, though," Lem Morgan licked the grease from his fingers. "Better watch out, Kelan, or you'll wake up some morning with one of her knives in your belly and missing a few of your important parts."

Dellay snorted in disdain while the other men chuckled at Morgan's crude remark. The door banged on the woman's departure and the men continued to eat and drink until Dellay pushed his empty plate away and refilled his mug. He picked up the scrap of paper with Hunter's tallies.

"So, not many men we can use." He tapped the paper absently against the handle of his mug and pursed his lips in thought.

Hunter swallowed his last bite and wiped his mouth on the back of his hand. He took a long swallow of ale and reached for the pitcher to refill his mug.

"Not more than ten at the most during the last fourteen, fifteen days. Maybe not even that many. Most coming over now are either too old or too young. More women coming, too."

Dellay grunted his irritation and turned to the man seated next to Hunter. "Lem, how many have you recruited for the mine?"

"Altogether?"

Dellay nodded.

"So far, forty-seven, and fifteen of those are women."

"Women?" Dellay asked.

Morgan shrugged. "Why not? These women have no men, no children to care for. And they're strong and reasonably healthy. They said if it means regular food and shelter, they'll go down in the pit and dig."

Dellay took another swallow of ale and set his mug down hard. "All right, then. Do it. Get 'em working. The old man will show them what to do. What about the smelters?"

Morgan filled his empty mug and took a drink before answering Dellay's question. "Got six men working on 'em. That old miner says he should be able to get one going by taking pieces from the other one, but it will be a while before he's ready to fire up the furnace."

"Good. Keep pushing. We finally have the numbers I think we need not only to get the mine operational, but to form the raiding parties that will take what we need from the west side of the mountains. "

"What about weapons? Food?" Hunter asked.

Dellay shook his head and waved a hand in dismissal. "All in good time, Hunter. The first raiding parties will be small and aimed at specific targets to get us the weapons we need. We'll hit Riversend in Kaenolir first and then later Timthurlen. I got men in Ross Harbor gettin' the Arlanders organized."

Hunter opened his mouth to speak, but Dellay anticipated his question. "I have two boats and two captains who don't care what they do or where they do it." A sly smile curved his hard mouth. "I also have another card to play, one that involves the Warders, but I'll tell you about that later when it's all set. Now," he said looking around the table at each of the men, "the seven of us leave for Riversend in the morning. There'll be a boat waiting for us at Waytown. It will take us to Riversend and the Guardian armory. I have a man in place there who knows Riversend very well. They've become complacent over the years since Finton sicced the pirates on 'em. They're too busy building and making money. The armory is a ripe plum waiting for us to pick it." He laughed, a harsh sound in the otherwise quiet room. The men looked at each other and turned back to Dellay when he banged the table with a fist. "That's all for now. Meet here at first light with what weapons you have and be prepared to ride to Waytown." He pushed away from the table and stood in dismissal. "Until tomorrow."

A scruffy figure slipped into the shadows as the men left the cottage. He had been hiding near the woodpile by the back door of Dellay's cottage, a back door that stood ajar. When the woman left, he had pressed closer so he could hear what the men inside were saying. He smiled as he moved from one cottage to the next, always staying beyond the reach of lighted windows and doors, until he passed the outskirts of the village. He paused to look back, waited several minutes to make sure he wasn't being followed, then turned sharply west toward the mountains. A long, hard journey lay ahead of him, but Gadred Aember waited for him at the end of it, and the information he had to give the leader of the Warders would be most welcomed. It seemed the Warders would soon have armed men at their disposal. The man smiled again and picked up his pace.

chapter nine

The setting sun colored the snow of the Dalrudd Mountains with a pale golden hue and painted the exposed stone ribs of the peaks delicate shades of pink and purple. Camron Thorpe stood at the tall windows of his office looking out toward the mountains, much as his friend, Tiernan Irworth, had done during the many years he wore the chain of chieftaincy. For Tiernan, the mountains soothed his soul, brought him peace. In all the years they had known each other, Camron had never known Tiernan to be a man who prayed, but if he had done so, Camron was certain those prayers would have been directed to the spirits that inhabited the mountains of Timis. The light slowly faded; shadows settled over the mountains and ushered in the darkness.

Now the golden chain of Timis rested about Camron's neck, and at times Camron felt he would be crushed beneath its weight. There had been many days during this past year when he cursed his old friend for laying the burden of chieftaincy on his shoulders. There were times when Camron desperately longed for the quiet, tranquil life he and his family had lived on Lorn Isle. With a deep sigh he turned away from the encroaching night and returned to his desk. He should read the latest report from Loren Lamond, captain of the Highland Guardians in Kaenolir, before joining Kitra for the evening meal. He lit the lamp on the center of his desk and settled into the chair at the long narrow table he used for a desk.

He had read only a few minutes when a soft knock on the door interrupted his concentration. "Come," he called. He continued to the bottom of the page he'd been reading and turned the page before looking up. Hugh Carlsby stood just inside the wide doorway, waiting to gain Camron's attention.

Camron leaned back in his chair and motioned Hugh to the chair near his desk. "What brings you into the bear's den, Hugh?"

Hugh laughed at the chieftain's comment. "So, you do know what some call this office."

Camron responded with a weary grunt and rubbed a hand over his forehead. "I don't know how Tiernan handled all the details and the requests and the demands and the reports and the complaints, and on and on and on," he muttered. "I'd rather be out tramping the mountains and finding out for myself just what's going on."

"Ah, but Lady Kitra would not be pleased to have you doing that."

Camron sighed gustily. "No indeed, she would not, especially if I said she couldn't come along."

Hugh laughed again and moved to settle more comfortably in his chair. "Couldn't you find a chair a man could sit in with some comfort, Camron? Or perhaps it's your way to make people state their business, get up and leave." He raised an eyebrow in question

"Well, now you know my secret." He pushed his chair back from the desk and stood. "Come, there are comfortable chairs by the fireplace. I take it you have something you want to tell me and knowing you, it will take a while."

While Hugh took one of the chairs set in front of the empty fireplace, Camron stepped to a cupboard and removed a distinctive dark green bottle of Highland whiskey and two small cups. He placed the cups on the table between the chairs and uncorked the bottle. "Help yourself," he said, placing the bottle within easy reach. He took the chair opposite Hugh.

Hugh filled his cup and Camron's, then eased back in his chair. He lifted his cup in silent toast to Camron and took a sip. With a satisfied sigh, he sat for a moment contemplating the amber liquid. "Wonder how much longer we'll be able to get this," he murmured before lifting the cup to his mouth for another sip. He set the cup on the table and turned to Camron. "I've been poking around Cragon Mine," he said. "You won't like what I found."

"So," Camron said after taking a sip of his whiskey. "Tell me. What do you know about the fellow helping the Arlanders operate the mine?"

"Bran Kemp. I remember him as being a quiet fellow, a loner. He was responsible for mapping the tunnels as we went and good at what he did. Bran could 'read' stone; he knew if the rock we were planning to dig was stable. And somehow he had an uncanny sense of danger, when there might be a rock fall, when the air was getting bad. When the Warders attacked Banning and took over the mine, he showed the miners how to slow the digging way down."

Camron got up from his chair and knelt before the fireplace to light the kindling placed there earlier in the day. When the fire crackled merrily, he added another log and returned to his chair.

"Why do you think he would help the Arlanders now?"

"Don't really know. I did hear that Dellay was willing to pay to restart the mining operation. Kemp's an old man now; his wife died several years ago. Don't think they had any kids and no other family I'm aware of." Hugh shrugged. "Why not take the Arlanders' money if it's offered. However, I wouldn't trust Kelan Dellay to keep a bargain."

A soft knock interrupted the conversation and Kitra Fairchild entered. Camron held out a hand to her as she came to stand beside him. Hugh rose and smiled a greeting.

"Sit," she waved Hugh back to his chair. She looked down at Camron and leaned over to kiss him lightly on the forehead. "Do you two plan to talk all night, or would you like some supper?" She looked to the table with the bottle and now empty cups. "You need some food to soak up that whiskey," she smiled.

"Food would be good, love. Do you mind having some sent up to us?"

"Of course. Good to see you Hugh. Tell Megan hello for me. I understand she's about to become a grandmother for the second time."

"Aye, and that's all she can think about. The babe should be arriving any day now."

"Tell her I'm envious," Kitra laughed. "No wee bairns in sight for us yet and not likely to be for some time." She looked down at Camron and squeezed his shoulder. "I'll have supper sent up," she said and left the room.

The men sat in silence for a moment after Kitra left. Camron got up to put another log on the fire. When he returned to his chair, Hugh had refilled their cups.

"What more did you find out about Kelan Dellay? You've been watching him for a long time. What do you think he's trying to do?"

"If you'd asked me that question five years ago, I would have said he's trying to cause as much trouble as he can, just because he can. Now, I think there's more to what he's doing than just lawlessness and mischief. I think he has a plan and that plan includes controlling the mine and using gold to establish himself as the leader of the Arlanders. The eastern side of the mountains really belongs to the Arlanders, as you are all too aware. I don't think he's satisfied with just the eastern part of Timis; I think he wants it all. And the gold from the mine is a key element."

"Sheevers," Camron muttered. "Will Kemp be able to get the furnaces operating again? They've been cold for a long time. There are reports from years ago that said anything that could be salvaged from the smelters and used elsewhere had left the furnaces inoperable without new parts."

"The word I've picked up is that he thinks he can get one of the furnaces back up by taking what he needs from the second furnace. I don't know much about the smelting aspect, so maybe he can get a furnace going."

The men's conversation was interrupted with the arrival of their evening meal. They ate in silence for a time before Camron asked the question that had been gnawing at him ever since his arrival at Camlanrein.

"How are we going to keep Timisians and Arlanders from killing each other, Hugh? Did Tiernan have ideas that he shared with you or that you were privy to?"

Hugh finished eating and set his plate away before answering. "Camron, I don't think Tiernan realized the full extent of the Arlander. . . 'situation' I'll call it for want of a better word." Hugh shrugged. "Tiernan, I believe, really felt that the people of Timis would make room for the Arlanders, and we did, for a time, right after the war with Finton and his Warders. Tiernan was more concerned about getting our people settled again, and the Arlanders just seemed to slip quietly into the landscape without his being aware of what they were doing or how many there were. When people came home to find Arlanders in their houses and on their land, the skirmishes that came about sent the Arlanders packing at first, but more kept coming and taking land and homes. And the 'squatting' was happening almost entirely in eastern Timis, somewhat out-of-sight-out-of-mind, so to speak. Sad to say, Camron, I think Tiernan had lost touch the last few years. He'd fought his war; he didn't want to fight another."

"You think then that war is inevitable," Camron said flatly.

Hugh sighed deeply and let his breath out slowly. "There's more going on than meets the eye, Camron. There are Warders living in a valley near the site of Finton's castle. What they're doing there, no one knows. And knowing what the Warders have done in the past, perhaps we should have some idea of what they're doing in that valley. Now, do I think war is inevitable? I pray it is not, but I think we must do something to stop Kelan Dellay from organizing the Arlanders into any kind of a fighting force. And, Camron, I think we will be hard pressed to do so, especially if we have Warders to contend with again."

Camron was silent for a long time. At last he looked away and scrubbed his face with his hands. "Sheevers," he muttered angrily. "Not again." He rose to pace the quiet room. "So. We need to know what the Warders are doing; we need to know what Kelan Dellay is up to. I need someone in the mountains to find out just what's going on. You know the area of the mine, but I know the rest of the mountains. At least, I once knew the mountains, knew them better than anyone." He turned to face Hugh. "It's been a long time, Hugh, since we found each other in a cave in Malhain Pass."

"I know. But there is someone you should talk to. You remember Dannen Vance? He helped get us out of Banning and down to Camlanrein."

"Yes, but wasn't he killed when Finton attacked Ross Harbor?"

"Yes, he was, but there is a younger brother, Cass. Soldiering doesn't appeal to Cass, but roaming the northern reaches of the Dalrudds does. If you decide you must be the one to scout the mountains, I suggest you take Cass with you. We'll need to find him first, however. I'll get the word out. It may be weeks, though, before he decides to come back to Ross Harbor."

"Do we have weeks, Hugh?"

"I don't know, Camron, I don't know. I hope we do."

The hour was late when Hugh Carlsby finally left Camron's office. Camron banked the fire before blowing out the lamp and candles he had lit while he and Hugh talked. He closed the office door behind him and made his way down the silent hall. Lamps in wall sconces cast flickering shadows as he passed. At the end of the hall he turned right and mounted the steps that led to his private chambers. The guard who stood watch at the top of the stairs saluted before stepping forward to open the wide door into the quiet sitting room.

"Good night, sir," the Trooper murmured.

Camron nodded a response and entered the large, comfortably furnished room. Kitra had left a lamp burning for him on the table near the door, and he extinguished the bright flame before moving through the room and down the hallway toward the equally large chamber where he and Kitra slept.

Heavy drapes were pushed back and moonlight brightened the room. A window near their bed was open to the cool autumn breeze. Beneath the coverlet Kitra stirred.

"Camron?"

"Hush, love. It's very late. Go back to sleep."

"Have you and Hugh been talking all this time?" she murmured.

"Afraid so, yes. I'll tell you about it tomorrow."

"Hm," she murmured.

He slipped into bed beside her and she nestled against him, one arm draped across his broad chest. He turned his head to kiss her hair and drew her close against his side.

Kitra sighed. "Tomorrow," she said and went back to sleep.

It would be a long time before Camron finally slept.

It took nearly four weeks before word reached Cass Vance that the chieftain of Timis wished to see him. Camron used the time to learn as much as he could about Kelan Dellay and what was happening in the High Champaign, but his time was also occupied with the increasing unrest among Timisians and Arlanders. More fights, more brawls, more violent deaths, more property theft—the dungeons and cells below Camlanrein were bursting at the seams. It seemed no matter what was done to appease the unemployed, usually homeless and always hungry Arlanders the more unsettled they became. Where would it end he wondered? How could he bring the two factions together?

Camron studied the latest maps of the mountains and read the disturbing reports of a Warder presence in a valley situated in the mountains above the area where Finton's castle had stood. How many Warders survived and banded together was unknown, but just the fact there was still an active group was disturbing. The information that Camron had access to indicated a hall had been built to house the men; they were self-sufficient; they were not seen except for a rare sighting on the beach near where the Stones of Destiny had once stood. Camron hoped Cass Vance would be able to tell him more.

Then there was the matter of Kelan Dellay. Imprisoned in the dungeons of Camlanrein for robbery and murder, he had escaped by killing the guard who came to bring him a meal. Dellay had feigned intense stomach pains and when the guard entered to see what was wrong, Dellay had overpowered and strangled the unsuspecting man. The brief report indicated Dellay had fled to the Dalrudd Mountains, but little was known about him during the ensuing years until he appeared in Malhain Village. He had gathered together a gang of thugs, mostly Arlanders but also a few disenfranchised Timisians, who made life miserable for the remaining Timisians in the High Champaign. The few fishermen and their families still living in isolated villages along the Balagorn Sea were repeatedly harassed by Dellay's thugs. Over time, he had brought more Arlanders into his fold although the exact number of men who followed his orders was not known. The Troopers stationed in a small garrison near Stonetown were outnumbered, their training inadequate, and their ability to capture or detain the marauding Arlanders limited. It would only be a matter of time before the garrison would be recalled for safety's sake. Once the Troopers were gone, Dellay would have the entire High Champaign under his control.

Camron had sent Hugh Carlsby into the mountains near the Cragon Mine on two occasions, and he'd come back with disturbing news that the mine was up and running with one of the smelting furnaces soon to be operational, perhaps before spring. Dellay had found the old miner Bran Kemp, who had helped the Arlanders learn to operate the mine. If the rumor was correct, Bran Kemp would soon be able to restore a furnace for smelting the gold.

That meant Dellay had the men and soon he would have the gold. It would only be a matter of time before he crossed the mountains into western Timis. How was he to be stopped?

Camron pushed the papers he'd been reading aside and rose to pace. He thought best when he was moving, and there was much to think about. He needed to get into the mountains and if Cass Vance didn't come to Camlanrein soon, he would go alone. He'd wait another two days, three at the most. He needed information, needed to know what the Warders were doing, needed more knowledge of what Kelan Dellay was doing, needed to know how many Arlanders were still coming across the Balagorn Channel and what they intended to do— establish homes and livelihoods, or push into western Timis with force.

He paused in his pacing and stood before one of the large windows looking out to the mountains.

"What are you hiding in your peaks?" he whispered. "What will I find?"

He would find no answers sitting behind his desk, and he needed answers. Otherwise, how could he keep his people safe and secure?

His ruminating was interrupted by a polite cough. When he turned away from the window, he found a tall, lean, deeply tanned man with dark, nearly black hair falling to his shoulders waiting in the doorway.

"M'lord," the man said quietly, his voice deep and almost melodic. "You wanted to see me?"

"Cass Vance, I take it," Camron replied in answer and moved to welcome him. The two men shook hands and Camron motioned Vance to the chairs near the fireplace. "Hugh Carlsby said that if I want to go into the mountains, you are the man to take with me. I knew your brother, but I only remember you as a little boy tagging after Dannen whenever you got the chance."

Cass Vance grinned before moving to take the chair Camron offered. "He was a good man, a good soldier, the best big brother. He taught me much of what I know about the mountains."

"Then you had a very good teacher."

"Hugh told me you want to retrace your footsteps in the Dalrudds. How long since you've been in the mountains, m'lord?"

Camron sighed and his mouth quirked in answer. "Too long, I'm afraid. I used to know them very well, but, yes, as you might know, it's been many years since I left Timis."

Cass nodded. "It will come back to you. The mountains don't let you forget, but they also do not forgive."

"I need information, Cass. I need to know what's happening in the High Champaign, and I need to know about the Warders. I want to see for myself what we're up against."

Cass pursed his lips and crossed his arms over his chest. "Well then," he said quietly. "When do you want to leave?"

The mountains do not forget. . .

Camron thought of Cass Vance's words as they climbed. They were not far from Malhain Pass. At the rate they were moving, and if the weather held, they would be able to reach Malhain Village in two or three days. The sun began to lower behind them as they made their way down out of the high peaks, and the wind blew cold and strong.

"M'lord, I know where there's a cave where we can spend the night. It's not a steep climb down from here, but it's a difficult one. I think there was a landslide a long time ago and whenever it rains or the snows melt, more rocks come down."

Camron paused to get his bearings and catch his breath. If they had come down out of the high reaches where he thought they had, he knew which cave and which rock slide Cass referred to.

"If we are where I think we are, this is Hugh Carlsby's rock slide, Cass, the one that blocked the pass many years ago."

"The one Hugh had to get down when he got away from the Warders and was coming to Camlanrein for help?"

"Yes, that one. And I know the cave you're referring to."

"It's a tough stretch of the pass to navigate. I think people tried to clear the slide, but the rocks kept falling and they gave up."

"Have you stayed in the cave before?"

"Only once, m'lord," Cass said with a shake of his head. "It's a strange place."

Before Camron could ask Cass to explain why he thought it so, he motioned Camron to follow him. Moving carefully, the two men tried not to dislodge the rocks and gravel as they gradually made their way downward. Once beyond the slide area they headed east.

"The cave is just up ahead," Cass said. "I think it's on the left side."

"Yes," Camron replied. "Just there. Do you see the cleft?"

Cass slowed and Camron took the lead. When he realized Cass had come to a stop behind him, he paused and turned toward the younger man.

"Come on, Cass. Let's get out of the wind. It will soon be too dark to see where we're going."

Reluctantly, Cass joined Camron at the mouth of the small cave. "Sheevers, I shouldn't have mentioned the cave," he muttered to himself.

Camron stepped into the cave and felt his heart beat faster. His breath caught in his chest for a moment as memories came rushing back, memories of coming to this cave because he could not turn away from a voice in his mind. His fire beast had led him here. It seemed a lifetime ago.

"If I come to the cave again, would I find you there?"

No, Caretaker. You will find only a memory of me in Malhain Pass.

"So'Kol," he whispered. "Are you still here?"

There was no answer. After a moment, he took a deep breath, swung his pack off his shoulder and set it on the ground. He rummaged among the contents until he found a small shuttered lantern. When he lit it, the glow from the little flame drew Cass inside until he stood next to Camron.

"It's all right, Cass," Camron said softly. "I know the spirit that dwells in this cave."

Cass looked at his chieftain for a long moment and then toward the back wall of the small cave. He turned to face Camron, looked more closely at the tall, dark man, remembered the stories he had heard about the exploits of his chieftain. This man, Camron Thorpe, had found a dragon in the Dalrudd Mountains and saved his people from death and enslavement. This man had ridden a dragon and destroyed an evil that other men could not.

"I know the story," Cass murmured. "You found So'Kol here in the mountains. In this cave?"

"Yes," Camron said. "He called me here."

"Is he still here?"

"Not as the dragon that came to save Timis. He is but a memory here."

"But you feel him."

"Yes," Camron said and turned away. "I feel him."

"Would he come again if you needed him?"

Camron shook his head. "I don't know," he said simply. "When all else fails," he murmured with a sigh and turned once more to face Cass. "Come, let's eat and then get some rest."

Caretaker.

Camron sighed and stirred in his sleep.

Caretaker.

"So'Kol?" Camron whispered. Moving quietly, he pushed his blanket aside and rose. The shuttered lantern still burned beside Cass. The cave made the younger man uneasy and Camron knew it had taken him a long time to fall asleep. Taking a deep breath Camron walked to the back of the cave, much as he had done that first time when So'Kol called him here. A section of the wall had collapsed inward since he had been here, and jagged pieces of stone lay strewn about the floor.

"So'Kol," he murmured and stepped around the rubble to reach the wall. "I'm here," he whispered. And this time, he knew what lay beyond the stone barrier.

Caretaker. The voice of his fire beast whispered in his mind. *Caretaker, the fire beasts need you. There is one who possesses a token that is a danger to us.*

"Who, So'Kol? What token?"

You must find him, you and the other Caretakers.

For a moment, Camron stood in confusion. What other Caretakers? And then he realized who they were—Rayce and KaynaRee. His Caretaker blood was part of them.

"How will we know him?"

You will know him. He wears a black robe.

"A Warder? Like Aldward Finton?"

There is a book, Caretaker. Rheena Aleen wrote a book long ago. She took us through the Portal to memory. The book will show the way.

"But, So'Kol, we can't read the book."

You must. Go now. Find the black robe. Stop him.

With those ominous words, Camron felt So'Kol slipping away once more into the memory of this cave.

"M'lord?" Cass's sleepy voice called.

Camron reached out to touch the wall, then turned to retrace his steps.

There was another Warder threatening not only Timis but the dragons as well.

"Damn Aldward Finton," he muttered. What price would his country pay this time for one man's greed and hatred?

"Are you all right, m'lord?" Cass tossed his blanket aside and rose as Camron stepped back into the small circle of light. "I thought I heard you talking."

"I'm fine, Cass. Just couldn't sleep. When it gets light, I want you to head to Malhain Village and determine, if you can, what Dellay is up to. We must know what he is planning to do. I need to find the Warders. "

"But, m'lord. . ."

"No more now, Cass. It will soon be daylight. Let's get what rest we can. We each have a long way to go tomorrow."

Cass looked at Camron for a moment before reluctantly turning away. He didn't like the thought of his chieftain going on alone, but the man still knew his way about the Dalrudds. His lordship had proved that already, but what if he encountered someone who wished Timis ill? Someone who threatened Camron Thorpe? Cass sighed and pulled his blanket around his shoulders and settled against the cold stone wall. He knew he would not sleep and with the dawn they'd be on their separate ways.

Had he heard Camron Thorpe talking? Or was it merely a dream? Cass shook his head. No, he'd heard Camron say 'So'Kol,' he was sure of it. So'Kol, the name of the dragon Camron Thorpe had found in the Dalrudds, had found here in this cave. There were forces here he did not understand.

Cass shivered. He knew it was not just from the cold.

Camron and Cass parted in the early hour just before dawn, Cass to Malhain Village; Camron to find the Warders. Camron knew that a long, difficult journey lay before him. He thought again of Cass's comment that the mountains do not forget, and he was grateful that he had not forgotten the knowledge he had gained during the years he had roamed these rugged peaks and hidden valleys, the knowledge that had once been second nature to him and returned in full force now as he pushed ever deeper into the uncharted Dalrudds.

The sunlight shimmered on the snowy peaks above him as he climbed. Wind whistled, making an odd kind of musical accompaniment. From time to time eagles soared on currents of air, sometimes above him, sometimes below him, as he climbed steadily moving south away from Malhain pass. If he continued on this route, he would bypass the Cragon Mine, staying well above it, before slipping through Cragon Pass and back into the high reaches above the location where Dunadd and the Stones of Destiny had once stood. Somewhere within those peaks, the Warders' valley lay hidden.

Camron paused only to rest when it became too dark to see. His food supply had dwindled to crusts of bread and a few slivers of dried meat. Water to drink was never an issue with the snow and the many streams and rivers that rushed ever onward down the mountains to the sea. Unnoticed, he moved past the mine and into Cragon Pass on the fifth day. He might have been able to add to his food pouch at Banning Village but dared not take the risk of being seen or recognized; thus, he pressed on, weary, footsore, and hungry.

And always So'Kol's words were on his mind.

Caretaker, the fire beasts need you.

A token, So'Kol said. What kind of token? How could a token be a danger to the fire beasts. The fire beasts were but memory now. Or were they? They had come when Timis needed them. They had come when men could not destroy the force of evil that threatened them. Did that same evil, but perhaps in a different form, threaten them again. Another Warder? Another evil?

Evil always finds a way, Talanor Rowan had said.

You must find him, you and the other Caretakers.

A sudden gust of wind pushed against him and he stumbled. Pausing for a moment to get his bearings, he looked back the way he had come. He saw a figure, or was it merely a shadow, slip from one large outcropping to another. He waited but he saw nothing more. Shaking his head to clear his mind, he hastened onward.

It was during the sixth day that he knew for certain he was not alone. He'd set a snare the night before and managed to catch a small weasel, an animal that lived on tiny rodents and an occasional hare that crossed its path. Roasted on a spit it would provide a good meal or two, not the best but good enough to satisfy his hunger. Clouds had been amassing for much of the day and the wind had grown decidedly colder. A storm was coming and he needed to find shelter and wood for a fire before he lost the light.

Camron climbed down to a lower elevation where scrub pines grew, blasted into grotesque shapes by the winds. This time when a figure flitted on the edge of his sight, he knew he was not mistaken: he was being followed. He began to pick up wood for his fire, purposely keeping his back to the area where he had seen the figure of a man slip behind a pile of rocks scattered among the trees. Camron turned his head at the last moment as he straightened and saw the man move away from one boulder to take up a position behind another.

"Well," he thought. "Who are you?"

When he had gathered enough wood for a fire that would last long enough to roast his catch, he headed toward an exposed wall of rock. An overhang on the back side offered protection from the weather. The storm was moving fast across the sky from the north; the dark clouds enveloped the last of the daylight, bringing wind, rain, and at this elevation, perhaps even some snow. Dropping the wood, he slipped his pack from his shoulder and set about skinning and gutting the weasel. Once that task was done and the fire burning well, he fashioned a spit and set the meat above the flames. It wasn't long before the scent of roasting meat churned the juices of his stomach and Camron's mouth watered.

Clouds massed directly overhead now and the wind moaned and shrieked as it whipped around the outcropping. Rain began to fall, but below him, through the curtain of slashing rain, Camron saw his follower slip from one rock to another, coming closer.

When the meat was roasted, Camron slid the carcass from the spit onto a flat rock beside the fire. He looked out into the darkness as the rain mixed with sleet rattled against the overhang.

"I know you're there," he called. "There's enough meat here for the two of us. Come and get some." He waited for several minutes, but got no response. "Suit yourself," he called again and settled down beside the fire to enjoy his repast. The knife he'd used to cut apart the meat lay close at hand.

He heard the rattle of the scree around the base of the outcropping and knew his 'guest' was making his way toward the fire and the tantalizing smell of roasted meat. After a moment, the man appeared and stopped at the edge of the circle of firelight. Camron motioned him closer.

The man was dirty, ragged and thin; an unkempt beard did not hide the deep scratches and bruises on his face. Perhaps from a recent tumble as he followed Camron. His lank hair, once black but now mostly gray, hung in greasy, wet strings down his back. A tattered cloak slung about his shoulders did little to keep out the cold; one boot had lost its sole.

"Do you have some water?" the man asked, his voice hardly more than a croak.

Camron handed him his water flask.

The man reached out with dirty, scratched hands to take the proffered water and drank hungrily. He wiped his mouth on the back of one hand and pushed the hair out of his eyes with the other.

"Better have some meat," Camron said.

The man hunkered down by the fire and took the meat Camron held out to him. "Thank you," he whispered around a mouthful. He closed his eyes as he chewed and sighed in satisfaction.

"When was the last time you had something to eat?"

The man shook his head. "Don't know." He reached for the water flask again and took a sip. "I've lost track of the days."

Camron nodded. "Easy to do up here."

The two men continued to eat in silence until the meat was gone. With another sip from the water flask before handing it back to Camron, the man pulled his soggy cloak closer around his shoulders. The fire crackled and sparked as Camron added more wood.

"Mind if I ask your name?" Camron said as he sat back against the stone wall that formed the base of the overhang.

"Why do you want to know?" the man asked with a suspicious glance.

"Oh, I don't know. I usually like to know who I'm sharing a meal with. More friendly that way."

A smile, quickly gone, flitted across the man's mouth. "My name is Orly. Desmond Orly."

Camron nodded in response. "You going any place in particular?"

"Why do you want to know?" he asked again.

"The mountains can be a dangerous place."

The man nodded and touched the large bruise on his cheek. "In more ways than one," he murmured. He sat for a long moment, staring into the fire. "I've given you my name. What about yours?"

"Camron Thorpe."

The man started and made as if to rise. As he moved, Camron reached down and grasped the knife. "Easy," he murmured. "I mean you no harm." Slowly Orly sank back down. From the wild almost feral look in his eyes Camron realized the man was not a threat—he was frightened. Camron wondered why.

"You're on the run, aren't you?"

After a long pause, Orly nodded.

"Can you tell me why? Perhaps I can help you."

Orly shook his head. "I don't think anyone can help me. I have to get away, get out of the mountains. I thought I could find a way out, but I keep getting lost. You're the first person I've seen in days. I had to get away in a hurry and couldn't take time to pack some food and water. I was afraid I would have been next." He would have kept babbling, almost hysterically, if Camron had not held out a soothing hand.

"You're safe here with me," Camron said quietly. He placed his knife on the ground beside him and waited. Carefully, showing his hands, he added more wood to the fire. The crackle and spark of the fire seemed to calm the other man. Orly sat watching the fire for a long time before he finally looked up.

"Do you know there are Warders still living in a valley west of Dunadd?" Orly asked, his voice so low Camron had to lean forward to hear him above the noise of the storm.

At Camron's nod, Orly shifted and rubbed his hands together. After a moment he held them out to the heat of the fire before clenching them together in his lap. "I've come from there." He shivered. "I. . .I ran away from there." After a long pause, he looked once more at the flickering flames. "Aember killed my friend," he whispered. "I know he did it, and he knows I know."

"Who is Aember?"

And then the words came pouring out of Desmond Orly: the Warders' hidden valley, Gadred Aember, the strange token Aember found, the death of Morton Cassel.

"I had to get away or Aember would have killed me, too. With Cassel dead, no one will stand up to him. Aember wants the Warders to be powerful again, like we were with Aldward Finton." Orly shrugged and looked away into the night. "He sent some of the brothers into the High Champaign, to spy, I think. Into Timthurlen, too, maybe even Ross Harbor. But I don't know what he has learned other than he thinks the Warders can use the Arlanders to get what he wants. I believe he has made contact with the leader of the Arlanders. I don't know for sure what his name is, Dellay, I think. Yes, that's it, Dellay. I heard his name mentioned in a conversation Aember had with Conn Regan."

"And what does Aember want?" Camron asked quietly.

"Timis. Gadred Aember wants Timis, all of it."

"Can you take me to the Warders' valley?" Camron finally asked.

Orly shook his head. "You don't want to go there. Aember will kill you. Anyone coming to the valley is run off." He looked down at his clenched hands. "Sometimes men have been killed." He looked up at Camron. "I can show you where it is and you can maybe find a place where you could observe the valley, but you must. . ." He shifted and looked away, then turned his gaze on Camron once more. "You must not go down into the valley, Camron Thorpe." He wiped his running nose on his sleeve. "You must not, not alone," he whispered.

The wind whipped around the men's shelter and scattered sparks from the fire high into the air. Camron thought he heard the cry of a wolf, but the wind carried it away almost as soon as he was conscious of the sound. Orly shivered, wiped his nose again and held his hands out to the heat of the dying fire. Camron added a few sticks to the blaze and watched as the dry wood caught and flamed.

"I need information, Desmond. If the Warders pose a threat again, I need to know what kind of threat."

Orly thought for a moment, then crossed his arms against his chest and leaned forward. "I'll take you to a spot where you can see what's going on in the compound without being seen." He sat thus for a long time. Finally, he came to a decision and hesitantly began to speak.

"There is a way into the hall that few remember now." He paused for a moment, then straightened and looked out into the dark night. He nodded. "It's an escape hatch built into the back wall, a tunnel that runs under part of the hall. I designed it and built it at Aember's direction. A day may come when you can get into the hall that way." He sat quietly, rubbing a finger back and forth over his lower lip.

Both men sat in silence with their thoughts. Camron might well make some decisions based on what Orly told him. But what Orly told him might not be true. Only time would tell.

Camron poked the fire with a last stick, tossed it into the flames and sat back to stare at Desmond Orly. He was a good judge of the character of men and he was faced with deciding if what Orly told him was a trap.

At last Camron stirred and sighed deeply. "What do you hope to gain by telling me this?"

"Morton Cassel was my friend, more like a brother. I left my family when I was very young to follow Finton's Way. I followed the path carefully, believing fully in what Finton told us. I carried his gold into the cellars of Dunadd; I marched in his army and killed Timisians who stood in the Warders' path. I watched the dragons—I watched you—destroy Finton and all that he stood for. Morton found me on the battlefield, badly wounded, nearly dead, and took care of me. When Aember found this valley and led a few of us into its safety, Morton was by my side. I had nowhere else to go; Aember offered direction and leadership; Morton offered stability and friendship. His was a calming influence on several of us. Aember was all for going out into Timis, killing and taking what we wanted, but Morton's voice prevailed. We learned to live without being noticed, but all the while Gadred Aember wanted more." Orly's earnest expression gave Camron pause.

"I'll ask you again, Desmond Orly, what do you hope to gain by telling me all this?"

"Morton Cassel came to believe that what the Warders had done in Finton's name was wrong. He wanted to live peacefully and he thought Aember was on the way to becoming another Finton. Morton and Aember argued often, more so these past months. Over the years, I came to believe that a peaceful life here in the valley was what I wanted. No more a Warder, just a man wanting to live out his life in a calm, reasonable way.

"What do I hope to gain by telling you this? I hope that the death of my friend Morton Cassel will lead to Aember's downfall."

"All right. Tomorrow at first light will you take me to the valley?"

He nodded. "With your help I think I can find the way."

"And show me how to get into the Warders Hall?"

"I can draw a map for you. Will you show me how to get down out of the mountains?"

Camron smiled. "Once you take me to the valley, I'll draw a map that will get you out of the Dalrudds and point you toward Timthurlen. I'll also have a message that I want to reach my wife at Camlanrein. Will you see that the message gets to a Trooper in Timthurlen?"

"Yes," Orly said quietly after only a moment.

The storm had subsided during the early hours of the morning. It left behind a cold wind and frozen puddles. Camron placed the meager remnants of his bread and dried meat on the flat rock beside the dead fire. "It's all I have left, Desmond. We'll split it between us."

Orly shook his head. "I can't take your food. You need it."

"We both need it." Camron divided the few crusts and slivers of meat and gave half to Orly and took the rest for himself. He lifted his pack to his shoulder, pulled up the hood of his cloak and set off. After a moment, Orly picked up the remaining scraps, stuffed them in his pack, and followed Camron.

It was well past midday and the men had been climbing steadily. For the last hour or so, they'd been aware of the rushing sound of a waterfall and Camron knew they were nearing the Warders' valley.

"We're nearly directly east of Finton's castle and the Stones of Destiny. Do you recognize any landmarks?"

"Yes, I know the waterfall. Once we reach it, we head south. The valley lies between two jagged peaks."

Camron nodded. "I know those peaks. I can find the valley from the waterfall. If you want to draw a map of the compound, I'll show you how to find your way to Timthurlen. Let's find the waterfall and then rest there for a bit."

With the water thundering at their backs, the two men drank icy cold water and ate a crust or two of bread while Orly painstakingly drew a map of the Warders' hall on a piece of parchment Camron had in his pack. With a piece of charcoal, Orly drew and labeled the layout of the compound. Then he carefully detailed the escape hatch built into the foundation on the back wall of the long hall.

"It will be hard to see in the dark because the bushes I planted along the foundation have grown very large. I've not checked the hatch," he shrugged, "in years, I guess. Use these windows as your guide. If you come down out of the mountains with the largest peak on your left, you'll come at the compound from the back. You'll go through an orchard and there's a large vegetable garden here." He marked the spot on his map. "You'll have to cross the garden, more or less in the open, so hope for a cloudy night if you decide to enter the hall this way. Once you've found the hatch—you'll feel the door frame—you'll have to work the latch open. It's in the center of the door and will no doubt be rusted after all this time. The door swings in; two steps down and you're in a passageway, a tunnel under the building. You'll have to feel your way along with one hand on the wall. Don't light a lantern because the light could be seen through cracks in the floorboards." Orly thought for a moment and then said, "It's about ten paces left to the common room. The passageway goes no further in that direction. The sleeping room for the Warders is roughly twenty paces to the right. The passage gets very narrow there, but it will lead you past the dormitory to Aember's chamber.

You'll know you're at his chamber when you come to two more steps up to another door. This one opens directly into his room." He handed the completed drawing to Camron. "May I ask you a question, Camron Thorpe?" At Camron's nod, Orly asked "Do you plan to kill him?"

Camron took the map and carefully stowed it in his pack. "I don't know, Desmond. It may well come to that."

Withdrawing another parchment, he began to draw a map to guide Orly down out of the Dalrudds. "Turn around," he said. "See the tallest peak among those three, to the northwest? That peak is just above Cragon Pass. Keep the peak in sight; sunrise on your right; sunset, of course, on your left. You should make the pass in two or three days. There are farms near the base of the mountains where you can ask for food and water, perhaps even a ride to Timthurlen." Camron folded the map and handed it to Orly. He took a folded letter from a pocket. "This," he said, "is for the Trooper commander in Timthurlen. Just leave the letter with him and disappear into the city. You should be safe enough if you don't draw attention to yourself. I suggest you shave off your beard and cut your hair; change your appearance as much as you can. If what you say is true, there may well be Warder spies wherever you go in Timis. When you can, come to Camlanrein. I could use your help when it comes to the Warders."

Orly took the letter and placed it, along with his map, in his pack. He shouldered the pack, stooped to take one last drink of water from the river, and turned to Camron. "Go with the Ancient Ones, Camron Thorpe," he said quietly.

Camron nodded. "Thank you, Desmond Orly."

"You can thank me in Camlanrein."

Camron watched until Orly was out of sight, then he filled his water flask, settled his pack on his back and set out for the

Warders' hidden valley. The wind seemed to push against his back and for a moment he heard a wild keening that he knew belonged to So'Kol.

Hurry, Caretaker. Hurry.

chapter ten

The faint light of dawn began to climb above the horizon as Kelan Dellay and his six men left the sleeping village behind. A raw, icy wind coming from the mountains swirled the dust their horses kicked up. Winter was coming and Dellay wanted to have men and weapons ready when spring came again. Snow and cold would keep Thorpe's spies out of the mountains, out of the High Champaign, and out of his business. He picked up the pace as the sky lightened; they needed to be at the Waytown dock by tomorrow afternoon. The captain taking them to Riversend wanted to leave as soon as Dellay arrived. They would sail only as far as Stonetown where they could moor for the night and leave in the morning as the tide turned. Kaenolir's fjords would force the captain to sail farther out to sea away from the rocks and strong currents. He wanted that part of the journey accomplished in daylight. This time of the year the weather could turn nasty in a hurry, not a good time to be sailing the dangerous waters off the coast of the Lowlands of Kaenolir. If the weather held and the winds were favorable, the boat should reach Riversend by nightfall of the third day. Darkness would cover their arrival and their movements once ashore.

A cold night's camp and the men were on their way again, grumbling and cursing at the fast pace Dellay set.

"He hardly even gave us time to take a piss," Hunter mumbled as he pulled up his hood and shrugged his ragged cape closer around his cold shoulders.

"Shut your mouth, Hunter, and ride," Dellay yelled.

Hunter swore under his breath and spurred his horse.

Dellay allowed the men to stop only to rest and feed the horses. After hastily making do on dry bread and hard cheese, they set off again. By late afternoon Waytown came into view. It had once been a small, vibrant village with a market place and busy fishing port. Now it was little more than a deserted shadow. A few of the once pristine cottages were ramshackle homes for Arlanders barely keeping body and soul together by scrounging what and where they could. Many of the cottages were abandoned derelicts, left to the ravages of time and weather.

As the seven horsemen drew near the harbor, Dellay saw the scruffy fishing boat that was to take them to Riversend and bring them back again. A man, scruffy as his boat, idly smoking a pipe, sat on an overturned keg on the dock. He stood as Dellay and his men rode up.

"Yer late."

"Well, we're here now. Where can we stable our horses so that they'll be here when we get back?" Dellay asked in a sour tone.

The old seaman shrugged. "Pay somebody to look after 'em. 'S about all ya can do."

Dellay swore and looked around. There were only two other boats tied up at the decrepit and rotting dock, both small rowboats. No one was in sight.

"You sail this thing alone?" Hunter asked.

The seaman spat and gave Hunter a rheumy-eyed look. "Deckhand ran off last week." He looked at Dellay. "One a yer men will have to handle the lines. If ya want to get to Riversend." He stuck the pipe back in his mouth and puffed with little concern for Dellay's predicament.

Dellay clenched and unclenched his big hands while he fumed and cursed. His face grew red with suppressed rage. He wanted to get to Riversend and this old bastard was about the only way he could get there. Dellay had already paid for the use of the boat, and now it appeared he would have to pay more for someone to look after their horses. There was a man waiting on the dock to get them into the armory, and Dellay needed all the weapons they could steal.

"All right, old man, we'll do it your way," Dellay said with a sour look. "How much?"

The pipe glowed red as the old man puffed away. Finally he removed the pipe from his mouth and pointed the stem at Dellay. "Another gold coin would pay for my grandson to care for yer horses. There's a stable, what's left of it, down the way. Horses will be out of the weather at least. Bit of feed there yet. I'll still need one of your men on the lines. Grandson can't do it if he's watching your horses." The pipe returned to his mouth and he clamped his teeth on the stem and looked out to sea. "Better make up your mind in a hurry. Might be some weather comin' in."

Given no choice, Dellay marched back to his horse and withdrew a small pouch from his saddle bag. He extracted a gold coin and walked back to the old man. "Here," he said through gritted teeth.

"I thank ye," the old seaman said with a smug smile as he took the coin. He gave a sharp whistle and a boy of about eleven, ragged and barefoot, trotted toward them from the direction of a dilapidated shed at the end of the dock. "Take care of the horses, boy."

The men dismounted and the boy gathered up the reins and led the tired animals away.

"Huh," Lem Morgan grunted. "Wonder if we'll ever see 'em again."

"Get on board," Dellay waved the men forward. "Who's done some sailing and can help sail this tub?"

"I've done a bit." Hunter stepped forward and Dellay nodded.

"All right, then," he said. "Let's get going."

The old seaman calmly knocked the spent tobacco from his pipe and stepped onto the bobbing deck of his boat. For an old man he moved easily and swiftly. He directed Dellay and his men to find a spot and stay there while Hunter cast off the lines, gave the stubby bow a shove and leapt on board.

At sundown three days later, the fishing boat slipped into an inconspicuous and out-of-the-way spot on the dock at Riversend near the armory of the Highland Guardians.

The sun had set hours earlier, but the dock still teemed with men; heavy wagons pulled by huge horses threaded their way through cursing seamen and around trade goods piled on the pier; men maneuvered carts loaded precariously high; women and children sold a variety of food and drink from small kiosks, even though the hour was late. Riversend had not only rebuilt its port, nearly destroyed by fire when Finton's pirates attacked, it had expanded. Warehouses lined the wharf; large ocean-going ships rode at anchor in the deep waters of the harbor waiting to be loaded or unloaded. Smaller fishing vessels vied for space and competed for moorage at the far end of the dock.

The Highland Guardian fort sat above the harbor on a knoll that overlooked the busy port. As the docks had been repaired and rebuilt, the number of Guardians needed to keep order had increased. The old Riversend fort had been destroyed in the fire; thus a new and much larger facility was built. The armory had grown in size to keep pace with the weapons needed by the expanding garrison. It was this armory that Kelan Dellay was planning to pilfer.

A tall man dressed in dark clothing materialized out of the shadows to meet Dellay as he climbed up the dock-side ladder from the fishing boat. Dellay looked up as the man held out a hand to help him up the last rung of the ladder onto the dock. The dark man's hood was pulled so low over his forehead Dellay could not see his features. The large hand that had helped him up onto the dock was rough and callused.

"Your men still on the boat?" he asked, his voice a low growl.

Dellay nodded. "They're ready whenever we need 'em."

"Good." He spat into the water. He nodded toward the boat Dellay had just left. "That old tub won't hold much cargo."

"It'll take all I need for now. When I need more I'll look you up again."

"Fair enough. Got the gold on you?"

Dellay smiled coldly.

"You'll see the gold when I see the goods," he said.

The other man grunted. "Let's go then. Get your men up here."

Dellay stepped over to the edge of the dock and motioned for his men.

"This way," the man turned and walked away at a leisurely pace when Dellay's six men stood on the dock. When they came abreast of the Guardian fort, he turned up a street that meandered up a hillside away from the harbor but parallel to the fort. After the men had walked a good distance, he turned again. This time he led the seven men down an alley that ran between two large warehouses, both dark and shuttered. He stopped and directed the men into the shadows provided by the building on their right.

"Wait for me here," he ordered.

He was gone only a short time before he returned to the silent group. "This way," he said. "And from here on, no talking."

They had gone perhaps a hundred paces, when the man stopped. He stepped to a large door and, with a key he drew from a pocket, unlocked it. At the click of the disengaged latch, he pulled the door open and motioned to the men. Once all were inside he closed the door and they stood silently in complete darkness. The man waited for several minutes, listening for any sound he couldn't identify. After several minutes of waiting in this manner, he struck a flint and lit a shuttered lantern he'd been carrying.

"Follow me," he whispered. "And be quiet."

A short time later he led them into a huge store room, stacked floor to ceiling with a variety of weaponry. "Take your pick," he said of the swords, spears, bows and arrows, lances. "Take only a few from each bin. Less likely to be noticed that something's missing."

"We need some of everything," Dellay said. "Here, Hunter, take only the swords you can carry without making a noise. Bring 'em back here to the door and go get some more." Dellay went on down the line directing the rest of his men on the weapons to take. The occasional soft clank made Dellay jump and pause what he was doing to listen intently. When they had assembled as much as they could carry back to the boat, the man came forward with large burlap bags, and the weapons were placed in seven bags and tied securely. Because of the length of the lances, the man directed that another bag be tied over the ends to completely cover them.

"Anything else that needs another bag?" At the negative response, he turned and led them back the way they had come. At the door he stopped. "I'll go first and make sure the way is clear. Remember," he muttered, "be quiet."

The man had been gone a long time and Dellay was getting anxious. Somewhere in the cavernous building a door slammed and he heard voices. He breathed heavily as the voices seemed to be coming closer. By the time the door opened behind him and the man returned, he sighed in relief.

"Come on. We have to be quick. There will be patrols in about twenty minutes," he motioned Dellay's group of thieves through the door, closed it quickly and quietly locked it again. With a rapid pace, made difficult by the heavy bags they carried, they maneuvered through the alley and turned the corner.

"Keep to the shadows," the man ordered.

He paused for a moment as they worked their way down the hill toward the dock. "Wait here and stay quiet," he directed and hurried away into the darkness. After another inordinate amount of time, he reappeared and they moved to follow him. They reached the old fishing boat and Dellay ordered Lem Morgan down the ladder and into the boat. One by one they handed him the burlap bags they carried, then clambered down to help him stow their night's work. When the bags were all on board, the man took Dellay by the arm as he was about to climb down to the boat.

"Aren't you forgetting something?" he growled. Dellay looked down to see a knife pressed to his side.

With a grimace he looked up into the man's cold eyes. "Hunter," he called over his shoulder. "Get my saddle bag. It's in the galley under the table there." He waited a moment. "Do you see it?"

A moment later, Hunter called up. "This one?" He was holding a brown leather pouch.

"Yes," Dellay called down. "Bring it up to me."

Hunter climbed the ladder and handed the pouch to Dellay.

"Get back below," Dellay ordered as he took the pouch.

Hunter eyed the dark man, turned and climbed down to the boat.

When his man was once more on the boat, Dellay opened the bag and carefully counted out the coins he and the man had agreed upon. He handed them over. The man sheathed his knife, recounted the gold coins and nodded.

"Good doing business with you," he said. "Now get the hell away from here before a patrol comes asking you what you're doing way down here." He turned and disappeared into the darkness.

"Arrogant bastard. I'd kill him and dump his body in the alley if I didn't need him again," Dellay muttered to himself as he climbed down the ladder.

chapter eleven

Cold wind whistled down out of the stone peaks of the Dalrudds. A weak sun, obscured now and then by dirty clouds that threatened snow, marked the time as midday. Cass found a place out of the wind where he could still observe the rough trail through Malhain Pass while he rested. He had seen no one since parting from Camron Thorpe; not many took this trail unless they hoped to find game in the lower reaches of the mountains. The absence of fellow travelers was to his advantage; if he wasn't seen, there could be no questions asked about why he was here.

Malhain Village was a place where he stopped occasionally, so his appearance there now should cause no undue interest, that is, unless Dellay was here. Cass knew the man had come to make Malhain Village his so-called headquarters and lived in the cottage that had belonged to a woman named Eithne and her family. Eithne's family was gone, dead at the hands of Arlander squatters. She did what she had to do to keep a roof over her head and food in her belly. Though Dellay forced her to cook and clean and do whatever else he wanted her to do, somehow she persevered, living a life of drudgery and sorrow. Eithne, Cass often found, was a source of information about what went on in the village and surrounding area. From time to time, she didn't mind sharing what she knew with Cass.

The daylight was starting to fade from a gray sky when Cass slipped unobserved to Eithne's back door. Only one light shone from the small window of the room Cass knew to be the kitchen of the cottage. The door was left slightly ajar and the warm, almost intoxicating smell of stew and fresh baked bread made his mouth water. He stood in the shadow created by the cottage and listened. The only sounds were those made by the woman as she moved about the room, singing softly to herself. No other lights, no other voices, no one about but Eithne.

Cass stepped forward and rapped lightly on the door. "Eithne," he called. "It's me, Cass Vance."

The singing stopped and a moment later Eithne stood framed in the doorway.

"What brings you here, Cass Vance?" She observed the tired lines of his face and then motioned him inside before he could answer. He dropped his pack and cloak near the door.

"You hungry? Of course you are," she said and closed the door behind him. "Take a seat by the fire." With the ease of a familiar task, she swung the pot of stew away from the flames and taking a long handled ladle scooped up two bowls of the delicious smelling stew. She set the bowls on a small table within reach of the chair Cass had taken and pulled another chair up close to the fire. Before she joined Cass she stepped to a narrow table under the window and took two spoons from a box and a loaf of crusty bread from a basket. She broke off two large chunks of bread and added one to each bowl, then handed Cass a spoon.

"What would you like to drink? Ale? Tea? I might even have a bit of Kaenolirian wine, too.

"Ale would serve me well," Cass said.

Eithne turned to a cupboard and took down mugs and a corked bottle. She set them on the table beside the rest of the meal. "Eat," she ordered.

Cass did not need a second invitation. The venison stew was rich in flavor and hot, the bread still warm from the oven, the ale mellow and cool.

Around mouthfuls, Cass managed to offer Eithne his thanks. "I can't remember my last hot meal, Eithne. I'm grateful to you." He wiped the bowl clean with a bite of bread and sat back with his mug of ale. He took a mouthful and let it set on his tongue for a long, satisfying moment. "Oh, that's good," he murmured as he set aside his empty mug.

"More stew?" Eithne asked.

"How about later, after I've chopped up some wood for you and filled the basket there by the hearth."

"I won't say no to the chopping. One less thing I have to do yet today."

"Good." Cass rose from his chair and stepped back out into the yard. There was still enough light for him to see the pile of wood dumped haphazardly near the back door with a hatchet stuck in the chopping block. He set to work splitting the logs into manageable pieces for the fireplace and soon filled the basket. He split more logs and stacked them in a neat pile before returning the ax to the block and loaded up an armful to carry inside to add to the fire burning in the fireplace. He laid his load of wood by the hearth and stepped back outside to get the basket he had filled. Eithne closed the door behind him and when he was seated once more, she filled another bowl of stew and brought a chunk of bread to go with it. She refilled both their mugs with amber ale and sat gazing into the fire while Cass ate.

"How are you, Eithne?" he asked when he finished the stew and bread. He picked up the mug of ale and raised it in a toast to Eithne. He emptied the mug in one long draught and set it aside.

In answer to his question, Eithne simple shrugged her shoulders. Once she might have been pretty, but hard work and sorrow had weighed her down. Deep lines ran from her nose to her mouth; lines of weariness marred her cheeks and forehead; dark circles shadowed her eyes. Her hair, once long and bright, had begun to turn gray and she wore it in an unkempt braid down her back. Her hands were rough and red from hard, bone-weary labor.

"I'm still alive," she sighed. "Though there are times I wonder why I keep struggling to live." She turned to look at him. "There are times I would prefer to sleep beside my man and my bairns up there on the hill." She motioned with her head toward the lonely place where the villagers had buried their dead for as long as there had been a village here.

The two sat in silence for some time before Eithne stirred herself again. "I don't imagine you just happened to come this way and stopped by to see me, Cass." She smiled as she said the words. "What do you want to know?"

Cass leaned forward with his arms resting on his thighs, his hands clasped loosely. He looked at his hands, then turned his head to look at the fire. With a sigh he sat up and watched Eithne for a moment. Finally he leaned forward and placed a hand lightly on her arm. "If what you might tell me puts you in harm's way, then tell me to leave. I don't want to make your life any harder than it is already."

"All right. I imagine you want to know what Dellay is up to."

"Yes."

She nodded and rose to stand staring down into the fire. "He and those six bastards who follow him about like he's the next king of Timis have gone to Riversend. Dellay knows someone there who can get him into the Guardian armory. His plan is to steal weapons from the armory—swords, spears, whatever he can get his hands on. He's got a boat that will bring the stuff to Blairtown. Better access to western Timis through Cragon Pass than up here through Malhain."

"How many men does he have, Eithne?"

"I'm not sure, Cass. He's been busy gathering Arlanders who are willing to fight with him and take whatever they want from wherever they want in Timis, maybe Kaenolir, too." She turned back and took her seat. "There are lots of unhappy people on the High Champaign, people who came here from Arland thinking they could make a new life. People still coming here, for that matter. Only they've found that living here is no better than it was in Arland, and they're willing to listen to what someone like Dellay has to tell them."

"And what is Dellay telling them?"

"Pickings are richer in western Timis. And, the biggest temptation of all—

I've gold to give you for joining me."

"The mine is fully operational, then."

"Soon will be, it seems. Old Bran Kemp's showing the ones Lem Morgan has rounded up how to dig. Dellay says one of the smelters will be working by spring, if not sooner."

"He paying the miners?"

"Says he is," she shrugged. "Also feeding 'em and putting 'em where there's room in what's left of Banning Village. None of our miners came back after the war, so the Arlanders took over the village. They scrounge food wherever they can, seafood, fish, what vegetables they're able to grow. So, where Dellay is getting all the food he needs, if he is getting food to feed the miners, I don't know. Stealing it, I suppose, maybe from up in Kaenolir. Kaenolir wasn't as hard hit by Finton like we were."

Eithne sat silently for a moment, biting her lip. "I don't know what to think about something else, Cass. Maybe it's something, maybe just Dellay blowin' in the wind." She paused again and put her hands together, steepling her fingers. "He says he's made contact with a bunch of Warders living up in the mountains, somewhere above the place where Finton had his castle."

Cass sat forward in his chair. "Warders?"

Eithne nodded. "One of the black robes claims to have found something powerful, something left behind in the destruction of Finton's castle. And something to do with dragons. At least, that's what Dellay said."

"Sheevers, Eithne, are you sure you heard right?" Cass rose to pace the room.

"Like I say, Cass, it could just be Dellay shootin' his mouth off when deep in his cups, but I think he's got something else going for him besides weapons for a bunch of hooligans. He's planning to build an army, and for sure whoever gets in his way will be sorry. Sometimes I think he's crazy, crazy mean, and it makes me afraid of what might happen again. But in his own way, he's smart, too."

"How did Dellay make contact with the Warders?"

"I don't know. He says someone came to him. I didn't see any Warder here, so maybe Dellay went somewhere to meet the Warders. I don't know. I'm sorry. I wish I could tell you more."

"Thank you, Eithne, you've told me a great deal, and I'll tell Camron Thorpe all that you've told me." He picked up his pack and cloak, but stopped and turned back to her. "You should think about leaving before Dellay gets back, before winter sets in and it's too hard to get through the pass. You should think about going to Ross Harbor, Eithne. You'd be safe there."

She smiled sadly, shaking her head as she got up from her chair. "This is my home, Cass. I'm a mountain woman, not one for the sea. And besides, I don't want to leave my man and my wee ones all alone up there on that lonely hill."

Cass nodded. "I understand, Eithne, but if life gets too dangerous here with Dellay, cross the mountains, will you?"

"Maybe I will," she said. "I won't ask you where you're going now; better I don't know, but let me pack up some food for you to take with you."

"I won't say no to that, and I thank you again for your kindness."

A few minutes later, Cass left by the back door and disappeared into the darkness. Eithne listened to his footsteps until she could hear him no longer. She continued to stand in the doorway, rubbing her arms against the night's chill. "Winter's coming," she murmured. Then, "Be safe, Cass Vance," she whispered.

She closed the door and went about the homely tasks of rinsing the supper dishes and putting them away in the cupboard, taking the stew pot from the fire and setting it on the narrow counter. She banked the fire. She blew out the candles burning about the room, all save one which she carried with her to her bedroom, grateful that she was sleeping alone tonight.

Cass shifted his pack to a more comfortable position on his back and moving from shadow to shadow made his way silently through the village toward the foothills of the Dalrudds. Most of the cottages were dark. Off in the distance a dog barked and was answered by another. An owl flew by on nearly silent wings. Clouds drifted over the moon from time to time, blocking out what little light the night offered.

Cass left the village behind, moving steadily back into the lower foothills of the Dalrudds. But after stumbling twice in the darkness over obstacles he didn't see, he decided he'd best find a hole to hide in; he'd wait until morning before going on. When he came upon a copse of scrub alder, he crawled into the dense undergrowth and hollowed out a nest where he was hidden from sight. Using his pack for a back rest, he settled down to wait for the sunrise.

Ruminating on all that Eithne had told him, he knew he needed to have more information on what Dellay was planning before heading back to Camlanrein. He would try to learn if there was credence to Eithne's contention that Dellay had made contact with the Warders and what that contact might mean. What had Eithne said? Something about one of the Warders having found 'something' from Finton's castle and something more about dragons. Somehow either Camron or Cass would have to try to get closer to the Warder enclave. He'd not spent much time in the southern Dalrudds. That part of the mountain range seemed tainted to him, the stench of evil still carried on the wind. If recollection of stories about Camron's prowess as a young man were at least partly true, then Camron would know the most about Finton's castle, the area where the Stones of Destiny had stood, about the Warders, and certainly about dragons. He thought for a moment of the night the two men had spent in the cave near Malhain Pass. Yes, Camron Thorpe knew a great deal about dragons.

He sighed and pushed thoughts of Warders and fire beasts aside and concentrated on what lay before him on the morrow. With an early start he could cross the River Roon and follow it down to the sea. Blairtown would be but a short trek from there. If Eithne was correct, Dellay would bring his stolen weapons to Blairtown by boat. And if he did, Cass would be there waiting for him.

After several days of rough seas, rain and cold wind, the old boat carrying Kelan Dellay and his stolen goods at last pulled alongside the decaying dock at Blairtown. The sun had already set; it would soon be dark and Dellay lost no time in off-loading his stolen armaments while there was still light to see by. He grudgingly paid the old sailor and sent Hunter to Banning Village to find a wagon and horses. Three of his crew headed back to Waytown with the fishing boat to retrieve the horses they'd left there and take them back to Malhain. The three were not pleased to be back on the water, but Dellay knew they needed those horses.

"Hope the horses are still there," he muttered.

The weapons would be safe enough here in the large shed behind the building that housed the smelter. The only people in Blairtown were the few men working on the smelter, but they'd already returned to Banning after working all day on the furnaces. When the time came, and that time would be soon, Dellay would dispense the weapons to the men he'd recruited over the years. He figured he'd have to make one more trip to the Riversend armory, two at the most.

"Have to use another boat, though," he mused. He didn't completely trust the man who owned the one they'd used this trip.

When Hunter returned, the weapons were loaded onto the rickety wagon pulled by two nags and taken to the storage shed. With everything safely stored, Dellay directed Hunter and two others to stay with the weapons, taking turns guarding the cache day and night.

"Anybody comes snoopin' around, you know what to do. Stay out of sight and away from the smelter," he instructed Hunter. "We don't want anyone to know what's in that shed. I'll see to it you have food and whatever else you might need."

"How long we gonna have to be here?" Hunter asked.

"Depends on how soon we can get another boatload of stuff from Riversend. I need to contact the other boat I have lined up. Don't want to use this one again." He motioned in the direction of the dock.

Hunter snorted. "Doubt it would get us there and back a second time. Don't know if it will make it back to Waytown. You might want to think about making sure that old fart don't spread it around where we been."

Dellay smiled. There was a mean look in his eye. "My thoughts exactly. Now," he said reaching into the pouch he had secured to his belt, "this should be enough to get food and blankets at Banning. You might want to make people think you're coming to work in the mine and getting yourself set up. Now, get situated in the shed and set up the watches. It may be a couple of weeks before I get back here again."

Hunter pocketed the coins. "How come you're not sailing back to Waytown, too?"

Dellay shook his head. "I have to meet someone at the mine. Got some business to get settled. Don't worry. I'll be back before you know it."

"Well, don't be too long. This guard duty could get real boring."

Dellay laughed. "You'll survive." He turned to go then paused and turned back. "Another thing, Hunter, after you get the stuff you need, you three stay out of Banning."

Hunter swore and spat. "Like I said, Kelan, don't be too long."

Dellay laughed again as he walked away.

In the shadows of one of the many smaller buildings that made up the dock area of Blairtown, Cass Vance listened intently to the conversation between the two men, one of whom he knew to be Kelan Dellay. He'd watched the fishing boat being unloaded and several big burlap bags placed on a wagon and taken to a shed behind the smelter building. Everything Eithne had told him about Dellay's plan to steal weapons from Riversend and to bring them to Blairtown was correct.

"Thank you again, Eithne," Cass thought.

Keeping to the shadows, Cass silently followed Kelan Dellay past Banning Village and along the shore of the Balagorn Channel. The moon had risen, giving enough light for Cass to keep Dellay in sight. The man had said he was going to Cragon Mine to 'settle up some business,' but with the direction he was going, Cass knew he was not headed to the mine. He was headed toward a place Cass had always avoided as he roamed the Dalrudd Mountains because he felt evil still resided there: Kelan Dellay was going toward Dunadd.

chapter twelve

Kitra Fairchild paced the paths of the garden that was a blend of trees and bushes stripped of their leaves in preparation for winter's dormancy and the dark shades of a variety of conifers. The bulk of Camlanrein shaded parts of the path as it meandered through the acres of well-kept trees, bushes, flower beds, and a few vegetable patches closer to the kitchen door.

"Where are you Camron Thorpe?" she muttered as she walked. She had been cooped up all morning, listening to the various reports and requests that had come to fill her days since Camron and Cass Vance left for the mountains. In Camron's absence she took over his responsibilities as he had asked her to do.

"If I have to listen to one more report I shall scream," she continued to mutter. "How does he stand it?" She pulled her shawl more closely about her shoulders to ward off the chill of an errant breeze.

Another autumn had come; another winter would soon settle into rain and gray skies; another year gone from Lorn and filled with the problems and cares of Timis.

Worry etched fine lines around her mouth and eyes. Camron had been gone for more than a month. Her children were far away in Kaenolir and according to their last letters, treading paths she did not want them to have to take. Every day more word came of the anger and fear, of the worries that plagued the people of Timis. Arlanders had taken over eastern Timis, pushing out the Timisians who had lived there for generations. The mine, long a mainstay in the economy of Timis, was in the hands of Arlanders and renegade Timisians. There were reports of Warders once more making an appearance; whether there were facts to back up these reports, she did not know. No one seemed to know.

And therein lay her problem. She did not know where Camron was; she did not know how to find him; she did not know what her children would experience in their quests; she did not know how Camron would bring peace to Timis.

"My lady."

Kitra turned at the sound of the voice behind her.

"There is someone to see you. His name is Cass Vance and he asked for Camron Thorpe. When I told him the chieftain was not here, he asked whom he should speak to, and I told him you would see him."

"Thank you, Donan. Yes, of course, I will see him." She turned to walk beside the man who had served Tiernan Irworth and now served Camron in the capacity of adviser, friend, confidant; he was always at hand to do whatever needed doing for the Chieftain of Timis and his lady. He had grown old in Camlanrein, a bit stooped now, his pace somewhat slower and sometimes unsteady; but his mind was still sharp. He possessed a wealth of Timisian knowledge that Kitra relied on to help her shoulder the duties Camron had thrust upon her when he left to search the Dalrudds.

"He has come from the mountains, my lady, and he's very tired. I ordered a meal be brought to him and settled him in the chieftain's office."

"Good." Kitra chewed her bottom lip. "He said nothing of Camron's whereabouts?"

"No, lady, he thought Lord Camron would be here before him."

The two walked in silence until they reached the back entrance.

"I'm very worried, my lady," the old man murmured as he stepped aside to allow her to enter the door before him.

"I know, Donan. I'm worried, too. I hope Cass Vance can tell us where Camron might be."

Donan escorted Kitra up the great staircase to Camron's office. "Call me if you need me, my lady."

Kitra smiled. "Thank you, Donan. Later I'll share with you what Cass may have to tell me."

Donan nodded and turned away to attend to other duties, and with worry gnawing at her Kitra entered the office where Cass Vance waited for her. What would he be able to tell her about Camron's whereabouts?

"Cass?" Kitra eyed the travel-stained, obviously weary man who stood looking out the window onto the mountain vista. He turned at Kitra's entrance.

"My lady." He nodded in deference. His garments were soiled and tattered, one sleeve of his tunic half torn off at the shoulder, both knees of his trousers worn through, his boots scuffed.

"It looks as if you've had a hard journey. When was the last time you ate a hot meal?" She smiled at the tall, dark haired man who looked as if he'd fall over any minute. "And had a bath and a night's sleep in a bed?"

"Too long ago to remember the particulars, I'm afraid."

"Sit," Kitra directed him to the armchairs where he and Camron had sat talking before going into the mountains.

"I'm too dirty to sit, Lady Fairchild."

"Sit," she commanded. "Donan is having some food brought up and you can eat while you're telling me where you and Camron Thorpe have been."

"Thank you," Cass sighed as he eased himself into one of the comfortable chairs.

Before taking the chair across from Cass, Kitra stepped to the cupboard and brought out Camron's bottle of Highland whiskey and a cup. She set the two items on the table beside Cass's chair and poured a cup for Cass. He lifted the cup in salute to Kitra and took a cautious sip. It burned and warmed all the way down. He closed his eyes in gratitude.

"Where have you been and what did you find?" she asked. "But first tell me where you think Camron Thorp might be."

"We left each other at Malhain Pass. While I searched for Kelan Dellay, Lord Camron went south to find the Warders."

Cass took another sip from his cup and told Kitra what he had learned from Eithne and what he had found when he followed Dellay to Blairtown. He interrupted his tale only when his dinner arrived. Kitra poured tea for both of them while Cass ate.

"Thank you," he said with a satisfied sigh as he sat back to resume telling Kitra all he had learned. At last when he'd given her all the details he could think of, he grew silent.

"You said that you and Camron parted ways at Malhain Pass."

"Yes. We sought shelter from the cold and the wind in a small cave." He paused for a moment. "I think you know the cave, my lady," he said thoughtfully.

"So'Kol's cave?"

"Yes." Cass drank the last of his tea and set the cup aside on the dinner tray.

"Help yourself to the whiskey, Cass," Kitra motioned to the bottle.

"Thank you, no. I'm dead on my feet as it is. I'd rather not fall asleep in your chair," he smiled.

"I'll not keep you much longer. Donan is preparing a chamber for you, but I would like to hear about the cave."

"I asked Lord Camron if So'Kol was still in the cave, but he said no, that only a memory remained of the dragon. But, my lady, I'm sure I heard the chieftain talking during the night. I'm also sure I heard him say 'So'Kol.' He came from the back of the cave as I woke up, said he couldn't sleep. I've only stayed in that cave one other time, and then only because there was no other place to find some shelter from a storm. It's a place. . .I've never found another place like it in the mountains. It's a place. . .a place of magic. . ." He shrugged.

"You know the story, then, of Camron's ties to that cave."

"Yes, my lady. I was only a child when you and Lord Camron came with your dragons, but I shall never forget them, how beautiful they were, how their fire destroyed the evil Aldward Finton had created."

"I thought both you and Camron planned to learn what the Warders are up to."

"That was the plan, but after the night in the cave, Lord Camron sent me to Malhain and he headed south. When I thought later about why we separated, I became more convinced that he'd talked with So'Kol, that he'd learned something important, something that had to do with the Warders. And with So'Kol." Cass scrubbed his hands over his face and yawned.

"Forgive me, my lady," he muttered, chagrined at his behavior. "I'm not making much sense."

Kitra rose. "No, forgive me, Cass. I did not mean to keep you so long. Come, I'll take you to Donan and he'll get you settled. We'll talk more in the morning."

Kita retired to her chamber, but found that sleep would not come. She mulled over all that Cass Vance had told her. It seemed certain that Kelan Dellay and the Warders were linked in some kind of partnership, their reason for doing so almost certainly control of all Timis. Finally, she took a heavy shawl from a drawer and, wrapping it closely around her head and shoulders, she left her chamber and walked silently down the hall to the back staircase.

"My lady?" a Trooper spoke as she neared his post.

"I need some air, Gavin. I won't be long."

"May I attend you, lady?"

"Thank you, Gavin, but that won't be necessary."

The young Trooper opened the door and stood hesitantly aside as she stepped out into the night. "I'll leave the door open for you, my lady. Call me if you need me."

Kitra waved her hand to acknowledge him as she walked down the graveled path toward the bench that stood under a huge old oak tree. She sat down and with the wind sifting through the nearly bare branches of the canopy above her, she called to Samar.

The great black wolf of Faerie that had been by her side since she'd gone to Lorn Isle so long ago seldom joined her here in Camlanrein. But she needed him now.

"Samar," she whispered.

A shadow, darker than the shadow in which it stood, moved toward her. The wolf came to her and she reached out to take his head in her hands. "Can you find Camron? Does he need us?"

"He has found the Warders."

"Is he in danger?"

"He went to the mountains to learn what the Warder found."

"Why? What did the Warder find?"

"Your fire beasts know. They will tell you. They are in danger. Call to them."

"My fire beasts?" she whispered. "What threatens them? What does the Warder have?" But the wolf did not answer her questions.

She rose to walk farther down the graveled path with Samar at her side. It was very cold and the air smelled of snow.

"It will soon be winter in the mountains," she murmured.

She walked on for a short distance before turning back toward the warmth offered by the hall. A few snowflakes drifted down out of the black sky as she reached the door.

Samar was no longer by her side.

When Kitra looked out on the mountains from Camron's office windows the following morning, she saw that winter had, indeed, arrived in the Dalrudds. The mountains were serene and beautiful in their winter dressing, but what did they hide in their majestic heights?

Here in Camlanrein the snow that had come during the night rapidly melted in the bright sunshine. Eaves and branches dripped rhythmically and puddles appeared on the pathways.

"Where are you, Camron? Are you some place safe and warm?" she thought.

What had the wolf said?

"He must learn what the Warder has found." And then, *"Your fire beasts know. They will tell you. Call to them."*

But she had not heard the magical voices of her dragons in her mind since she told them goodbye. She was far from the place where they first spoke to her. Responsibility for Timis rested heavily on her shoulders until Camron's return; thus she could not go back to Lorn nor could she leave Camlanrein to try to find her dragons' cave again. The power and the magic of the three dragons pulled at her still, at the odd moments when her mind wandered or she remembered what it had been like to speak with dragons, to fly with them, and to feel their fire. There were times when the Fire Song hummed through her blood, made her heart pound with the joy of the music. She knew she would forever be tied to the fire beasts who had called her to come to them.

How could she find them again? Where could she go in Timis to call to them so they would hear her? Malhain cave? Something niggled at the back of her mind, something connected to Camron. . .

"My lady?" Donan interrupted her thoughts and entered the office with a sheaf of papers for her perusal. She absently took the papers and placed them on her desk.

"Donan, you know Timis very well. Other than the Stones of Destiny, are there other places in Timis like the Stones? Not with their evil context of course, but some ancient sacred place or one that was once thought to be a sacred place? Perhaps still is?"

"Yes, Lady Fairchild. There is such a place, north of Camlanrein on the coast, not far from the village of Lisburn. The place is called the Round Stones. Many believe the circle there is a sacred place infused with light and ancient knowledge. The guardian of the Stones is said to be a woman named Liadia. "

"Liadia. The same as the historian?"

Donan shrugged. "I know of the Liadian historian, of course, so perhaps the guardian of the Stones is the writer of the histories." Donan thought for a moment. "I went there for the first time when I was about sixteen or seventeen. It's a beautiful spot, very peaceful. It's as if the Stones are sleeping and whatever power is there simply waits. The grasses almost sing as the ocean breezes pass through them. There is an ancient grove of trees nearby that many believe is as sacred as the circle. I only know it felt as if someone were watching me from the grove as I entered the circle, making sure I was not there to desecrate the Stones in any way. The Stones are so weathered and the grass grown so tall that at first I could not find them. Once I found one, though, I was able to find the others. I have been there many times since and always come away feeling glad that I went.

"You know that Lord Camron went to the Round Stones to search for answers. Tiernan Irworth believed he found the way to his dragon there." Donan was silent for a moment before asking, "Why do you want to know about a sacred place?"

Kitra turned once more to contemplate the mountains before answering Donan.

"Donan," she said finally, "will you take me to the Round Stones?"

"Of course, Lady Fairchild, if you wish. When would you like to go?"

"As soon as possible. And, Donan, I would like to see Cass Vance as soon as he is awake and had something to eat."

"Lady Fairchild?"

Kitra turned from her vigil at the window to see Cass Vance in the doorway. She smiled in welcome and motioned him into the room.

"You look rested and," she smiled, "much cleaner. Come, sit by the fire. Would you care for some tea?"

Cass smiled in answer to Kitra's comment about his appearance and took the armchair he had occupied yesterday. "Will you join me, my lady?"

"I never say no to a cup of tea." She stepped to the door and asked the Trooper there to send for tea and a sweet to go with it. When she was settled in the chair across from him, she asked after his rest and the comfort of his quarters. Was there anything more he needed? Their rather desultory conversation was interrupted with the arrival of a large pot of tea and a plate of biscuits. Kitra poured a cup for Cass, then one for herself.

"Help yourself to the biscuits, Cass," she said as she took one of the almond sweets.

The two sat quietly for a time, enjoying the tea and biscuits and a moment of quiet. Kitra finished her treat and dusted the crumbs from her fingers. "I have another task for you," she said quietly. "I want you to go back to the mountains to find Lord Camron."

Cass nodded. "I thought you might want me to do that. How soon do you want me to leave?"

"I would like to say immediately, but you've another hard journey ahead of you, so take some more time to rest and get together whatever supplies you think necessary. I'll be gone from Camlanrein for a short time, but when I return I'll send you on your way again." She rose in dismissal.

He paused as he reached the door and turned back to her. "If the Ancient Ones are kind, my lady, I will find him and bring him home."

"Thank you, Cass."

Kitra, Donan, and a patrol of twelve Troopers left Camlanrein soon after sunrise the next day. The snow had all melted but the night had been cold. Frost glittered on the trees and a thin sheet of ice covered yesterday's puddles. Clouds of vapor rose above the horses in the cold morning air as the group headed out. They planned to cross the River Comtarse, spend the night at the old inn in Lisburn Village, and visit the Round Stones the next morning.

They followed an easy track that at times lay along the Trayonian coastline; at other times the track moved inland a distance of a mile or two. After a short stop at midday to eat a quick meal and let the horses rest, the group was on its way again.

"How much farther, Donan?" Kitra asked as she came abreast of the bay Donan rode. By her reckoning, they were about three hours from sunset.

"Lisburn is just over that next hill then a bit to the east, Lady Fairchild. We'll be there well before the sun sets."

The village of Lisburn was old, a bit ragged around the edges, but people greeted them with friendly waves. When Finton threatened western Timis, Tiernan Irworth had evacuated the village. At the war's end the people all returned from wherever they had sought safety from war. The Arlanders had not come this far west; thus homes were still secure when their owners came back to claim them.

The inn was on the ocean side of the track that skirted the cluster of stone cottages making up the village. The inn, too, was old, a bit run-down, but its furniture and floorboards gleamed with cleanliness. If the mouthwatering smells emanating from the kitchen were any indication, their dinner would be delicious. Donan saw to the arrangements for settling the travelers and seeing that Lady Fairchild was comfortable. He suggested to the Troopers that Lady Fairchild's name not be spoken when others were within earshot.

"Just a safety precaution," he said at their startled expressions. "The people here are good people, as far as I know, but there may be others about who might not be so good."

Sleep would not come to Kitra. She was very tired and more than a bit sore from riding. She was much more accustomed to a boat, tiller, sails and wind, rather than a horse and saddle. Once Donan mentioned the Stones and what he believed Camron had found there, she remembered Camron telling her about his encounter at the Round Stones with a woman who named herself Liadia. Camron had found a dragon carved in stone in the center of what had once been revered as a sacred circle. Later he had found So'Kol in a cave high in the mountains.

What did she expect to find in the circle of Stones? Would she find Liadia there as Camron had? Would she find her own dragons there?

Then, soft as a feather's touch.

Come. I will show you.

"Ke'Shan," Kitra whispered. "Ga'Vrill? Jho'Son?"

Come to the Stones, lady. We wait for you.

Tears came quickly and ran into her hair at the voices she remembered so well. She sat up and pushed her blankets away. Her fire beasts called and she must go to them.

Kitra closed the front door of the inn as quietly as she could and with a cautious backward glance she hurried away from the inn and through the sleeping village. A full moon gave her light to see by. An owl somewhere close by called to another. Off to her right large trees lifted bare branches to the sky. For a brief moment a cloud covered the moon and Kitra walked in darkness hearing sea breezes rustle stalks of long, dry grass. She felt she was close now to the Round Stones. When the cloud moved away, the moonlight helped her see more clearly. A few more steps and she stood at the edge of a rough circle. She closed her eyes and silently asked to be allowed to enter. The breeze died, a hush fell all around her. Magic slept here.

She waited.

"Why have you come, Kitra Fairchild?" The voice was low, melodious, almost a whisper.

When Kitra opened her eyes, she saw a woman standing just within the circle. Her hair, braided and wound like a crown on top of her head, seemed to glisten in the otherworldly light.

"Because I must," Kitra murmured. "I came to find my dragons once more. They are in danger, but I do not know where the danger comes from."

"But why did you come to this place?"

"Because it is a sacred place."

"Ah. Yes. It is that. Your Camron came here to find what he searched for. Do your fire beasts call to you?"

"I must call to them."

"So you must." The woman stepped away. "Enter," floated back to Kitra on the still air.

Kitra stood breathing deeply for long minutes before stepping beyond the boundary of the circle. The breeze through the grass whispered her name. With careful steps she moved to the center of the circle. There in the shadows created by the grass and the moonlight, she saw a stone, the stone that was a dragon with wings uplifted.

"Ke'Shan," she whispered. "Ga'Vrill. Jho'Son."

Only the wind answered her.

With a heavy heart she reached out to touch the stone dragon. "Please, come. I must know what to do." She murmured a prayer though she knew not to whom or to what she prayed only that her dragons would hear her call. She placed her hands on either side of the stone dragon's head. "Come, come to me, dear ones," she prayed.

She waited a moment more; then she closed her eyes and began to sing. Music filled the air, the music of her Song. Her voice strengthened. Fire Song wrapped her in magic, lifted her spirit, filled her with the power of Faerie.

When the Song ended, there was a soft, almost imperceptible sound. She opened her eyes to see the circle shrouded in a silver mist. Within the mist, she saw shimmers of blue and gold and green.

And heard her dragons singing.

"You came," she murmured.

We have come, lady.

Ke'Shan moved out of the mist and dipped his head to her. With trembling fingers she reached up to touch the great blue dragon. Ga'Vrill came to her next, then Jho'Son. She touched each of them in turn, laughing and crying at the joy that poured out of her in seeing them again, in touching them, in singing her Song.

"What must I do?" she asked them. "Why do I fear for you?"

Find the black robe. He has found our essence buried in the dust of the Stones. He brings evil with him. He would make us his.

"A Warder? We thought we had stopped the evil of the Warders when we destroyed Finton and his Pales."

Ga'Vrill touched Kitra's cheek with her warm breath

"How can he make you his? For what purpose? How can we stop the evil?"

Jho'Son gently nuzzled Kitra's hand. *Your children have the answers.*

"Rayce and KaynaRee?"

They come to you.

You will find a way, from Ke'Shan.

"You came when all else failed. Will you come again?"

Ke'Shan bowed his head and Kitra reached up to touch him once more. She breathed his name as she touched him. Then she turned to Ga'Vrill and Jho'Son, murmuring their names as she touched each of them.

When all else fails she heard Ke'Shan say. Or was it the wind? She closed her eyes, bowed her head, and said their names again.

When she opened her eyes they were gone.

She stood in the silent circle, her sorrow like a weight on her heart and mind. Wind from the sea shifted the grass until it again covered the stone in the center of the circle. She turned away and saw a man standing near one of the Stones at the outer edge of the circle.

"Mother."

"Rayce?" She began to run. "Rayce," she cried as he took her in his arms and hugged her. At last he set her away so he could look into her eyes. "What are you doing here? How did you know where I was?" she said when she could speak again.

"They told me at Camlanrein where you were. I've translated father's book. "

"Ah. Your book, now, too, then."

"Yes, my book, too."

Kitra nodded. "Caretaker," she breathed. Her son stood tall before her, the near image of his father, strong and powerful in the knowledge he had come to possess.

"Our dragons are in danger, Mother, from an ancient evil. Their fire destroyed an evil power, but it left their essence bound up with the evil that pervaded the Stones of Destiny and the evil Finton called from the Abyss."

"Ke'Shan said that one of the Warders has found something, some powerful piece that threatens the dragons. It is the Warder we must find and when we find him, we will find what endangers the fire beasts."

"Kitra Fairchild. Rayce Thorpe." The woman stood just beyond the edge of the circle within the shadows. "You must go now," she said. "You have found your answers. You know what you must do."

"Yes, Liadia," Kitra said. She looked once more toward the center of the circle and then to her son. "We know what we must do."

Kitra and Rayce turned away. Dawn was not far off, she thought, as they walked away from the circle of Round Stones.

Wind from the sea rustled the grass of the circle. *Caretaker*, it seemed to whisper.

"Yes," Kitra thought again. "We know what we must do."

They left Lisburn at dawn and pushed hard to arrive at Camlanrein some time after midnight. Kitra sent the men off to bed for a few hours rest and retired to her chamber. Exhausted, she fell asleep almost immediately, but something awakened her with a start a short time later. Samar sat on his haunches at the foot of her bed. Pushing aside the coverlet, she rose.

"Samar? What is it?"

"Caretaker needs help."

"Will you go to him? Can you find him?"

"Yes, lady. I know where he is. An ancient one looks after him."

Pulling on a robe as she left the room, she called for Donan. The Trooper on duty outside the chamber door was sent to fetch him, even though the hour was late. On second thought she called after the Trooper, "Send for my son and Cass Vance, too."

"Yes, my lady," the Trooper said over his shoulder as he hurried away.

Kitra returned to her sleeping chamber to dress and found Samar waiting there for her. "Rayce and the man who was with Camron in the mountains will go with you."

"I will find them in the mountains. Together we'll bring Caretaker back to you, lady." On silent feet the wolf slipped away.

"Bring them all back to me, Samar," she whispered.

In the darkness, just before dawn the next day, Rayce and Cass mounted and turned to tell Kitra goodbye. Each man held the lead ropes of two horses, one loaded with provisions and one that would serve as a reserve mount. They needed to go fast and far.

"Samar will find you when you reach the mountains. He knows where Camron is." Kitra reached up to squeeze Rayce's hand on the reins. He smiled and nodded to her.

With Cass leading the way, the men urged their horses through the gates of Camlanrein and out into the darkness.

"May the Ancient Ones watch over you and may you find Camron quickly," she whispered. With a heavy heart she turned away to begin the duties that awaited her.

chapter thirteen

Conn Regan sat before the fire in Gadred Aember's chambers, waiting quietly as the Warder checked a map Conn had drawn for him. The map of the Dalrudd Mountains was drawn with meticulous attention to detail, showing every cave, every valley, every peak, every river and stream, even the animal trails that Conn had explored in his months-long travels. A second map of western Timis was also drawn with detailed features. Cities and villages, small settlements, individual farms were listed. Well-traveled roads were drawn with precise mileage charts. Less traveled tracks and paths that wandered through Timis and connected with the major roads or wound through the foothills were also carefully charted.

"You have done very well," Aember said as he sat back and eyed the younger man. He'd sent a scholarly man into the mountains, a man who had returned lean and muscled, his skin tanned from summer sun and harsh wind. His brown hair, pulled back and tied with a leather thong, was streaked with reddish tints; his dark eyes perused everything, missed nothing. He was a man Aember would want to keep close, but not so close that he knew all Aember's secrets. While he did not doubt the younger man's loyalty to the Warder cause, Conn Regan was also privy to knowledge the other Warders were not. Aember deemed it necessary to make sure it stayed that way.

"I'm pleased with the maps and what you've learned about this Arlander, Dellay," Aember complimented Regan and smiled to show his pleasure at Regan's accomplishments. "Your contact with him sets the stage for our move into the west. The Warders I sent into the High Champaign and western

Timis tell me the people are very restive. Life is not what they expected and getting more difficult all the time. But I want to hear more about Kelan Dellay."

"He's a mean one, he is. Follow his orders or there will be severe consequences. He's crafty, too, and not afraid to take chances. I met with him just before he was planning to go to Riversend. He has a contact in the armory, and a boat and captain to take him there and bring back the weapons he's able to steal. He seems to feel he can break into the armory whenever he needs to."

"How many men do you think he has who are willing to follow him?"

"At least three hundred, possibly closer to four hundred."

"Hm, yes. That's the estimate I've been given by the Warders gathering information in the Champaign. Has this Dellay fellow told you where he plans to store the weapons until he's ready to distribute them? In Malhain Village?"

"No. There are a couple of large storage sheds near the smelting furnaces in Blairtown and he plans to use one of those. He'll leave some trusted cohorts to guard his cache."

"Do you think there is credence to his contention he can get into and out of the Riversend armory unseen? Surely the armory is well guarded."

Conn shrugged. "I never know when he's just bragging or when to take him seriously. I do know that there are many men scattered throughout eastern Timis who are ready to follow him. Maybe he's just a braggart but there is also something about the man that makes other men feel they want what he wants. There is something else about him, m'lord, something I can't quite put my finger on."

Regan paused and pursed his lips as he thought what to say next. Aember let him take his time to think through what was on his mind.

"Dellay's a powerfully built man, capable of defeating any man in hand to hand combat, whether by fair means or otherwise. There is something almost, hm, I'm not sure how to phrase it, something almost sinister about him, something very devious. I think he'd slip a knife into the ribs of any man, or woman, who crossed him or got in his way, and no one would dare to point him out as the one doing the killing. I saw him in a fight once in Banning Village. Three miners took him on when he wouldn't pay them what they thought he owed them. Before the dust settled, two of them were dead and one so badly hurt he died the next day. Dellay used nothing but his fists and his feet. The miners were all big men, strong men, but they didn't stand a chance against him."

"It seems we will have to proceed with caution in our association with him. We want him to provide the distraction in western Timis while we gain control of the dragons. When will you be in contact with him again, Conn?"

"There is a place along the Channel near the old Stones where I've met him before, an old shack that's not been used for years. I'm to meet him there tomorrow. He'll either be there, or he won't, depending on how his raid on the Riversend armory went." Regan shrugged. "Or if he feels an association with us will be to his benefit."

Aember paced back and forth in front of the fireplace for several minutes before turning back to Regan. "Do you think, Conn, that we can control him?"

"I think, Lord Aember, you can control him, but we must move carefully. If he even suspects what we're up to, he will turn on us. If he believes you have the power of dragons, he will want it. He won't hesitate to try to kill you."

"We won't need him, Conn, once we have the dragons, but we'll need his men to keep Timis under our thumb. With him gone, the mine will also be ours. It will be important to gain control of the mine quickly. With the dragons and the gold, no one in western Timis will be able to stop us. From Camlanrein it's not far from there to Kaenolir." His dark eyes took on a hooded look and he smiled with satisfaction.

"Now," Aember said quietly, "tell me more about the caves in the mountains. Where do you think the dragons sleep?"

The two men returned to Regan's map of the Dalrudds, and Regan pointed out three places he'd marked with an X.

"As I've indicated on the map, the peaks are riddled with caves, but these three are definite possibilities. This one in particular." Regan pointed to an X marking a cave near the old Malhain Pass.

"Yes, you told me when you first found the cave that something did not want you there."

Regan nodded. "I've been back to each of these three caves on separate occasions, the Malhain cave just before I came back here. The feeling of something being there, something powerful, m'lord, was very strong. And, I found tracks in the sand that has accumulated inside the entrance of the cave. Someone else had been there just recently."

"Do you know who? Could it have been Desmond Orly?"

"Orly? Why would he have been there?'

"Never mind, I'll tell you about Orly later." Aember moved to stand before the fire with his back to Regan, his hands held out to the warmth of the flames. "Are there others who either live in or near the mountains who would frequent the cave?"

Regan rubbed his hand over his chin. "Not that I'm aware of. There is a fellow I've encountered a time or two in the northern mountains, but he's a wanderer. Spends most of his time in the mountains by himself, away from people; he's nobody to be concerned about. The people who live in Malhain Village are mostly Arlanders just trying to get by. I've not seen any of them in the higher elevations; once in a while a few men hunt deer and whatever else they can find but always in the lower regions."

"You've no idea who might have been in the cave then."

"No, m'lord. I did not see them nor did I find any tracks that I would term suspicious."

"Anything near the valley?"

"No, nothing."

"I want to go to the Malhain cave as soon as possible, Conn."

"My lord, winter has already come to the high peaks. In Malhain Pass, where the cave is, snow can be chest deep in many places. It will be difficult to get to the cave."

Aember ground his teeth and cursed in frustration. Finally, breathing deeply, he turned to Regan. "Nevertheless, we must get to that cave as soon as possible." He thought for a moment. "And, Conn, bring Dellay here. I want to take the measure of the man myself."

Regan blinked in surprise. "Yes, my lord, as you wish."

"Yes, I do wish. That's all for now, Conn," Aember said with a dismissive gesture.

Conn Regan rose and quietly left the chamber. He wondered what Aember had meant about Desmond Orly. Regan had not seen the man since his return two days ago. Come to think of it, he hadn't seen Morton Cassel either.

"Hm," he grunted. What had happened in his absence? He made his way to the communal room, planning to find Jaston Sonne. Sonne was the best source of gossip among the Warders. As he went in search of Sonne, he thought of his lord's command about bringing Dellay here to the compound. It did not seem a wise thing to do. Regan shrugged, but then who was he to question Gadred Aember?

From a notch in a steep cliff on the lower elevation of a peak that reared above the Warders' compound, Camron Thorpe watched the activity that passed below him. Desmond Orly had suggested he watch from the top of the cliff, but as a winter storm blew in, he had to find a more protected spot, not only from the snow but also from the wind. He'd found the cleft by accident as he attempted to climb down the steep face of the cliff. His foot slipped and he nearly landed headfirst in the rocks shielding a small crevasse. With a bruised shoulder and a badly sprained wrist, Camron managed to pull himself into the narrow opening. He discovered that it widened just enough for him to enter a space about the size of a room. Here he was out of the wind. The ceiling of the cave soared so high into the darkness that he could not see where it ended; the walls and floor of the cave were smooth with an iridescent gleam here and there where light from the opening touched the stone. When he placed a hand against a wall to steady himself, it felt warm to his touch. He felt something else, too, something ancient and still but watchful.

A kindred spirit like the one that lived in memory in Malhain Pass.

He smiled at the thought as he absently rubbed his aching shoulder.

"Now if I could just find something here to eat," he sighed.

He'd eaten the last of the bread yesterday. The slivers of meat had been gone since the day before that. Camron knew he could not stay here long. From the initial view from the top of the cliff, he determined that the compound was guarded day and night by patrolling Warders, at least six at a time. There was no way he could get into the hall by way of the escape hatch Orly had told him about. He filed the knowledge away. There might come a time when he needed it.

Standing in the shadows, he looked down into the compound below him. There were about thirty-five to forty Warders he thought, but it was difficult to get an accurate count since they did not all gather together where he could see them. He counted a few as they chopped wood, a few more as they dug root vegetables from the garden behind the hall, still a few more who left the compound ostensibly to either fish or dig clams. Probably the latter. The seas would not give up many fish this time of the year.

Then this morning a man in a dark cloak carrying a large pack and a long bow slung over one shoulder came down the trail into the compound. He was greeted enthusiastically by several of the men. Camron watched as a tall man in a black robe came out the front door to greet the newcomer with outstretched arms.

"Aember," Camron guessed. "And the other, from Orly's comments, must be Regan. What was it Orly called him? Conn? Mm, yes, Conn Regan. The one who's been out scouting for Aember. Wonder if I've ever encountered him?" he thought, then shrugged the question aside.

There was little activity in the compound until the half dozen Warders returned with loaded sacks. He had been right in thinking they had gone down to the shore to clam. The men went around the hall to the back as lights began to appear in the windows. The wind picked up and whistled through the peaks, bringing the threat of more snow. Dark clouds sailed overhead and it soon grew too dark to see any activity below him. He turned away from the opening, cold and weary and very hungry. He eased himself down against the wall at the back of the cave with a sigh and leaned back against the stone. He took a drink of water and shook the bottle to estimate how much remained in it.

"Not much left," he muttered. The dull ache in his wrist brought a groan as he rubbed it. His shoulder, too, throbbed from his fall. With long legs stretched out before him, his back against stone that was definitely warming him, he soon slept.

Weak sunlight filtered into the little cave, waking Camron from an uneasy sleep that had been suffused with dreams. As he pushed himself awake, his dreams of So'Kol, of Rayce, of Ree drifted through his mind. He rubbed his face with his cold hands, trying to bring one image that lingered in his wakefulness more clearly into focus: he had seen Kitra with her dragons. He closed his eyes and tried to see the details of the dream.

In the dream she stood in a sacred circle, a circle defined with round, weathered Stones. In its center, the grass obscuring it from view until Kitra touched it, was the stone dragon he had found in that same circle in his quest for answers.

He'd seen Rayce with the Caretaker's Book, then with his mother.

And Ree?

"Sheevers," he whispered as he opened his eyes in surprise. "KaynaRee with a fire beast, a red dragon."

Had he really seen her with a dragon? He shook his head in wonder and pushed himself slowly erect.

He'd been asleep for many hours; while he slept the warmth of the stones beneath him eased most of the soreness he had experienced after his tumble down the cliff. He rotated his shoulder and felt only a mild discomfort when he did so; his wrist still ached but not with the pain of yesterday. Taking a sip of water from the nearly empty flask, he moved to take up a position near the cave's entrance. As he did so the world spun in a dizzy circle and he reached out to steady himself with a hand against the wall. His stomach lurched and he feared he would throw up the water he had just drunk. Breathing deeply through his nose, waiting for the spinning sensation to cease, Camron leaned against the wall until he could move again without being dizzy. "Need to eat," he muttered. "Too long."

Shouts from below brought his attention back to the activity in the compound. With careful movements he placed himself in the shadow of the cave's entrance and watched as four men moved into sight.

The man he'd seen greeted by Aember—had it been just yesterday? He'd lost track of time. That man—Regan perhaps—and another, larger man descended the trail leading into the Warders' compound. They were escorted by two Warders.

"Hm. Dellay?" From Cass Vance's description of the Arlander, he felt certain the large man was indeed Kelan Dellay.

"So, it would appear that Dellay and the Warders are joining forces." The two men were greeted at the front door by Gadred Aember and ushered into the hall.

The day wore on. Camron slumped beside the entrance, trying in vain to keep his attention on the compound and to stay awake.

"Nothing going on. I'll sleep for just a few minutes," he muttered as he yawned.

When he opened his eyes again, it was dark. A cold wind blew icy pellets through the opening and he found he was soaked to the skin.

"Sheevers," he muttered and tried to crawl farther into the cave. His limbs did not want to do his bidding. He knew he must get away from the entrance of the cave, knew he must get out of his wet clothing, get to the back of the cave where it was warmer. Summoning all his strength he rolled to his knees, supported himself with his hands and began to crawl slowly back to the wall where he had slept last night. Groaning with exhaustion, shaking with cold, he fell to the floor near his pack. After resting for a few minutes, he pushed himself up and began removing his wet garments. Free of his clothes, he wrapped himself in his cloak and rolled against the warm stones.

Sleep now, Caretaker, I will watch over you.

"So'Kol?" he whispered.

No. Another. Rest.

chapter fourteen

Conn Regan and Kelan Dellay were greeted at the top of the trail leading into the valley by two Warders. Garbed in black robes with hoods pulled down to obscure their faces, they nodded to Regan before glancing at the stocky man who puffed from exertion as he came up beside Regan. With backs ramrod straight they turned and began the trek down to the compound.

"Wait, slow down," Dellay huffed, but their escorts didn't slow their rapid pace or stop to wait for him.

Regan grinned at Dellay. "You're lucky you can still walk, Dellay. Others trying to enter this valley were dead before they reached this spot." Without further comment, he set off after the Warders.

With a savage oath, Dellay hurried to keep up with Regan. "What do you mean, Regan?" he muttered. "Who's dead? Dammit, slow down," he swore.

Regan ignored him but did slow his pace enough for Dellay to catch up to him.

"Who's dead?" Dellay demanded again, breathing rapidly.

"Anyone who came snooping." He turned to give Dellay a piercing glance. "I suggest you watch yourself while you're a guest of Gadred Aember's Warders. If Aember hadn't invited you, your bones would lie back there in the rocks, making a feast for the vultures."

Dellay merely grunted in response, but he did turn for a moment to glance back the way they had come.

The two Warders ushered Dellay and Regan into the common room where Aember and the rest of the brothers waited for them. Aember stood at the head of the table, tall and resplendent in a black robe, a belt of gold links about his waist. His long black hair, pulled back from his forehead, fell to his shoulders; a black neatly trimmed beard covered the lower half of his face. His dark eyes gave no suggestion of his thoughts as he scrutinized his guest.

The Warders stood at their places around the table observing Dellay. If Regan were surprised at what he saw, he did not show it. They, too, were garbed in heavy black robes that gave them the appearance of soldiers dressed in uniform, their hair clean and combed, beards trimmed, hands clasped behind their backs. Each man wore either a sheathed knife or short sword on a heavy leather belt. They stood straight and silent, eyeing the man who accompanied Conn Regan into their midst.

"Welcome, Kelan Dellay." Aember's deep voice drew Dellay's attention back to the man at the head of the table. "Please," Aember gestured to the chair on his right, "come sit here. You must be tired and hungry from your journey." At his nod, three of the Warders left the room and the rest took their seats. "Conn, sit, here on my left."

"My lord, please excuse me for a short time while I refresh myself."

"Of course, of course, Conn. Do not be long," he said with a smile. "We've much to discuss with our friend."

Dellay eased his bulk into the proffered chair and when a mug of ale was placed before him, he took it and immediately drained it. He set the mug down on the table, wiped the back of his hand across his mouth and belched. He soon raised his mug for a refill. "That was hardly a drop in the bucket. It's been a long dry trip."

Aember smiled again, a knowing smirk, that didn't reach his eyes. "Good, isn't it? We brew it from grain and fruit we grow ourselves." He motioned to one of the servers. "Jaston, more ale for our guest," he instructed. "Leave the pitcher."

Aember waited for the last vestiges of the meal to be removed before he excused the brothers to their rest. A fire had been kept burning in the large fireplace while the men ate, and Aember rose from the table, asking Dellay and Regan to join him in more comfortable chairs near the hearth. Dellay refilled his mug before leaving the table to join the two Warders. Aember noted with pleasure that the Arlander was unsteady on his feet; with a knowing glance to Regan he suggested that Regan bring the pitcher and place it on the table near Dellay's chair.

When Dellay was seated across from him, his mug brimming once more, Aember deftly turned the conversation to the number of men Dellay had brought to his cause.

Even drunk on the Warders' ale, Dellay was crafty enough to give only a vague estimate. When Aember broached the subject of weapons, Dellay smiled knowingly.

"I've men aplenty and weapons enough, Warder. Now let's get down to business. Why did you bring me here? If you wanted me dead, you could have killed me at any time during the trek into your valley or during the meal."

Drunk? Perhaps, Aember thought, but a man to be reckoned with nonetheless. He smiled at Dellay as he toyed with the links of his belt.

"We have need of each other, Kelan Dellay. You may have the weapons and the men, but I have the wherewithal to teach those men how to use them. My Warders are soldiers, warriors of the Way. They fought alongside Aldward Finton and would have taken Timis. . ." He grimaced with distaste.

Dellay laughed, a short bark of sound. "Except for the dragons," he said and laughed again. He raised the mug to his lips and some of the ale dribbled down his chin. Wiping the liquid away with his sleeve, he eyed the Warder leader. "Your men are good soldiers; I'll give you that. I'll also give you the fact that my men need training. Arlanders are good brawlers, good with our fists, but I'll admit we know little about fighting with swords. Knives in close quarters we can handle, but not swords or spears." He paused for another drink. "What are you offering, Warder? What do you want in return?"

Aember's mouth curved in a sly, malevolent smile. "I'm offering to train your riffraff army in return for western Timis."

Dellay grunted as he set aside his mug. "Well, then. Here's what you'll get when the Arlanders take the rest of Timis."

It was nearly dawn when the bargaining between the two men ended. Regan showed Dellay where he could sleep for a few hours before leaving to find his own rest. Aember made his way to his chamber, not to rest—he didn't feel the need for rest—but to plan. Dellay, he decided, was a worthy opponent, an ally for a time, but he would die all the same. Just when and how was not yet fixed, but die Dellay would. Timis belonged to Gadred Aember.

And the dragons would make it so. It was time to find the cave in Malhain Pass.

From the brooding mist-covered peak that looked down on the Warder compound, a wolf howled once. On a narrow, treacherous ledge that zigzagged down the face of a cliff, the wolf, darker than the night around it, made its way down the mountainside. It stopped, waiting for two men to catch up. As the darkness began to shift to daylight the wolf continued to descend the cliff, his claws clicking against the stone.

Wind swirled the mist around the wolf and the men, obscuring all but the narrow path they followed. Snow, more ice than snow, began to pelt the climbers. Neither Cass nor Rayce knew where on this mountain the wolf would lead them; wherever he led they must follow. Camron Thorpe was somewhere close by and Samar knew where.

"Sheevers," Cass muttered as his foot slipped, and he clung desperately to the wall of rock, almost overbalanced by the heavy pack on his back, before righting himself.

"Cass, are you all right?" Rayce called softly.

"I'm okay," Cass gasped as he tried to catch his breath.

The wolf paused. With a glance back at the men, Samar stepped onto a wider, rock-strewn ledge and disappeared.

"Sheevers," Cass swore again. "Samar, where did you go?"

"Can you see anything?"

"No. Be careful. One step at a time. Samar is somewhere up ahead."

A moment later Cass saw where Samar had disappeared to: a narrow cleft in the rock. "Looks like he found a cave, Rayce." Cass carefully made his way, sliding his feet with each step until he stepped through the opening and found himself in a cave. A moment later, Rayce joined him.

Out of the wind, the air in the cave was warm. Not only was the air warm it was brighter; it was almost as if the space was lighted from within. "What is this place?" Cass whispered. Then he turned to find Samar and saw him hunkered down next to a form lying curled against the wall at the back of the cave.

"Rayce," he called as he hurried to take his pack off.

A hand reached out to touch the wolf. Samar whimpered and licked the hand.

"Samar," a voice croaked. "You found me."

"Father!" Rayce slipped his pack off and knelt beside Cass.

"Lord Camron, it's me, Cass Vance. My god, man, how long have you been here?"

"Rayce? Cass? Water, do you have water?"

"Yes, and food. Water first." Cass reached back to open his pack and pulled out a water flask and handed it to Rayce. He maneuvered around until he was able to lift Camron's head so that Rayce could give him water.

"Just sips," Rayce said quietly. After a little more water, he set the flask aside. Cass eased Camron back down.

"Rayce, find some bread and cheese. There's a bottle of ale in the right pouch of my pack. Should be a cup with it. Dip the bread into the ale and give it to him, just a little at a time."

Rayce hurried to do as Cass bid, his hand shaking. He took bread and some cheese from his pack, then found the bottle of ale and cup from Cass's. He poured ale into the cup and dipped some bread into it. Once again Cass lifted Camron's head while Rayce fed his father small morsels. Next Rayce placed a bit of cheese on some bread and Camron ate it hungrily.

"Not much at first, my lord."

Camron sighed as Cass eased his head back down. "Thank you," he murmured. "My clothes, Rayce. They should be dry. Help me get dressed."

"Can you stand, Father?"

"Don't know," Camron muttered. "We'll find out."

It took several minutes for Rayce and Cass to help Camron into his clothes. Once the task was completed he sat down with his back resting against the wall, breathing deeply from the exertion. Rayce hunkered down on one side of him while Samar lay beside him on the other, his ears cocked, his eyes watching as Cass sat cross-legged near them.

"Would you like something more to eat?" Rayce asked

"Yes, please."

"We've dried meat as well as more bread and cheese. Do you think your stomach can handle that?"

Camron nodded. "Some ale, too, Rayce."

As Camron ate, Cass studied him, trying to figure how long Camron might have been here. They had separated, he calculated, at least ten days ago, perhaps more. How long it had taken Camron to find this cave, Cass didn't know, nor did he know how many days Camron had been here, nor how long he might have been without food. His chieftain was thinner, his face haggard; he was certainly weaker. However, he did not seem injured in any way.

"What's going on down in the compound? Is it too dark to see?" Camron asked.

"The Warder compound?" Cass asked. "You found it then."

"Yes. From this part of the mountain you are able to look down into the Warders' compound. Didn't you see it as you came in? And how did you find me?"

"Samar led us to you, Father. Mother sent Cass and me with him to find you. She's worried and frightened, especially after Cass came back to Camlanrein and you weren't there ahead of him."

"When did you come to Camlanrein?" Camron asked Rayce curiously. "According to your last letter you were going to Cathorn Isle." Camron reached out and took his son's arm. "The book," he whispered.

"I translated it, Father."

Camron breathed deeply and closed his eyes. "You did well, Rayce," he said when he opened his eyes. "Those words have not been read for centuries."

Rayce smiled at his father and Camron saw in his son's eyes the knowledge he possessed.

Camron smiled back. "Your dragon told you what you must do."

"Yes. Mother went to the Round Stones," he said softly. "Her dragons came to her there."

"So, she knows, too." He looked away for a moment toward the opening of the cave. "It has to do with the Warders."

"One Warder in particular, Father. He found a token that joined the essence and power of the dragons with the evil power that Finton possessed for a time. It is this token that he believes will allow him to call the dragons and control them."

"His name, Rayce, is Gadred Aember, the leader of the Warders. According to a man I met after leaving you, Cass, Aember wants all of Timis. And probably Kaenolir, too. And this fellow, Desmond Orly, believed Aember found something buried in the sand near the place where the Stones of Destiny once stood."

"We must find him, this Gadred Aember. The token must be taken to the Caretaker's Circle," Rayce said softly.

"The Caretaker's Circle?" Cass asked.

Rayce looked to his father to answer.

Camron thought for a moment before replying. "The Round Stones," he said. "The sacred circle near Lisburn."

"Of course. Where Lady Fairchild went," Cass said as he nodded his head, some of the pieces of the puzzle beginning to fit together for him.

"Cass, can you see what's going on down below?" Camron asked.

Cass took a position that allowed him to look down into the Warder compound. Mist no longer concealed the valley and Cass had a clear view. "Huh," he grunted. "There's Dellay. I'm sure that's him. The Warders are with him." He counted silently for a moment. "About thirty-five, thirty-six of them I'd judge. They're heading up the trail out of the valley." He heard a rustling behind him and turned to find Camron and Rayce coming to see for themselves.

"They have their black robes on," Camron stated. "I've not seen them wear them since I've been watching. No, I'll take that back; I've seen the one I think is Gadred Aember in a black robe. And there he is, the one leading them. He's bigger, taller than the other Warders."

Camron, Rayce and Cass watched in silence until the men were out of sight.

"There's still smoke coming from the chimney," Cass said. "I don't think all of them left."

"Orly said there were fifty of them living in the valley. One is dead, Orly left, so that makes forty-eight. Cass, you counted about thirty-six who left with Dellay, which leaves maybe a dozen still in the hall," Camron said. "Except I don't think all forty-eight have been here lately. So maybe a half dozen left in the hall. Orly believed Aember had sent some of the Warders out to spy on the High Champaign. Perhaps there are Aember's spies in western Timis, too, Orly believed."

Thick gray fog began to drift through the mountains once more, hiding the valley and the distant peaks. The three watchers turned away when they could no longer see below.

"My lord, who is this Orly fellow you mentioned?" Cass asked.

Camron quickly told Cass and Rayce about his encounter with Desmond Orly. "I suggested he find his way to Camlanrein. If he is able to get there, he'll contact me. He was to leave a letter I wrote with the Troopers in Timis. Do you know if the letter made its way to Ross Harbor?"

"Mother never mentioned a letter from you, so I doubt she received it. Cass, did my mother say anything to you about a letter?"

Cass shook his head in answer to Rayce's question.

Rayce thought for a moment before speaking again.

"This Orly fellow, you said he showed you a way into the hall." He watched his father intently. "And that he believed this Gadred Aember found something buried in the sand somewhere along the Balagorn Channel?"

At Camron's nod, Rayce continued. "You have a map Orly drew showing a secret way into the hall. Do you still have the map?"

"I think so, yes." Camron rummaged through his pack and brought out the folded piece of parchment. "Here it is." He unfolded the paper and handed it to Rayce. "Rayce?" he asked, already realizing why his son asked about the map.

"If you are sure Aember was one of the men we saw leaving the compound, perhaps there is something he left behind that will tell us what he found." Rayce walked to the opening where there was a bit more light and studied the map. "Maybe he even left it hidden in his chamber."

"Rayce, I know what you're thinking but it's too risky. I had considered finding the passage and trying to find out more about Aember's plans, but I decided against it. First, there's the problem of getting near the hall unseen; second, finding the passageway. If it even exists after all this time."

Rayce looked back at his father with a slight smile. "And third?"

Camron came to stand beside Rayce. "Getting out unseen."

"Ah, yes, the getting out would be important." He folded the map and placed it in a pocket. "But I must try to get in and get out. If the token is here, then we can thwart Aember's plans quickly. If not, well, then, I'll need to find Aember."

Camron opened his mouth to tell his son how dangerous it would be and then closed it again. He reached out to grasp Rayce by the shoulder. "All right," he said quietly. When he turned to include Cass in the plans that he'd begun to formulate when Rayce asked to see the map, Cass was already shaking his head even before he heard what Camron planned.

"It's just too risky, my lord."

"It is that, Cass."

Cass rose and went to stand in the opening, looking out into the swirling grayness. "We won't be able to see our hands in front of our faces out there," he muttered, before turning away to finish fastening his pack. He lifted it and settled it on his back.

"How did you get here, Cass?"

"Samar led us down that blasted cliff out there. How did you find this place?"

"You might say I fell into it. Literally." Camron pulled his cloak around his shoulders. "Now, Samar led you in; he'll lead us out. You trusted him all the way here. You'll need to trust him a little longer."

Cass shrugged and gave his chieftain a lopsided smile. "I do, my lord. I do trust the wolf, but he should be with you and Rayce, not me."

"Don't worry, Cass," Rayce said as he shouldered his pack. "We'll not be alone."

Cass looked first to Rayce, then to Camron but said no more.

The wolf came to stand beside Camron and looked up into the man's eyes. Camron smiled at him and placed his hand on Samar's head. "All right, old friend. Lead us out of here." Samar stepped through the cave entrance and into the fog. Cass followed him out.

"Father?"

Camron stood in the middle of the small cave, taking one last look around him. "Go on, Rayce. I'll be right behind you."

Rayce nodded and slipped out the opening. As he left the protection of the warm cave, he thought he heard a voice whisper *Caretaker*. It could have been the wind, he thought, but he smiled, knowing it was not. He had felt the presence of the spirit of the cave when he stepped into it. He knew why his father was alive and remarkably healthy after the long days he had spent in the cave, days without food and water; he also knew why his father lingered still.

Camron stepped to the cleft in the stone, reached out to touch the wall near the opening, and whispered, "Thank you." A pulse throbbed beneath his fingers.

Caretaker.

Samar led the three men down into the valley through mist and heavy fog and gathering darkness. Cass grumbled about being unable to see a thing, but the wolf led them unerringly downward. When Camron judged that they were nearly to the orchard behind the Warders' hall, he softly called Samar to him.

"We'll stop here for a while. Rayce, catch your breath and then we'll make our way to the back wall of the building. Cass, when you've rested, Samar will lead you away from the valley and back into the mountains. You should make it to Cragon Pass within a day or so."

"I still don't like leaving you behind, my lord."

"Rayce and I won't be far behind, Cass. We don't plan to spend much time looking for Aember's token."

Cass sighed deeply. "I'll do as you say, my lord, but it doesn't mean I have to like it."

Camron smiled. "I know. But I want you to get to Camlanrein as quickly as you can. Lady Fairchild needs to know what has happened." He took Cass by his arm. "Thank you for all you've done for Timis and for me. Go safely and go quickly. I'll see you in Camlanrein, Cass." He squeezed Cass's arm gently, then looked to Samar. "Take Cass to your lady, Samar." He turned to Rayce. "Ready?"

At Rayce's nod, the two men moved away.

"May the Ancient Ones go with you," Cass said quietly as Camron and Rayce disappeared into the darkness.

In a surreal world of swirling, diaphanous fog, Camron and Rayce left the protection of the orchard and began to cross the no-man's land of the Warders' garden. Snow had begun to fall adding to the silent grayness through which they trespassed; they moved with as little sound as possible, picking their way carefully along the cultivated rows. Pinpricks of light, visible from time to time in the fog and snowflakes, marked the windows of the hall. The two men came to an abrupt halt when the back door suddenly opened, and one of the Warders stepped out into the darkness, leaving the door open behind him. Wood was stacked not far from the door and he loaded a basket he carried with logs before returning to the hall. He closed the door behind him and all was gray and silent once more.

Rayce realized he was holding his breath and remembered to breathe only when the Warder closed the door. Camron touched his arm and once more they moved stealthily toward the hall. They reached the end of the garden and angled to the right toward the two middle windows. If Desmond Orly's memory was correct, they would find the escape hatch below those two windows.

Bushes had grown tall in the intervening years since the hall was built. Their bare branches were woven together forming an almost impenetrable hedge. Camron motioned for Rayce to drop down, and the two men crawled the last few feet to the place where they hoped to find the passage door. Camron slipped off his pack and pushed it under a bush, and Rayce followed suit. Dropping down to his belly, Camron slithered under the intertwining branches of two bushes that he thought might hide the door. A twig snapped, caught on his clothing, and he came to an abrupt halt, barely breathing. Rayce hunkered down, not daring to move. A figure came to stand in one of the windows, looking out into the heavily falling snow. After a few moments he moved away, calling to someone close by.

"Can't see anything out there. Probably a raccoon. I saw their tracks by the back door yesterday."

Camron lay without moving for several minutes, waiting to make sure no one was coming out to investigate. Then he continued to crawl, moving only a few inches at a time, taking care that his clothing didn't snag another branch. He reached the foundation and felt along the stone exterior, searching for a wooden door. His fingers encountered nothing but stone. He nearly gave up, but moved a little more to the right. As he did so he touched what he believed was wood. Checking the surface carefully, he knew he'd found a wooden door frame.

Over the years, the building had settled, pushing the rock foundation deeper into the ground. The bottom of the door was buried in several inches of dirt and an accumulation of decomposing leaves from the bushes. Slowly and as quietly as he possibly could, he began to dig with his hands, pushing the dirt off to the side of the door. It took several agonizing minutes of surreptitious digging before he cleared the last of the dirt away from the bottom of the doorway.

Orly said the door swung in. Feeling all around the door, he found the heavy metal latch in the center, as the Warder had remembered. With no light to see it and judging by what his fingers felt he knew it was corroded.

There were more voices coming from above the two men hidden in the bushes, and Camron paused to listen to the conversation .

"We have packed food enough for seven days," a voice said. "Providing we don't get caught in a storm, that should be ample."

"We can get more supplies at Banning if need be," another voice from almost directly above Camron.

"Once we're through Cragon Pass, we should be able to get to Timthurlen within two or three days. There will be little snow to contend with once we're down out of the mountains."

The voices moved away and Camron was left to wonder what the conversation he had overheard meant. The remaining Warders were planning to go to Timthurlen. Why? He felt certain he knew the answer, and that answer meant he and Rayce didn't have much time—they needed to get into the passage way and out as quickly as possible.

The latch slipped a little. As quietly as possible, he worked the latch in almost infinitesimal increments. Sweat beaded his forehead and ran down into his eyes. He blinked rapidly and continued to move the latch. With a sudden, soft snick the latch slipped back. Breathing heavily, Camron placed his hands on the door and began to push ever so gently. The door moved. He dug away more dirt before giving the door another gentle push to open it a few inches further. Now he could get his hands around the edge of the door. His arms trembling with the strain, he held the door back as well as pushed it open, keeping his movements slow and even. He paused to catch his breath and rest his arms; then once more he pushed against the old door until it finally stood open enough for them to enter.

"Thank you, Desmond Orly," he murmured under his breath.

Feeling his way, still on his belly, he pulled himself through the door and down two steps. At the bottom he was able to push himself to his knees. After resting a moment, he turned back to the open door to help Rayce.

Darkness in the passage was almost absolute, except here and there light from the room directly above them filtered down through the cracks between the boards of the rough floor. The air was stale and musty, smelling of earth and damp and old food. Cobwebs dangled from the ceiling of the tunnel and Camron brushed the feathery softness away from his face.

With their hands feeling along the wall and moving their feet slowly one careful step at a time, if Orly's memory still served, they had gone about ten paces to the left and were positioned below the common room.

The soft clink of dishes and the smell of food indicated the Warders were eating their evening meal directly above them. Camron placed his hand on Rayce's shoulder, turned him to his right. "Go," Camron barely breathed the word, and Rayce moved away toward Aember's sleeping chamber. He would have to get through another door to get access to whatever Aember may have left behind.

Camron moved so that he could hear the Warders' conversation more clearly. A small chink between the planks of the floor allowed him not only a limited view of the room, but also allowed him to hear what the Warders were saying.

"This snow may set back our timetable."

"Rather than set out through the mountain track to the pass, perhaps it would save us time if we went down our track to Dunadd and from there take the route through the pass."

"Yes, I agree with you," this from one of the voices Camron had heard earlier.

Conversation ceased for a time as the men ate. From where he stood, Camron could see four men, but from the number of voices he'd heard he was quite sure there were at least two more. He tried to find another place where he could see into the room, but there was no other vantage point that offered him the view this one did.

"With our brothers training the Arlanders in the High Champaign, the hall seems very empty," one of the men said. "And colder. Do you feel that draft?"

"The wind has picked up," another said

"Once we've organized the Arlanders in the west and prepared them for the raids to come, we'll soon be gone. Perhaps we'll be able to return here for a time." The first man sighed. "But I feel it may be a long while before we live here again, my brothers. We've much to accomplish."

Chairs scraped back and dishes clattered.

"Get some rest. We have a busy day tomorrow."

"Do you think the snow will delay our leaving?"

"I hope not. Lord Aember is counting on us and we must leave day after tomorrow if we are to follow his plan."

The men cleared away their dishes and left the room. In the passageway below, Camron leaned back against the wall and rubbed his forehead.

"Damn the Warders," he swore silently. "Will they never leave us in peace?" He looked into the dark in the direction Rayce had gone. He waited several long minutes before he heard Rayce's near silent approach.

"Rayce," he whispered.

A moment later he felt more than heard Rayce moving along the wall toward him. "Here," he whispered again. He extended his arm toward the sound and touched his son. "Come."

The two men made their way back the way they had come and slipped through the door. Camron hurriedly pushed the dirt around the bottom of the door frame, but he did not take the many minutes needed to close the warped door. Time was short and they must get back to Camlanrein.

Heavy snow and cold wind greeted them as they slipped under the bushes. They waited several minutes before they retrieved their packs and set off across the garden. The silence was complete; there were no lights in the windows; there was no one standing guard outside the hall. They had not been heard nor seen. There was no need to cover their tracks, for the snow filled their footprints almost immediately. They were well into the orchard before Camron paused.

"Did you find anything?"

"No," Rayce replied. "It was as if no one had ever spent any time in that room. Everything orderly, swept clean. Without tearing the room apart, I can't say for certain that Aember didn't leave something hidden there, but I think he'd not want to leave the dragon token behind for any of his Warders to find. Did you learn anything?"

"Yes." Camron quickly told his son what he had overheard. "We must get back to Camlanrein as soon as we can. We're ahead of the Warders at this point." He shifted his pack to ease his back. "I hope we can stay that way," he muttered and set out at a brisk pace, as brisk as the deep snow allowed.

Camron led the way in a circuitous route around the Warders' compound. He was heading toward the area where Dunadd had stood, the same route the remaining Warders planned to take. From there they, too, would slip through Cragon Pass. Once out of the mountains Camron hoped they could find someone willing to lend them horses. With horses, Timthurlen could be reached in a long day, two at the most.

They pressed on through the deep snow, stumbling often in their haste. With the sky beginning to lighten, the snow stopped, and the two men elected to find a place to rest for a short time and eat.

"How long do you think it will take us to reach the pass?" Rayce asked as he finished his bread and dried meat.

Camron took a swallow of water before replying. "It depends. We don't want to be seen. If Dellay has men watching the pass, he may also have them spread out in the mountains. And it also depends on how deep the snow is. I'm hoping we can make it by nightfall. Our chances of getting through in the dark are better than in the daylight."

Rayce nodded. "Father," he said quietly, "I'll be leaving you at the pass."

Camron sighed deeply. "I was afraid of that. I could try to dissuade you by saying you don't know these mountains, nor do you know the High Champaign. I don't like to think of you trying to find your way alone."

Rayce smiled. "I won't be alone, Father." He shifted to a more comfortable position. "I must find Aember."

"I know. But if he's surrounded by Warders and Arlanders, how will you get to him?"

"There will be a way."

Camron grunted. "Well. If I can't dissuade you, think how upset your mother will be if you don't come back with me."

"Ah, but Mother will understand."

Camron sighed and nodded. "So she will. Well, then, let's go." Camron and Rayce stood, swung their packs to their backs and set out once more.

chapter fifteen

Wind-whipped waves of the Trayonian Sea sent the white sloop down into deep troughs and up onto towering peaks carrying the boat ever onward, south to Timis. KaynaRee began to sing and music, wild and free like the sea, surrounded the woman at the tiller of the *Highland Guardian*. A path through the waves smoothed, flowed, lifted the sloop, sent it on its journey.

Caretaker, hurry. Words repeated over and over, urgent, fearful. Dreams, just on the edge of her consciousness, repeated as well, waking or sleeping. At times she walked alone; other times Rayce accompanied her. In the shadows a man in a black robe lurked, his features hidden.

And always a dragon called, and then another and another. She knew the voice of Ja'Anee. The others she did not know, but they called out the same message. *Caretaker, hurry, we need you.*

She sailed past the port of Fairtown on the Kaenolirian coast, past a village she knew from her map was Lisburn in Timis, past the confluence of Trayonian Sea and Comtarse River, without resting. She stayed beyond the jagged rocks and columns of stone cut off from the cliffs by time and water, and came at last to the breakers that marked the surge of the River Bray out of Brayner Bay and into the sea. The *Highland Guardian* slipped through the mouth of the bay and into calmer waters. She was startled to see light and smoke from several fires burning along the docks of Ross Harbor as she made her way up the river toward the landing at Camlanrein. A Trooper ran toward her as she guided her boat to a mooring slot.

"It's not safe here right now, miss. You shouldn't go into Ross Harbor."

"I need to get to Camlanrein. Can you take me there?"

"I must ask you your business, miss. We're not to let anyone enter the hall."

She tossed the Trooper a rope and he hesitated before catching it and tying it to a piling.

"I'm KaynaRee Fairchild, Trooper, and I've come to see my parents."

"You're the chieftain's daughter?"

"Yes." She took the hand he offered her and stepped up onto the landing.

"What's happening? What are all the fires about?"

"It's a riot, my lady. Come, I'll take you to Lady Fairchild."

"Isn't my father here?"

"No, lady, he is not." He hurried away and Ree had to run to keep up with him. Soldiers met them at the door to Camlanrein and the Trooper saluted.

"Take this lady to Lady Fairchild. At once," he said. Then he turned to Ree, saluted her and hurried back into the night.

"This way," one of the Troopers said, leading her inside, up the staircase and down the hall where another Trooper stood guard outside a door that stood open. KaynaRee heard voices, loud and angry, as she stepped into the room. She had been a child when she first entered this room and Tiernan Irworth greeted her in his booming voice.

"Enough, enough," she heard her mother command in a voice that brooked no disobedience. Ree almost smiled at the tone, but this was a much more serious situation than an argument between siblings.

"Sit down, all of you, and I'll listen to one at a time. Now, you," she pointed to the man who'd taken a seat in a huff, "what's going on?" At that moment she looked up to see her daughter standing in the doorway. Surprise and relief registered briefly before she motioned Ree into the room.

"It's Arlanders, my lady," the disgruntled man said. "They're breaking into the stores of grain at the harbor. They're setting fires and destroying property as they make off with everything they can carry."

"And you are?" Kitra asked.

"I'm the Harbor Master Elden. I'm. . ."

"If you are the harbor master," she emphasized the last word, "why aren't you at your post at the harbor? I suggest you get back down there and help the Troopers. Get those fires put out. We'll deal with the thieves later."

"Well," the man blustered, but nevertheless he rose and stomped out of the room, muttering something about the chieftain needed to get back here.

"Now, then, the rest of you," she turned to the other two. "What can you tell me about what's going on other than what I can see for myself? Adam?"

"My lady," Adam Carland said. "There were three separate bands of men, who, from the information I have from Troopers, have been identified as Arlanders. They demanded access to the grain storage bins. When that was denied them, they assaulted the guards and Troopers. I believe we also have men killed, on both sides."

"Do you know what set them off now?"

"Yes, I think I do," Adam continued. "Our Troopers have been reporting unrest among the Arlander immigrants for some time: not enough food, no adequate shelter, no jobs. We have not responded to their needs in a way we should, perhaps, but the Timisians are undergoing hard times, too. There's not enough to go around. Added to the conditions all of us are living under, there are agitators stirring up the Arlanders. The situation is fast becoming untenable."

The man in a Trooper uniform with a bar on his collar spoke up. "We don't have enough Troopers to adequately patrol the cities, villages and outlying areas. We've never had enough Troopers to do that, as you will remember, my lady, I'm sure, from what we suffered at the hands of Aldward Finton and his Warders." Sergeant Noonan, in charge of the Troopers in Ross Harbor, shrugged. "We're faced with many more Arlanders not only in Ross Harbor but also the rest of western Timis, and more coming all the time, mostly men, my lady. Very few women, no children that I've seen in the last few weeks. The Arlanders seem to be organizing into specific groups. I've seen the same men talking to groups of the immigrants. Whenever the Troopers happen to see them, they disperse. Later, these same men are seen talking to other groups of men."

"Lord Camron knows of a Kelan Dellay, an Arlander. Is he here, do you think?"

"I know of this Dellay fellow. He's been a thorn in our side for some years. Broke out of our prison by killing a guard. If I were to say who's organizing the Arlanders, I'd say that Dellay is behind this. Lady," Sergeant Noonan said quietly, "any word from Lord Camron? I don't discredit your leadership and you've done well in his absence, but we need him and whatever information he may have secured in the mountains."

Kitra shook her head and moved away from behind Camron's desk to stand looking out the window. She could see little in the darkness but the reflected glare of the fires burning in Ross Harbor. After a moment she turned back to the two officials.

"Organize firefighting units of townspeople to help. Get the Troopers organized so they can fight back efficiently. Whenever possible arrest the rioters. You may have to use one of the warehouses for a jail if there are too many for the cells here in Camlanrein."

The men rose, giving Kitra silent nods as they left to try to quell the riots and capture the men responsible for them.

Kitra turned then to KaynaRee, held out her arms to her daughter and with a near sob enfolded her in a tight embrace. At last Kitra stepped back to look into her daughter's eyes. In them she saw the knowledge that she and her daughter shared: knowledge of dragons and Songs.

"Father is on his way out of the mountains, but Rayce is not with him, Mother," Ree said with a soft smile. "Father will be here soon."

"What about Rayce?" Kitra asked. "Why did he remain behind?"

"He's gone after the Warder who has the dragon token."

"Alone?" Fear tinged the single word.

"No, no longer alone, Mother. His dragon is with him."

"What about you? Will you remain here?"

"No, Mother. My place is with Rayce."

Kitra sighed and smiled sadly. She took her daughter by her shoulders and held her for a moment. "At least stay and rest a bit. Would you like something to eat?"

Ree laughed. "Always worried about my stomach. Yes, I would like something to eat. I don't really remember when I ate last."

Kitra stepped to the door to call for Donan.

"Mother," Ree said quietly

Kitra looked at her daughter.

"Samar will be here soon. Father is not far behind him."

Kitra merely nodded her head but she breathed a silent prayer of gratitude.

By midmorning of the next day, most of the fires had been put out; nearly twenty Arlanders were residing in a makeshift jail in one of the warehouses near the dock; ten Arlanders had been killed, several people wounded; two Troopers were dead; and there were several with wounds, some serious. Much to Donan's chagrin and downright fear, both Lady Kitra and her daughter left the safety of Camlanrein for the docks early in the morning to assess the damage for themselves. They crossed the bridge over the River Bray and made their way to the docks of Ross Harbor. Along the way Kitra stopped to talk to one of the Troopers on patrol. His left arm was bandaged and he limped as he came toward the two women.

"Lady," he said, his voice raspy, "'tis not safe for you here. Please go back to Camlanrein."

"We won't be long. Have you been on the docks all night?"

"Yes, lady. I've been fighting fires."

"Be sure you take care of that arm. You're limping, too."

"I fell through a hole in the floor of one of the warehouses. It's just a sprained ankle. Lady," he said after a moment's hesitation, "at least let me come with you, if you won't go back."

"All right, Trooper. I'd like to see the rest of the damage here on the docks."

They had not gone far when a familiar black four-footed protector appeared beside Kitra. He seemed to have come out of the smoke and ruin of the building they'd just passed. The startled Trooper reached for his short sword, but KaynaRee laid a restraining hand on his arm.

"That's a wolf," the Trooper said, shock and alarm visible in his stance.

"He's a friend," Kitra said quietly as she took the wolf's head in her hands and gently pressed her forehead against him. Samar whined softly and licked her cheek. "Welcome back, Samar."

She looked up to see Cass Vance coming toward them leading a tired horse. "There you are," she said in welcome. A brief flicker of fear passed over her features before she held out her hand to the travel-weary man.

"I see Samar found you, my lady," he said as his eyes slid from the wolf over to KaynaRee. "My lady," he said in acknowledgement.

"Ree, this is Cass Vance. I sent Samar and Rayce and Cass into the mountains to find your father. I see Samar, Cass, but where is Lord Camron?"

"He should be here soon. I've much to tell you, Lady Fairchild."

Kitra nodded before she turned to the Trooper. "Thank you. Take care of yourself," she said in dismissal. The Trooper saluted and watched as they retraced their steps along the wharf back to Camlanrein. He breathed a sigh of relief. There was no way he could have explained to the Chieftain if something had happened to Lady Fairchild, either of them, while they were with him.

"I think the chieftain should only be a day or so behind me, two at the most. Do you know if this Desmond Orly fellow

Lord Camron happened upon while he was searching for the Warders' hall has come to Camlanrein?" At the negative shake of Kitra's head, he went on. "These Arlander 'organizers' as you called them may well have Warders mixed in among them. We saw the Warders and Dellay leave the compound together. Lord Camron and Rayce hoped to find out more about what the Warders are up to."

Cass, Kitra and Ree sat before the fire blazing in the hearth in the sitting room of the chieftain's private chambers. They had talked through much of the afternoon and into the evening except for the times Kitra left to return to the office to talk and plan with the various men whose responsibilities were the orderly governing and protection of Ross Harbor.

"Do you know what Desmond Orly looks like?" Ree asked. "You said he was a Warder. It seems a black robe would be noticed if he had come to Ross Harbor. Someone would surely remember seeing him."

"I doubt his appearance would be that of a Warder, lady. If Warders are here spying, organizing, whatever, he would not want to encounter any of his former brothers in black. If I were a run-away-Warder, I'd burn the robe, get different clothes, shave my beard if I had one, and cut my hair, too. A black robe would advertise, 'Here I am' to any other Warder who might be on the lookout for him."

"Mm, true," Ree murmured. "He would probably never tell anyone his name, at least his real name. If father told him to come to Camlanrein, perhaps he's waiting until the chieftain returns."

"That seems reasonable." Cass rose and stood before the hearth, one hand resting on the mantel. "You have something you've been circling around as we've talked, my lady." He looked at her over his shoulder. "Do you want to tell me about it, or wait for your mother to come back?"

Ree smiled. "You are very perceptive, Cass Vance."

"Huh," Cass grunted. "Your mother once said the same thing to me, so it must be true. When," he said as he turned to face her, "do you want to leave for the mountains?"

"Father will be here tomorrow."

"And you know this because. . .?" Cass asked.

"Father will be here tomorrow night," she stated again. "I want to leave before either he or Mother can try to convince me I mustn't go."

"You want to go to the mountains to find Rayce," Cass stated flatly.

"Yes."

"I won't ask you why you want to go. I doubt I'd understand your reasons, or if you'd even tell me; but I know a wolf led me to your father and then brought me here to your mother. I know you are a Golden One like your mother and a Caretaker like you father. Rayce, the same. I know dragons are part and parcel of who you are. So," he sighed gustily, "I will take you to find Rayce. I suggest we take a boat from Ross Harbor to Timthurlen and cross to the mountains from there. It will be much quicker. We'll leave at first light. In the meantime, we should both get some rest."

"I'm sorry to take you back out so soon, but, Cass, I must go."

"I know, Ree, I know," he said softly and gave her a rather weary smile.

"My boat is tied up at the landing. We'll take it."

"I'll sleep while you handle the boat. Fair enough?"

Ree nodded. "I know boats, you know the mountains."

Her mother entered the room. She looked tired and drained, the long hours of turmoil and worry taking their toll. KaynaRee went to her and hugged her. "You need to get some sleep, Mother."

"Yes, I suppose I do." She looked to both Ree and Cass. "What did I miss?"

"Nothing you don't already know," Cass said. "We were talking about Desmond Orly, wondering if he made it to Camlanrein."

Kitra nodded absently.

"Go to bed, Mother," Ree took her mother by the shoulders and shook her gently. "You're exhausted. Father will be here soon. Go." She gave her mother another shake.

"Yes. Both of you get some rest, too. I'll see you in the morning," she said as she turned away, her proud carriage slumped in weariness.

Beyond the boundary that marked the limits of Ross Harbor, darkness hid two figures standing in the protection of a stone wall that ran for some distance along the shore of the River Bray, quietly talking. Both were dressed in dark clothing, hoods pulled low over their foreheads.

"How many did we lose?"

"Too many. Ten dead, twice that many injured, and nearly twenty in jail."

"Can we free the ones in jail?"

"I'd say not now. Too many guards."

"Where do they have the ones who are hurt?"

"In another part of the warehouse they're using for a jail."

"What's next then?"

"We wait for word from Dellay. Should be hearing from him soon. Just be ready."

The two shadows crept away, one headed farther up the river, the other back into Ross Harbor.

Camron Thorpe came back to Camlanrein under the cover of darkness. Two Troopers stopped him as he entered the outskirts of Ross Harbor and when they realized who he was, they insisted upon escorting him through a city in panic. The smell of charred wood, carried by the wind from the burned out areas on the waterfront, was everywhere. As they rode through streets of barricaded businesses and homes with armed men standing watch over their property, Camron took in the full extent of the damage the Arlanders had caused. Not only had they destroyed warehouses and stolen whatever they could carry away, they had stolen the peace that once belonged to the people of Ross Harbor.

From what the Troopers described, Camron saw a clever organization behind the thievery and the destruction: the attack was meant to cause fear and disorder. The Timisians were not prepared for such an assault, and Camron knew this riot might well be first of many. Kitra had not had an easy time while he was in the mountains.

At the Bray River bridge, Camron dismissed the two Troopers and sent them back to their posts. He clattered across the bridge and rode into the central courtyard of Camlanrein where he was halted by more Troopers. When he pushed back his hood and the light from flickering torches identified their chieftain, the soldiers' relief at seeing him was obvious. Camron was reminded again of the difficulties Kitra had faced without him.

He found her still in his office conversing with Donan. He was aware immediately of her exhaustion, the added lines of fatigue in her face, and the deepened shadows under her eyes. Donan, too, showed every year of his age, his voice hoarse with weariness. When she looked up to see Camron standing in the doorway, she stood up, her hand across her mouth, her shoulders shaking with silent sobs. Donan turned to see what caused his lady's agitation and found his chieftain entering the room.

"My lord," the old man whispered as he rose and stepped aside. With a slight nod of his head, he left the room, knowing that for now, his presence was not needed. He silently closed the door behind him.

Camron let his pack slide to the floor with a thump and held out his arms as Kitra came around the desk to step into his embrace. She shook with the force of her emotion and Camron simply held her, murmuring soothing words of comfort. Finally she stepped back and wiped her cheeks with the palms of her hands.

"I don't know whether to kiss you or hit you," she said. "I had begun to despair of ever seeing you again, Camron." She sniffed the last of her tears away and smiled at him. "You've gotten thin," she murmured as her eyes took in the deep lines of his wind-burned face. He removed his cloak and laid it across a chair and she saw that he was, in fact, very thin. "Oh, Camron," she whispered, "what have you endured?" She grasped Camron by the arm.

He covered her hand with his. "I will tell you all while we eat. I asked the Trooper on duty at the door to bring a late supper for us. He said that he had not been able to persuade you to eat earlier, but I am very hungry." He took her back in his arms and breathed in the scent of her, the fragrance of wild alpine flowers. "Ah, love," he whispered as he gently tipped up her face to meet his mouth.

The meal finished, Kitra sat with a cup of tea and Camron with a mug of Highland whiskey. A fire burned low in the hearth adding to the somnolence of the room, lit now with only a single candle on the table beside Kitra's chair and the flickering flames of the fire. They had asked Donan to join them for a time, to add his insight to what Kitra told Camron of the situation here in Ross Harbor.

Camron told Kitra and Donan all he knew about the alliance between Warders and Arlanders. Warder spies would soon be in place in both Timthurlen and Ross Harbor, if they weren't in position already. He spoke of meeting Desmond Orly and that he hoped the man had made it to this side of the mountains. He spared no details of his dangerous surveillance of the Warder compound nor of his and Rayce's search of the tunnel beneath the hall to learn more of Aember's plans. Only when Donan left to find his rest did Camron tell Kitra what their son faced as he sought out Gadred Aember and the dragon token. Finally he spoke of his time in the small cave and of the dragon spirit that watched over him until Samar, Rayce and Cass found him.

Kitra smiled as she told him of her reunion with her dragons at the Round Stones. "They know we will do everything we can to keep them safe, Camron," she murmured. "But my heart aches for our children."

And then she told him of KaynaRee. "She has her dragon, Camron," she said softly. "But she and Cass left yesterday. While I still slept," she shook her head and looked toward the dark windows. "They left before I could try to stop them, I suppose," she said, her voice thick with suppressed tears. "She did leave a letter for us and I'll show it to you tomorrow. She asked Cass to take her into the mountains. So she could find Rayce. "

Camron nodded. "They are not alone, love. They have their dragons."

"When all else fails," Kitra whispered.

Smoke hung over the ruins of three warehouses and several businesses destroyed by fire during the riots. Boats had burned at their moorage or drifted out into the harbor and sank as they burned, leaving the bay littered with hulks that would endanger shipping for a long time to come. Much to his relief, Camron saw the damage was not as extensive as he had feared. Troopers worked to extinguish the last of the smoldering fires; townspeople were busy boarding up buildings that still stood and might yet be saved. Others hauled debris away from the docks by the cartful. Fishermen were repairing their boats and equipment.

The acrid stink of charred wood hung heavy in the air as Camron walked along the docks. He stopped often to talk with people working to salvage what they could from the destruction or pitched in to help where he was needed. The chieftain had come home; surely now the Arlanders would find there would be consequences for what they had done.

He spent the day on the docks and as he was about to return to Camlanrein, he saw someone duck quickly behind a pile of debris and scurry away, someone who did not want to be seen. Camron called to a Trooper working nearby. "Come with me," he directed and the two men set off after the man, running along the dock, dodging people and carts. The man crashed into a loaded cart and fell, but before he could get back up,

Camron and the Trooper were on him. Two other Troopers heard the commotion and dashed to their aid.

"Watch out," the Trooper who had accompanied Camron shouted as he was knocked backwards. "Knife, knife! He's got a knife."

Camron blocked the man's arm as the cornered man raised the knife to strike and struck him in the stomach, hard enough to double the man over. The knife was wrenched away by one of the Troopers and the man pinned roughly to the planks of the dock by another. The second Trooper helped secure the man's hands behind his back after handing the knife to Camron. "We'll want to talk to this one," Camron said as he took the knife. "Are you hurt?" He turned to the Trooper and helped him regain his feet.

"No, my lord." The Trooper touched the back of his hand to his mouth and it came away bloody. "Just a busted lip." He wiped more blood away. "Do you know who our friend here is?"

"No, but I've a good idea who sent him here. Lock him up; put a guard on him and if I've time, I'll talk to him later. Let me know where you put him."

The Trooper saluted and the three of them moved off with the trussed up man toward the warehouse they'd been using as a jail.

Camron watched until the men were out of sight before turning away. Torches were being lit along the waterfront and men and women continued the task of clearing the docks and the more difficult task of picking up the pieces of ruined lives. With a deep, disheartened sigh, Camron walked on, leaving the waterfront with all its destruction behind. He saluted the Troopers at the foot of the bridge and crossed the river. Ahead of him the lights of Camlanrein beckoned.

"So it begins," he muttered under his breath. "So it begins."

chapter sixteen

Gadred Aember and Conn Regan left the Warders and Kelan Dellay at a training camp Dellay had organized on a wide plain north of Malhain Village. Men, along with some women, eager for the spoils to be had across the mountains, came to the camp in response to Dellay's call to arms. The Warders had divided the Arlanders into roughly twenty training sections, each section under the leadership of one or two Warders. The training was proceeding as Aember wanted; now was the time to reach the cave Regan had determined was the best place to discover a dragon's lair. Regan knew the way to the cave would still be locked in snow, but Aember was determined to set out immediately. The two men left Dellay's camp soon after sunset, hoping to reach the pass by midday of the next day.

Drifts of knee-deep snow, in some places nearly hip deep, filled the trail that wound through jagged, plunging cliffs of stone so high they seemed to lean toward each other. Bitter cold wind whistled through the narrow chasm as the two men made the slow, torturous climb. They were nearly halfway through the pass when they heard the first ominous rumble, followed quickly by the sharp, explosive crack of fracturing stone. The earth wrenched under their feet, tossing them from side to side. Dust mixed with snow filled the air around them. Stone walls hundreds of feet high swayed, fell in against each other like warriors in battle, and tumbled into the chasm. Gadred Aember screamed as he was thrust about like so much detritus on a sea of heaving earth. Boulders and rocks of all sizes, thick slabs of stone, gravel, ice and snow crashed down the mountainside to fill the fissure called Malhain Pass.

When the rumbling of the mountain's fury finally stopped and the dust began to clear, the silence was absolute except for an occasional moan coming from the two men who had been caught in the throes of the earth's upheaval. Conn Regan slowly pushed himself to his knees; he coughed to clear the dust from his throat before staggering to his feet. He pressed a hand against his left side and caught his breath as pain cut sharply through his ribs. He was sure he'd broken at least one rib, maybe more. His hands were scrapped raw as were his knees. When he put a hand up to his aching head, it came away bloody. He coughed again and hissed with the pain that raced down his side and back.

"Lord Aember," he called hoarsely. "Lord Aember, where are you?"

"Here, Conn," came the weak reply and Regan turned to see Aember pushing himself to a sitting position.

Conn stumbled to Aember's side as another section of the mountain slid away in the distance.

"What happened?" Aember breathed.

"Earthquake, avalanche," Regan croaked. He looked around and groaned. "The mountain has collapsed and closed the pass."

"No," Aember moaned. "The cave," he muttered, "what about the cave?" He fumbled at his neck and sighed with relief when his fingers touched the pouch.

Regan shook his head. "It's buried under the mountain. We can't get to it, my lord. The mountain fell in on itself. There is no pass and probably no cave anymore."

Aember's rage boiled up inside him at Regan's answer. They had been close, so close; he was sure of it.

More rock slithered down toward them, accompanied by several large chunks of ice.

"We need to get out of here, my lord, back the way we came, before the mountain closes in behind us."

Aember swore in frustration, but with Regan's help gained his feet.

"Can you walk?"

"Yes, I think so," Aember said as he looked at Regan. "Your head is bleeding rather badly. Where are our packs? Have you seen them?"

Regan looked about and saw his pack nearby, Aember's a short way beyond. With painful steps, Regan retrieved them and rummaged in his for something to wrap around his head to staunch the bleeding. Aember picked up his pack and took out his water flask. He rinsed his mouth, spat, and then drank thirstily. With his head now roughly bandaged, Regan followed suit. After quenching his thirst, he put his flask back in his pack and turned to head back down the trail that wound east through what was left of Malhain Pass. He looked back once to make sure Aember was coming.

"How far were we from the cave?" Aember suddenly asked after they had been walking for some time.

"We were more than halfway there."

"So close," Aember muttered as he stumbled along after Regan.

Night was fast approaching when Aember and Regan finally came down out of the pass. In the distance they could see the scattered lights of Malhain Village. Regan paused so they could rest and get their bearings.

"We need to find shelter, my lord, and replenish our food pouches. There are several abandoned cottages in Malhain. We should be able to find one that will offer us some protection from the wind and the cold. While you rest, I'll see if I can't find someone willing to share or sell us the supplies we need. I might find an unguarded food cache, for that matter, and we'll help ourselves." He put away his water flask after taking a drink and pushed himself to his feet. He sucked in his breath as a wave of pain washed over him.

"You're hurt?" Aember asked. "More than the cut on your head?"

"I think I broke some ribs, my lord," he said through clenched teeth. He stood for a few moments until the pain eased somewhat.

"You need something to bind yourself. That will help a bit, I think. Can you make it down to the village?"

"Yes, but I'll need to go slowly."

Aember nodded. "If you're ready, shall we go then?"

They found an unoccupied cottage off by itself about a half mile from the village, its windows boarded up against intrusion. The door, however, yielded easily and once inside, they were able to light a shuttered lantern. The earthen floors and rough walls showed no sign of recent occupancy except for a few logs dumped beside the small rock fireplace at the end of the single room. A rickety bench sat near the fireplace and a chair with a broken leg lay near it.

"I'll get a fire started, my lord, and see if there is some wood close by. It would be best if I waited until most of the villagers are asleep before I try to find more food."

"All right. Yes, a fire would be most welcome, Conn."

With a fire burning brightly, Regan went back outside and found a small woodpile around the side of the dwelling. It took him several painful minutes before he had gathered enough wood to keep the fire burning through the night. When he completed that task, he left the cottage. He knew if he didn't keep moving, he would stiffen so much he couldn't move.

Everything hurt, he thought. Scrapes on his hands and knees burned; his head throbbed; and his ribs hurt so badly he found it difficult at times to breathe. Wind whistled and moaned its way down out of the mountains as he made his way toward the sleeping village, and he shivered with cold. He could smell snow and pulled his hood far down on his forehead, careful not to disturb the untidy bandage.

His steps were slow and painful, and it took Regan over an hour to reach the outskirts of Malhain Village. He remembered Dellay mentioning he lived here, but Regan had no idea where. He noticed a lighted window in the cottage off to his right and made his way toward it. Far off, toward the Dalrudds, he heard a distant rumbling and cracking. The ground trembled beneath his feet, and the lighted window of the nearby cottage swayed for a moment. The back door of the cottage opened and a large woman stepped out, turning toward the mountains. She stood listening for a long moment. When the night was quiet again except for the wind, she stepped back inside and closed the door.

Regan moved with stealthy steps and stood beside the window. He could see much of the room and the woman appeared to be the only one in the cottage. Here might be his best opportunity to find someone willing to sell the supplies he needed, but he decided on a different route as he stood there watching the woman.

He knocked softly, but when there was no answer he knocked again, harder this time.

"Who's there?" the woman called out.

"I'm looking for Kelan Dellay," Regan answered. "Do you know where I can find him?"

The door opened enough for the woman to look out. "Why do you want Dellay?"

"I was scouting for him. In the mountains. Up there," he gestured toward the pass. "I got caught in an avalanche when the earth shook. Have to tell him there isn't much of the pass open anymore. Just this end." He leaned against the doorframe on one arm and moaned softly.

"Are you hurt?"

"Broke some ribs," he muttered and staggered to the back step and tried to sit, but yelped in pain.

"Here, let me help you." The woman moved down the step and took him gently by the arm. "Come inside. Let's have a look at those ribs. The head, too."

Leaning heavily on the woman's arm, Regan stumbled up the step and into the small cottage. She maneuvered him to a bench beside the fireplace and helped him down before pulling a stool over to sit in front of him. Regan breathed a careful sigh of relief.

"Thank you," he whispered. "What do I call you?"

"Eithne," she said as she pushed his hood back and carefully peeled away the bloody bandage. He flinched as the bandage stuck to the wound.

"You have a name?" Eithne asked as she turned away to fill a basin with water. With a wet cloth she gently loosened the crusty bandage and cleaned the wound. She set the basin and cloth away and picked up a small jar; its contents smelled of herbs. "This will sting a bit."

As the salve touched his raw skin, he sucked in his breath and let it out with a curse. "A bit?" he said when he had his breath back.

Eithne merely smiled. She set the jar aside and wound a narrow strip of clean cloth around his head. "There. That should help. Now, if you'd remove you tunic, I'll take a look at those ribs. Can you do it by yourself or do you need some help?"

When the tunic proved more than he could handle, Eithne helped him out of the garment. "You have a name?" she asked again as she slipped the tunic over his head. "Well," she said as his chest was exposed. Bruises covered his chest and down his left side, across his shoulders and down his back. "How much of that mountain fell on you?" she said softly.

"Most of it," he whispered as he clenched his teeth against the pain of his ribs.

Eithne grunted and picked up the salve. With gentle fingers Regan found unusual for hands so large, she smoothed it over his chest, his side and then moved behind him and did the same for his shoulders and back. This time the salve did not sting, except in the scratches on his shoulders. "Sit for a bit," she said and rose to rummage in a small cupboard near the window. She found a long woven scarf and folded it in half.

"Here, hold this end."

When she finished winding the scarf around his upper body and crisscrossed it over his shoulders, she sat down and looked at him. "Now, let's take a look at your hands and knees." She filled the basin with water again and cleaned the scrapes on his hands and knees before removing the sand and grit from some of the deeper scratches. More of the salve rubbed into the cuts and scrapes soothed after the initial stinging.

"You didn't tell me your name," she said. "But never mind, lots of folks this side of Timis don't have names." She placed her competent hands on her knees and stood upright. "You hungry?" she asked.

When Regan left the cottage as it began to get dark the next day, he carried a pouch of bread, cheese, some dried apples, a little dried venison, and two water flasks filled with fresh water from the village well. Eithne now had a few gold coins hidden away.

Though his body still ached, the binding helped to give his broken ribs some stability. He moved slowly and carefully as Eithne had warned him to do. "It's a wonder you didn't puncture a lung," she had said. Even with his slow pace, it took him less time to return to the cottage where he'd left Aember.

"My lord," he called as he neared the door. "It's Conn. I have food and water."

The door opened and Aember stood silhouetted in the light from the fire. "I had begun to think you had deserted me," he said angrily.

"No, my lord. Surely you know I would never do that."

Aember grunted. "Yes, yes. Come in. What did you find?" Aember glanced at the clean bandage on Regan's head as the Warder pushed his hood back and set his pack and a pouch filled with the food and water from Eithne on the bench Aember had pulled before the fire

Regan opened the pouch and placed a loaf of bread and a chunk of hard yellow cheese on the bench. "I've some dried meat and a few dried apples, too."

Aember tore a hunk of bread from the loaf and cut off a large piece of cheese with the knife from his belt. He chewed for several minutes before speaking.

"Someone took care of your head," he said around a mouthful of bread. He reached for more cheese, but Regan moved it out of reach.

"We need to be careful with the food," Regan said under Aember's resentful glare. "We don't know how long we'll need to make this last."

Aember swallowed and picked up one of the bottles. "No more where this came from?" he asked with a sour expression.

"No," Regan said simply.

"I suppose you're right," Aember reluctantly agreed. "How are your ribs?"

"I can move," Regan said.

"Hm. Good." Aember took a swallow of water and set the bottle aside. "We'll go back to the compound for now to rest up. Spring isn't far off and as soon as you can, I want you to go to Ross Harbor. Find out what you can from Camlanrein. But stay out of the way of Dellay and the Arlanders."

"What will you do, my lord, while I'm gone?"

"Me? Oh, I'll keep busy around the compound." He wiped his mouth with the back of his hand. "Get some rest," he commanded. "We'll leave in the morning."

When winter at last began to loosen its grip, spring rushed in icy torrents down the mountainsides; trees began to show new growth; and wild flowers bloomed in a riot of color. Conn

Regan settled his pack once more on his back and prepared to leave the confines of the Warder compound. His ribs were nearly healed, and if he did so with care, he could move without much pain. He planned to pass through Cragon Pass and head for Timthurlen on the western coast. He'd find a ship there bound for Ross Harbor. Before leaving the Warders' compound, he'd shaved, cut his hair and placed his black Warder robe in the chest at the foot of his bed.

It was his plan never to wear it again.

He had spent the last weeks of winter healing and contemplating what he would do next. For years he had followed Gadred Aember with unquestioned allegiance, but during the time spent alone with no other company but himself and occasionally with Aember, he began to question that blind obedience.

There were other questions, too. Jaston Sonne suggested the possibility that Morton Cassel had not died a natural death. There was also the strange disappearance of Desmond Orly. Jaston insisted that Orly had been seen fleeing from the hall. Why? Had he killed Cassel? Regan doubted it; the two men had been close friends.

Then there was the token that he had found buried in the sand. He had come to think of it as the dragon token. Why had Aember kept it for himself? If Aember were able to find the dragons, with Regan's help, and bring them under his control, where did that leave the rest of the Warders? Aember had callously dismissed the need for Dellay once he controlled the dragons—why would he need the rest of the brothers, Regan included?

Why couldn't Regan be the one to take the riches of Timis for his own? Why should it be Gadred Aember who had it all? Morten Cassel may well have been right in his belief that

Aldward Finton had taken the gold for himself, that he had no intention of sharing it with the Warders he commanded.

And Gadred Amber was cut from the same bolt of cloth as Aldward Finton.

After Malhain Pass was blocked by landslides prohibiting them from reaching the cave that Regan thought might be a dragon's lair, his thoughts had turned more and more to the legends surrounding the fire beasts, specifically, how the beasts had come to the aid of the Timisians and the Kaenolirians. Camron Thorpe and Kitra Fairchild had found the dragons, had ridden them as Aldward Finton, Dunadd, and the Stones of Destiny were all destroyed. Surely Thorpe and Fairchild knew where to find the dragons.

And they were in Ross Harbor, in Camlanrein.

The strength and power that Regan believed Aember possessed had begun to erode while the two men were living in the old hall, waiting for spring. Aember rarely spoke, seldom left his chamber, and finally, as the winter wore on, he became more and more lethargic, sinking deeper and deeper into silence. The daily work was left to Regan. Regan prepared their meals, though Aember rarely ate. Days and then weeks went by without the two men ever seeing each other. Regan continued to keep the fire burning in the common room, set snares to catch the occasional rabbit or squirrel for the stew he then prepared, and filled the water bucket from the well behind the hall.

It was when the snow had melted all around the hall and he'd gone to bring in more firewood that he noticed the earth had been disturbed about midway along the building's foundation. It was possible that a wild animal had sought to enter the hall and he went to investigate. When he found the opening under the bushes, his first impulse was to tell Aember, but then he thought better of it.

Who had opened the door? He squatted on his haunches to look in the opening. Curious to see where this led, he dropped to his belly and gingerly crawled under the bushes, slipped through the opening, then down two steps wet from melting snow, littered with dirt and leaves blown in by the wind. When he could stand upright, he found he was in passageway hacked out of the earth, high enough to let him stand, wide enough to pass without difficulty. He'd not known this tunnel beneath the hall existed. He'd never heard anyone speak of it. Where did it lead? What was its purpose?

With a hand on the wall he followed the cold, dank passage to the left and found it ended after a short distance. Dim light filtered through cracks in the floor above his head, and he could make out the furniture in the common room. Turning around, he retraced his steps to the opening. The tunnel continued and he moved cautiously along its length, wanting to see where it ended. It narrowed, but he could still squeeze through. After a few more steps of feeling his way in the darkness and the cold, he encountered another door. Dim light from the room beyond shone through several cracks in the door. Regan silently mounted the steps, being careful to place his weight in such a way that the old boards did not squeak. He pressed his face close to one of the larger cracks and looked into the shadowed chamber.

Regan had not seen Aember for several weeks, but the man who lay stretched out on the bed gave no indication he was the robust leader of the Warders. His hair was matted and snarled; his robe covered an almost skeletal frame; his cheeks and eyes were sunken, giving his head a skull-like form. Regan gagged at the smell emanating from the room.

Regan watched for several minutes. He heard Aember mumble incoherently, saw him clasp a claw-like hand around the pouch at his neck, and mumble something about the fire beasts. Then his hand fell away from the pouch; his legs twitched and he lay still.

The minutes dragged by. There was only the slightest movement of Aember's chest as he breathed.

This was the man who would command dragons, who thought to order and control Dellay and the Arlanders? This spectral, filthy creature?

Regan nearly laughed aloud.

He'd seen enough; it was time to take his leave of Gadred Aember and the Warders' hall.

But first there was something he wanted.

With careful, furtive movements, he ran his hands over the door. There was no latch, nothing to indicate the door was locked. He found the hinges and moved to the opposite edge of the door and began to apply pressure. Tensing his muscles, holding his breath, he began to push. The door moved inward with no sound. He continued to push until he had enough space to step through the door and into the room.

He stood absolutely still for many minutes, watching the half-dead man on the bed. Aember neither spoke nor moved other than the slight movement to indicate he still breathed.

Regan had a decision to make: did he take the dragon token and silently leave? Or did he kill Aember, the man who had for so many years been the one to lead the rudderless Warders, himself included?

He stepped to the bed and removed the knife sheathed on his belt; he bent down and slipped the knife under the cord around Aember's neck and with a deft movement sliced through the cord. At the same time he lifted the pouch and stepped back.

Aember mumbled something and tried to lift a hand to his neck, but he could not. His hand fell away; his mouth fell open; his eyes fluttered once or twice, but they did not open. His breathing now was agitated, but though he may have tried, he did not, could not rise from his filthy bed.

Regan turned and quickly moved away through the chamber door and into the dormitory. He stopped at his own bed to finish packing his few possessions. With that task swiftly completed, he took the silken pouch with its dangling cord into his hands. He stood for several moments fingering the pouch before he carefully tied a knot in the cord and slipped it over his head and under his shirt and tunic. The pouch pulsed gently against his chest, and he smiled as he pulled on his cloak before swinging the pack onto his back. Several days ago he had packed a food pouch with the remaining supplies he'd need for his journey to Ross Harbor. On his way out through the kitchen, he paused to retrieve the pouch and filled his water flask, adding it to his pack.

The sun was shining and a warm breeze greeted him as he closed the heavy front door of the hall. With purposeful steps, he left the compound and set out toward the narrow breach in the walls of the mountains. He soon left the Warder valley behind without looking back, heading into the mountains he had come to love. At this pace he would reach Cragon Pass by nightfall. Once through the pass he'd make his way to Timthurlen and from there to Ross Harbor.

Conn Regan needed no map to show him the way to find the dragons. He knew how he would find them, knew how he would gain their power and control their fire for his purposes.

Yes, he knew the way.

The way lay through Camlanrein.

chapter seventeen

Rayce Thorpe paused before entering the shabby square in the center of Banning Village. Booths were set up around the edges of the square, though the goods they displayed were as tattered and worn as the people offering them. A wiry-haired man in a dirty tunic squatted on his haunches beside a basket of shellfish and shouted to be heard above the noise and chatter of people moving through the market. A woman stopped to check the basket, wrinkled her nose in distaste and moved away. The man shouted after her and spat at her retreating back. As Rayce approached, the man gave him a black-toothed grin.

"Fresh clams, good sir. Fresh from the sea just this morning."

Rayce stopped and gave the man a hard look. "Which morning?"

"Well," the man, still grinning, said, "Perhaps it wasn't just this morning."

"By the smell, I'd say your merchandise is a few mornings past fresh." Rayce nodded and moved on. Behind him he heard the man swear.

There were a few good smells in the air, and Rayce headed for a booth selling loaves of bread. This merchandise was definitely fresh just this morning, and Rayce bought two large, crusty, round loaves. He spotted a cheese booth next and made another purchase. The pretty girl in charge of the booth, no more than twelve, smiled shyly and ducked her head.

"I ain't seen you around here before."

"Just passing through on my way to Malhain."

"Ah," the young miss said knowingly, "Goin' off to join Dellay's army, are you?"

"I'm giving it some thought. Waiting for a friend to join with me."

"Well, you best buy some more cheese. You've a fair journey yet."

Rayce looked over the cheese selection and chose a small round of hard yellow cheese. "You haven't perchance seen him? My friend? Tall, black hair and beard, probably wearing a black robe."

"There's lotsa black robes passed through. Going up to Malhain."

"My friend would be hard to miss. He fancies himself the leader of the men in the robes," Rayce said with a little grin.

The girl grinned back but then shook her head. "Didn't see no leader. Just a bunch of men in robes. Weren't friendly at all. Didn't stop to buy nothin'. All had swords, so mostly folks stayed out of their way."

Another coin exchanged hands, and Rayce turned to leave.

"I'd watch out for those black robes if I was you."

Rayce laughed and nodded. "You're probably right." With a wave he turned and left.

He wandered through the rest of the market. There was little to choose from, but he did add some dried meat, venison he hoped, to his small cache. If he recalled his history of Timis, Banning had long been a mining town but never a prosperous one. The miners and their families had fled Banning when the Warders came, and the Timisians never came back. Instead, the Arlanders came, took over the mine and apparently had it operating again. Maybe the little village of Banning and the people who had come here might see better times. But he doubted it.

At the head of the next lane over from the square he saw a decrepit looking inn, the faded sign above the front door declaring it to be the Wayfarer's Inn. Since there was only an hour or so of daylight left, he decided to stop. Perhaps he'd be able to get a hot meal and a halfway decent bed for the night. He'd been out in the open since leaving his father at Cragon Pass, sleeping where he could find shelter, eating cold rations. He'd encountered few travelers, and those he'd asked about 'his friend' had seen no one of such a description.

Rayce mounted the steps of the porch that extended across the front of the inn. When he pushed open the wide battered door into the common room, he was greeted by an old man with a gray beard who was nearly as wide as he was tall. If the man's size was any indication of the quality of the food served in the inn, perhaps there was reason to hope for a decent meal.

"What can I offer ya, young man?" The man rose from a chair near the fireplace and moved behind the long bar at the end of the room. He eyed Rayce up and down, then nodded as if satisfied with what he saw.

"A hot meal and a bed for the night for starters. Perhaps a bath later." Rayce looked around the deserted room. "Not many guests tonight I take it."

The innkeeper laughed, more a cackle than a laugh. "Yer my first guest in many a night, but, yes, there's hot food, good ale, and a clean bed. The bath can be arranged for an extra coin. Now, what would ya like first?"

"I'll take the ale and the food," Rayce said wearily, digging in his pocket for two coins. "Is that enough?"

The man nodded and motioned Rayce to a table near the fireplace. He poured a large mug of ale and brought it over to the table. "I'll go see to yer supper. My woman made a stew today, not much meat in it, I'm sorry to say, but it's tasty and fillin'. There's bread baked just this morning as well." He thumped the brimming mug on the table. "Ya look to have traveled far."

"Far enough," Rayce said without adding any particulars.

The old man grunted and turned away. He pushed through a door behind the bar into what Rayce assumed was the kitchen.

There was a clatter of dishes and the voice of a woman, who, by the sound of it, apparently felt the old fellow needed a good scolding for some transgression he had committed.

Rayce sampled the ale. It was good, as the innkeeper had said. He took another swallow and sighed. If the food lived up to the ale, he'd be satisfied. He listened to the altercation going on in the kitchen, and smiled as an equally wide older woman opened the kitchen door with a shove from her hip. She carried a large bowl and a plate with a round loaf of bread on it.

"Of course the old fool would give ya the ale without nary a bite of food in yer belly to soak it up. Here now, have some of the stew and bread before ya drink anymore."

She plunked the bowl of savory smelling stew, thick with vegetables and gravy, down on the table in front of him. She set the bread off to the side and pulled a spoon from her apron pocket.

"There, now. When ya finish that, there's more if ya want. It will take a bowl or two or three to fill up that long frame, and I've more in the pot."

She stood by the table, her red roughened hands on her hips to make sure Rayce ate before drinking anymore of the ale. When he broke off a chunk of the bread and dipped it in the bowl, she nodded in approval and turned to leave.

Rayce closed his eyes with pleasure at the taste of the rich, spicy stew.

"This is wonderful," he said around a mouthful. "Thank you."

"Huh, not just handsome, but polite, too. I dare say yer mother taught ya well." The woman pushed a strand of gray hair back in place behind her ear and smiled.

"She did indeed," Rayce said as he scooped up a spoonful of stew. "Have you and your husband eaten your evening meal yet? Why don't you come join me since there are no other guests at the moment?"

"Why, thank ye. We'd like that. Not many stop by here anymore, not like in the old days before our miners left. Be right back."

Rayce noted that the woman had said 'our' miners.

The innkeeper and his wife soon joined Rayce, and the three ate in companionable silence for a time. When Rayce emptied his bowl, it was quickly refilled.

Finally, hunger and thirst satisfied, Rayce leaned back in his chair with the last of his ale in hand.

"Ya one of them?" the old man asked as he brushed bread crumbs from his beard. He gave Rayce a penetrating look before reaching for his mug of ale.

"One of which?"

"Ya don't look like an Arlander," the woman said. "Yer one of us." She gave an approving nod. "Yes."

"How long have you been here, in the inn?"

"My pa built the inn," the innkeeper said. "I grew up helpin' him and my ma run the place. We was always busy then, day and night. Miners come by after their shifts in the mine. Sometimes they'd bring their women in for a cordial mug or two of ale, and the place would be filled to bustin'. There'd be music, fiddles and pipes, and singin', always singin'. Lots of people passin' through, too, goin' from the High Champaign to the west side of the mountains." He gave a deep sigh. "Ain't no more of that nowadays. Them Arlanders don't have the coin or the time to come here," he said sadly. "I do miss the old days, I surely do."

"Why do you stay?" Rayce asked softly.

"Where else would we go?" the woman responded. "We didn't leave it when the black robes come through and threatened to burn us down; we stayed when everybody else left. I guess we'll stay a little longer. We're old now, too old to start some place new," she said with downcast eyes.

Rayce set his empty mug on the table, and when the old man moved to pick it up and refill it, Rayce shook his head.

"When I stopped at the market earlier, a young girl asked me if I was going to join Dellay's army. What can you tell me about him and this army of his?"

"Faw," the woman spat. "He's an Arlander, been causin' trouble here for years. Thinks he's going to take this riffraff bunch he's roundin' up and train 'em to be real soldiers. He's got his eye set on what's west of the mountains. Only thing is, he doesn't know the first thing about leadin' an army. He's real good, though, at causin' trouble, and that's what he mostly does, cause trouble."

"Ya thinkin' about joinin' him, are ya?" the old man half rose out of his chair, angry now to think that Rayce might not be what he appeared.

Rayce raised his hands in a placating manner. "No, definitely not," he assured the two. He turned to the woman, gave her a long look, and finally nodded, as if he'd come to a decision. "You asked if I was an Arlander. I was born and raised on Lorn Isle off the coast of Kaenolir. My father is a Timisian, my mother a Kaenolirian.

"Lorn Isle?" the old man asked quizzically. And then he sucked in his breath in surprise. "Yer father, lad, is he by chance Camron Thorpe?"

At Rayce's nod, the old man began to laugh. He laughed until tears ran down his cheeks, clapping his hands together in a paroxysm of joy. His wife looked at him in wonder. "What?" she cried. "What are ya laughin' like a crazy man for?" She reached out and gave his shoulder a shake.

"Dragon rider," he wheezed. "This boy's pa is one of them dragon riders who killed Finton." And he laughed some more.

The woman turned to Rayce, her eyes wide with wonder.

"I knew you wasn't one of them Arlanders," she said with a decisive nod of her head. "I just knew." She turned back to her husband, who had finally stopped laughing and was wiping his cheeks with the back of his hands.

"Now then," she turned again to Rayce. "Yer not just travelin' through this forsaken place for the fun of it."

Rayce gave the old pair another long look before replying.

"I'm looking for a man. He's tall, dark hair and beard, walks with a slight limp. He may be with the men who are with Dellay in the High Champaign, the black robes. The man I'm looking for is their leader. He may or may not be wearing a black robe." Rayce paused and looked from one to the other. "It's very important that I find him. He has something that may put all of Timis in danger, maybe Kaenolir, too."

"Danger?" the old man asked. "Like the Warders again?"

"Yes, like that again," Rayce said. "Have you seen him?"

Both the innkeeper and his wife shook their heads.

"We saw the black robes come through here with Dellay, but if there was one of them who was their leader, he didn't stand out as such. They didn't stay here, just passed through. On their way to the camp Dellay has north of Malhain Village. From all accounts, he's trainin' his army there. He's a mean one, that Dellay. Stay clear of him," the innkeeper warned. "Another thing. We heard that Malhain Pass is completely blocked now. There was an earthquake folks are sayin', though we didn't feel nothin' much but a bit of shakin'. Thought it was something they was doin' at the mine. So most like it was avalanche that blocked the pass. The chieftain needs to know that, I'd say."

"Dellay will have to go through Cragon Pass then. That's good to know."

Rayce sat forward in his chair. "Now," he said quietly. "I must extract a pledge from you. Tell no one that I was your guest here at the inn. It will be dangerous for you and for me."

The couple turned to each other and nodded. When they turned back to Rayce, the man said, "Ya have our pledge."

"Good." He looked at the two people who'd spent their lives in this village, most of those years right here in this inn. "I would like to know under whose roof I'll sleep tonight."

The woman smiled. "I'm Maeve," she said. "This old fool next to me is Owen."

"Well, then, Maeve and Owen, I thank you for this fine supper and your companionship. I would take that bed if you'd be so kind as to point me in the right direction."

Owen nodded and picked up a candle from one of the other tables. "This way," he said as he lumbered across the room and up the stairs.

Rayce pulled his shirt and tunic over his head, sat on the bed to pull off his boots before standing to shuck his trousers. With a yawn, he stretched out on the narrow but surprisingly comfortable bed. He pulled the covers up over his chest, then reached over to the small bedside table to snuff out the candle. A window on the other side of the room offered only a dim light in the dark. He sighed, closed his eyes, and was asleep almost immediately.

How long he had been asleep he did not know, but the dream was there, just on the edge of his consciousness.

Caretaker.

Mist coiled and swirled in a dizzying pattern, allowing the dreamer only a glimpse at what it hid. But he knew who called, knew whose voice he heard waking and sleeping.

"I'm here, Far'lin."

You must seek elsewhere.

"I know, but where? No one I've talked with remembers Gadred Aember."

He is not the one you seek. Another took the token.

"Who? Who has the dragon token?"

He wore a black robe, but no more. Time grows short.

And then, *Another Caretaker will know.*

The silver/black dragon slipped away into the mist of his dream. As the swirling mist parted again, two figures came toward him. He heard KaynaRee's voice and saw her emerge from the mists for a brief moment. The other figure came to stand beside Ree and Rayce recognized Cass Vance, but he soon turned away and Ree stood alone.

He heard Ree say, *"We must hurry, Rayce. The Arlanders are coming. Timis needs us. We must find the token. It's not here. We must look elsewhere. There isn't much time."*

The dream changed yet again. Rayce saw a man with a heavy pack climbing up out of the Warders' valley. The hood of his cloak was pulled low over his forehead, hiding his face from scrutiny. Was this man the one who had the dragon token? But who was he? One of the Warders, but which one? He didn't appear to be Gadred Aember. Aember was taller, bigger. And Far'Lin said 'another' had the token.

Maybe Conn Regan? Wasn't he the one Orly had told his father about? Regan was something of a right-hand man for Aember, if what Orly said was indeed the case.

And where would he go, this other Warder? Where was Aember?

Malhain Pass was blocked. Did that mean that So'Kol's cave was no longer accessible? Would either Aember or Regan have known about the cave's location?

Maybe. If they knew the events leading up to Finton's death and the destruction of Dunadd. And they surely would have since they had been part of Finton's army of Warders.

Hurry, Caretaker. Hurry.

"But where do I go? Show me where to go."

Rayce slipped in and out of sleep and dreams until finally, he came fully awake. The window on the other side of the room was bright with early morning light, and gratefully he rose from his restless bed. A pitcher and basin stood on a chest under the window, and Rayce washed his face and hands and dried them on the thin towel lying alongside the basin. When he had once more donned his clothes, he left the room.

"There ya are," Owen said as Rayce came down the stairs. "Hot tea and oat cakes. More comin'." He nodded his head toward the table Rayce had shared with him and Maeve for last night's supper.

"You are a mind reader, Owen." Rayce smiled as he dropped his pack and cloak beside the table and took the proffered chair.

The tea was hot and the oat cakes just out of the oven. He looked up to see Maeve coming through the kitchen door with more cakes and a small pot of honey.

"What ya don't eat now," she said cheerfully, "take with ya."

Rayce laughed as the round woman set the plate and honey before him.

"I dare not stay here long," he grinned at her, "or I would be the same size as Owen there."

Maeve answered his grin with one of her own and a wink. She turned to bustle back to the kitchen and left Rayce to finish his meal. When he had eaten his fill and drunk the last swallow of tea, he pushed back his chair and stood. He fished in his pocket for more coins and placed them on the table beside his empty plate.

"I don't know where yer headed now, young Thorpe, but we heard this mornin' that they got a furnace over at Blairtown up and runnin'. They're diggin' up more gold every day and now they've got the wherewithal to smelt it. Dellay is promisin' gold to anyone who will join him, and that means just about every able-bodied man or boy, or woman for that matter, in this part of Timis, the Arlanders, that is. The chieftain needs to know that we heard Dellay is gettin' set to send raidin' parties across the mountains, just as soon as the snow melts in the pass. Timthurlen is probably in the line of fire, wouldn't ya say? It'll be soon now that the weather is warmin' up."

Maeve came in from the kitchen with the remaining oat cakes wrapped in a soft cloth. She had another packet for him, too, and a full water flask. She laid them on the bar and smiled at him.

"Ya've brought some light back into this dark ol' place, Rayce Thorpe. We thank ya for that. If the Ancient Ones are kind, we'll meet again one day." She reached out and gently touched his hand, then turned and quickly disappeared through the kitchen door.

"Aye, the old woman speaks true," Owen murmured.

Rayce nodded. "Keep yourself safe, you and Maeve." He took the food Maeve had given him and stooped to place it in his pouch. He stood and pulled on his cloak, then swung his pack up on his back. He settled it into a comfortable position and turned away. At the door, he turned back to see that Maeve had joined Owen behind the bar. He lifted his hand in farewell and stepped out into the sunshine.

"May the Ancient Ones look after ye, young Thorpe," Owen whispered.

"Be safe," Maeve murmured. She gave Owen's arm a squeeze and returned to the kitchen. There she could wipe away her tears without Owen seeing them.

Rayce had a decision to make: continue north toward Malhain or west to Camlanrein. He left the inn and started across the village square. The merchants were already setting up their stalls and he spotted the same ragged man squatting beside a basket of clams.

"Probably the same ones he had yesterday," Rayce mused and moved on.

He had nearly crossed the square when he saw a familiar figure coming toward him from one of the lanes leading into the square. The figure stopped for a moment, taking in the activity around her, before spotting Rayce.

Rayce grinned and waited for his sister to come to him.

"There you are," KaynaRee said. "I've been looking for you."

"And now you've found me."

They gave each other a quick hug.

Rayce looked over Ree's shoulder. "Where's Cass?"

"If he follows his plan, he's gone to scout out the camp the Arlander, Kelan Dellay, has set up near Malhain Village. Dellay is the fellow. . ."

"I know who Dellay is, Ree, and I know why you've come to find me."

"The token, Rayce. We haven't much time."

"I know. Come, we can talk as we walk."

They walked down a lane leading away from the square and eventually out of the village.

"We must look elsewhere. It's not where we thought it would be, and the one I thought had it doesn't have it now. Someone else does."

Another Caretaker will know.

Rayce heard the words again. He stopped and turned to Ree.

"Do you know where the token is, Ree?"

"It's not here, Rayce. We must go back."

"Back?"

"Yes. Back to Camlanrein. We'll find it there."

The dream had been more vivid than any dream she'd had since leaving the Singers' Hall. Even as she remembered what the dream had revealed, she could feel the urgency, the fear that the dream projected.

"Cass and I set out from Ross Harbor in the *Highland Guardian*. We sailed to Timthurlen and left for the mountains from there. He thought you'd be somewhere near Cragon Pass, since that's where he'd parted from you and father. We rode to a farm in the foothills where we left the horses. Cass knows the farmer and his family and has stopped there often. They told us they'd heard from two other travelers that Malhain Pass is blocked, that there is no way through the northern Dalrudds. They'd heard, too, that Dellay is forming an army and training it north of Malhain Village. Cass said as soon as we found you, he was going to check out the camp and get back to Camlanrein as quickly as he could.

"We planned to avoid Cragon Pass and the mine and come down into Banning Village from the mountains. If you had come through the village, Cass thought someone would have seen you and remembered you. Then we'd head north. But I told him I wouldn't be going into the High Champaign with him, told him I knew I would find you here in Banning. He was not pleased to let me go off alone, but he also felt he needed to ferret out as much information as he could about Dellay and this training camp.

"We camped in the hills not far from Banning last night. It had been a rough climb down out of the mountains, and I was tired and cold. Cass got a fire going and we had hot tea to warm us a bit, but Cass was worried about someone seeing the fire and put it out.

"The dreams began almost as soon as I went to sleep. Or maybe I didn't really sleep, I don't know. I'd never experienced the dreams like this before.

"She came to me, my beautiful Ja'Anee. She was so very real I could reach out and touch her, feel the heat of her fire. She took me to a place I've never been. Not like the Horn of Kalora, not like the Singers' Hall, a place of rough, round stones set in a circle. Tall grass shifted as the wind blew through it, and as I walked through the grass, I could hear the sea. An eagle cried as it soared above me. But it was also peacefully quiet, as if this place were just there, waiting.

"Ja'Anee led me to a large stone in the middle of the circle. It stood upright among the round stones. And it was carved in the shape of a dragon.

"Bring the token here, Ja'Anee said, here to the Caretaker's Circle. Here the evil it possesses will be destroyed. Here the fire beasts will be remembered by all the Caretakers who come after.

"She told me then of the one who possesses the token. He is a 'black robe,' she said. Though he has put aside the robe, his heart is still that of one who would bring evil to this ancient land. He comes, Ja'Anee said, across the mountains to the sea. He comes soon.

"The token somehow contains the essence of the fire beasts. That is how the black robe will find them. He will use the dark power of the token, the power that comes from the Abyss, the power Finton used in his quest to take Timis and Kaenolir, to force the fire beasts to obey him. But he needs to find the dragons. Once he has the dragons, the evil becomes the dominant power.

"Then, Rayce, she told me another Caretaker waited for me, that together we would find the token, but we must hurry.

"When I woke up, it was still dark and still cold. Oddly enough I felt warm. I had been so cold when I lay down to sleep. Then I realized why I felt warm: I lay with my back against a warm body." She gave Rayce a little grin.

"Torar lay against me," she said, "keeping me warm. I knew then I had to leave Cass behind and get to Banning Village, that I'd find you here."

The two walked in silence for some time before Rayce stopped and turned to Ree.

"The place in your dream, Ree, is the Caretaker's Circle, the place where we are to take the token when we recover it. I met mother there. She'd gone to the circle to call her dragons. And you're right; it is a very peaceful place. It has been a sacred place for a very long time."

Rayce told her then of his dream and that he'd been shown a man leaving the Warders' valley.

"I don't think the man was the leader of the Warders that father and I saw. I think the Warder we're looking for is Conn Regan."

"Cass told me about how the two of you found father and about the Warders. By the way, father should have returned to Camlanrein a few days ago."

Rayce nodded his head. "He and mother will have their hands full." He looked away toward the mountains. "We're nearly to the pass. I'd like to get through it in daylight if we can, but I'd also like to avoid other travelers."

Deep snow still covered much of the track through Cragon Pass, making the trek especially difficult in some places. Sunset found the Caretakers slogging through a stretch of snow that had begun to melt.

"This part," Ree said, breathing with the exertion, "is the worst part."

With each step they took, they sank into wet, knee-deep snow that made every step an effort.

"How much farther?" Rayce muttered.

"Not far now. Just about through this."

They stopped to rest when they reached firmer ground. It had grown dark while they traversed the last part of the melting snow. Rayce opened his food pouch and handed Ree an oat cake. "More where that came from." They munched in silence for a moment. "I'd like to get down into the hills a ways before we stop for the night." He finished his cake and handed Ree a second one and took another for himself.

"How far to the farm, Ree?"

"We left the farm about midday and camped overnight. We reached the pass the next day about midmorning." She brushed the crumbs from her fingers. "These are really good. Got any more?"

Rayce opened his food pouch and as he handed Ree another cake, a dark form stepped up behind Ree.

"Well, hello. We have a guest, Ree," he said. He nodded his head toward Ree.

She turned and saw Torar come to stand beside her. She leaned her head against his flank and sighed. It was a moment before she realized there was another wolf beside Torar.

"Rayce?"

Rayce smiled. "We have two guests, it seems. This is Jagar, Ree. He was with me on Cathorn."

"Ah," she murmured. "We each have a guardian then."

"Well," Rayce said as he put the food pouch away. He rose and offered a hand to Ree. "Let's go. The wolves will show us the way."

The River Roon rushed in spring frenzy down out of the Dalrudd Mountains, carrying logs, rocks, chunks of ice, and anything else that fell into the water. Since leaving Ree near Banning Village, Cass Vance had kept to the foothills. He'd tried to argue with her that they could find Rayce and learn more about Dellay's camp at Malhain.

"Obviously," he thought, "I lost that argument."

But somehow, he felt Ree would find Rayce in Banning; she had been so certain she would that he had to trust her judgment. What was it about the Thorpes and Fairchilds? He shook his head in puzzlement.

He followed the wild river east for several miles, aiming to cross the Roon where it narrowed enough for a bridge to span the water.

"Huh," he muttered. "Hope the darn thing is still there."

He'd not been over this route for a year or two. If the bridge, which had begun to show its age, had given in to the weight of time and hard usage, he had a long way to go to find a place to cross the river: either back higher into the mountains where it had its beginning in the snow and ice of the peaks, or all the way down to the coast where it emptied into the sea. Either way would take time, time he felt he did not have. He needed to find out what Dellay was up to, needed to learn, if he could, when the Arlanders planned to begin their assault on western Timis.

Time. How much time did the Timisians have before they were once again in the middle of a fight for their lives?

Cass trudged on, keeping alert for other travelers. This was not a well-traveled route since the sea and Balagorn Channel were much more expeditious in getting people and goods from the High Champaign to the mining area. He reached the bridge by late afternoon and was relieved to see it still stood. It creaked and groaned as he hurried across, the water below him eating away at the banks that constrained it. It seemed doubtful the bridge supports could stand much more abuse.

"Glad I got here when I did," he thought.

Ahead of him lay the high plain's expanse. Malhain Village was still a half-day's journey or more away. He thought of Eithne, but knew that he dare not impose on her again— Dellay was too close. Deserted cottages stood here and there on the outskirts of the village, but perhaps they, too, were now occupied by members of Dellay's army.

There was no choice but to make a cold camp, and he veered back toward the foothills. The hills offered the best place to stay out of sight and also a vantage point to watch the action in Dellay's camp.

By nightfall he had gained the lower hills. He continued on until it was too dark to see before he found a place where low bushes grew among fair sized rocks. Here he would be out of sight and have some protection from the wind. After pushing his way through a copse of evergreen shrubs, he settled down with his back against a tall, smooth stone, pulled out his food pouch and water flask and ate a cold, solitary supper.

A full, yellowish moon rose up above the plain, casting shadows among the hills. Wind whistled, somewhat mournfully he thought, through the stones that sheltered him. He soon heard the calls of night hawks, hunting the small prey that lived in these hills. There would be owls on the hunt, too, he knew.

He remembered another time when he wandered this way down out of the mountains. There were many stones scattered throughout this section of the foothills with strange markings on them, pictures of large birds in flight, probably eagles or buzzards who lived and hunted in the hills and mountains. Deer with tails raised in danger, bull elk with massive racks pitted against each other in combat, smaller creatures, like badgers and weasels.

But then he recalled one particular stone that stood by itself, tall and imposing, a silent sentinel, almost as if it had been carefully placed on top of the hill. On this stone, furled in full and glorious flight, was a fire beast, a fire beast breathing fire.

Cass shook his head. He'd not thought of that stone in a long time. He wondered why he remembered it now.

He sighed and pulled his cloak closer about his shoulders, pulled his hood down over his forehead, leaned his head back against the hard stone, and fell asleep.

Dellay's camp, on the plain to the north beyond Malhain Village, stretched for more than a mile in all directions. There were tents set up, fires burning, and men milling about, eating and drinking, preparing for the day.

"Sheevers," Cass breathed when it had grown light enough for him to see the camp in its entirety.

How many men were down there? Several hundred at least. Perhaps a thousand or more.

Men on horseback—Where had Dellay procured that many horses?—began to advance, broke ranks and circled, all the while slashing downward with swords or driving with spears. There were many circles of men with swords and what Cass supposed were axes, though he could not be certain at this distance. They fought each other, forcing one another back or down until the opponent yielded. Then they formed another circle and did it again. And again.

In other circles, men used pikes, others used fighting staffs, driving each other back until at a command, they stepped back, only to begin again with a different weapon.

Cass even saw women wielding pitchforks and clubs.

The cacophonous roar of shouting men, the clash of weapons, the thunder of hooves—they were the sounds of battle, and Cass shuddered, lowered his head and closed his eyes for a moment. From what he could determine, this was an army, an army who had used the winter to become an army that was battle ready.

He slithered back away from his vantage point and staying low ran as fast as he could. When he felt he would not be seen, he straightened and kept running at a steady, ground-covering pace. There was a trail that snaked through the mountains, a trail his brother had used to lead the miners and their families away from Banning Village. He had used it on a few occasions, but not this time of the year. It was not an easy trek but it would get him back to Camlanrein more quickly than going south to Cragon Pass.

Snow still covered the trail in long stretches, but the drifts were not as deep as in Cragon Pass. In many spots the snow had already melted and left behind muddy puddles. Cass stopped counting the number of times he slipped and fell. He was wet and cold, bruised and battered; but he kept going. He had to get to Camlanrein.

He stopped only briefly to eat and rest before moving on again. He paused to fill his water flask at a stream and kept going. By nightfall he had nearly reached the summit of the trail. When it was too dark to see, he stopped, ate and slept for a few hours. When there was just barely enough light to see his way, he started out again. He reached the summit soon after sunrise and began to wend his way down

He came out of the mountains just to the north of the River Somlech. A friend still lived on a farm at the foot of low lying hills along the river. There would be food there, he knew, and a place to rest for a few hours, before asking the favor of a horse to take him to Camlanrein.

The Arlanders were coming. May the Ancient Ones have mercy. The Arlanders were coming.

He took the stairs two at a time and raced down the hall to the chieftain's office. He burst through the door before the startled Trooper could open it and announce him. Camron, Kitra, Rayce and Ree looked up at the commotion to find a dirty and tattered Cass Vance. He had stopped at his friend's farm to borrow a horse; his information was too important to take time to rest or eat. Both he and the horse were ready to collapse when they clattered over the River Bray bridge and entered the courtyard of Camlanrein.

"They're coming, my lord. They're coming. Several hundred. With horses and weapons." He paused to catch his breath. "And they know how to use them."

Camron was the first to jump up. "Sweet merciful gods, Cass, what did you find?"

chapter eighteen

The shadows of night slipped away with the rising sun. The hidden valley, freed at last of its winter snow and cold, was alive with the evidence of spring. Life burgeoned and bloomed, sang and flowed.

A beam of sunlight flashed on the window of the chamber at the end of the long low building in the hidden valley and illuminated the figure on the bed. As the sun warmed him, his eyes fluttered; his chest heaved; he drew in a deep breath and slowly expelled it. Then another and another.

Gadred Aember awoke from his winter sleep.

His eyes opened to take in his surroundings. For a long time he lay quietly gathering his strength. Slowly, the torpor of many weeks began to dissipate, and he rolled to the edge of the narrow bed. With careful, studied movements he sat up and rested until the sudden dizziness caused by his movement eased. Then he pushed himself upright and stood for several minutes, gradually regaining his balance, feeling his blood surging throughout his body, feeling his strength returning. He reached up with both hands and pushed his hair back from his face. He looked down at his soiled garments and grimaced with distaste.

He walked somewhat unsteadily toward his chamber door, opened it and walked out of the foul-smelling room. He passed through the dormitory and the common room and left the hall through the back door. Once outside he went to the well and drew up a pail of water. After removing his soiled robe, undergarments and trousers, he began to wash himself. He drew pail after pail of fresh water from the well and scrubbed until he was clean. Aember stooped to pick up the pile of clothing, extracting the chain of gold links.

The pouch containing the dragon token was gone from his neck. Perhaps that is what had finally awakened him. He also knew that Conn Regan was no longer in the valley and that it was Regan who had taken the token while he slept through the last weeks of winter, gathering strength for the conquest of Timis.

A cruel smile creased his mouth as he walked naked back into the hall. He tossed the soiled clothing near the back door. Once more in his chamber, he took fresh clothes from the chest at the end of his bed, dressed in trousers, shirt and tunic. He also removed a sword with an intricately carved hilt, a sheathed knife, and a heavy leather belt. After dressing he secured the gold chain around his waist under his tunic before buckling on the sword and slipping the knife into a pocket of his trousers. Next he turned to the table beneath the window where he'd left the maps that Conn Regan had drawn. Aember folded them carefully, placed them in an inner pocket of his tunic, looked around the room, then left the chamber.

He found a pack in the larder and filled it with the last of the dried fruit and meat. There wasn't much left on the shelves, but then he didn't require much food. Back at the well he filled a water flask before entering the hall once more. He took a cloak from a hook by the front door, opened the door and set his pack and cloak on the front step. Inside the hall, he removed a lantern from its stand near the fireplace and set it by the front door. He took the small barrel of oil that sat next to the stand and began to move through the hall, room by room, sprinkling the oil on furniture, splashing it on the walls and floors until the barrel was empty. He walked to the front door, struck a flint and lit the lantern, turned and tossed it into the hall.

For a moment a small flame seemed to float over the broken lantern until the single flame became fingers of fire spreading out over the floor. With a whoosh, the common room erupted in flames. Aember stooped to pick up his cloak and pack and hastily moved away. From a safe distance he watched fire shoot high into the morning sky, black smoke billowing and swirling among the red flames. When he was assured that the entire building was burning, he turned away.

He looked back only once to see the thatched roof of the hall collapse and heard the roar of the fire as it devoured the old building. He grunted with satisfaction, wheeled about and left the Warders' Valley behind.

Conn Regan, hood pulled low over his forehead, moved through the crowded streets of Timthurlen, furtively searching for familiar faces. When he encountered a fellow Warder, he made himself known and together they continued through the busy streets.

"What are you doing here, Conn?" Jaston Sonne asked quietly. "Did Lord Aember send you here?"

"You might say I'm merely passing through on my way to Ross Harbor, Jaston. Are there other brothers here?"

"There are three of us in Timthurlen, including me. Three in Ross Harbor last I knew. Lord Aember sent us west to learn what Thorpe was doing to prepare his people for whatever Dellay decided to do. We were also charged with organizing the Arlanders and planning raids in both cities. We were to cause as much trouble as we could. If people are frightened they want to run, not stand and fight. How is Thorpe going to deal with that?"

Regan nodded. "Where can we find the other two here with you?"

"We meet every night after it gets dark in one of the taverns down by the docks. It's off the beaten path and few go there. Nobody asks your business or wants to know your name."

"Good. Let's go there now. I need to talk to you. And I could use something to eat."

The tavern was tucked away at the end of a dark alley between two weather-beaten buildings. The alley stunk of rotting fish, decaying refuse, and excrement. A rat scurried ahead of the two men before it disappeared into a pile of garbage.

"No wonder few go here," Regan muttered.

Beside him, Sonne merely grunted.

They took a table in a dark corner of the tavern where they could observe the dimly lighted room. One man stood behind the scuffed bar watching them. Two other men leaned against the bar, drinking silently and paying them no mind.

A slovenly woman of indistinguishable age slouched over to them.

"Waddya want?" she muttered.

"Anything safe to eat in this place?" Regan asked.

The woman snorted. "There's stew. Made it meself. Bread fresh yesterday.

Regan grimaced. "We'll have stew and bread. Bring us a pitcher of ale."

The woman turned and slouched back to the bar to get the ale and two mugs. She thumped them on the table in front of

Regan. "I'll bring the stew in a minute. Ya got coin to pay for this?"

Regan dug in a pocket of his tunic and slapped a coin on the table.

"Two more for the stew," the woman muttered as she scooped up the coin, but waited for Regan to give her the extra for the stew.

"Bring the food and you'll get the coins," Regan said, his voice edged with irritation.

The woman harrumphed and left the men to their ale.

"How did you find this place?" Regan asked Sonne.

His companion merely laughed and poured each of them a mug of ale. "Like I said, Conn, few come here and nobody's interested in who you are or what you're doing here."

For two more coins, steaming bowls of a thick stew were plunked on the table. A loaf of rather stale bread was added to the meal and the woman disappeared through a door behind the bar.

The stew was actually quite tasty and the two Warders ate their fill before pushing the bowls aside and refilling their mugs.

"Now, then, Conn, what are you doing in Timthurlen?" Sonne asked, his voice pitched low.

"As I said, I'm on my way to Ross Harbor." He sat contemplating his mug of ale for several moments. How much should he tell Jaston Sonne? How much did he want the other Warders to know? Most of it, he decided, or they might not be able to accomplish what he had in mind.

Regan set his mug aside and slipped the pouch from under his shirt. He leaned forward, clasping Aember's treasure, now his treasure, in his hands.

"Gadred Aember is dead, Jaston. The dragon token is ours, as it should have been from the day I found it." He opened the pouch just enough for Sonne to see the tip of gold and granite treasure he'd found buried in the sand along the Balagorn Channel. "The seven of us here in western Timis are going to use it to bring the dragons to us."

Sonne's eyes grew large as he took in the token and what Regan had just said. "Sheevers, Conn, how will we do that?" he finally breathed.

"Here's how, Jaston."

"We need to be even more careful than we've been in the past. Camron Thorpe knows the Arlanders are on their way. There are more joining Dellay all the time, from what we hear. We know many of the Arlanders who were here in Timthurlen have gone east. Do you have a rough estimate, Conn, of how many there are in Dellay's camp?"

"There were about four hundred, maybe a few more, when Aember and I went with him to the High Champaign camp he set up."

"From the gossip, many more than that now," Jaston Sonne replied. "I've heard seven, eight hundred. I've also heard a thousand or more." He shrugged.

As Conn Regan and the three Warder spies Aember had sent to Timthurlen made their way toward one of the few remaining ships tied up midway along the dock, Regan noted the activity along the waterfront. Warehouse and businesses were being boarded up; piles of sand with stacks of pails were ready to put out fires; barricades closed off streets leading away from the docks. Ships were being loaded with trade goods and sent out to sea for safety. Beyond the city, earthen bulwarks were being built, much as they had been when Finton threatened, using soil, logs, rocks. Troopers were much in evidence, directing traffic, helping people load carts, questioning men they thought looked suspicious, organizing patrols.

Timthurlen was a city preparing for an Arlander attack, an attack that would come crashing down on them out of Cragon Pass.

A Trooper suddenly called out a command to halt. "Where are you going?" he demanded of the four men.

"Sir," Regan stepped forward. "We are on our way to Ross Harbor with important information for Camlanrein. We're about to board that ship there," he gestured toward the large vessel where men were hurrying up and down the two gangplanks, loading the last of the goods from a nearby warehouse."

"I don't think I've seen you around here before."

"No, we've just come through the pass. We've been watching what's happening on the High Champaign. The chieftain needs our reports as soon as possible. That's the last ship," he pointed to the ship in question, "bound for Ross Harbor. It will be faster by sea than by horseback."

"All right," the harried Trooper motioned them on. "On your way then." He hurried away when someone called his name, either satisfied with their answer or with no means to check the accuracy of it.

Within minutes the Warders were on board the ship, helping to stow the bundles and crates headed for Ross Harbor. The story told to the Trooper had also been told to the captain of the ship, but a few gold coins had helped to insure their passage from Timthurlen. If the wind and weather held, the ship would reach its destination within two or three days.

From Ross Harbor they had but to cross the River Bray to reach Camlanrein.

A tall dark figure briefly perused a map before returning it to an inner pocket in his tunic. Cragon Pass lay behind him, Timthurlen to the west. He was not, however, going to that city. Conn Regan would not be found there but in Ross Harbor, and his dragon token would be found wherever Regan was. With a mile-eating stride Gadred Aember set off on a course that would bypass Lake Lech and take him cross country to Ross Harbor.

"Clever of you, Conn Regan," he mused as he walked. "Clever of you to take the token while I slept. And clever to think the way to the dragons lay through Camlanrein. At least that is what I assume you deduced." He smiled, more grimace than smile. "I'm sorry I didn't think of it first," he muttered. "But, never mind, I've thought of it now, and I know where to find you. And the dragons."

chapter nineteen

Camron Thorpe buckled on his long sword, slipped a knife into the sheath in his boot and picked up his saddle bags. He turned toward the door of his office as Kitra entered.

"The Troopers are ready and waiting," she said quietly as she came to stand by him.

Camron nodded and set his bags aside. He held out his arms and Kitra stepped into his embrace.

"I'm sorry to leave you here, but you and Donan and the rest of the officials know what needs to be done," he said, his face pressed against her hair. "Cass will remain with you and give you a hand wherever you need him."

She gave him one last hard hug and then stepped back. "I know. The Arlanders are nearly to the pass and you're needed in Timthurlen."

"You should be hearing from Loren Lamond within a few days. The courier to Kaenolir left five days ago."

Camron picked up his bags again and together they left the chieftain's office.

In the courtyard of Camlanrein the Troopers going with Camron waited, ready to mount up. Camron strapped on his saddle bags and swung into the saddle, and the Troopers, some twenty-five of them, followed suit. With a last look and a salute to Kitra, the Troopers set out with Camron in the lead. Several volunteers brought up the rear of the column, leading extra horses. The march to Timthurlen was to be swift, allowing only a few short rest stops to eat and exchange mounts. As the sun rose over the Dalrudds, the men clattered across the bridge and through the streets of Ross Harbor. Once beyond the city, Camron set a grueling pace.

From the shadows of a cluster of trees just off the road, a man watched the Troopers go by. He smiled with satisfaction and waited for the last horseman to pass by before leaving his hiding place. Camron Thorpe was leaving, taking the majority of the Troopers who patrolled the area with him; and Kitra Fairchild was still at Camlanrein.

He couldn't have planned it better himself.

KaynaRee and Rayce met their mother in the chieftain's office to share the evening meal and details of the day's events.

"He's here. I'm sure of it," Ree said again in answer to her mother's question concerning the Warder who had the dragon token. "Rayce and I searched everywhere that we thought he might be. He may have changed his appearance since coming here, but something will tell us when we've found him. We're going out again tonight."

Kitra shook her head, her forehead furrowed in worry. "I don't like the idea of the two of you out late in the city. There have been several arrests lately of thugs and hooligans who prefer the night for their mischief."

"We'll be fine, Mother. Torar and Jagar are always close by."

Rayce had been silent throughout the meal and the conversation between his mother and sister. He sat back with a mug of ale, lost in thought.

"Mother," he finally said. "Do you know if Desmond Orly ever contacted father?"

"No," Kitra shook her head. "I'm sure Camron would have told me if Orly had come to him. Why do you ask about him?"

"Just a thought." He looked at Ree and then back at his mother. "Maybe we need to be looking for Orly as well as Conn Regan."

"But, Rayce, you said. . ."

"I know what I said," Rayce interrupted Ree. "But think about it for a moment: Orly was a member of the Warders for many years, going back to Finton. He knows all the Warders who lived at the hall. Father told him to make his way here from Timthurlen. He may have stayed in Timthurlen for a time, or even in one of the smaller settlements in the outlying areas between the mountains and the coast."

"What are you suggesting?" Kitra asked.

"He knows there are Warders in western Timis, and according to Father he suggested to Orly that he would be safer if he wasn't seen by the brothers; he should just disappear. In that case, he may or may not come to Camlanrein, or if he is here, he's hesitant to come forward. Who knows where all the Warders are, or how many there are here in Ross Harbor? They could have infiltrated a number of places—businesses, homes of officials, maybe even here in Camlanrein itself."

"Do you think he's here, Rayce?"

"I don't know, Ree," he shrugged. "But somehow I have the feeling he is. Everything he told Father—about the location of the Warders' hall, about the escape tunnel, about Aember and Regan, about the spies Aember sent throughout Timis— seems to have been the truth." He paused for a moment before continuing with his line of thought. "I guess the point I'm coming to in a round-about way is that perhaps we should be looking for him, too."

"And if we find him, he could help us find the other Warders and Conn Regan," Ree said, nodding her head. "You may have a good idea, Rayce. "

"But a very dangerous one, Rayce, dangerous for you, for Ree, and certainly for Orly."

"I'm aware of that, Mother, but we're running out of time."

A knock on the door interrupted their conversation and Donan entered. "Cass Vance is here, my lady. There's more trouble in the city."

"We're ready whenever you say, Conn."

Darkness hid the men gathered in a burned out, disserted area of the harbor. Seven Warders and ten or so Arlanders, carrying torches ready to be lit, listened intently as he gave them their instructions.

"Remember, scatter throughout the streets above the harbor before you light the torches. We want fires going in several areas so that the Troopers will be spread thin. There aren't that many Troopers left here anyway. Once you've set a fire or two, don't stick around. If people try to stop you, run. Don't stay to fight. Get away and lay low until I contact you again." He looked around the group. "All right, let's go."

It took no more than a few minutes before there were several fires burning throughout Ross Harbor. Soon there were people running through the streets, shouting for help, calling out to each other. Water brigades were set up; sand was used to try to smother small blazes before they could begin to burn out of control. Two men seen setting a business afire were tackled and beaten into unconsciousness before being dragged off to the makeshift jail near the dock. Others were seen running away, but putting out the flames was more important than trying to stop the perpetrators.

Conn Regan ran down a narrow lane that wound through a congested warren of small, rough cottages. He tossed his torch onto the thatched roof of one building and knew that the flames would spread quickly from there. He ran until he came to one of the main thoroughfares, turned and headed toward a fire being fought at the intersection with another main street. He saw a lone Trooper coming toward him, running at full speed. As they were about to meet, Regan veered into the soldier, knocking him down. He was on him in a second, his knife at his throat.

"Come with me, or you are a dead man."

Regan pulled the Trooper roughly to his feet, keeping the knife pressed to his side, and took him down a dark alley that separated two buildings.

"Take off your uniform."

"What?"

"You heard me. Take your uniform off." Regan pressed the knife against the man's throat. "Throw it on the ground away from you. Your sword first."

"All right, all right," the frightened man said and hastened to comply.

When the uniform and sword were removed, Regan pushed the man deeper into the alley and with a vicious chop on his exposed neck knocked him to the ground. Regan didn't pause to see if the Trooper still breathed, but quickly stripped off his own clothes and donned the Trooper's. They were close in size and the uniform fit fairly well. He made sure the dragon token was still safely around his neck, slipped his knife into his boot, buckled on the soldier's sword, picked up his own clothes and stuffed them behind a dilapidated bin, and ran from the alley.

For several hours, Conn Regan kept on the move, down first one street and then another, moving ever closer to the bridge over the River Bray. He stopped now and then, keeping up the disguise of the Trooper—directing fire fighters, even sending other Troopers to places where they were needed—before slipping away again. As the sky began to brighten, he trotted into the courtyard of Camlanrein and saluted the Trooper on duty.

"I was told you needed me here as an extra guard for Lady Fairchild."

"Good. I'm by myself. The rest have gone into Ross Harbor to help fight fires. It looks like half the city is burning."

"Where do you want me?"

"Take this end of the bridge. No one comes into the courtyard without finding out who they are and what they want. By the way, what's your name?"

"Garrett. Coel Garrett. I've been patrolling the River Bray and was just sent here to Ross Harbor."

"All right. Go back to the bridge and don't be afraid to use that sword."

Regan, now Garrett, turned and dashed back to the bridge.

"It's bad, Lady Fairchild," Cass Vance said, wiping his smoke-stained face on the sleeve of his shirt. It didn't help much because his shirt was stained, too. "This time they set fires on streets away from the harbor. That section of cottages just above the harbor where most of the dock workers live? That whole section is on fire. Those cottages are packed tight in there and most have thatch roofs. Once the fire got started it was impossible to stop. I'm afraid we'll find many dead once we can get into the area."

Kitra pressed her fingers against her mouth and stepped to the open window to look across the river toward Ross Harbor. The sky above the city was colored with garish red-orange flames. She could hear shouts and screams of terror and the roar of fire.

She leaned her head tiredly against the window frame. Finally she turned to her children. "Find him. Find Conn Regan." she said. "This can't go on, but leave Camlanrein as unobtrusively as you can. I suggest you take a skiff from the landing and cross the river. We don't know who might be watching out there. But whoever they are, they know that Camron and many of the Troopers have left the city."

She turned to Cass. "Get what you need and go with Ree and Rayce. Another pair of eyes will be helpful. You saw the Warders, too, and can identify Conn Regan. Find him or anyone else you think might be a Warder. I want them locked up."

The three left Camlanrein by an underground passage, rarely used, that led from the lower level of the great hall to the river landing. Rayce remembered a visit to Timis when he was very young and Tiernan Irworth had taken him through the tunnel. It had been an adventure then.

"Not unlike the tunnel under the Warders' Hall," Rayce thought as he led the way through the passage with a lantern. His shadow flickered along the wall and their footsteps echoed as they hurried along the hard-packed floor. When they came to the door at the end of the passage, Rayce slid the latch back. The door clicked open, but before they stepped out he doused the lantern. One by one they slipped out of the door and hurried to the landing.

Three skiffs, Ree's *Highland Guardian,* and Rayce's *Dragon Keeper* bobbed at their mooring lines tied to cleats on the large landing. Cass took the smaller of the skiffs and Rayce and Ree took the larger one. The river's current was running fast and full with spring run-off from the Dalrudd Mountains, making the usually quick trip across the river particularly difficult. In the summer the boats' square sails could carry them leisurely down the river, but tonight the oars would be used.

Cass pushed off first, followed closely by the second skiff with Rayce at the oars. The current caught the boats quickly and sent them into the middle of the river. It took all the oarsmen's strength and nearly half an hour to defeat the swift current and reach the opposite shore.

Cass nosed his skiff into the bank and sat bent over the oars, waiting a few minutes to ease his quivering muscles and regain his breath. Rayce bumped his boat into the shore a short distance from Cass, and Ree jumped out to pull the boat up onto the bank. Like Cass, it took Rayce a few minutes before he had the strength and the breath to get himself out of the boat.

"These boats weren't meant for running the river," Rayce puffed.

"Better you, brother, manning the oars than me." Ree patted her sibling on the shoulder. "I might have wound up in the bay on my way out to sea."

They pulled the two skiffs as far as they could onto the shore, turned them over and stowed the oars under them.

"Which way, Cass, back up the river a ways and enter Ross Harbor well beyond the harbor? Or this way," Rayce gestured down river, "and come through the dock area?"

Cass looked around for a moment. "This time the fires were started away from the waterfront. If I had been one of the ones setting fires, and if I wasn't caught in the act, I'd hightail it to a place where there were no fires."

"In other words, you'd head for the docks. Lots of burned out buildings and lots of rebuilding going on down there. You'd have any number of places to hide," Ree said.

"Right."

"There would be places near the outskirts of the city, too," Rayce said. "But we're closer to the docks, so let's head that way first."

"I have one suggestion," Cass said, looking first at Ree and then at Rayce. "We should stick together. This is not an area to be poking around alone."

Ree smiled. "We'll not be alone, Cass, but I agree: I think we should stick together."

Cass gave her an oddly speculative look. "Huh," was all he said.

The three kept to the shadows, moving cautiously, stopping often to listen to the noises around them. The tide was coming in and slapped noisily against pilings and the few boats, mostly burned out hulks, still moored here. Acrid smoke burned their noses and stung their eyes. They heard men shouting, women screaming from time to time, and once Ree thought she heard a child crying for his mother. Flames seemed to be everywhere in the streets above the harbor.

"May the Ancient Ones help us," she thought.

Cass stopped suddenly, squatting down beside a partially constructed wall, and motioned to Ree and Rayce who were already moving into deeper shadows.

Two men came down a street, laughing and talking and passing a jug back and forth between them as they came. One of the men stumbled and fell to one knee, giggling drunkenly. The other man swore good-naturedly and leaned over to help his friend, nearly falling down in the process.

"Come on, you stupid clod," he said as he helped his companion to his feet. "We need to get to our li'l ol' hidey hole before Regan gets back."

"Yeah, yeah," the other man said and giggled again. "We shudda grabbed two jugs." He sloshed the contents of the jug he was holding. "This one ain't gonna last all night."

"Maybe that Warder will bring us a couple."

"Wonder if we'll see him again," the other mumbled. "Or the other ones for that matter."

After they had stumbled on out of sight, Cass stood up from his hiding place. Ree joined him moments later, but Rayce set out after the two drunken men.

"He wants to know where their gathering place is so we can tell the Troopers where to look."

The two waited in silence for several minutes. Finally Cass asked, "Should we continue to wait for Rayce, do you think?"

But as Cass asked the question, Rayce came into view.

"What did you find, Rayce?" Ree asked her brother.

"They're just down there, along this same alleyway, in a burned out warehouse. There's nothing else around it, so they picked a good hiding spot. While I watched a couple more showed up, all Arlanders."

"Do you think the Warders will be there, too?"

"Little love between the two groups," Cass said. "My thought is the Warders will be elsewhere."

"Let's keep moving," Rayce said quietly. "When we encounter Troopers, we'll tell them what we found."

The night was spent in a fruitless search, and when the sky began to brighten, the exhausted trio headed back the way they had come. They found the skiffs where they'd left them, pushed them back into the river, and began the arduous task of rowing back to the landing. The current carried them under the bridge, and they put in well below Camlanrein and the landing. They pulled the skiffs up onto the bank, tied them to a tree near the water's edge, and began the long hike back to the hall. Cass led the way through the trees that grew in a thick cover on the Camlanrein side of the river, through the gardens surrounding the back of the hall, and to the back door. A Trooper recognized the three and stepped aside to let them enter.

Donan, showing every year of his advanced age, met them at the head of the stairs.

"I finally convinced Lady Fairchild to get some rest. Cass, there is a chamber prepared for you, too. You know where it is." He gave Rayce and Ree a weary smile. "I assume you were not successful," he said.

"We didn't find any of the Warders," Rayce said as he rubbed a tired hand over his forehead. "Ree, Cass, I'm off to bed. Donan, you should retire, too." He gave the old man a nod, turned and headed toward his chamber.

"Donan," Ree said softly, "I'm going to stand here until you take yourself off to bed. Go."

The old man gave her one of the sweet smiles he reserved for the Ladies Fairchild, nodded and made his way down the stairs with slow, tired steps.

"You, too, Cass," she said.

"You don't have to tell me twice." He gave her a mock salute and followed Donan back down the stairs.

Rayce dropped his sword on the floor beside his bed, pulled off his clothes, and sat on the side of his bed. He leaned forward and rested his elbows on his knees, his head hanging in weariness. He needed a bath and something to eat, but he had the energy for neither.

Caretaker.

A glimmer of silver and black emerged and Rayce's dragon stood just there, at the edge of his sight, immense, powerful.

"We didn't find him, Far'Lin," Rayce whispered.

She will find him soon. Ja'Anee comes. Rest now. You are needed elsewhere. With your father.

"In Timthurlen."

Yes. Go to Dragon Head Point. I will take you to him.

The silver dragon with black wings turned his head and Rayce saw his own reflection in the glittering eye.

Call us with your Song. When all else fails.

The silver image slipped away and Rayce was left alone.

"When all else fails," Rayce murmured, stretched out, pulled up the coverlet, and drifted into dreamless sleep.

Too restless to sleep, her golden hair tousled from pushing her fingers through the strands, a robe hastily slipped on over her night dress, KaynaRee stood at the open window, watching the River Bray in its wild rush past Camlanrein. It would soon escape its banks and send flood waters into the sections of Ross Harbor not protected by earthen dikes. First fire, then flood. She sighed and would have turned away but for a brilliant red shimmer of color.

"Ja'Anee," she breathed as the shimmer became dragon.

Caretaker.

"I am here, Ja'Anee," she whispered.

Trust Torar. He knows where the black robe hides. In plain sight. When you call me with your Song, I will come.

When she looked again trying to catch a glimpse of Ja'Anee, she saw instead the silver wolf, looking up at her from below.

"Torar."

Come, Caretaker. We must go.

Rayce gave his mother one last hug and turned to find KaynaRee standing in the doorway. She came into the office as he stepped back from Kitra.

"You're leaving."

"Yes. To join father. I was coming to tell you goodbye. Far'Lin said you will find the one who has the dragon token soon."

"I know. He's hiding in plain sight."

"Do you know what that means, Ree?" Kitra asked quietly.

"I'm to trust Torar, Mother. So that is what I will do."

Rayce stooped to pick up his pack and the fur lined cloak, hat and gloves his mother had found for him. "It's time for me to go," he said quietly. "I'll find Far'Lin at Dragon Head Point." He smiled at Kitra, then looked long into Ree's eyes before leaving the chieftain's office.

"May the Ancient Ones go with you, Rayce. Go with you both," Kitra murmured as Ree stepped up beside her mother. Kitra reached up to touch her daughter's cheek. Ree smiled and laid her palm against her mother's hand. They stood so for a moment before Ree stepped back. She gave her mother one last smile and left the room.

"Kailie," Kitra whispered, "be with her. Watch over her."

The Trooper saluted Rayce as he rode over the bridge and took the road that led away from the still-smoldering city. The Trooper had been there all night and now through much of the day. He was growing weary, weary of standing in one spot for hours and weary of his Trooper disguise. Perhaps that was why he did not see the man who stood in deep shadow on the opposite side of the river.

The sight of the Trooper had made the man stop to look more carefully at the guard at the other end of the bridge more carefully. There was something familiar about him, even though the uniform and the cap proclaimed him to be a soldier. The man watched for several minutes, saw Rayce ride across the bridge, saw the Trooper salute the rider. He watched until he saw the Trooper leave his post and head over the bridge, watched until the Trooper disappeared down the street leading into the city.

The man nodded. The distinctive walk confirmed it: Conn Regan was here in Ross Harbor, nearly on the doorstep of Camlanrein. He set off after the Trooper, staying well back, ducking into shadows, slipping between buildings. He had promised Camron Thorpe he would come to Camlanrein. He would do so when he knew what Conn Regan was doing in a Trooper's uniform.

Neither the man nor the Trooper saw the young woman who also watched the Trooper leave his post and hurry away. They did not see her set out after the man who trailed the Trooper, keeping to the lengthening shadows among the buildings near the road.

Nor did they see the silver wolf at her side.

chapter twenty

"Just tell me what it says, Donan," Kitra said as she accepted yet another report.

"This is from a scout Camron sent into the Dalrudds two weeks ago. He came in to report a storm in the mountains. Several more feet of snow have accumulated in the eastern end of Cragon Pass. The snow is to our advantage, Lady Fairchild. Dellay's advance will be slowed, and that will give Lord Thorpe more time to prepare."

"And for Rayce to reach Timthurlen." She pushed her chair back from the desk and rose, rolling her tired shoulders and arching her back to help relieve the tension and stiffness she felt. Darkness had descended again but so far there were no new fires; however, flood waters were now the threat.

"I want a message to go out, Donan, to the people of Ross Harbor. Anyone who wants to leave the city for safety elsewhere should head north, to Lisburn, to Clomnell, or on into Kaenolir, even the mountains. They should not wait but pack up what they need and leave. There is no way we can protect the city." She rubbed her forehead with a tired gesture. "Pray that Camron will stop the Arlander army at Timthurlen," she murmured.

"He will, my lady. We must have faith that we will survive even this. We did before; we will do so again."

"I pray you are right, Donan. Now, let's get people moving away from Ross Harbor toward safe havens."

A few hours earlier, Troopers had descended on the warehouse the Arlanders were using as a hiding place. In the fight that ensued, although it was more a roundup than a fight, eight drunken men were captured and taken to the cells beneath Camlanrein. Two others were found in an alley, badly beaten. They were being guarded until they were well enough to be put in a cell. Two men, described as possible Warders, were taken by a patrol as they came down the alley to the warehouse and placed in separate cells away from the drunken bunch.

"Donan, is Cass in the hall?"

"Yes, lady, he helped bring in the hooligans believed to have started the fires. He is certain that there are two Warders among them."

"Good, find him and bring him to me. I'll want the two Cass believes are Warders taken to a room where he and I can question them."

Donan nodded and left the office.

Much as Camron did when he was thinking, Kitra paced, circling the large room. Do the two Warders know where Conn Regan is? Do they know what he has planned next? How many Warders are there in Ross Harbor? And where are they? Where is Gadred Aember? Is he here, too, or yet to come? Is he with Dellay? How will they know when the Arlanders will strike Ross Harbor next?

And what about the people whose homes and businesses had been destroyed in the fire, or were threatened now by the flooding river? How could they all be accommodated? Would they willingly stay and fight when the time came, or would they, too, pack up and leave the city?

So many questions, so few answers.

Hearing a noise she looked up to see Cass Vance in the doorway.

"Cass," she said, "Come in. Donan said you were with the Troopers who brought in the Arlanders responsible for setting the fires." She moved to the chairs by the fireplace. "Here, sit for a moment. I asked Donan to have the two you think might be Warders placed in a room for questioning, but I wanted to talk to you first."

Cass took one of the chairs while Kitra settled into the other. "Would you like something to drink? Tea? Wine? Some whiskey?"

"No, my lady. I'm fine. Donan told me you planned to question the Warders."

Kitra nodded. "Yes. I would like both of us to question them. I think you know what information we want from them. But you feel certain these two are Warders, not Arlanders? Is there a possibility that one of them is Conn Regan?"

"Definitely Warders, my lady. The swords we took from them are old Warder swords. The men are Timisian in looks, not Arlander. But no, Regan is not one of them."

"All right then." She hesitated, looking away from Cass. "I don't like to have to do this, but. . . Do whatever is necessary to get them to answer your questions. I have a trick or two up my sleeve, but let's see how cooperative they are first. Now, besides their swords and the certainty they are Timisian, what are your impressions of the two?"

"These two have been here in Ross Harbor for some time, I think. It's a good possibility they've been the organizers behind the fires, at least the first one. Like Rayce and KaynaRee, I think Conn Regan is here, too, and he's the one making the decisions now. I believe the Warders and Arlanders were following his orders, not acting on their own. If Aember sent Warder spies here, he did so for a purpose. But Conn Regan's purpose may be different from Aember's. However, it's all conjecture at this point, at least on my part."

"My lady," Donan called from the doorway. The old man smiled as he said, "The Warders are ready for you."

"Thank you, Donan," she said with a smile in return. For the first time in many long days, and nights, she felt she was closer to some answers.

Lamps flickered on brackets along the long, dark hallway through the level below the hall. Halfway down the hall there were two Troopers stationed by each of two doors. When Donan stopped outside the first door, he stepped aside and one of the Troopers unlocked the door before he and his fellow Trooper entered, taking up positions on either side of the door, hands on their sword hilts. Cass stepped into the small room carrying a lantern, and when Kitra entered Donan closed the door after her.

The room was perhaps twelve feet square. It smelled of mold and rot and dampness and the leavings of small rodents. A small rough table and two chairs had been placed in the center of the room, where a prisoner sat shivering stripped of his clothes except his undergarments. When Cass swung the lantern in front of the man's face before placing it on the table, the man flinched and brought his bound hands up to shield his eyes.

Cass pulled the other chair out and faced the man. Kitra stayed back at the door between the two Troopers.

"Do you have a name?" Cass asked.

The man stared down at his bound hands and did not answer.

"Do you have a name?" Cass asked again

This time when the prisoner did not answer, Cass gave the side of the man's head a hard open-handed slap. It nearly knocked him off his chair. One of the Troopers stepped forward to steady the man.

"I will ask you one more time: do you have a name?" Cass's voice had taken on a low, menacing quality.

"Bres, my name is Bres," the man mumbled.

"Very good, Bres. That wasn't so hard, was it. Now I have some more questions for you. Do you follow the Way of Aldward Finton? I suggest you answer quickly."

The questioning went on into the night. When Bres refused to answer, he paid dearly for his silence; but it soon became evident to both Kitra and Cass that Bres knew nothing of the whereabouts of Conn Regan, nor could he tell them the whereabouts of two of the brothers Aember sent to Timthurlen. They had been instructed to separate and hide until Regan needed them again.

"All right, Bres, enough for now," Cass said and turned to the Troopers. "Bring in the other prisoner."

Lugh, upon seeing the bloodied Bres, readily confessed to being one of the organizers of the Arlanders in Ross Harbor, to setting the fires that had destroyed so much of the city, to the fact that, yes, Conn Regan was with them the night of this fire, but he had no idea where Conn Regan might be now. For all Lugh knew, he'd left the city. Nor did he know where the two Warders who had been sent with him to Ross Harbor were. They had separated after the fire and he hadn't seen them since.

It was Kitra who asked about the dragon token.

Lugh looked to Bres and shrugged.

"Conn Regan has it. He showed it to me," Bres finally said.

"And what does he plan to do with it?" she asked, very softly.

Bres sat for a long moment, his head bowed. Tears leaked out of his closed eyes.

"Bres?" she asked again, a note of command underlying the soft tone of his name.

"He plans to. . . He plans to kidnap you and force you to call your dragons. He remembers the dragons you and Thorpe rode, when you killed our Lord Finton and destroyed his castle." Bres was openly sobbing now.

"Do you know when or how Regan plans to kidnap Lady Fairchild?" Cass asked.

Bres shook his head while Lugh looked at his fellow brother with wide eyes. "No, he didn't share that with me. Only when the time came he would let us know where we should meet him."

"Were the Arlanders who set the fires to be part of his plan?"

Bres shook his head. "No, only us Warders."

"If Regan has the token and he is the one with plans for the dragons, what does that mean about Gadred Aember? I thought he was the leader of the Warder survivors?" Cass asked.

Once more Bres shook his head. "Regan didn't say. When I asked after Lord Aember, Regan said he had been ill and had not survived the winter. Regan left the hall soon after he found the master dead in his bed. That's all I know." He looked to Cass, his eyes pleading with Cass to believe him. "I swear that's all I know."

Cass looked at Kitra and she nodded. She turned to the Troopers guarding the door. "Take them back to their cells for now," she said. And to Bres, "If you remember anything else, we want to know about it. Be assured," she said quietly, "the Warders will pay for their greed and their hatred."

Bres and Lugh dumbly nodded their heads.

Kitra stood at the window in the chieftain's office, arms folded tightly across her stomach. Cass stood in front of the fireplace, his hands wrapped around a mug of Highland whiskey. They'd spent much of the night questioning the two Warders, and now with dawn beginning to chase away the darkness, the two tried to come to grips with the information they'd gained.

"Cass." Kitra came away from the window and joined Cass near the fireplace. "KaynaRee is searching for Conn Regan. If Regan plans to try to kidnap me, if he encounters Ree, he may believe she can call the dragons as easily as I. Or he may use her as a way to get to me." She turned to face Cass. "She is in danger, too," she whispered, tears filling her eyes. She blinked them away and turned away to pace.

"My lady," Donan spoke from the doorway, "I'm sorry to intrude, but there is someone here you must see." He turned away before Kitra could say aye or nay, and a tall, broad shouldered man with silvered hair stepped into the room.

Kitra and Cass both stared at him.

"Lady Kitra?" he asked, his voice a deep, rich baritone.

"Baskers," she whispered. She sighed deeply and stepped forward to meet him. "Captain." She held out her hands to him. "Loren Lamond," she smiled. "What are you doing here?"

He took her elegant hands in his large, capable ones and smiled in greeting.

"It seemed a good time to visit," he said amiably. "We've some Arlanders to discuss."

Kitra asked Cass to stay, and the three sat back with cups of tea after the dishes of a meal had been removed.

"I am very glad to see you, Loren. You can't know how much it means to see you."

"Camron has kept me informed about the activities of the Arlanders here in Timis since he became chieftain. The last few years, there were only intermittent reports from Tiernan, but I am not surprised that there has been an increase in the Arlanders' destructive behavior here. In the past week or so, we caught about a half dozen Arlanders breaking into the Riversend armory with the help of a former night watchman. When I ordered an inventory, we found it wasn't the first time they'd helped themselves to Guardian weapons.

"We've been dealing with more of them pushing into the Lowlands from the High Champaign. They steal whatever they can, and in the process they often destroy homes, even small settlements along the Hranor Hills. They've been coming in by sea closer to Riversend, and we've been hard pressed to protect the villages along the coast." Loren set his mug aside. "When I received the message that Camron was on his way to Timthurlen, expecting an attack there, I wanted to come to determine for myself just what you're facing here.

"And I got a good picture of what's been going on when we tied up at the dock. I know the duties of chieftain have been placed squarely in your hands, so, Kitra, tell me what you can about the situation in western Timis."

The rest of the morning and most of the afternoon were spent telling the Guardian Captain what they knew, what Camron and Cass had found in the mountains, what they were dealing with, and what they feared was coming. At this point Donan and the city's Harbor Master Elden and Sergeant Noonan were asked to join the group and share their knowledge of a situation that was quickly becoming dire.

"Many of the food storage warehouses have either been broken into or destroyed," the harbor master explained. "Since we no longer have the benefits of goods, or gold, from the High Champaign, much of our grain and meat now come from Kaenolir. I'm sure you are aware, Captain, that your own needs may soon take precedence over ours. I fear we are in for some difficult times ahead."

After more discussion of the situation in Ross Harbor that resulted in no new information, Kitra soon excused the two men so they could return to their duties. She thanked them for coming and escorted them to the door.

"Anything you think I should know, even if it seems out of place or inconsequential, don't hesitate to come to me or send me word."

"My lady, there is one thing that I've noticed just since the last fire." The sergeant thought for a moment before continuing. "A couple of the Troopers have noticed a man who seems out of place here. Big man, uses a walking staff, blazing eyes, black hair with streaks of gray, asking lots of questions about you and Lord Camron. He's interested, so he says, in the history of both Timis and Kaenolir, but his questions seem to center more on Finton's war and the part the dragons played."

"Does he walk with a slight limp?" Cass asked.

"Yes, as a matter of fact, he does. Do you know him, Cass?"

"Hm, I may." He looked to Kitra and gave a slight shake of his head.

290 K. J. Olson

"Thank you, Sergeant," she said. "If you or your Troopers see him again, let me or Donan know immediately. If neither of us is available, tell Cass. He is someone we want to keep an eye on."

Noonan saluted her and left. When he was gone, Kitra turned to Cass.

"What do you think?"

"I'd say there's a good possibility that Gadred Aember is here in Ross Harbor," he said in a flat, toneless voice.

"My lady, do you want me to inform the hall guards of the situation, or would you prefer to do so? I can arrange a time in their schedules and yours to meet with you."

"Thank you, Donan. Yes, it appears the Warders have even more devious plans for Timis, and for me in particular. We need to prepare for all contingencies."

"If you'll excuse me, my lady, I'll continue to search for Regan and now Aember as well." He turned to Loren Lamond. "Captain," he said with a nod and a salute and left the office.

Kitra sighed and joined the Guardian Captain by the fireplace. For a moment she was overwhelmed by the events surrounding her and her shoulders slumped. She closed her eyes and breathed deeply.

"Can you call your dragons again, Kitra?" Loren asked quietly.

She opened her eyes and sat up straighter. "I don't know if they will hear me, Loren. But I do have Samar by my side whenever I need him."

"Samar?"

"One of the great wolves of Faerie. He has been with me on Lorn Isle."

"Ah, yes, I remember now."

The two sat quietly, remembering events of twenty-five years ago, before Loren spoke again.

"When I leave here, which I will do when the tide turns, I plan to stop at Fairtown and proceed cross country to the Lowlands. My Guardians are assembling just beyond the Hranor Hills; in fact, they should be in place by the time I reach them. It is my intent to push into the High Champaign and do as much damage to the amassed Arlanders as we can, pull back, and then come at them again once we've regrouped. That is the main reason I came: to tell Camron, and now you, what the Kaenolirians plan to do. That plan will change only slightly, Kitra.

"Since it appears the Arlander camp is or soon will be on the move, we'll continue to harass them. Swift attacks on the fringes, day or night, when they least expect it, from behind, from the foothills, when they're trying to get across the River Roon, wherever and however it's to our advantage to hit and run.

"When the army reaches Cragon Pass, we'll assess the damage we've done to them and continue to come at them from behind.

"I sent a courier to Timthurlen this morning, advising Camron of my plans. My troops should be in place and ready to move when I get to the staging area near the border. Which means we should be on the move in another three to four days.

"The late snow storm in the Dalrudds gives us a little more time to get into position, ready to hit them as they prepare to march to the pass. The element of surprise, I hope, will be entirely with us, at least in the beginning."

"Thank you, Loren. Perhaps, once and for all, we will find a lasting peace. I don't understand the nature of men like Kelan

292

Dellay and Gadred Aember, nor shall I ever understand what drives men to want what others have so they can have more."

"Nor I, Kitra. Though for generations the Lamond men and the Highland Guardians have struggled to find and maintain that elusive peace. We attain it for a time, but then it slips away to be replaced by hate and greed. All we can do is try to find a common understanding, but, unfortunately, that often results in war. And war is never the answer; history has shown us that."

Loren rose and offered his hand to Kitra, and she rose to take it.

"I must get to my ship. We'll be setting sail in an hour or so."

"May the Ancient Ones go with you, Loren, you and your Highland Guardians. The Timisians offer their thanks for what you are doing. When this is settled. . ." she paused and shook her head.

"I know, Kitra, I know. Stay safe. Now," he said, "get some rest, and be sure someone is guarding you at all times."

She smiled in farewell and walked with Loren to the door. After closing the door behind him, she turned to the windows and watched the play of light over the Dalrudd Mountains. The sun was about to set on another day. She had loved this time of day on Lorn Isle, feeling the daylight slip away to be replaced by the peace of night. Her life there seemed to have occurred in another time. She wondered if she would ever find such peace again.

"Samar," she murmured. "I need you beside me." When she turned away from her solitary vigil after a few minutes, the wolf sat on his haunches nearby. She held out her hand to him, and he came to stand in front of her. "Thank you, old friend," she murmured as she took his head in her hands and bent to press her forehead against him. "Thank you."

She left the office with the wolf beside her to find two Troopers, one on either side of the door. "We are to escort you and guard you, Lady Fairchild."

Kitra nodded. "I'm going to my chambers and get some sleep. The wolf will remain with me at all times from now on."

"We'll be at your door while you sleep, lady."

At the door of her private chambers, one of the Troopers entered first, checked the rooms, and when all appeared to be well, he saluted and the two left Kitra alone.

He might have been noticed at another time, this ragged figure who moved from one seemingly empty or burned out building to another, always keeping to shadows when he could, moving unobtrusively, hood pulled down to hide much of his face; but not here, not today. He paused from time to time to listen at windows, then crept to another shack, another shed, another building, always listening, searching for a voice or figure he would recognize. This once crowded street was all but deserted; people had lived and worked here on the outskirts of Ross Harbor, people who eked out a living as best they could.

But no longer.

The fire and the Arlanders had taken what little they did have; and the Timisians were forced to move on, drifting away, to be carried by the tide of poverty to the next hovel, the next hut that could provide a bit of shelter until that too was taken from them.

Desmond Orly stopped at the sound of quiet voices, slipped deeper into the shadows cast by the late afternoon sun, and squatted unmoving as the voices passed him by. He watched as two men turned toward one of the shacks that had somehow escaped the fire.

"So," he thought as the men's faces where momentarily silhouetted as they paused before entering the shack to determine there was no one about. "There you are, my brothers."

He waited until the sun began to set, the smoke turning the horizon into burning red flames. With cautious steps, moving only a step or two at a time, he approached the shack. One of the men laughed at whatever the other said, and Orly settled down to wait a little longer.

"We're going to have to get s'more of this stuff," one of them hiccupped.

"Tomorrow," the other said. "Too tired to go out now. Trooper might catch us," he said and laughed again.

"Shh," the one muttered. "Someone might hear you."

"Nobody home, Ross, you know that. Tha's why we picked this place. 'Member?"

"Go to sleep, you dunderhead."

"Gotta piss first."

"Okay."

The door opened with a squeal of old wood against stone and one of the men stepped out. He moved to the corner of the shack and pushed his clothing aside to relieve himself. As the stream of urine hit the dust, he shivered and then sighed. He never saw the man slip up behind him, didn't know anyone was there until a hand was clasped tightly over his mouth. Surprise froze him in place long enough for a knife to slide quickly across his throat and spill his life's blood. It mingled in the dirt with his urine.

Orly carefully let the body drop to the ground before he slipped back into the shadows, but not before removing the short sword Corm carried.

"Corm, how long does it take to piss?"

The other Warder stepped out of the door and looked around. "Where did you go, back to town?"

"Corm?" he called again and then saw the crumpled figure on the ground.

"That's a hell of a place to sleep," he muttered and bent over to give Corm a shake.

It was the last movement he would make. The knife, still red with Corm's blood slid effortlessly into his back, once, then again. Orly leaned down to wipe the blade on the Warder's tunic. Breathing deeply he pulled Corm's body back into the shack, then went out to retrieve Ross's body.

"Two that Camron Thorpe won't have to worry about," he thought as he threaded his way back, back into the city toward Camlanrein, back where he had seen Conn Regan. "And two for my friend Morton Cassel."

The darkness covered him, and he wondered for a moment if he had the courage to continue on the path that circumstances had forced him to take. He had killed as a soldier, as a soldier of the Way, but never one of his own comrades. He knew, however, that Aember would not have hesitated to kill him if he had not run from the valley. He would be dead, his bones slowly becoming part of the mountains, if not for Camron Thorpe.

Conn Regan's death would be his final payment of the debt he owed the chieftain of Timis.

chapter twenty-one

Hammers rang in the early morning air as men built defensive walls along the flanks of the city; there were the sounds of saws, men shouting and swearing, shovels thunking into hard-packed soil. Men and draft horses pulled large timbers into position, dumped wagonloads of sand and gravel in piles, hauled large sledges filled with rocks of every size and shape.

Timthurlen was preparing for an attack by the Arlander army.

Barrels and buckets full of water were added to piles of sand placed every few yards along the streets and lanes of the outskirts of the city. Weapons were distributed to men, older boys, and women—to anyone who wanted them and knew how to use them. Archers had been ordered into the mountains directly above Cragon Pass with instructions to discourage anyone trying to cross into western Timis at that point. Other scouts patrolled the foothills north and south of the pass.

The few Arlander men remaining in the city were rounded up and sent back across the mountains, urged on by the archers when they reached the pass. Their women and children were allowed to stay but warned to keep to a designated area near the harbor. The women of Timthurlen were to keep an eye on them and make sure they offered no help to their men.

It was obvious to Camron Thorpe that people were frightened, but they also worked diligently, day and night, to shore up the defenses of their city: they built defensive walls; they reinforced existing buildings to provide safe havens for women and children; they boarded up buildings and tore down buildings that could offer the enemy any advantage. They moved animals except for the cows and goats needed for their milk to safer pastures to the north near Timis Bay. Hunters were sent along with the scouts into the foothills to bring down what prey they might find. They butchered animals and salted the meat, preserved what vegetables and fruits were available, baked bread by the hundreds of loaves, made soft cheese and stored it in cool cellars, cooked up large pots of fish and shellfish and fed all the workers and anyone else who might be hungry. They chopped and stacked firewood; they filled every jar and can and small barrel with water for drinking and collected them in their homes and other strategic places throughout the city. Those who lived on the outskirts of Timthurlen were moved into buildings, large and small, along the waterfront. Ships were anchored away from the docks.

"There's a courier coming in, Lord Camron," one of the men working on fitting rocks into place along the outer wall called down to Camron.

Camron waved to the man, letting him know he'd heard, before pitching a few more rocks against the base of the wall for added support. He wiped his hands on his trousers and turned to signal the man carrying a leather pouch over his shoulder.

With a salute, the courier handed Camron his packet of messages. Camron took note of the Highland Guardian emblem on his tunic.

"You're coming from Captain Lamond?"

"Yes, m'lord. He has been with Lady Fairchild in Ross Harbor and he sent me by ship from there. It was imperative to advise you of his plans. The message requires your immediate attention and a response."

"Thank you," Camron said as he took the packet. "There's a cook shack down that lane," he gestured with his head. "Get some food and find a place to rest for a while. When I've got a response ready, I'll let you know, just tell someone at the shack where I can find you or you come here to me. I'll see what Captain Lamond has to say and then we'll decide how to get you back as quickly as possible with my response to him."

The courier saluted again and turned to the lane where he'd find the cook shack.

"Shane," Camron called to one of the workmen nearby. "Will you find Hugh Carlsby and send him to me? I'll be at the command hut."

The workman saluted and hurried away on his errand.

A small cottage had been set aside for the chieftain's use, somewhat beyond the noise and crush of workmen, wagons and horses. However, there was no time, day or night, that had been quiet since Camron's arrival in the city. He entered the cottage and paused to get a drink of water and light a candle before sitting down at a small, roughly built table that served as a makeshift desk. He brushed the sweat off his brow with the heel of his hand and opened the packet.

He read for several minutes, then laid the message on the table with an audible sigh of relief.

"Thank you, Loren Lamond," he said.

"Talking to yourself, m'lord?" Hugh Carlsby asked as he entered the dimly lighted cottage. He smiled and pulled a barrel that served as a chair closer to the table.

"For the first time in weeks, Hugh, I see a small glimmer of hope for us." He handed the Guardian's message to Hugh. "Read that and see for yourself."

Hugh read silently for a few minutes. He looked up from the paper with a smile on his face. "Thank the gods for the Highland Guardians," he said quietly and handed the message back.

Camron looked down at the message and read it again.

"With the Guardians harassing Dellay's army from the north, we may be able to buy some more time to get everything in place here. We're got to stop them here, Hugh. Ross Harbor can't mount any kind of offensive and the defense of the city is left almost entirely to the people, since I pulled out most of the troops. Kitra would be hard pressed to stop an attack. The fires have destroyed so much of the city.

"In Kitra's last message, she had begun to evacuate those who were the most vulnerable as well as anyone who wished to leave, but it appears the people had already figured that out. Many had left at her writing, heading to the villages to the north as well as Fairtown in Kaenolir." He paused at a rap on the open door and turned to see the Kaenolirian courier.

"Ah, you're here. Come in," he called. "I'll have a written message for Captain Lamond shortly, but let me tell you what we're doing here and what I have in place in Cragon Pass."

Rayce came to a halt at the base of the rock outcropping that rose stark and jagged above the waters of Timis Bay. Perhaps, he thought, it had been called Dragon's Head Point even in the time when fire beasts roamed freely. He dismounted and retrieved his pack and the warm outer garments his mother had given him.

"You will find the time you spend riding on a dragon's back to be the coldest in your life," she had said with a smile. "And also the most thrilling. I wish I'd been able to have saddles made for you and Ree. Since I don't have a saddle to give you, you'll just have to hang on for dear life." She had laughed at the rather disconcerted look she received from her son.

He removed the saddle and bridle from his horse and gave it a swat on the rump to send it trotting back toward Ross Harbor. He bent to hoist the awkward pack onto his back, and though the light was rapidly fading he began to climb.

Caretaker, I am here.

"I'm coming, Far'Lin."

He heard the dragon snort, he thought, and then he heard, much to his amusement as well as apprehension, *Don't fall.*

"Thanks for the advice," he muttered.

The climb proved to be very difficult. At one point he feared he was stuck with no way down or up, but then he was able to find a narrow toehold that helped him bypass a deep fissure in the stone that had blocked his way upward.

Night deepened around him as he climbed. The surge and crash of the waves at the base of the cliff provided a counterpoint to the music he had begun to hum. Somewhere close to the ancient rock he heard the cry of a night hawk, a familiar night sound he'd heard all his life. For the moment, it brought him a modicum of comfort.

He paused to rest. A ghostly white shape, its wings spread wide sailed by him, so close he could see the individual feathers of a great white owl and feel the soft brush of air created by the owl's flight. Off for a night's hunting, he surmised, wondering if he had scared it away from its nest, a nest he might not have noticed in the dark. After a few more minutes, he began again to move upward, searching for and finding handholds and toeholds.

Finally, after what seemed hours to him, he pulled himself up over the lip of the outcropping and lay face down on his belly. He lay quietly for a few minutes, resting his forehead against his folded arms, thanking whatever ancient spirits inhabited this pile of rock before turning over onto his back, his pack making an uncomfortable resting place. A dark shape moved off to his left, its distinctive horned head lifted to observe the Caretaker.

"I'm wondering," Rayce said, "could you have found a more accessible spot for me to join you?"

He heard the snort again and couldn't tell if it was a sound of derision or humor. He settled on a mixture of both.

This is a place we used to gather. When fire beasts roamed freely. The winds lifted us off the rock and sent us spiraling into the sky. When the warm days came after the cold winds, the sea dragons dropped into the water from here.

"Ah," Rayce said. "A dragon playground."

Rayce rolled onto his knees and pushed himself up.

"All right, Far'Lin, now what?"

Now, Caretaker, I teach you to fly.

"Baskers," was all Rayce could think to mutter.

With his fur lined cloak, a leather cap lined with the same fur pulled down over his ears and tied under his chin, a second pair of heavy woolen trousers, and leather gloves lined with warm wool, he stood by Far'Lin's front leg.

Climb onto my knee.

With more effort than grace, he pulled himself up onto the dragon's knee with a grunt.

Now, up on my back. Between my wings.

"Where do I put my legs?" he wondered aloud.

The dragon's massive head swung around and Rayce was observed with his glittering eye.

Like a horse.

"Oh."

When he was situated on Far'Lin's back at the base of his neck just to the front of his wings, he found two narrow horn-like protrusions on either side of the fire beast's neck. Without a saddle, these horns would have to serve as something to hold onto and, he hoped, keep him from falling from a great height.

Hang on.

Gripping with his knees, hanging onto the horns, Rayce let out a shout of sheer elation as the dragon, his dragon in this time and place, lifted off the outcropping. With starlight above and the pounding sea below, they flew.

And his mother was right: he had never experienced such cold.

Or such joy.

His blood pounded through his body keeping time with the wild music of his Song. Up here in the clouds there were no sounds of marching men, men marching to slaughter each other. No, here the rushing wind, the strong beat of Far'Lin's massive wings, and the surging of waves against a distant shore beneath them were the only sounds. For this time, his only thoughts were of the fire beast he rode.

His laughter rang out, but as Far'Lin banked and turned toward the land, he experienced a moment of fear.

I will not let you fall, Caretaker. Do not be afraid.

After flying for some time, but all too soon it seemed, Rayce could see the lights of Timthurlen. They came in low over the city and Rayce looked down to see men working by torchlight on an earthen wall. Other lights burned throughout the city, and he could see people and horse-drawn wagons moving through the streets.

Slowly the dragon circled downward until he settled into a field not far from the city.

I will leave you here, Caretaker, and return to Dragon's Head. I will come when you call.

Rayce slipped clumsily down from his high perch, so stiff from the cold his knees buckled and he knelt for several minutes before he could push himself upright, his heart still racing with what he had just experienced.

"Tomorrow," he said and then thought, *or is it today?* "Tomorrow, we will need to fly over the mountains to see where the Arlanders are. Can we do that when it is light, or will it be safer to fly during the night?"

You will see more when the sun shines. Now go. Find your father.

With a running leap the dragon flew away and Rayce removed his hat and gloves and began the short trek into Timthurlen. Growing warmer as he walked, he slipped the cloak from his shoulders. A Trooper patrolling a section of the road into the city halted when he saw Rayce.

"I'm a friend," Rayce called, dropping his cloak and holding his empty hands out to his side. "My name is Rayce Thorpe. I need to find my father. Can you direct me to him?"

His shoulders drooping in weariness, haggard from lack of sleep, Camron Thorpe helped put the last of the logs into place making a barricade he hoped would keep the Arlanders from overrunning this section of the wall.

"I think we're done here," he said, stepping back and perusing the work. "Where next, Hugh?"

"That's the last work on the wall," Hugh said as he wiped the dirt and sweat from his face with an equally dirty, wet sleeve of his tunic. "We're as ready as we can be," he said and spat to clear his mouth of dirt before taking a drink from his water flask. He wiped his mouth with the back of his hand and took another swallow. "I'm going to get something to eat and sleep for a few hours. You should, too. You're dead on your feet."

The two men turned at a shout and saw a Trooper hurrying toward them. Following close behind was a somewhat disheveled young man. Camron suddenly laughed as the Trooper, with a grin he couldn't stop, said with a flourish of his hand, "Your son, my lord."

"Sheevers, Rayce, what are you doing here?"

"So, Rayce," Camron said as he pushed away his plate and picked up his mug of ale. "How do you like riding a dragon?" he asked with a grin.

"Now I know why Mother and you, and Kailie sometimes, would get this faraway look in your eyes when you spoke about your dragons." He grinned back at his father. "Even if I live to be a very old man, I'll never forget what it feels like to ride on the back of a dragon—damn cold and unbelievably uncomfortable!" he laughed, his pleasure and joy, and pride, at the recollection of his first ride shining in his eyes. He set his ale mug aside and yawned. "And now," he said, "if I don't get a little sleep I won't be much help to you. And the way you look, you need about twenty-four hours of uninterrupted sleep."

"I'd settle for three or four, but there's more work to be done."

"No, Father, you need to get some rest or you'll not be any good for anything." He stood and pulled his father to his feet. "Where do we bunk?" he said.

"You're right. I do need a little sleep," Camron admitted through a huge yawn. Now that he'd stopped moving for a time, he felt his exhaustion. He yawned again. "Wake me at dawn."

"I hate to tell you this," Rayce said with a smile. "It's already dawn."

He led his father to the bunk he'd been using, only sparingly, since his arrival in Timthurlen and pushed him down to sit on the rough pallet.

"Give me your foot."

"What?" Camron asked unable to comprehend why Rayce would want his foot.

"Give me your foot so I can pull your boot off."

"Oh." He complied and Rayce pulled off the boot and with it a bootful of sand.

"Now the other one."

With his boots off, Camron sat for a moment, his hands hanging limply between his thighs. He yawned again, swung around and stretched out, asleep almost before his head hit the stained, lumpy pillow. Rayce covered him with the rumpled blanket at the foot of the bed.

Rayce looked around the small room, found a spot on the floor that would accommodate his long length, rolled himself into his cloak and using his cap and gloves for a pillow, sighed deeply, yawned once more and drifted into sleep.

Neither man was aware that Hugh Carlsby stopped to look in on them, pulled the door shut behind him, and called a Trooper over to stand watch while his chieftain finally stopped long enough to get some much needed sleep.

"Don't wake him unless it's absolutely necessary," he admonished the young Trooper.

Only then did Hugh turn away to find his own rest.

The sun stood high overhead as Rayce and Camron walked to the field not far from Timis Bay where Rayce had left Far'Lin the night before. Rayce stood quietly for a moment, closed his eyes, and then began to sing. The music of his Song swirled around him before rising toward the cloudless sky. When he heard Far'Lin's answering Song, he smiled and opened his eyes. The music spun away on errant breezes to be replaced by the sound of the beating of powerful wings.

"Sheevers," Camron whispered as Far'Lin came into sight. "He's magnificent."

The dragon spiraled slowly downward and landed a short distance away. He lowered his head and flicked Rayce with his warm breath before turning his glittering black eyes to take in Camron.

Caretaker he said as he bowed his great head in homage.

Camron grinned upon hearing the fire beast's voice in his head. "Far'Lin," he murmured and lifted his hand in greeting.

Rayce pulled on his 'dragon garments' as he'd begun to think of them.

"We'll fly over the pass and then north until we encounter Dellay's army. I should be able to estimate its size and how fast it's moving. I'll continue north until I can find the Highland Guardians and see what their position is."

"Good. I've sent word to the archers so that when they see you they'll know who you are and not take any potshots at you and Far'Lin."

Camron watched as Rayce rather clumsily mounted and positioned himself at the base of Far'Lin's neck. He couldn't help grinning and then he laughed out loud.

"I remember how uncomfortable it was the first time I rode So'Kol," he said. "While you're gone, maybe I can come up with some kind of a saddle for you."

"If you do, make two. Ree's going to need one, too."

Camron nodded and stepped back. He watched as the dragon lifted into the air with his son, and his throat tightened at the memories that came rushing. He could have sworn he heard So'Kol's whispered *Caretaker* in his mind. Or was it just the wind?

When all else fails.

No. It wasn't the wind.

He stood for another moment and then turned to walk across the field and back to Timthurlen. There was work to be done.

Rayce and Far'Lin flew above the Dalrudd Mountains catching the uplift winds to carry them high and swiftly along Cragon Pass. Snow looked to be disappearing quickly throughout the narrow passage. With the wind whistling coldly and loudly in his ears, Rayce noted the activity around the mine as they passed over Banning Village and Blairtown. Far'Lin flew lower and flew along the River Roon for a time before turning northward again to fly along the foothills.

"Far'Lin, I want to see what activity there is in Malhain before flying over the plains."

The dragon angled eastward but rose even higher to keep from being seen as he flew directly over the village. They hadn't gone far when they came upon the dust raised by men and horses, wagons and carts as they moved slowly through the High Champaign, heading south.

"Baskers," Rayce muttered through frozen lips and chattering teeth. "Where did they all come from?"

Dellay's army, numbering a thousand or more, had broken camp and was on the move.

Far'Lin flew high, lazy circles giving Rayce a good look at what the Timisians were about to face.

"All right, Far'Lin, I've seen enough here. I want to find the Highland Guardians. But you need to set down. I'm about frozen solid."

Once beyond the Arlander army, Far'Lin skimmed along the lower reaches of the mountains. Still some distance from the Hranor Hills, he circled ever lower and settled gently to the ground.

Rayce groaned as he loosened the frozen grip he'd had on the slender horns he was using to keep his balance. Far'Lin folded his wings and lowered his belly down on the ground.

"I don't think I can move, Far'Lin," he muttered. "I'm so cold."

Close your eyes, Caretaker, the dragon said as he turned his head to look at Rayce. With a soft flicker of enveloping flame he warmed his rider. As feeling began to make his limbs tingle, Rayce sighed.

"Thanks," he murmured, and the flames ceased.

Rayce swung his leg over Far'Lin's neck and slid down to the bent knee and then to the ground. He landed clumsily and off balance and had to lean against the dragon for support.

"When I get back to Timthurlen, I'm going to have to find more clothes to wear. Baskers, I've never been so cold."

He heard a snort and thought the dragon was probably laughing at him.

"Easy for you," he muttered. "Not so easy for me."

Rayce stomped around for a time, getting feeling back into his legs; he swung his arms and rolled his shoulders to ease the stiffness there. When he finally felt warm enough, he was ready to go again.

"Ready?" he asked. "We'll continue north until we spot the Kaenolirians. If we can, I want to land and talk with Captain Lamond, tell him what I've seen today."

Far'Lin grunted and bent a knee for Rayce to remount. This time, as he clamored up onto the dragon's back, it took a little less effort, and he didn't feel quite so clumsy. They circled slowly a few times, all the while moving ever higher before once again heading north. Below them lay the rough line of the Dalrudd foothills which they followed for some time until the low-lying Hranor Hills could be seen in the distance.

"There, Far'Lin. That must be Captain Lamond and the Guardians."

A double column of horsemen, numbering about sixty Rayce thought, followed by several pack horses came into view.

"Find a place to set down ahead of them."

Far'Lin swooped down quickly, came in low and landed about a mile in front of the Kaenolirians. Rayce dismounted and waited.

The Guardians came to a halt a short distance from the waiting pair. The leading rider dismounted and came toward Rayce. He stopped, eyed first the dragon, then Rayce.

"Rayce Thorpe, I presume," he said. Then with a grin, he looked up at the dragon. "Accompanied by his fire beast."

Rayce stepped forward and offered his hand. "Captain Lamond. My father sends his greetings and his thanks. He also sent a message pouch by courier."

"Yes, the courier caught up with me last night. What can you tell me about the Arlander army?"

As succinctly as possible Rayce told the Guardian captain what he thought was the approximate number of the army, how fast they were moving and where they were when he saw them.

"I'd say they're only two or three hours ahead of you, but moving very slowly. About a hundred mounted men, the rest on foot. Supply wagons and carts bringing up the rear. Some men on horseback accompanying the supply train."

"Good. We'll get into position when it grows dark and give them a little surprise. Will you be coming with us?"

"Yes. Far'Lin and I can keep them in sight for you and maybe do a bit of harassing of our own."

Captain Lamond saluted and turned away.

"Okay, Far'Lin. We want to keep the Arlanders in sight, but not so they notice us."

I will have to fly high, Caretaker.

"Baskers," Rayce muttered as he clamored up on the dragon's knee. "Any warm air up there?"

Far'Lin merely snorted.

Rayce and his dragon flew in and out of scattered clouds as they kept the long line of the Arlander army in sight. The mist of the clouds clung to Rayce's garments and his exposed face and added to the bone-deep cold. When they reached the end of the supply train, Rayce told Far'Lin to turn and come in low.

"Just the sight of you flying at them will scare not only the men, but the horses, too."

The dragon banked and came down swiftly, passing very low over the supply wagons and the line of men riding alongside. He screamed and sent flames shooting toward the startled men. Horses answered him with their own screams, of terror, plunging and bucking and unseating their riders. Horses pulling the wagons bolted and went careening into the foot soldiers strung out in front of them. Wagons tipped, spilling their drivers and contents. Rayce heard men and horses cry out in pain and fear. All was confusion on the ground.

"Enough for now, Far'Lin, before they can regroup." The feeling of exhilaration he had experienced as the powerful fire beast spewed fire began to turn to deep sadness. "Why," he wondered "must we kill to stop them?"

Because, Caretaker, they want what is not theirs. Long ago we could fly without fear, but no more.

Dragon and rider turned in a wide, slow circle before flying away into the clouds.

It will soon be time to sing your Song, Caretaker.

"I know. When all else fails. Has Ree found the dragon token?"

Ja'Anee says soon. First she must help the Golden One.

"The Golden One? Mother? What is happening, Far'Lin? I must go back to Ross Harbor!"

Not yet. Call her fire beasts from the sea to come to her aid. The one from the mountain top, too. The Golden One will not be harmed.

"Mother's dragons. So'Kol," he whispered.

Soldiers below us, Caretaker.

Unable to see because of the clouds, Rayce told the dragon to descend so he could join Captain Lamond and his soldiers.

They settled in a field ahead of the column and Rayce slid down off the dragon's back. Stiff with cold, he leaned against Far'Lin's warm belly and waited for feeling to return to his frozen body. Once again his dragon warmed him with a gentle breath of fire.

Sing your Song, Caretaker. Call the fire beasts for the Golden One now.

chapter twenty-two

"So, that's where you've gone to ground, Conn Regan," Desmond Orly thought.

The Warder had slipped in the side door of a run-down tavern that was far enough away from the harbor to have escaped the first fire but close enough to the harbor not to have burned in the second one. Orly found a place among the debris of the alley where he could watch the door but remain hidden, and he settled down to wait.

He'd been following Regan for two days, but last night he'd been surprised to see Regan head down an alley not far from the harbor and come out a short time later dressed not in a Trooper's uniform but in trousers, shirt and tunic. Nor was he carrying a weapon Orly could see.

"Probably a knife under the tunic. Maybe one in his boot," he mused.

Now Orly watched and waited, dozing from time to time until he heard someone else coming down the street.

"Well, well, Jaston Sonne," Orly muttered to himself as the light from the opened door briefly let Orly see who entered the tavern. "So what are you doing here?"

For a moment he contemplated slipping into the tavern and trying to hear what the two men might be talking about, but decided after only a moment that such an action would likely result in his death. He'd wait, and when they left the tavern he'd follow them.

He wondered if his shadow was waiting somewhere in the dark.

The tired barmaid plopped a platter of roasted meat and bread on the table where the two Warders sat. She'd brought a pitcher of ale and mugs and waited now to see if they wanted anything more.

"Well?" she grumbled, hands fisted on her ample hips.

"That's all," Regan said with a dismissive wave of his hand.

She turned and made her way back to the kitchen, her bare feet slapping the dirty floor with each step.

The men ate in silence for a time until Regan pushed back and picked up his mug.

"What have you found out about our brothers?" he said so softly that the second man had to lean close to hear him.

"Both Bres and Lugh are in the Camlanrein jail. Most of the Arlanders who helped us light the fires are in jail, too. My source for Trooper gossip didn't know any more than that. Bres was with me in Timthurlen, but Lugh was here in Ross Harbor. That means one who was with me and two here are unaccounted for. They all know to come to this tavern, but I've not seen them since the fire. "

Regan swore softly. "That leaves just you and me, Jaston."

"You're still planning to. . .do what you planned?" Jaston Sonne said in a whisper behind his hand.

"Yes," Regan answered. "It will be more difficult, but all we need to do is wait for the right opportunity to present itself." He reached for the pitcher and refilled their mugs. "Now, here is what we'll do."

No one had seen the dark haired man who walked with a limp. Troopers were to watch for him, of course, but with the congestion and confusion that dominated the streets as people began to flee the city, the soldiers had little time to spare for one man who might or might not be in Ross Harbor. In fact, at least three Troopers had seen the man just this morning, but his appearance was very different from that of the man who had been asking questions about the history of Timis and its dragons. Although he still walked with a slight limp, he did not carry a walking staff. His long hair had been shorn close to his head; his face was clean shaven. He wore an inconspicuous tunic of gray material; his black trousers were of a similar fabric; his knee high boots were scuffed black leather. The hilt of the sword he wore sparkled with gems, but its scabbard was purposely plain. He kept his left hand on the hilt as he walked along the waterfront, looking and behaving as a wealthy merchant intent on his business.

Gadred Aember made his way through the crowded thoroughfare down to the nearly deserted harbor. When he found a small rowboat tied to a piling at the far end of the dock, there was no one to question why he was taking the boat or what he was doing there. He smiled to himself as he tossed the line away, stepped down into the boat keeping a hand on the dock planking to steady himself. With a shove, he pushed away, secured the oars in their locks and set out up the river toward Camlanrein.

He rowed with easy, strong strokes along the west shore of the River Bray. Though the current was swift and the river very high, even this close to the shore, he made good headway. When he passed under the bridge, the Trooper on duty paid him little mind, too busy making certain that people did not loiter and kept moving north toward the next bridge that would take them across the river near Clomnell Village or still farther north into Kaenolir.

He passed Camlanrein, then the boat landing below the hall, but he kept on until the river narrowed. Here he put in to shore, tied the boat to a tree, though he thought it unlikely he would need it again, and set off the way he had come back towards Camlanrein. If he had timed it right, he would reach the hall after dark. He needed the darkness for what he planned to do.

A well-defined trail took him away from the river through a forest of fir and hemlock. Huge maple trees with thick trunks attesting to great age grew on either side of the trail, creating an arched canopy of dense branches whose leaves rustled in the warm wind. Small birds flitted through the branches, their songs a warning to trespassers; sunlight dappled the trail as he walked. Aember noticed none of these things. He was preoccupied with what he would need to do to gain admittance to Camlanrein and proximity to Kitra Fairchild. It should not be difficult, after all, for he had information concerning the Arlander army and how soon the enemy would reach Ross Harbor. He also carried a letter, written in such haste by Camron Thorpe the handwriting was nearly illegible, urging Lady Fairchild to call her dragons to protect the people of Ross Harbor.

"Such a clever ploy," he thought. How could she ignore a directive from the chieftain?

And when the dragons answered her call and came to her, Conn Regan would come, too. Or perhaps he was there already. Either way, when Aember found him he would kill him. Just that simple, kill him and take back the dragon token. With the token in his possession Lady Fairchild would join Conn Regan in death and the power over the dragons would be his.

He laughed softly, with pleasure.

The sun began to set, bathing the path he walked in a golden glow. Ahead of him, not far now, was Camlanrein. Soon, soon, it would be his, his seat from which he would rule all of Timis.

First Timis, then Kaenolir.

His.

So close. So close.

The same litany had been spoken years before by Aldward Finton.

Conn Regan, dressed again in his Trooper disguise, walked across the bridge and into the courtyard of Camlanrein with Jaston Sonne at his side. They paused at the front door to salute the guard and asked to see Lady Fairchild.

"This man," Regan jerked his thumb in Sonne's direction, "has some information about the fires and the whereabouts of a Warder here in the city. I'm sure the information will be helpful to her."

The Trooper on guard looked them over carefully before nodding his head and opening the door for them to enter. Once inside another Trooper met them at the foot of the main staircase. Again Regan stated their business with Lady Fairchild.

"Wait here."

The Trooper turned to mount the stairs, but with his back to Sonne, the Warder hit him on the back of his head with a small cudgel he had concealed in his sleeve. Regan caught the unconscious man as he fell and drug him out of sight of anyone coming down the stairs. Mounting the stairs two at a time, they reached the upper landing, found an open door into an empty room and slipped inside. Now they stood, breathing deeply, for several minutes, listening for any indication that they had been detected.

The upper hall was silent until an older man hurried from a room at the end of the hall. He entered a room across from where the two waited and closed the door behind him.

"Let's go," Regan whispered.

They left the room and walked purposefully toward the large room at the end of the hall where a woman moved in and out of their sight through the open door as she paced.

"My lady," Regan said respectfully.

Her head jerked up at his intrusion. "I'm sorry to disturb you, but I think you should hear what this man has to say about a man he thinks is a Warder."

Kitra looked first at Regan, then at Sonne. Behind her a black wolf rose to his feet to take his place beside her.

"How did you get up here without an escort?"

"The Trooper at the stairs told us to come on up. He was alone and said he couldn't leave his post. This fellow has information I think you may want to hear."

"About?"

"He's been following a man he finds very suspicious." He looked away from Kitra to the huge wolf at her side and frowned.

"Does he walk with a limp?"

Taken aback, Regan blinked. "A limp?" he thought. "But he's dead," was his next thought.

The wolf growled low in his throat.

"Why, yes, yes he does," Sonne answered. He didn't know where this was going, but he would play it along. However, that was the biggest wolf he'd ever seen. Nervous now, Sonne cleared his throat.

"What does he look like?" Kitra asked as she placed her hand on the wolf's head.

The only man Sonne knew who walked with a limp was Lord Aember. Was he here after all?

"He's tall, dark haired, uses a walking staff."

As the man began to talk he moved slightly toward Kitra. Samar bared his teeth and growled, more loudly this time.

"I think you better tell me who you are," Kitra said quietly.

Just then Donan came to the door. Kitra shook her head slightly and he quickly took in the situation and hurriedly turned away to find the Troopers she had sent on an errand a few minutes before.

With her attention momentarily diverted, Regan rushed forward to grab her by the arm, but Samar leaped at him with a ferocious snarl. Regan screamed at the wolf's teeth sank into his shoulder. Sonne, eyes wide, backed away, but he was jerked upright by a man behind him, a tall man with dark hair, who wielded a bloody knife.

Regan's screams were cut short as Samar, with one violent shake, tossed him aside, his muzzle stained red. The dark man let Sonne's body fall, then stepped back, dropped his knife, held his arms out away from his body.

"I'm a friend, Lady Fairchild, I'm a friend. I've come from Lord Camron, with a letter."

Kitra backed away, Samar moving with her, growling savagely.

"Who are you?" she asked.

"I told you, I'm a friend with a letter from Camron Thorpe. It's here in the pocket of my tunic. May I get it and hand it to you?"

Kitra nodded. "But if you make a move toward me, the wolf will tear your throat out as he did this one." She pointed to Regan's crumpled form.

"I understand. Please, don't be afraid."

He continued a soothing patter in his deep, melodious voice while he carefully removed a letter from an outer pocket of his tunic. He was about to step forward with it, but Samar growled a warning.

"No, stay there," Kitra commanded. "Throw the letter on the floor and step back several steps."

The man nodded in acknowledgement, tossed the letter toward Kitra and stepped back. As he did so, Donan and two Troopers charged in through the door. With swords drawn, the Troopers immediately backed the man toward the wall and farther away from Kitra. They took up positions to either side of him.

"My lady!"

"I'm all right, Donan. Samar took down one man and this man," she pointed to the stranger, "took down the other. He contends the letter he's just given me comes from Lord Camron."

She stooped and retrieved the letter, but when she opened it, she frowned in puzzlement.

"This isn't Camron's handwriting," she accused as she handed the letter to Donan.

"He wrote it in a great hurry, Lady Fairchild. He tells you to call your dragons. The Arlanders are attacking and he needs their aid."

Kitra handed the letter to Donan who read it and shook his head.

"Lord Camron did not write this, lady."

Donan turned and with the letter in hand confronted the man.

"Who are you? What do you want?" Donan said, shaking the letter in the man's face.

With a sudden, violent move the man pushed away the two Troopers and grabbed Donan with an arm around his neck and a knife at his throat. The movement was so swift the Troopers had no time to react.

"If the wolf attacks, the old man dies," the man said as Samar snapped in frustration.

"Samar," Kitra said quietly, "no. Come to me."

"Tell the soldiers to drop their swords and move away." When the two Troopers hesitated, the man pricked Donan's neck and a drop of blood slid down his throat.

"Do as he says," Kitra commanded.

"Now, the man your wolf killed has something that belongs to me. It's probably around his neck. A pouch. Bring it to me. Very carefully."

Another drop of Donan's blood trickled down his neck.

Kitra began to understand then. This man was the Warder leader and the pouch contained the dragon token. She knelt beside the dead man and pushed aside the bloody shirt to expose the cord around his neck. Samar's teeth had cut through the cord and the pouch had slipped to the floor in the blood pooling beneath the man's head and shoulders. She rose, gore coloring her hands red, holding the pouch.

"Bring it to me."

"First, let Donan and the Troopers go, unharmed, and I will come with you."

"Lady, no!" Donan cried.

"It's all right, Donan. Trust me," she smiled at the old man, whose cheeks were wet with tears of frustration. She turned to the dark man. "The pouch for their lives or I let the wolf loose on you."

"Fair enough." He pushed Donan aside and signaled the Troopers to step away.

"I assume, Gadred Aember, that you want me to call the dragons for you."

He smiled, a triumphant, ugly smile.

Caretaker, the Golden One needs us. The black robe has come.

Torar trotted ahead, but stopped to look back at KaynaRee.

Call your fire beast. She will be needed.

As Ree and Torar crossed the bridge and ran into the courtyard of Camlanrein, Ree began to sing. She stopped to let the Song envelope her in the magic of the ancient Faerie. Mist suddenly shrouded the courtyard with gleaming tendrils of light while the music soared into the dark night, building and building, until with a final, crashing chord the swirling mist coalesced into a shimmering red shape. Ja'Anee, huge, powerful, beautiful in her power, stepped toward KaynaRee and lowered her head to the Caretaker who called her.

I have come. We will wait in the shadows until it is time.

A shadowy figure slipped into the courtyard, following the woman and the wolf, but he stopped in his tracks as music began to fill the night.

"Sheevers," Desmond Orly whispered, a word of wonderment he had not uttered since he had watched dragons come out of the sky and destroy Aldward Finton and all he had built. "Sheevers," he said again, in awe of the magnificent fire beast that came to the young woman he'd been following. He watched them move away from the center of the courtyard and disappear into the shadows.

Lady Fairchild stepped from the front door of the hall, closely followed by a tall man.

"Gadred Aember," Orly grimaced. Aember had changed his appearance, but Orly recognized him nevertheless. "What is he doing here?" he wondered.

Orly hunkered down where he was, not wishing to draw attention to himself.

"Call them now, Lady Fairchild, or your life is forfeit."

"But that won't get you what you want, Aember, and I have the token," she stated. "Step away," she commanded. "They will not come with evil so close by."

Aember hesitated, but did as she commanded.

The night grew still, as if in the small world of the courtyard time did not move forward. Kitra clutched the pouch in her bloodied fingers, threw back her head and began to sing. From far away, an answering Song. She knew her dragons came, not just at her call, but also a call from a Caretaker.

A call from Rayce.

The Song changed, grew darker and more menacing. The Singer turned to face the Warder and with a wild and powerful surge, the Warrior Song burst from the throat of a Warrior Singer. The music beat against the dark man, forcing him to his knees. He screamed and clasped his hands over his ears. From the night sky fire beasts—sapphire of a summer sea, gold of sunshine on the curls of the waves, green of the sea's depths—trumpeted in answer to the red dragon on the ground. Their Songs soon mingled with the Warrior Song as the Song of a Caretaker added yet another layer of power with its harmony.

Desmond Orly stared in disbelief at the scene before him. While the music obviously brought severe pain to Aember, Orly felt no such pain only a constant pounding in his ears, but the fierceness and wildness of the Songs brought him from the shadows. Troopers came running from several directions; Donan hurried through the front door with two more Troopers. The runners slowed and came to a stop, taking in the fantastical scene before them. Cass Vance dashed across the bridge and came to a skidding stop as he watched the sea dragons settle gently to the ground and a dragon the color of a blazing sun at sunset come from the shadows cast by the hall.

Cass realized the cringing man screaming in pain and rage was Gadred Aember. He came forward slowly, saw KaynaRee join her mother, saw, too late, a man race from the shadows, short sword in hand, saw the sword descend with such force it nearly severed Aember's head from his shoulders. A last, high scream, cut short, mingled with the ancient music, and the Warder who would be king slumped in death. The resentment of what he had and lost, the envy of what he never had but wanted, the evil that coiled in his heart and mind died with him.

"For Morten," the knife wielder murmured. "For all who will die in your name." Orly dropped the knife and stepped away, bloodied hands held palm out at his side.

Slowly the echoes of ancient music, sung by Golden Ones and fire beasts, drifted away and the courtyard of Camlanrein was silent once more. Sunlight mounted the peaks of the Dalrudds and steadily, gently spread its glow over the land, turning all it touched, for one brief moment, to gold. The night had passed.

With a sob, Kitra shook herself and then sighed deeply. Ke'Shan lowered his head and bathed her with his gentle flame to comfort her.

"You came," she whispered as she reached up to touch his splendid head.

Come, lady, we must go to Caretaker's Circle. So'Kol waits for us there. We will destroy the token. Caretaker, come too.

Ke'Shan knelt and offered Kitra his knee.

I will fly low, lady. You will not be cold.

Ja'Anee lowered herself and gave Ree her knee. Ree scrambled up and positioned herself between the dragon's wings. With all the horror of the past days forgotten for the moment, she grinned down at Cass and Donan. Cass grinned back and saluted her.

"Donan," Kitra said, turning to find the old man smiling at her. "I'll return as quickly as I can."

"I will see to this," he said as he nodded toward the body of the Warder, "and to that upstairs. But what of him?" he asked pointing to Orly.

"Do what you think is best. Hear his story, though, before you decide." She turned then to the Troopers. "Help Donan as he needs it and then return to your duties. Cass, when I get back I'll call for you. Be ready to go to Timthurlen."

With a nod to both Cass and Donan, she turned to Ke'Shan and mounted her dragon. She looked to her daughter, mounted between Ja'Anee's wings and clinging to the slender horns at the base of the dragon's neck. She gazed at the pair for a moment, struck by the golden beauty of her daughter and the gleaming red of her daughter's dragon. She smiled and was answered by Ree's wide grin.

The four dragons flew low but swiftly, winging their way along the coast of the Trayonian Sea north toward the ancient circle of Round Stones. They soon turned, their wings beating slowly, almost lazily, and spiraled downward, trumpeting to the great white fire beast that waited for them near the carved dragon in the circle's center.

Golden One, Caretaker.

So'Kol lowered his head to the two women, so alike, who slid down from their high perches and came to stand before him. Ree gazed on her father's dragon, her mother's sea dragons, her own glorious red dragon—all had come to their aid. The magical creatures of her parents' and Kailie's stories here now, in this time, to help the people of Timis as the dragons had been helped by the Golden One and the Caretaker.

"The evil one is dead," Kitra said softly. "I have the dragon token."

She removed the pouch from a pocket of her gown where she had secured it while she flew. Carefully, with trembling fingers, she opened the bloody pouch and without touching the token in it, turned it upside down and dropped the piece of gold and black granite on the back of the carved fire beast. She stepped aside to give the dragons room.

So'Kol grunted deep in his throat. The four dragons joined So'Kol around the stone, and with a keening sound vibrating up from the depths of the ancient magic within them, lowered their heads toward the token. Jets of fire erupted violently from each of them, pinning the lump of black and gold to the stone.

A wild, eerie shriek split the air as the flames grew to towering pillars. A grotesque black shape rose up within the flames, struggling to break free. So'Kol screamed in answer and his fire and that of the others intensified so fiercely that Kitra and KaynaRee had to turn their heads away, shielding their eyes.

As she turned away, Kitra began to sing. The Warrior Song rang out over the Stones to be answered by Ree's Caretaker Song. Wind, hot and strong, suddenly blew over the ancient place, carrying with it the Song of another Caretaker, another fire beast.

Once again time ceased to move, and the power and magic of Faerie beat against the evil embedded in the token, beat and burned until all that remained was a bit of black sand and a small pool of liquid gold. Wind howled through the circle and lifted the sand and carried it away to fall heedlessly into the churning sea, evil for this time and in this place defeated and burned to tiny sifts of sand to lie forever now beneath the crushing waves. The gold slowly sank into the stone of the carved dragon, the essence of the fire beasts becoming one with the ancient carving, hidden here in this timeless circle whose stones were slowly sinking into the earth.

The singing stopped. The wind died down. The sea settled back into its timeless rhythm.

The dragon token was no more.

It is done, lady, So'Kol said. *Thank you.*

With solemn, dignified grace, a king of legend, he bowed first to Kitra, then to KaynaRee.

It is time to join the other Caretakers.

All else failed.

Ke'Shan and Ja'Anee lowered themselves to the ground and Kitra and KaynaRee mounted. They were needed in Timthurlen.

Kitra and KaynaRee returned to Camlanrein and quickly gathered a few items of clothing and warm cloaks, trousers, caps and gloves for the times they would fly their dragons. The four dragons waited for their riders in the courtyard.

"Are you ready, Mother?" Ree asked, donning her cloak.

"Nearly so, Ree. I've some instructions to give Donan and I'm waiting for Cass Vance. See what you can find that will cushion the ride on our dragons."

Ree turned to leave as Donan, Master Elden, Sergeant Noonan and Adam Carland entered.

"Ah, there you are. Good. I'm leaving you in charge here." She looked at each of the men. "I suggest you meet at least once a day to fix your agendas. I'm trusting you, Lord Camron is trusting you, to do your duties. Keep in contact with the people left here in Ross Harbor. If there are Arlander troublemakers taking advantage of the situation, use your best judgment as to how much force to use to quell any disturbances they cause. Don't hesitate. Be firm."

She sighed.

"I'm sorry to put all this on the four of you, but Ree and I must go to Timthurlen. Our dragons and our Songs are needed to stop the Arlanders there. If they should break through, well. . ." She shrugged and pursed her lips, her forehead furrowing in sorrow. "Do what you can to save Ross Harbor," she said softly.

"Now, I'm taking Cass Vance with Ree and me. I assume you've sent for him, Donan?"

"Yes, my lady. He's on his way."

"All right then." She looked into each man's eyes for a moment. "I'm counting on you," she said quietly.

Each man came forward to shake her hand.

"We'll do our best, Lady Fairchild," Master Elden said.

"You have my word that I'll do all I can to keep Ross Harbor from falling into Arlander hands," Adam Carland said as he clasped her hand in both of his before stepping back.

"Stay safe, my lady," Sergeant Noonan responded and saluted her. "May the Ancient Ones watch over you."

When Donan stepped forward, she reached out to give the old man a hug.

"Come back to us, my lady," he whispered. He stepped away, but stopped at the door to look once more at his chieftain's lady; then he turned and walked sadly away, followed by the other three men.

She raised her hand in farewell, or in benediction; she knew not which.

By the time Cass came to find her, both Kitra and Ree were ready to go to Timthurlen. Kitra prepared another make-shift saddle for the dragon Cass was to ride. He could, of course, decide that riding a horse would get him where he needed to go easier than flying on a dragon's back, but she smiled to herself as she put the finishing touches to the padding.

"My lady," Cass said from the doorway.

"Ah, Cass, good. I have a proposition for you," she said as she tightened the last strap. "What do you think about riding a dragon?"

He gave her a puzzled look.

"I don't know. I've not thought much about it. Maybe when I was young and heard the stories of you and Lord Camron."

"Well, think about it now. I want you to accompany KaynaRee and me to Timthurlen. You know the Dalrudds so well and I'm sure Camron can use your help. You'll get to the city much more quickly if you ride one of the dragons. Are you up for a dragon ride?"

Cass's mouth dropped open in surprise. He shut it after a moment with a sharp click.

"Well, hm. Huh."

Ree smiled at his consternation.

"You have your choice of dragon—gold or green."

Cass sighed deeply and then laughed.

"I've always favored green, my lady."

"Jho'Son it is then."

chapter twenty-three

Far'Lin settled gently to the ground in a field some distance from the outskirts of Timthurlen. He lowered himself to his belly and canted his leg for Rayce to dismount. Rayce swung his leg over the dragon's neck and slid to the ground from the saddle his father had fashioned for him. Along with the Highland Guardians, Rayce and Far'Lin had spent the last few days harassing the Arlander army as it wound its way laboriously down the Champaign plain toward Cragon Pass.

The harassment had killed many Arlanders, wounded many others, and disconcerted the men marching at the rear of the column so much they scattered and ran screaming when they saw the dragon's shadow. The Guardians took advantage of the confusion and fear generated not only by the dragon but also by their own lightning attacks.

Wagonloads of supplies were left behind to catch up to the main column as best they could, and the Guardians pounced on the vulnerable supply train. Without ready access to food and weapons, Dellay would have a harder time of it. While the skirmishes slowed the wagons, they did not stop but rumbled inexorably on toward Timthurlen.

Camron cantered across the field leading a saddled mount.

"I saw you come in," he said as he slowed his horse to a walk. "Thought you might like a ride into Timthurlen."

Rayce patted Far'Lin's side and took off the saddle before walking away to meet his father. He was exhausted and had not relished the thought of the long walk to the city. He'd asked Far'Lin to land closer, but the dragon didn't always do as Rayce requested.

"What does Far'Lin know of your mother and sister?" Camron asked with a worried frown as he halted near Rayce.

"She and Ree are safe," he assured his father, "and they'll be here soon. Aember and Regan are both dead," Rayce said as he removed his cap and gloves.

"Huh. Well. Does Far'Lin know how they died?"

"Samar killed Regan, but a man unknown to the dragons killed Aember when he threatened Mother. Mother and Ree took the dragon token to Caretaker's Circle. All Far'Lin said was that the token had been destroyed. He didn't say how, and he chose not to answer me when I asked him how." Rayce cocked an eyebrow at his dragon but the dragon merely grunted.

"Well, we'll get the particulars when they get here. The important thing is they're safe and the token destroyed," he said with obvious relief. "Now, tell me about the Arlanders," Camron said as Rayce removed his heavy cloak and tossed it and Far'Lin's saddle across the horse's neck before mounting.

"The vanguard of the army will reach the pass within two, possibly three days, the city in another five or six days, I'd think," he said as they turned around to return to Timthurlen. "The Guardians have caused enough damage to slow the supply wagons, and the more heavily damaged wagons have been left behind. The horses panic when they see Far'Lin's shadow, and the Guardians have time to get to the men riding guard on the train. They attacked the main column at the River Roon crossing, and several more Arlanders were killed or wounded, but there are still too many of them to stop." He sighed and shook his head at the immensity of what faced them.

"Yesterday the Guardians were on the receiving end of a nasty surprise," he continued, "when the last four wagons were loaded with archers under the tarps instead of supplies. Three Guardians were wounded seriously, one man killed before they could get away.

"Now, tell me about the situation here in Timthurlen."

"We're as ready as we can be," Camron said with a shake of his head. "I'm grateful for the men and women who have elected to stay and fight, but our numbers are not large enough to cope with a thousand or more Arlanders." He shrugged.

"The fire beasts will come, Father," Rayce said quietly.

"And many men on both sides will die," Camron said flatly. "Die because of envy and hate and greed."

Father and son rode on in silence until they reached the outskirts of the city. They stopped at a paddock on the other side of a large, well-built stable, dismounted, and turned the horses over to a boy who had run out to them from the building. With a quiet word to the animals he led them away.

"You must be hungry," Camron said. "Let's get something to eat while we discuss what I have in mind. I want your opinion about the feasibility of getting a message to Dellay."

They headed for the cook shack where huge pots of soup and stew, spits of roasting meat, and piles of freshly baked breads where available day and night.

"How is the food supply?" Rayce asked as he loaded a bowl with stew and bread on which a helper had placed a large slab of meat.

"We're managing for now. Ships are still coming from and going to Kaenolir. However, if the Arlanders manage to break through and take the harbor our food supply will dwindle rapidly. What about the food situation in Ross Harbor?"

"Much worse than here," Rayce said around a spoonful of the filling stew. "The Arlanders managed to break into several food stores, took what they could carry from the bins, and foolishly burned some others. The harbor is in such bad shape now that it's hard for ships of any size to dock. And you know that if this continues with the Arlanders, Kaenolir will be running short, too. "

"Damn the Arlanders," Camron muttered. "Damn the Warders."

Rayce looked up in surprise, for his father rarely spoke disparagingly of anyone.

A shout from outside calling for Camron preceded Hugh Carlsby's hurried entrance.

"Dragons, Camron." He grinned at Rayce. "Lovely, lovely dragons coming our way."

"That would be mother and Ree," Rayce grinned back at Hugh.

Camron pushed back his chair and rose. He, too, smiled broadly.

"Let's go greet them."

An excited chorus of voices greeted the three men as they ran from the cook shack. Coming from the north, flying low and majestically, came six dragons with So'Kol in the lead, their scales shining and glimmering, their powerful wings thrumming. White, blue, gold, green, silver/black and red. They flew once over the city, trumpeting and singing as they circled, before landing just on the far side of the defensive wall.

Many of the people of Timthurlen were of an age to remember the dragons ridden by Lady Fairchild and Lord Camron, but others were too young to have seen the sight of fire beasts filling the skies. However, nearly all of the younger ones had grown up with stories of the fire beasts' destruction of Aldward Finton's army and the monstrous Pales.

Laughter and tears greeted these glorious beasts and their riders. There was joy at their coming, for their presence in Timthurlen meant hope, hope that Timis might yet survive another war.

The dragon riders slid to the ground and came to meet Camron and Rayce. Camron hugged Kitra and then turned to embrace Ree. He grinned and saluted Cass who grinned back.

"Glad you could join us, Cass," Camron said.

"What a wonderful sight," Rayce said. "All our dragons in one place."

More will come, Caretaker, when you sing your Song.

"Yes, I know. When all else fails."

When all else fails, Ke'Shan echoed.

Much later, when the excitement caused by the dragons' arrival had abated and the sun had set, Camron, Kitra, Rayce, Ree, Cass and Hugh gathered in the small cottage that had become the command post. Candles were lit and chairs were found to accommodate everyone.

"This is what I'm thinking," Camron said after a time. "I believe it's something we must try." He looked down at his hands, clasped loosely together as he leaned forward, his forearms resting on his thighs. "I'd like to get a message to Dellay, drop a pouch from the back of whichever dragon is best obscured in the darkness. Remind him of what the dragons did to the Arlanders who fought with Finton, remind him of what they will do to his forces now. But," he said as he sat up, "I don't want him to know yet that there are more fire beasts than just Far'Lin.

"I'd like to meet with him, just Dellay and me, try to negotiate a lasting peace between Timisians and Arlanders."

"Do you think he's interested in peace, m'lord?" Hugh asked. "He has nearly a thousand men. We have, what? Maybe three hundred at the most. He wants Timis, all of it, not just the eastern half. If he takes us, he has a clear path to Kaenolir."

"What will you offer him, Camron?" Kitra asked.

"I'll offer to help the Arlander people who have settled in Timis as well as any of them who wish to return to their homeland. To work together to build something where we can all live."

"I'll take the pouch, Father," Rayce said.

"And I'll go with him," Ree replied. "I want to see what our fire beasts are up against."

"Kitra?"

"It's worth a try, Camron. I doubt that Dellay will be willing to listen, but talking together is always better than fighting."

Camron looked to Hugh who merely shrugged.

"Cass?"

Cass folded his arms across his chest and thought for a long moment before speaking. "We've little to lose and much to gain if he's willing to talk. However, I've known Kelan Dellay for a long time and I doubt he'll be interested in anything you have to say, Lord Camron. He may pause for a moment when he remembers what dragons can do, but I imagine he thinks he has the upper hand here, especially after the devastation in Ross Harbor." He looked to Rayce and nodded. "As far as Dellay knows, there's only the one dragon, one dragon that can't fly very low because of the archers."

"By the way, Cass, how did you like riding Jho'Son?" Camron smiled.

Cass laughed. "My lord," he said. "I may never walk the mountains again or ride a horse anywhere. The only way to go is on the back of a dragon."

The dragon riders smiled in agreement.

"I know what you mean, Cass. How well I know what you mean."

Hugh looked from one to the other of the group with chagrin.

"Damn," he muttered.

It was decided that Rayce would ride Ke'Shan and Ree would be mounted on Jho'Son, the blue and the green deemed best to blend with the dark skies. Camron's letter to Dellay was secured in a pouch at Rayce's waist.

As his children dressed for the cold night ride, Camron took the rough saddle he'd had made to Ree.

"It's not nearly as comfortable as the ones your mother and I had, but it will serve for the time being. I'll have the saddle makers start making two more. The two we used are back on Lorn. Had no idea we'd have need of them again. I'll go see about saddling Jho'Son for you."

"Thanks, Father. Anything will be more comfortable than the blankets we used for padding on our way here."

As Camron turned to go, Ree called out to him.

"Father, do you think Dellay will be interested in talking with you?"

"I think, KaynaRee, I'm sending you and Rayce on a fool's errand. But," he sighed, "I have to try."

When all else fails.

The darkness was complete with no moon and clouds covering the stars. Ke'Shan and Jho'Son launched into the air, their wings beating a rhythmic accompaniment to the whistling wind. The dragons flew high, skimming the Dalrudd peaks, and soon found the fires of the army just south of the River Roon. Rayce pointed downward.

"Tell Ree we need to find the center of the camp. From what I have observed, Dellay has a big white tent he sets up in the middle of the army so he has tents and men on all sides of him."

Ree soon signaled that she had heard and the two dragons began to fly in a wide circle until they saw the white tent. Flaming torches set to either side of the entrance to the tent silhouetted two soldiers keeping guard.

Slowly Ke'Shan and Rayce closed the circle.

"All right, Ke'Shan, get me close to the tent."

As the great blue settled closer to the targeted tent, Ree and Jho'Son stayed above them, the dragons' wings beating with a slow, loud rhythm.

Rayce removed the pouch with his father's message.

"Just a little lower, Ke'Shan. I want to drop the pouch as close to the tent's front entrance as I can."

On the ground, men standing guard duty around the camp began to call out and look about for the source of the sound created by the dragons' wings. This was Rayce's signal to go no closer. He aimed the pouch for the ground between the two guards at Dellay's tent and let it fall.

"Go, Ke'Shan! Get us out of here!"

Hang on, Caretaker, Ke'Shan replied.

With strength and power that never ceased to amaze the dragon riders, the two dragons shot upwards above the enemy camp. On the ground, the shouts and cries of alarm did not reach the climbing fire beasts, but Rayce let out his own shout, of exhilaration, which was carried away by the rushing wind as he hung on for dear life.

The pouch had narrowly missed one of the guards outside Dellay's tent, and as he bent to pick it up, Dellay pushed the tent flap aside.

"What the hell's going on?" he swore. Then he noticed the pouch. "What's that?"

"It came out of the sky."

"You fool. How could it come out of the sky? Give it to me."

And he swore again as he grabbed the pouch and went back inside. He slumped in a chair near a table littered with leftovers from a meal, a large jug of whiskey and several cups. He reached for a cup and tossed its contents on the ground before filling it to the brim from the jug at his elbow. He drank deeply, wiped his mouth with the back of his hand and filled the cup again. After emptying the cup a second time, he sat back, picked up the pouch, opened it, and dumped out its contents. He frowned in puzzlement as several small rocks clattered on the table until he realized the few rocks had been added for extra weight.

"Huh," he muttered and picked up the letter. "It did come out of the sky after all." As he read, he began to laugh.

"So," he finally said. "You want to talk, do you now, Lord Camron Thorpe." His lip curled in disdain. "And you offer to help the Arlander people. Too late, boy-o, you're too damn late. Remember the dragons, you say? Well, yer one and only dragon ain't gonna stop a thousand men."

And he laughed again as he poured another cupful.

"Hunter," he yelled. "Get in here. I have a job for you."

Some four days later, a horse and rider bearing a white flag galloped toward Timthurlen. When he was within a hundred yards of the wall, he stopped and waited. It wasn't long before a lone horseman came from the city toward him. When the Timisian was still a few yards away, the other man threw down a pouch, turned and galloped back toward Cragon Pass.

Camron slowed his horse to a trot, and when he came to the pouch, the same one he had sent to Dellay, he stopped and dismounted. He stooped to pick up the pouch and opened it. Inside were the same small rocks and a letter. When he opened the letter and read it, he sighed.

The letter consisted of one short, explicit, profane phrase.

He folded it, stuffed it back in the pouch and tossed the pouch on the ground.

"So be it, Dellay, so be it."

chapter twenty-four

A cloud of dust hung over the long column of men, horses and wagons as Dellay's army wound its way around Banning Village and on toward Cragon Pass. It took two days, once they crossed the River Roon, to get the column to the mouth of the narrow pass. Here the column slowed and came to a halt, for Dellay suspected there might be archers in the pass and sent two groups of men into the rocks, a group on either side of the pass, to come in above anyone hidden in the steep cliffs. He sent a few horsemen charging through and smiled grimly when a barrage of arrows rained down on them. He'd been right. The archers, however, were few in number and were eliminated quickly. Once the dead and wounded horsemen were pulled out of the way, the column began to move.

Summer's heat had not yet reached the mountains; however, as the army began to come down out of the Dalrudds the temperatures climbed. Men and horses needed water and Dellay turned northwesterly toward Lake Lech. One half of the army would camp there while the other half marched south. When all were in position, they would move on Timthurlen; the city would be squeezed between the two forces, crushed in the vise of Dellay's army.

High above the dust cloud, silver/black and green dragons rode the currents of air created as the wind flowed down the mountain sides and arrowed upward again when meeting the incoming winds from the sea. Rayce eyed the splitting army with consternation and dread.

"There are so many, Far'Lin. Bad enough if they come against us straight on at the wall, but they'll be coming from two directions."

Others will come, Caretaker.

"What do you mean, others will come?"

As before. Sing your Song when all else fails.

"I will," he said after a time.

Jho'Son, with Cass aboard, came into Rayce's view and the two dragons flew side by side back to the city. They landed in the field just beyond the end of the defensive wall.

"Sheevers," Cass said breathlessly, "do you ever get used to it?" He laughed as he slid awkwardly down to Jho'Son's knee and then jumped to the ground, jarring his hips, knees and ankles. He grunted and swore as he landed.

"I don't think so," Rayce laughed in response.

They removed the saddles, slung them on their backs and trudged into Timthurlen. The two dragons took to the air once more to find a sheltered place to rest until they were called again.

Camron met the two men as they came toward the command cottage.

"What did you find?"

"It's not good," said Rayce. "Dellay is splitting his army to come at us from both the north and the south."

"We're in for it, Lord Camron," said Cass.

"Sheevers," Camron sighed.

Kitra, Ree, and Hugh joined the three men a short time later. After hearing the grim news, a plan was put in motion. All of them, with Hugh up on Ga'Vrill, much to his delight and trepidation, would leave Timthurlen when it was dark. Three of them would fly north, the other three south. They would give no quarter. Dragon fire would be loosed on the sleeping army.

As the sun set in a blaze of red and orange, Hugh was given a quick lesson in dragon riding. Warm clothes had been found for him, and another make-shift saddle hurriedly assembled. He was hoisted up on Ga'Vrill's knee and then clambered up to a seat between her wings. He gulped a bit when he looked back down to the ground and saw how far away it was. Kitra stood by helping him get situated as comfortably as he could. At her direction, he grasped the small, slender horns at the base of the dragon's neck to give himself stability. She suggested he lean forward as far as he could this first time in the air; the wind would not push quite so strongly against him if he did so.

So'Kol had come at Camron's call, and as the huge white fire beast settled down near Ga'Vrill, Camron's heart seemed to expand in his chest and his blood sang.

"Hello, old friend," he murmured as the dragon lowered his head. He reached out and laid a hand on the powerful neck.

Caretaker. Ga'Vrill says to tell her rider that she won't let him fall. He shouldn't be afraid.

Camron chuckled before passing the message to Hugh.

"Easy for you to say, Ga'Vrill," he muttered and tightened his grip on the horns until his knuckles were white with pressure.

The golden dragon responded with a lady-like snort that Hugh took for a laugh.

"'Tis not funny," he muttered.

"Okay, Hugh. Remember to lean in the direction of Ga'Vrill's head as much as you can; stay low; and hang on." Kitra gave Hugh his last instructions. "She's a gentle lady and she'll take care of you."

"It is my sincerest hope that she will do so, Lady Fairchild," Hugh said fervently.

With a last wave, the two dragons lifted off into the sky and flew in ever widening circles above Timthurlen. With the wind whistling in his ears and tears streaming down his cheeks, Hugh laughed and shouted with excitement.

Camron told So'Kol and Ga'Vrill to make some tight turns, climb upward and then drop downward so Hugh could experience how a dragon moved.

Bending low and holding on tightly, he thrilled to the adventure of flying on the back of a dragon.

"I am a dragon rider!" he shouted. What stories he would have to tell his grandchildren! That is, if he survived to tell the tale. He sobered when he thought what waited for them below, what waited for all of Timis if they did not defeat the Arlanders here at Timthurlen.

When Camron felt there was no more time to teach Hugh how to fly, he told So'Kol to take them back.

"Well, Hugh," Camron said when they were back on the ground. "What do you think about flying with dragons? Actually, you don't have to answer that. Your grin says it all."

"Sheevers, it's cold up there!" Hugh replied, but he said it with laughter in his voice.

When the darkness was deepest and most of the Arlanders were sleeping, the dragons took to the air again. Kitra and her sea dragons with Hugh on Ga'Vrill and Cass on Jho'Son headed south, Camron, Ree and Rayce on their dragons to the northern camp.

"There is no moonlight for them to see us, and there will be no light until the dragons use their fire. They may, however, hear us. As we planned, only one pass," Camron had advised. "Our dragons know what is expected of them, and they will sense danger from below. The Arlanders may be on the lookout for one dragon but not three. Don't take unnecessary chances. No matter how many we injure or kill tonight, there will still be too many coming at us all too soon.

When Caretaker sings, others will come. As they did before.

Camron sighed at So'Kol's reassurance.

"May it be so," he whispered.

High above Lake Lech the dragons began to descend. The encamped army lay just beyond the shores of the lake.

"Drop down lower, So'Kol. Tell Ja'Anee and Far'Lin to spread out so we come over the camp together."

The three dragons skimmed the still, deep waters, their wings thrumming a slow, steady beat, the sound not unlike rolling thunder. The sentry fires of the sleeping army were visible in a circle around the camp, but, too late, the sentries heard the sound of the dragons and screamed a warning.

"All right, So'Kol, use your fire."

Side by side the fire beasts launched their attack. With fierce and terrible roars, jets of flame lanced into the tents and men bunched below. Screams of terror and pain floated up to the dragon riders as they raced through the camp. After one swift and deadly pass, the dragons lifted away into the night skies and headed back to Timthurlen, arrows falling harmlessly behind them.

In the camp south of Timthurlen, all was chaos. Tents burned and men died in agony. Their task completed, Kitra ordered her sea dragons away. Somehow Dellay's white tent escaped the conflagration rained down by the fire beasts. He ran from the tent screaming and cursing to shake his fists impotently as the dragons winged away, their terrible damage done.

It was a silent group who dismounted in the field near the city. They unsaddled their dragons, rubbed them down where the saddles had been strapped to their backs, and murmured quiet words of praise. The wild excitement the flaming had generated in the fire beasts began to dissipate under the gentle hands of their riders. Finally, when the dragons stopped trumpeting and settled down to sleep with their heads under their wings, their six riders made their way to Camron's command cottage. The saddles were left on the ground nearby, and they entered to find a large platter of roasted meat and warm bread and pots of steaming sweetened tea waiting for them.

When they were all seated, either in the chairs available or on the floor, when food had been eaten and a second or third cup of tea drunk, Camron offered praise for the newest dragon riders, Hugh and Cass.

"You did well. You all did well. It's not easy to ride a flaming fire beast and know what that fire is doing to men and animals on the ground. It is my hope with this initial foray that Dellay will see the light and come to negotiate with us. I doubt it, but I hope so. I pray so." He sat quietly for a moment, took a last swallow of tea, and set the mug aside. "Now, if you're done eating, get some rest. Once they've assessed the damage we caused today, they'll either come with peace offerings or come to fight." He rose in dismissal and all except Kitra filed out.

She stood next to him, his arm around her waist, her head resting on his shoulder.

"When we flew our dragons against Finton, I thought we would never again fly with flaming dragons," she said quietly. "Men died today, needlessly, because of their greed. I know for some, it's their desperation that drives them. You offered to help, but I doubt that offer made it to the men who fight out of need for home and hearth. Dellay wants it all. He'll have it all or die trying."

"And so many will die because of it, so many on both sides." He sighed when Kitra stepped back to pour another cup of tea for both of them. "Fighting each other is such a waste, such a needless waste. I'm going to talk with Rayce. So'Kol says others will come, as they did when we fought Finton and his Warders. I want Rayce to sing his Song quickly. Maybe seeing many dragons and knowing what is against them will send most of the Arlanders running back across the mountains."

"Yes, Ke'Shan says the same. Both Rayce and Ree have indicated their dragons also told them others will come."

"Perhaps more lives, on both sides, can be saved when Dellay sees he cannot win." She emptied the last of the tea into a mug and handed it to Camron.

"I'm going to send out scouts to see what's happening in both enemy camps; then I'll wake Rayce. Get some rest, love. We've a long day ahead of us."

Camron sent Kitra off to bed, gave the four scouts their instructions, and rested briefly himself. He woke from a nap and went out to find Rayce. He found both Rayce and Ree sleeping on the ground beside their dragons. So'Kol opened one eye at his approach, gave a gargantuan sigh and went back to sleep. Camron smiled and stepped over to Rayce. He knelt and laid his hand on his son's shoulder.

Rayce grunted and shook off his father's hand, too deeply asleep to realize who was beside him.

"Rayce, I'm sorry to wake you, but I need to talk to you."

Rayce rolled over and opened his eyes. He stared up at his father with an unfocused stare.

"Rayce, wake up."

Rayce closed his eyes again, sighed deeply and yawned. He scrubbed his face with his hands before sitting up. He pulled his knees up and laid his arms across them, his head hanging. With another yawn, he focused on his father.

"Hello," Camron smiled. Rayce had, even as a boy, been a deep sleeper who found it hard to awaken.

Rayce smiled back. "What time is it?" He frowned and looked skyward.

Camron glanced up at the sun. "About midday. I am sorry to wake you, but I wanted to talk to you about your Song and about your dragon. Let's go back to the cottage and let Ree sleep for a while longer."

"Lucky Ree," Rayce grumbled under his breath.

"Yes, she is. Lucky to have such a brother," Camron laughed. He sobered after a moment and helped Rayce to his feet.

"Now, then," Camron said when they were seated at the table he used for a desk. "Tell me about your Song."

Rayce thought for a moment before looking at his father. "I think it is a replication of Far'Lin's Song with an added element of Faerie magic. If I understand the mythology of the ancient fire beasts correctly, and from what you and mother told Ree and me, each dragon had his or her individual Song, but when they sang together it combined their enormous power. When I sing, then, with Far'Lin, his Song will be blended with the other five dragons that have come to help us. When I add my Song to theirs, it will call more dragons to come to us. How many more I do not know. You said that the sky was filled with dragons when So'Kol and mother's sea dragons sang. You sang the Caretaker's Song, which blended and harmonized with So'Kol's, and mother's Warrior Song blended and added to the power of her three dragons' Songs."

"Yes, I believe you are right," Camron nodded his head in agreement. "If Dellay does not capitulate and come to us offering peace but chooses instead to attack, I want the six of us in the air, the four of us singing our Songs. If other fire beasts hear us and come quickly, Dellay should realize he has no chance against such numbers and give up the fight."

"What will that mean for his army, do you think? Will they disperse peacefully, or will Timis be forever under the threat of another Arlander attack? Perhaps Kaenolir would be a target for a dispossessed people, too."

"I think we are nearly to the time when all else has failed," Camron said sadly.

In the Arlanders' southern camp Dellay stomped and fumed and raged. He damned the dragons and heaped a measure of profane promises on the heads of the Highland Guardians. Kaenolir was next after Ross Harbor, he swore.

His army was in chaos; he'd lost count of the number of men killed or burned too badly to fight. At least a hundred in this camp and probably as many in the northern camp. He also knew men had deserted him, heading back to the other side of the mountains and safety. But even in his fury, he set in motion his plans for the attack on Timthurlen.

Before the fires were completely extinguished, the dead and wounded shunted aside, Dellay sent a courier with orders for the northern contingent of his army to move at dawn of the next day and be in position to attack Timthurlen the day following. There was no thought in his mind of turning tail and running or going to Camron Thorpe with an offering of peace. He still had the forces to sack the city and move on to take Ross Harbor and everything in between. Six dragons, he scoffed, could not stop eight hundred men.

Dellay roamed the camp, shouting advice, encouragement, and calling down retribution on any who broke and ran. They could not be defeated, he screamed time and time again, until his men once more began to believe they were invincible. When he felt all was in order and this section of his army would advance as he ordered, he left instructions he expected to be followed to the letter with the Warders embedded among the Arlanders and raced to the northern camp.

He exhorted the soldiers he had assembled into a force to be reckoned with to carry on the fight they had begun. The dragons had dealt them a blow, true, but they were not defeated. They would be on the lookout now for dragons, and his archers were prepared to bring the beasts down.

When he paused for food and drink, he wondered now and then, what had become of Gadred Aember? The Warder, Dellay had learned, had found a token he believed could control the dragons. Either the token didn't work after all, or Aember was dead. He snorted in disdain. So much for the Warders and their token. However, he still needed them, at least for a time. Three of them had died in his camp, one in the other he learned later; four were badly burned.

When he had no further need of them, they would all die. And the day was coming soon when he had no further need of the black robes.

At dawn the following day, the army began moving slowly from their camps. Above them, out of range of archers' arrows, six dragons circled, letting themselves be seen, reminding the marching men of the power of their fire. The dragons made the marchers nervous, but still they marched on. At the end of the day, they massed on the outskirts of Timthurlen, waiting for a new dawn, when the two units would close the vise and take the city for their own.

Neither the Timisians nor the Arlanders slept much that night. Dellay drank most of the night, stumbling about among his men, promising and exhorting, cajoling and encouraging. Before another day had dawned, he swore solemnly slurring his words, Timthurlen would be theirs. Think of all they could do with the riches that would confiscate. Think about possessing all of Timis, never having to be poor or hungry or homeless again, their families secure and well cared for. He painted dreams with his drunken words.

And the Arlanders, for the most part, desperate to believe almost anything, believed Dellay. The Warders smiled knowingly, still believing that it would be they with the dragons at Aember's command, they who would possess all of Timis.

In Timthurlen, men and women clung together, gathered their children about them for a final goodbye, before sending them to what they hoped was the safety of the waterfront. Defenses were checked and re-checked; water barrels filled to the brim, food prepared; bandages and the herbs and salves to heal wounds and fight infection gathered in one place. Everything they could do to prepare for battle had been done.

But there was little rest. All they could do was wait.

The Arlanders were coming at dawn.

May the Ancients Ones hear our cries and protect us or help us to die swiftly and without anguish.

An hour after midnight, the sound of thundering hooves was heard and those on watch at the wall peered into the darkness, trying to determine what new threat was coming at them. They drew their swords; others drew their bows in readiness. Just beyond arrow range, the horsemen stopped.

"Ho, the wall," a voice shouted. "We've come to help. We're the Highland Guardians."

A ragged cheer greeted the friends from Kaenolir.

"Come in, come in," a guard shouted.

Someone ran ahead of the Guardians as they entered the city, leading them through the crowded, narrow streets to the command cottage. Camron and Hugh came running.

"Loren, praise the gods," Camron called. "Hugh, show the Guardians to the stable. When their horses have been taken of, take them to the cook shack. They're welcome to bed down wherever they can find a spot." He turned back to Loren and escorted him into the cottage. "Would you like something to eat? Or a cup of whiskey?"

"The whiskey first, Camron, then I'll take some food."

Camron poured a cup for each of them and offered one to Loren, just as Kitra came in.

"Loren," she murmured and held out her hands to him. He set down his cup and took them. "Welcome," she said simply.

He smiled at her as he loosed her hands and picked up his cup again.

"I cannot say I'm not glad you came, Loren, but I fear you and your men may come to harm here," Camron said.

"Surely, Camron, you of all people should have faith in your dragons." He cocked an eyebrow at his Timisian counterpart and took a sip from his cup.

"Huh," Camron said as he motioned Loren to sit.

"We watched your dragons the night before last and came in after you left the northern camp to add a bit of our brand of fire to the Arlanders. It was a hit and run kind of skirmish, but we got away unscathed and caused a bit of damage in the process. At least I assume it was you. I saw a white dragon anyway, and the only white dragon I know is your So'Kol." He waved his hand away as Loren offered to refill his cup. "So, tell me what you've done to prepare and where you want my Guardians and where are your dragons? We didn't see them as we came in."

The dragons had flown to the mountains when the enemy began moving into position around the city. There they were safe; in the protective heights of the Dalrudds they could rest until the Singers called them.

They came then, just before dawn, with the singing of the magic Songs that called them, came trumpeting and singing their own Songs, and landed in the city's main square. With a last word to each other their riders mounted and the dragons again took to the sky.

They circled above the army and as the sun breached the mountain peaks, they came in behind the massed Arlanders, flinging their flames and immediately pulling up and away out of reach of the enemy's arrows before they could be hit. Again and again they came with fire until the archers anticipated their attacks and forced them away. But the dragons would not be denied and several archers died where they stood.

Dellay signaled and with a battle cry that was heard in the city, his army converged on Timthurlen. They came in waves, men with spears, with pikes and axes; they came with swords and knives and clubs. And the Timisians and Guardians fought with desperation, fought and died, and somehow managed to drive the Arlanders back, but at great cost. Dellay cursed and swore, sending his men into position for another assault. He sent the nearly one hundred mounted troops to rush the wall.

This time, the defenders at the wall were not able to drive the attackers back.

It was the dragons who halted the mounted rush.

They came in low behind the horses, their wingtips almost touching, and with a wild cry they sent their fire. Horses and men fell, screaming in anguish. The dragons flew almost straight up and came diving in again, this time from the front before the men could turn their mounts away.

"Sheevers," a man watching the annihilation whispered in horror as men and animals found no avenue of escape, only flames.

Now, Caretaker! Sing your Song!

Far'Lin hovered in the air above the dead and dying, and Rayce in his own anguish, began to sing. The music poured out over the battle below. His father and sister joined his Song with their Caretaker Songs; his mother with her Warrior Song blended with the Songs of her sea dragons.

And time stood still.

The sounds of battle drifted away. From the caves in mountain peaks, from secrets valleys, from the sea, fire beasts slipped through the portal of memory and once more rode the currents of the sky.

And they came at their Caretakers' calling, more than a hundred of them, their glorious colors shimmering and glittering in the sunlight. They called and sang and trumpeted as they swept toward the men waiting to push forward the final assault on Timthurlen.

And time stood still.

Or perhaps it moved backwards, back to a time when fire beasts sang and ruled the skies, the seas, the mountains.

The music that flowed over the battlefield surged in volume, until the men who would be conquerors could bear it no longer. Some fell to the ground, crying out for mercy; others ran screaming away from such torment. Dellay grabbed the dangling reins of a horse that ran by in panic, mounted, and drove his heels into the animal's side. He raced away, leaving his scattered army behind to fend for itself.

But the music was relentless and as the dragons circled low over the battle field, their fire burst out. Those who tried to escape died as they ran. Others cowered and begged for their lives.

When Rayce saw that the Arlander army was shattered, he stopped singing, and slowly the music drifted away over the battlefield. He looked at the havoc and death the power and magic of the combined Songs had wrought, and he cried out with sorrow and grief.

"It need not have come to this!"

He felt Far'Lin sigh. *Men have ever fought each other for dominance,* the dragon answered. *And so it shall always be as long as they walk the earth. But a time will come when fire beasts can no longer come when Caretakers call. That is as it should be. Men must learn. But I fear they never will.*

Rayce heard Ree singing. It was a Song of thanksgiving for the fire beasts' aid. Then one by one, the other fire beasts that had come in answer to Rayce's Song lifted into the sky and slipped away, through the portal, to their places of memory.

When all else failed.

The next several days were a blur of burying the dead, caring for the wounded, tending to families and friends who had lost loved ones. Nor were the Arlanders left to fend for themselves; the people of Timthurlen pitched in to form burial details and help care for the wounded, provided horses and wagons to transport wounded Arlanders back across the mountains.

A group of men came to Camron to ask permission to stay in Timthurlen. When he asked them why they wished to stay, they told him there was nothing for them in eastern Timis. Were they willing to work if they stayed, abide by the laws in place here, stay out of trouble? When they solemnly promised to do whatever Camron asked of them, he allowed them to remain in the city, but he would not hesitate to put them on a ship bound for their homeland if they did not or could not live under the restrictions Timisian law placed on them.

He called to Hugh Carlsby and told the men to give Hugh their names; and after they had done all they could for their countrymen, they would be put to work repairing the damage their fellow Arlanders had done not only in Timthurlen, but also in Ross Harbor.

"Assign someone to keep an eye on them, Hugh. For now they'll have to bed down in the square. See that they have blankets and whatever else they may need." He looked each man in the eye. "Keep your word or you'll be on that ship," he said with a hard edge to his voice.

He sighed as he watched the beaten men walk away. If more of them had come to him to begin with, it might not have come to war.

"Foolish, greedy men. But desperate all the same." He spoke not just of the twenty or so who had come to him, but all of the Arlanders who had pushed their way into Timis. He shook his head, sighed, and watched Loren Lamond walk toward him, leading his horse. Camron had suggested the Highland Guardians wait for ships to carry them up the coast to Fairtown, but Loren declined.

"It's time for us to go home, Camron, but thanks for the offer. When my six wounded have recovered, I'd appreciate your sending them home by ship."

"Thank you, my friend," Camron said with emotion. "Words are not enough," he said as he clasped Loren's hand between his.

"You've a hard road ahead of you, Camron Thorpe. Timis will be a long time healing. Keep me informed." He turned away and mounted. With one last look at Camron, he raised his hand in farewell and trotted away.

The next morning just as the sun bathed the mountain peaks in gold, Kitra gathered her family and together the four of them rode away from the city toward the foothills of the Dalrudds. Six dragons rested in the shadows cast by the higher hills. As Caretakers and Golden Ones approached them, they rose and began to sing. The four answered them with the Songs they had been given by the Faerie; they dismounted and met their fire beasts.

When the Songs were finished, Ke'Shan, Ga'Vrill and Jho'Son bowed to Kitra, and she reached out to touch each of them in turn and whisper her goodbye. Sorrow at their leaving, sorrow because they must go, sorrow because she doubted she would ever see them again warred with the gratitude she felt for their coming to her one more time.

"Thank you," she whispered to each of them as she touched the great heads bent to her. Tears slipped down her cheeks and she whispered a prayer that one day she might see them again, touch them again, fly with them again. The Ancient Ones had blessed her with these three fire beasts, and they would live forever in her memory.

Golden One, Ke'Shan said. *We must return now. It is time.*

Do not be sad, lady, Ga'Vrill said as she sighed. Her large eyes glistened. *We would stay with you if we could.*

"I know, sweet Ga'Vrill, I know.

Jho'Son blew gently and flicked her with his warm breath. *Goodbye, lady. Walk in peace. Remember. Always.*

Kitra dried her tears then and stood back to give her sea dragons room to lift up and away. "Goodbye, my beautiful ones," she whispered. "I will remember."

Not far away, Camron stood leaning against So'Kol's massive side. "Well, my friend. I said goodbye to you once before and it broke my heart. How can I say goodbye a second time?"

But I must go now. I know you understand, Caretaker.

"Yes, I understand. That does not make it any easier." He pushed away and came around to touch the dragon's head.

"I will never forget, So'Kol, what you have done for Timis and what you did for Kaenolir. I will never forget. Never." He whispered the last word, unable to say more.

Live in peace, Caretaker. One day we may see each other again. Farewell, my Caretaker.

Nearby, KaynaRee stood with Ja'Anee, her hand resting against the powerful neck curled around her like a glorious red arm. She couldn't stop her tears or the sobs that silently shook her body.

We must go, lady. It is as it should be. Once we could have stayed with you. But no more.

"Will you ever come again, dear Ja'Anee?" she whispered.

Perhaps. Only time will tell. Walk in peace, my lady. I may still come to you in dreams.

"Goodbye, Ja'Anee. Thank you. I will never forget."

Rayce and Far'Lin had walked some distance away from the others, but Rayce was unable to say the words that filled his heart.

No tears, Caretaker, Far'Lin huffed. *I do not like tears.*

Rayce couldn't help but laugh at the gruff voice in his mind.

That's better. I would stay if I could, you know.

"Would you? I would like that very much, Far'Lin."

Or you could come with me.

Rayce sighed. "Perhaps," he said, his voice etched with sorrow, "when I have lived my life, you will ask that I come to you. I hope you will ask me then. Will you?"

Perhaps, Far'Lin murmured. *It would not be so lonely if you were with me. Goodbye, Caretaker. Be at peace.*

Rayce stepped back and watched Far'Lin take to the skies, followed by Ja'Anee, Ke'Shan, Ga'Vrill and Jho'Son. Last came So'Kol. Their wild trumpeting filled the skies as they circled higher and higher into the bright, clear sky.

And then they were gone.

A bedraggled, blubbering figure, by turns cursing and praying, staggering and falling, crossed the River Roon and stumbled on toward Malhain Village. His exhausted horse had collapsed under him before he reached the river, and he was forced to continue on foot. He limped through the cluster of cottages to the one he occupied at the edge of town, mumbling what he would do to Camron Thorpe, what he would do if he ever encountered Conn Regan.

"Damn Warders. All Aember's fault. Damn dragons."

If it hadn't been for the dragons, he'd be in Camlanrein by now.

He mounted the step to the back door of the cottage and shoved open the door, shouting for Eithne.

"What are you doing here?" she asked coldly. "We heard the dragons killed you. Too bad they didn't," she muttered and turned her back to him. She whipped around as Dellay grabbed her by the arm.

"Get me something to eat, you sow," he screamed.

"Go to hell, Dellay," she swore. "I'm done feedin' the likes of you."

He raised his fist to strike her and gasped. His eyes bulged and he stumbled back, a knife protruding from his chest. "You killed me, bitch," he whined as he staggered back. "You killed me." He fell, twitched only once and lay still.

"That's for me, my man and my boys, you bastard." She retrieved her butcher knife and wiped it on his shirt.

Under the cover of darkness, she dug a shallow pit some distance from her back door. When she was sure there were no prying eyes to see what she did, she drug Dellay's body out of her cottage by his shoulders and rolled him into the grave. With something bordering on relief, but no sadness and no remorse, she shoveled and tamped the earth over the hated figure.

"I shoulda killed you long ago," she muttered and spat. "Long ago."

As she stepped back into her cottage, free at last, she wondered how many had died because of Kelan Dellay.

chapter twenty-five

AND SO IT ENDS

The heat of summer had passed and winter had come and melted into spring once more and life moved on. New buildings in various stages of construction sprouted from the burned remains of the old; ships docked at Ross Harbor. The few Arlanders remaining in the city were given the choice of remaining to become part of the fabric of a productive Timis or returning to their homeland, but their former lawlessness would not be tolerated—their punishment would be swift and severe if they resorted to their old ways.

In Timthurlen, life moved on as well, never the same as before the dark day when the Arlander army mounted its attack, but life and living nevertheless. Families learned to cope without their loved ones, lost so needlessly to greed and evil. The few Arlander families who still lived in the outskirts of the city lived out of the way, quietly and unobtrusively, not wishing to bring retribution down upon themselves.

Work throughout western Timis was fostered by a sense of renewal. Life would never be the same for many, but children were brought up and taught how to live as good a life as was possible; adults learned to move beyond their pain. Slowly wounds healed and time passed as it must.

Once the news came to Timis that the rain had returned to Arland, ending the years-long drought, Camron Thorpe offered ships and supplies to people who wished to return home. There were Timisians who volunteered to accompany the returning Arlanders and help with resettlement. It would be many long years before Timis would forget, or forgive, the Arlanders for what some of them had done, but helping their former enemies build a new homeland was an encouraging part of the healing process. With Arlanders leaving Timis, particularly eastern Timis, Timisians were able to claim what they believed was theirs by right and heritage.

By the end of the second summer after the war, the gold mine was operated by Timisians. Camron sent Hugh Carlsby to the Cragon Mine where he managed the miners and saw to their wellbeing. He would do so, he told Camron, until the mine was running smoothly; then he wanted to return to Ross Harbor and his family. Several of the Arlanders who had been mining for Dellay elected to stay and work. They were offered a good wage, good food and a decent place to live. Hugh set about designing and building a second furnace and under his guidance the earth gave up its wealth to a peaceful Timis.

Many of the Arlanders living in Banning Village deserted the hard scrabble lives they had been living there for yet another promise of a good life in their homeland, but Hugh wondered if they would ever find the kind of life they so desperately sought. Or would they simply drift from nothing to nothing until they died.

No one knew for sure what became of the Warders. Several bodies dressed in bloodied, tattered black robes were found among the dead on the battlefield, and Desmond Orly was asked to help identify them if he could. He positively identified nineteen as his former brothers of the Way; they were buried together in a mass grave in the fields where the dragons had set down. No one seemed to know what might have happened to the others who had been sent to train Dellay's troops; they had simply disappeared, or so it would seem. The two captured after the second fire in Ross Harbor still moldered in a jail cell beneath Camlanrein, and they would end their wretched lives there in time.

And Desmond Orly, too, disappeared after saying goodbye to Camron Thorpe. He had paid his debt to the Timisian chieftain, and now he could live out his life in peace as he wished to do, no longer fettered by the dictates of Gadred Aember and the Way.

The lives of the Timisian chieftain and his wife changed from preparing for war to helping their people settle into a peace they hoped would last through the ages. They worked from dawn to dark and frequently on into the late night, laboring beside the men and women who were putting their city and lives back together. Camron often rode out into the countryside, checking to see what needed doing for rural families, offering supplies if they were available, promising to honor requests when at all feasible. Kitra, with her gentle ways, spent time with families who had lost fathers, husbands, brothers, and sometimes mothers, wives, and sisters to the needless, senseless slaughter of fire and battle. She knew time would eventually lessen the intense pain of the emotional wounds many suffered, lessen the pain until it became bearable, even though it would never go away until death released them.

She and Camron encouraged the building of two schools in Ross Harbor and one in Timthurlen, schools that would teach children how to read and write, how to reason and find solutions, how to analyze and solve problems they would face throughout their lives. They would learn, too, about the histories of Timis and Kaenolir, even Arland. If they came to an understanding of the past, Kitra hoped the future would be brighter for all of them.

Cass Vance was sent into eastern Timis to help Camron keep abreast of the situation there. People whose homes had been confiscated by Arland squatters were slowly returning to what had once been theirs. For most it would mean repairing, rebuilding, tearing down and starting anew. Cass was to offer the chieftain's aid wherever possible.

Rayce asked him to check in on the old innkeepers in Banning. Were they well, able to keep the inn open? Was there anything they needed?

They were well. No, they needed nothing, but please greet the young Thorpe for them when Cass saw him next. Tell him the inn was already busy with customers. Old friends and new were making the inn a gathering place, just as it had been in the past.

He stopped frequently to check on Eithne in Malhain Village. Only a few cottages were occupied now, the rest left empty of the Arlanders who had dwelled there. He urged her to go to Ross Harbor or to Timthurlen. He would take her wherever she wished to go and see her settled, but she refused his offer. As she told him once before when they'd had a similar conversation, she was still a mountain woman, not a woman of the sea. She never told him what happened the day Kelan Dellay returned to Malhain Village, nor did he ever ask her for any particulars. Cass was pretty sure he knew what lay under the rapidly settling mound behind Eithne's cottage.

And when time grew heavy for Cass, he escaped to his beloved Dalrudd Mountains, there to find the peace and solitude he needed.

When Rayce felt the situation in Timis was much improved, he came to his parents and asked for their permission to leave and for their blessings. He wanted to return to Cathorn. There was still so much for him to know, still so much for him to understand.

"Never fear, Mother," he laughed when his mother asked if he would come back to them from time to time. "You've not seen the last of me. *Dragon Keeper* knows its way to Camlanrein. I miss the sea." He sighed. "And," he whispered more to himself than to his parents, "I need to come to grips with all that has happened." KaynaRee had told him much the same thing yesterday as she readied the *Highland Guardian* for the sea.

Camron placed his hands on his son's shoulders and looked long into eyes so like his own. He merely nodded his head in understanding, pulled his son into a hard embrace, then released him and stepped back.

Rayce turned to his mother and smiled. She answered his smile through tears and he took her in his arms and held on tight. She, too, stepped back, letting go, sending him off to find his bliss. "Talanor will be with you in spirit," she said softly. "I know he will guide you."

"Ree and I will spend some time with Grandmother Mary in Shiptown before we go our separate ways. You know that Ree is planning to go to Lorn Isle for a time."

"Yes, she told us last night," Kitra said and couldn't quite keep the sadness from her voice. She understood, both she and Camron understood, but still it was hard to let them both go.

"Sail safely," Camron said as he tossed the mooring lines to Rayce as he pushed off from the dock. The tide was running swiftly; there was a fair wind from the south. The sun was shining; the air was redolent with the sounds and smells of spring.

Time to go.

Dawn brightened the sky when Ree and her parents stood together beside Ree's sloop for their final farewells. Dinner the night before had been a time of laughter and sharing stories, sharing dreams, questions asked and answered. Ree was excited about sailing to Lorn, of living there once more. Whenever she felt in need of companionship, she'd sail across the Strait of Tears and down to Landsend to visit friends, and she'd invite them to come to visit her as well. She promised her mother she would sing the Warrior Song each morning, just as her long-ago grandfather, Andrew Goldenhorn, had, just as Kitra had. Although Ree's Song was very different from those two Songs, hers too was a Warrior Song. She also promised to visit her grandmother, Mary Fairchild, often, and she would visit Rayce on Cathorn, too.

"I'll not be lonely, Mother. And once life is more settled here, I hope you will both come to Lorn."

"Oh, yes, sweet daughter. You've not seen the last of your parents by any means," Camron promised in a gruff voice that dissolved into laughter.

Ree laughed, too, and then grew serious. "You know that I must do this. There's so much I need to understand, but I'm curious, too. I dreamed of a dragon, I rode a dragon, a dragon whose fire I called. And people died when I did. I need to understand how I could do that; I need to understand why it was necessary to do that."

"I know, Ree, I know. Your father and I wrestled with the knowledge we caused so many deaths. And we still wrestle with the question of why it had to come to fire and death. You will find it is not easy at times to live with what has been done, what you have done, what we four have done." Kitra smiled and tears filled her eyes. "But, dear KaynaRee, you will find your bliss, as will your brother, as your father and I have found ours in each other." She took her daughter in her arms for one last, fierce hug, then surrendered her to her father.

"Go with the Ancient Ones guiding your way. Know that the Golden Ones and the Caretakers go with you," Camron whispered as he hugged her.

Camron and Kitra stepped back, Ree stepped into the boat, Camron cast off her lines, and Ree pushed off from the dock. She raised the sail and heard again the sighing of the wind, the cry of the seabirds that flew alongside and overhead, the singing of the waves as the *Highland Guardian* crossed the Brayner Harbor and headed for the Trayonian Sea. She turned and raised her hand in farewell and knew her parents would watch her until they could no long see her sail. She turned her face into the wind and then lifted it to the sun.

She was going home.

Mary Hamilton sent them off after visiting her for two weeks with smiles and hugs, with promises from them that they would visit again in the fall, and with their favorite cookies. Rayce steered across the sea to Cathorn; Ree had the longer journey around the Kaenolirian headlands and east to Lorn Isle.

The sky was a brilliant blue, so bright it was nearly colorless, when KaynaRee sailed into the Strait of Tears. The familiar crying, the agony of the wind, that always wept through the Strait greeted her, and Ree began to sing, first the Song of the sea that guided her through the turbulent waters and then her own Song. The wind, with a mind of its own, carried the *Highland Guardian* home to the dock of Lorn. The boat bumped gently against the old timbers; she hopped out to tie up, grabbed a couple of packs—she'd get the rest later—

and headed up the trail leading into the center of the island and the cottage.

It was all as she remembered, more than a little overgrown, but Lorn Isle as she remembered it. The cottage, shuttered and closed when Rayce left, stood waiting. With eager steps she hurried the last little way, dropped her packs at the door, and pushed it open.

Dust motes on narrow streams of sunlight slipped through the cracks in the shutters and lit the way into the interior. She heaved a deep sigh of contentment and just stood, smelling the dust mixed with scents of home—the heavy tang of salt air, the rich green smell of trees and grass and the sweet scent of flowers blooming profusely and wildly in her mother's flower beds.

For now, she would open the shutters, make up her bed, and wipe out a cupboard or two so she could store her food items. Tomorrow at dawn she would climb the eagles' pinnacle and sing her Warrior Song. Tonight she would sleep in her own bed in the cottage where she had grown up.

And perhaps dream again of Ja'Anee.

At dawn, KaynaRee climbed to the top of the pinnacle and walked nearly to the edge of the sheer cliffs that soared above a crashing sea, spray flying high enough to soak her if she stepped too close to the edge. She smiled and looked about her as the sun began to rise above the horizon, casting a golden sheen on all it touched.

KaynaRee Fairchild, daughter of Golden Ones, child of ancient Caretakers, lifted her head and her voice rang out in a glorious, exalted Warrior Song. The moaning of the winds and sea through the narrow channel between Lorn and the sunken isle of Sinnich ceased; the waters' roar quieted to a murmur.

She sang for all the Golden Ones, those Warrior Singers who had stood on the promontory that had long ago been buried beneath the sea by the rage of Maelorn, the darkling prince. She sang for Andrew Goldenhorn and Kailie Fairchild who had stood on this pinnacle, for Kitra Fairchild, and last of all for KaynaRee Fairchild. When the Song ended and the last notes drifted away, she turned.

Waiting for her was Torar.

She laughed with delight as the great silver wolf, who had been Kailie Fairchild's companion, who had been with Ree in Ross Harbor, came toward her. He stopped a few steps away and sat on his haunches, grinning his wolfish grin.

"Hello, my friend. I'm glad you decided to join me."

He nodded his head. "*I did not want you to be lonely, lady.*"

"Nor shall I be, Torar. Alone, perhaps, but never lonely."

Cathorn Isle materialized out of the mists that had protected it for all the ages when mages resided here. Rayce breathed a sigh of contentment as he guided *Dragon Keeper* to the old, worn dock. One of the first things he'd have to do was repair it, he thought. He secured the sloop and tossed three of the several bags in which he'd packed books, food and clothing onto the planking. There would be time later, perhaps tomorrow, to get everything down the long trail to the cottage. There was no hurry. For now he would take the essential things he needed.

He trudged along the path with the heavy packs and stopped once to catch his breath with the excuse of checking to make sure everything was as it should be. When he neared the cottage, he stopped again, just to look at it. Not so long ago he'd come here searching for answers and he'd found them. It seemed nearly a lifetime ago.

Now he came to find solace and peace. The tranquility of the island assured him he would find the comfort he needed.

And if the Ancient Ones were kind, he would dream once more of Far'Lin.

He dropped the packs on the front step and pushed open the door. It stuck a bit and the hinges squeaked. Another task to put on the list. He stepped back outside to pick up his packs; as he did so, he heard a soft 'woof,' and looked up to see the wolf who watched him. Rayce straightened and smiled.

"So, Jagar," he said softly "you are here."

"*I am here, Caretaker. I have waited for you. This is where we both belong.*"

"Yes, this is where we belong."

An ocean breeze ruffled the wolf's fur and brushed along Rayce's cheek. It was, he thought, not unlike the touch of human fingers.

"Talanor," he whispered and Jagar opened his mouth to grin at him.

The Caretaker's Song

As sung by Rayce Thorpe

Wake, you are needed.
Evil walks.
Good lies weak and hopeless,
Hear its petitions.
Come
Slip through the Door opened to your being.
Come
For you are needed.

Come from sea. Come from ice. Come from blackest night.
Dreams give rise and fire beasts sing.
Faerie hear and touch with magic those who listen
And know.
Hear the Songs of fire beast and Faerie.
Come.

When all else fails, memory serves.
The portal opens.
Come.
You are needed.
When all else fails.
When all else fails.

Would you like to see your manuscript become a book?

If you are interested in becoming a PublishAmerica author, please submit your manuscript for possible publication to us at:

acquisitions@publishamerica.com

You may also mail in your manuscript to:

**PublishAmerica
PO Box 151
Frederick, MD 21705**

We also offer free graphics for Children's Picture Books!

www.publishamerica.com

CPSIA information can be obtained at www.ICGtesting.com
Printed in the USA
BVOW031930181012

303389BV00001B/33/P

9 781462 694488